UNNATURAL RELATIONS

Mike Seabrook

Unnatural Relations

THE GAY MEN'S PRESS

First published 1989 by GMP Publishers Ltd
Reissued in The Gay Men's Press Collection 1996
Third impression 1998
GMP Publishers Ltd, P O Box 247,
Swaffham PE37 8PA, England

World Copyright © 1989 Mike Seabrook

British Library Cataloguing in Publication Data

Seabrook, Mike
Unnatural Relations.
I. Title
823'.914

ISBN 0 85449 116 3

Distributed in Europe by Central Books,
99 Wallis Rd, London E9 5LN

Distributed in North America by LPC Group,
1436 West Randolph Street, Chicago, IL 60607

Distributed in Australia by Bulldog Books,
P O Box 300, Beaconsfield, NSW 2014

Printed and bound in the EU by WSOY, Juva, Finland

Author's Note (June 1989)

All the descriptions of police and legal procedure in this story have been checked for authenticity, although I have taken occasional liberties, for which I plead the usual defence of dramatic licence. Readers would be forgiven for presuming that my portrait of the judge, in particular his conduct at the end of the court scene, must be one such liberty, and an extreme one at that. Much though I regret the fact, they would be wrong. This character is modelled closely on a judge who was sitting until a few years ago; and his conduct of the court case in this tale is based on a case that I watched that judge conduct less than ten years ago. At least he is not sitting now. I doubt if we shall ever look upon his like again.

I am grateful to Chris Chapman, Solicitor of Sheringham, for legal advice; to the Sheringham police for valuable advice when I needed it; to my friend Steve Speck for helpful comments; and most of all, as usual, to my wife Perviz, whose contribution to this book was so great that she ought to be on the front cover as co-author.

ONE

The lake was a sheet of beaten silver. The wind drove the clouds hard across the reluctant dawn sky and made a ceaseless dry hiss in the reeds and the alders, there were a few spots of cold rain in the air. Jamie Potten scrambled over the fence off the towpath and dropped on his belly. The hawthorn brakes were too dense for even a boy to force his way through; but if you were small it was possible to crawl between the ancient black boles, beneath most of the thorns. Dragging his rod and his old canvas tackle bag beside him, he came to a sheer twelve-foot bank, and began to clamber down, finding handholds in the roots of the hazels that grew out from it. He dropped the last few feet, rolled, got up and squeezed his way through a thick belt of alders and sallows, and he was there.

He had discovered the place two years ago, and it had been his private citadel ever since. He didn't think anyone else knew of it. He hoped not. It was quite invisible from the path, and even if you did know it was there, it was wholly inaccessible to anyone much bigger than Jamie, who was small for his fifteen years. The angling club that owned the fishing rights on the lake was not wealthy, and its members were not energetic. They hadn't restocked the lake after an outbreak of some devastating disease several years before, and most of the keen fishermen in the district fished elsewhere. They were equally indolent about cutting back the bushes and undergrowth surrounding the lake. Jamie hoped it would continue.

Certainly in his two years of fishing there he had never been disturbed by anyone. The alders and sallows gave way to a tiny sward of turf, almost smooth enough to be a lawn, which sloped gently down to the edge of the water of a small bay. The water here was deep: you could see the bottom for no more than a couple of feet, then it plunged, suddenly into blackness. The horns of the bay curved round, shaggy with bushes and small trees, in such a way that you could make a goodish long cast, and yet were hidden from view from any other point on the lake shore. For Jamie, who had discovered by the age of ten that privacy was the chief mercy the world had to offer, it was a personal paradise, big enough for him.

He knew that big carp, tench and chub fed in his bay, and sometimes he had glimpsed the form of a great pike cruising, just below the surface. He coveted the great fish more than anything else in his world. It was, he thought, just about the most beautiful object he had ever imagined: sleek, majestic, sublimely confident. Jamie, who, like most lonely, self-sufficient, unhappy boys, had written secret poems, had written dozens about the pike. Then he had read Ted Hughes's ideas and decided that since the last word had been written he would do better to concentrate on just catching the creature. Perhaps today would be the day. That would be something to show them, when he brought home that miraculous creature - in which, to be truthful, he only half believed. He had no clear idea how he would go about playing and landing such a fish, and none at all about how he would kill it, let alone get it home. But he was a good fisherman, and a confident boy in some things, among them his own resource. He hoped more than almost anything else that today, which had started badly even by his standards, he would take the ultimate symbol of himself home. There was only one thing he hoped even more: that Christopher would come.

***

They had started early that morning, before he was properly awake. It happened occasionally - less often than at the Great Crisis of last summer, when it had been going every morning when he awoke and continuing every evening, a continuous rumble downstairs, mostly muted, occasionally rising in a shout or even, now and again, a scream. Those rare crescendi were invariably followed by a lull, in which, oddly, he could hear the individual words more clearly. The words were always some exhortation on the lines of "Shhhhh! He'll hear *you*." The "you" whether it was in the rumbling growl of his father or the elocutioned mezzo of his mother, was always underlined. It had puzzled him why he could always hear the words in these interludes and not at any other time, but he quickly worked out to his own satisfaction that it was because they were the only moments when they weren't both talking at once. The conclusion had pleased him in an abstract sort of way, with the pure, impersonal pleasure of the mathematician who cracks some difficult problem. He had grinned to himself and gone to sleep. As usual he had been woken by the deafening silence as they called a cease-fire for the night. And then, as usual, he had cried himself back to sleep again. But there had still been some of the warm pleasure of triumph left, and the process hadn't taken as long as usual. That had been the moment of what he privately termed his divorce.

Over the past few months there had been much less of that, and correspondingly more silence - which, he thought, working it out on his own private scale, was rather worse. His father had taken to going off to the club early in the evening and returning late, after his mother was in bed. Then there was often nothing, sometimes a subdued murmur from their bedroom. That, he thought, was the worst of all. Another problem: why did the softest murmur from their room wake him with such unfailing efficacy, when sometimes he could drop off in the middle of tumult downstairs? He could find no answer to that one that satisfied his logical mind, and had to be content with the theory that there was somehow, in some subtle way, infinitely more menace in low voices than in raised ones, and that he himself must have some special sensors for picking up menace and distinguishing it from the mere pushing and hauling that was his conception of normality. That morning they had been speaking quietly.

He had experienced the familiar sequence. It was almost, some strange corner of his mind told him, as if he ticked the stages off on his fingers. The sudden transition from sleep to wakefulness, with no warm, cocooning few minutes coming to the surface. The instant cringing, crawling of the flesh and the draining of the blood. He had never quite been able to track *that* exact feeling to its lair, never been able to work out quite where the blood drained to. It was just a rush of the fluid that he felt conscious of inside his body, all of it, suddenly rushing, from some place to some other place. It was always over before he could get hold of it and start his analysis.

Then there was the sequence of thoughts, always the same, and their aftermath. And that, he was quite sure, was the worst item of all. God, I wish he was dead. No, I wish *she* was dead. It's her fault as much as his. No. I wish they were *both* bloody dead. That's the truth of it, isn't it, James Potten? Come on, now, you know you don't wish them dead. Where would that leave *you*? You? Is that all you can think about - where it would leave *you*? You selfish bastard, James Kieran Potten. Whose side are you on?

And the aftermath. Guilt. Get up, Jamie Potten. Get up, go on, get up, *now*. And perhaps if you're extra nice to both of them they'll never suspect what you've just been thinking about them. Get away with you! They know. That's why they do it. If they thought you cared about them they wouldn't be like this, would they?

At any rate, his systems invariably told him, get up, *now*, and go down and be nice to them. Bright smile. As if nothing's happened. At least, as if you haven't heard it happening. Then, maybe, just maybe, they'll forgive you.

That's how it used to be, Jamie thought to himself somewhere beneath the surface as he set up his rod-rest and screwed his rod together and prayed that the big pike would come today. Or that Christopher would come. Or both. Perhaps Christopher would help him catch the pike, help him land it. He'd know how to kill it, perhaps. That would need some doing. And some thought beforehand. He knew that it was Christopher that he wanted. But the pike would do. Yes, that's how it had used to be, but that was ages ago, when he had been a boy. At least, his mind added (for he was quite exceptionally honest, as all boys like him become) a *young* boy - when he was thirteen, say.

He was now grown up, or pretty close to it – the nagging bit of him insisted on adding – and now he knew the truth. It was simply nothing to do with him. They didn't forgive him, because there was nothing they had to forgive him for – unless for having been born to them. No, the truth was they were simply both bastards. It hadn't made a scrap of difference when he had got out of bed and gone down and been extra nice to them both, because they didn't give a damn whether he was nice to them or not. They hadn't even noticed. They were too fully occupied with their own problems, and he... he didn't even come into the equation; a phrase he had been very proud of when it had come into his mind one morning.

"They're just a pair of fucking bastards," he muttered to himself, and the words, drifting like steam in the cold morning air, made him feel good. They were somehow cleansing. He scanned the swim quickly, made a perfect fifty-foot cast, and smiled to himself as he sat down on the canvas bag to fish. He would have been astonished if anyone had told him, but when he smiled he was beautiful.

Over an hour later the wind had slackened and there were a few more spots of rain. Jamie was disgustedly taking a very

11

small gudgeon off the hook and throwing it back. There was a rustle in the alders and sallows behind him, and Christopher arrived. Jamie threw the gudgeon back with a curse on its parentage, looked over his shoulder, smiled a dazzling smile which almost curdled Christopher's blood, and laid his rod in its rest.

***

At about the time that Jamie Potten was laying down his rod and walking slowly towards Christopher with his arms outstretched, David and Annabel Potten were standing in two separate towering rages in the study of the headmaster of their son's school, both trying to make themselves heard above the other, and neither of them hearing or desiring to hear the headmaster's soothing suggestion that they be seated in the two Victorian chairs placed for their benefit before his enormous desk.

The headmaster allowed the commotion to go unchecked for a few moments, in which it told him a great deal. He had not met the Potten boy's parents before except for odd moments at school functions, and when he had politely but firmly required them to visit him he had not known what to expect. The opening few moments of any such meeting, especially a potentially difficult one such as this, were always most instructive, and this was even more so than the norm. The headmaster, who was a kind, intelligent and extremely worldly man, made a series of mental notes even as he stood with his arm still extended to indicate the chairs. Then, even as the voices began to rise and take on querulous tones, he spoke again, in a tone that he used rarely to the boys in his charge and almost never to anyone else. It was not loud, but it had the effect of a whipcrack.

12

"Mr and Mrs Potten, you will please *sit down* in those chairs which have been placed for you, and do me the kindness of listening, first of all, to what I have to say."

They were so astonished at being addressed in that tone, which he had selected especially, that they both stopped speaking at the same moment, and meekly sat down. The headmaster, mentally offering up a prayer of relief at the silence, stalked slowly round the desk and eased himself into his own throne-like chair. He had been a schoolmaster at very good schools for a very long time, and was well-versed in the many small ways of making himself impressive and holding people in awe; he exerted his powers to the full. He had already made his preliminary assessments of the Pottens, and concluded that every artifice of thirty years' experience would be called into the battle-line today. Accordingly he steepled his fingers, pursed his lips and looked coldly at the two parents over the top of his gold-rimmed glasses, much in the manner of a judge about to pass sentence. The silence grew in darkness and consistency. After fully half a minute he observed David Potten's face darkening. He waited. After a few more seconds the man's mouth opened. The headmaster spoke, ruthlessly drowning the first word before it was born.

"Mr and Mrs Potten, we are worried about your son, James. In fact we are *very* worried. I take it that this is not altogether a surprise to you."

"Worried? What do you mean, worried? He seems all right," said the father, sharply. The headmaster saw that he was darkening again, a deep red flush crawling up his cheeks and across his forehead. The wife, he saw with approval, had begun immediately to look worried and even furtive. Good, he thought, somebody's feeling guilty. He waited once more, watching the flush on Mr Potten's face darken. Eventually he said, "So it *does* surprise you, then?"

"I assume that if he's been up to no good you'll have dealt with it yourself. It's what we pay you for, isn't it? And if he isn't up to no good, what else is it that's worrying you? His work's all right, isn't it? Judging by his reports, anyway."

He fell silent under the headmaster's level gaze. "Mrs

13

Potten. Does it come as a surprise to *you* that we are worried?"

The woman, he thought, was superficially the harder case. The husband was aggressive, probably ruthless in business - that was his reputation, at any rate. Built like a bullock, wearing heavy farmer's tweeds and otherwise dressed in the kind of casual that doesn't reek of money but gently radiates it. Mrs Potten was sophisticated, dressed from Paris by the look of it, smelt very slightly of something very discreet and even more expensive, and spoke with a warm, beautifully modulated voice that could, he suspected, send shivers up the spines of many men, especially the wrong kinds. He waited, observing her carefully construct her reply.

"Ah... well, Doctor Lane, I don't assume automatically as my husband does that James has been up to no good, as he so elegantly puts it... but I, too, have seen no cause for complaint about his work, and he seems to be keen enough at games... is it his discipline, perhaps? No, I can't think so," she went on, giving the headmaster no chance to speak. "No, he's always been a *very* well-behaved little boy, right from when he was tiny. In fact, I've sometimes wondered if he had *enough* spirit, as boys go... I mean, we've always been at pains to bring him up to remember his manners and so forth, but I really can't think of anything he might have done..." She let the sentence fall to earth by itself, offering him a very faint smile.

David Potten drew a leather cigar case from his jacket, extracted a large cigar from it, rolled it, put the case away and prepared to light it. As a transparent afterthought (at least it wasn't a deliberate snub, reflected the headmaster) he said, "You mind if I smoke?" The headmaster caught the woman's eye. She raised her eyes slightly towards the ceiling, then slightly increased the voltage of the faint smile. He studiously kept his face neutral. "Not at all," he murmured. "I was about to offer you one of these..." He opened a cigarette box on the desk top and proffered it to Mrs Potten, who refused with an almost invisible shake of her head. Dr Lane lit one for himself and drew on it deeply.

"You will remember," he said eventually, "that I said we are worried *about* Jamie. He is, to begin with, a very self-possessed boy, would you agree?"

"I should hope so," said the father, snappishly. "Isn't that what we're paying you six thousand a year for, to *make* him able to stand on his own two feet? A boy should be able to look after himself, shouldn't he?"

Dr Lane heard him out. Then he said "That is true, to be sure. But he is, after all, only fifteen years old. Has it struck you that he is, perhaps, *unusually* self-possessed - for that age? That he is, perhaps, just a little, ah, *solitary*?"

This time he had to wait. After the pause Mrs Potten said, hesitantly, "I have thought he was something of a loner, Dr Lane. But I put that down to his being an only child..."

"I think," Lane said, "that there is a little more to this than the mere only-child syndrome. I think there is something seriously amiss."

The father flushed deeply, and rose all the way out of his chair. "Are you telling me there's something *wrong* with my boy? Something *wrong* with h..."

"Be *quiet*, David," snapped his wife, "and for God's sake *sit* DOWN." Her voice was by this time crackling with tension and unease. Lane noticed that when she relaxed her tight control on her voice, although the modulation cracked, the accent did not. He also noticed that as soon as she brought that tone into it her husband sat down as if he'd been shot. She's the tough one, he thought. Well-bred, though, I'd have said. Pity there's not much humanity underneath it all. She was speaking again, urgently, to her husband. "For Christ's sake forget about chucking your weight about for once and listen to what he's saying. Dr Lane, come to the point. What do you think is wrong with Jamie?"

He hesitated a long time before he answered, trying to gauge the best way to put it. "Frankly, Mrs Potten, I don't know for certain. I think it will require a psychiatrist to discover that..."

All hell broke loose. They were both on their feet, shouting alternately at him and each other. Eventually on sheer

15

volume the man won. "...you got the infernal bloody gall to sit there and tell me my bloody son's *mad*..."

"...Christ's sake sit *down*, David. He's not saying James is..."

"...this what we're paying this fancy fucking place thousands of pounds a year for, to have this, this... this..."

"...*down*, David. PLEASE..."

"...won't have it. I say, I will not have it. I'm suing. I'll have the boy out of here in five..."

The headmaster sat through the tirade impassively for a minute and a half, thanking the providence that set his study away in a remote part of the building where few if any pupils or even masters were likely to penetrate. Then he spoke. "Mr and Mrs Potten, I shall say this once to you, and once only. I will not have exhibitions of that kind in this room, or anywhere else in this school. I have called you to see me on a matter of the greatest importance to you both, to me, to the school, and most of all, to Jamie. I am not accustomed to trifling in such matters. I should never have asked you to come to see me had I not regarded the circumstances as quite exceptionally grave. I must now ask you to hear what I have to say, in its entirety, and to comment upon it as necessary.

"But you will kindly do so in the proper manner, as the extreme gravity, as I consider it, demands. And you will *not* again have recourse to the kind of disgraceful exhibition of a minute ago. That has nothing to do with my dignity, or with considerations of propriety. I say it because what I have to say is far too important to allow deplorable behaviour by either or both of you to distract us. Now, let's begin with today. Are you aware that Jamie is absent from school today?" They gazed at each other in surprise. "Well, Mr and Mrs Potten? Are you telling me you don't know whether your son is at school or not?"

"No. Well, I... He left for school this morning," faltered Annabel Potten. "He had his breakfast as usual, and left at the usual time. He was wearing his uniform, and he had his books with him. I can't think..."

"He's not here this morning, Mrs Potten, and he hasn't

been all week. This is not by any means the first time that he has been absent. In the past he has produced notes, ostensibly from you, excusing him on various pretexts."

"But, dammit, man," began David Potten explosively, "why haven't you got in touch with us before, if he's been going AWOL?"

"Because when it began, early this term, we accepted the notes. The explanations were reasonable; the occurrences were only very occasional; finally we had no reason to think that they were other than genuine. Later on, as the absences increased, we began to question the boy. He gave us assurances that it was a temporary thing, and stated - to me, in this room - that the real reason was that..." He hesitated, coughed and cleared his throat. "He declared that the cause of his problem was that your marriage was breaking down, and that the strain of it was such that he was unable to give his attention to his work, or to anything else. He stated that the only thing he felt able to do was to walk miles by himself, trying to sort ideas out in his own mind.

"He begged us," he continued in a dead, flat tone, "or rather, he *implored* us to take no action, most of all he implored me not to pass it back to you, saying that it would finish everything if I did so. On a strict promise from him that he would not absent himself once again, but that he would bring his problems to me without fail, I agreed to what he begged." He broke off, lit himself another cigarette, and went for a short walk round his study. He came to rest before the big windows looking out onto the school's impressive front drive, with its avenue of great trees, and stood gazing out for some moments.

Coming back to his seat, he resumed. "As I said, I acceded to what he asked. I believed that he was a quite extraordinarily mature and sensible boy. Of his exceptional intelligence I was already aware. I believed that he was sufficiently worldly-wise and possessed of so unusual a degree of honesty - that he almost certainly knew as well as anyone what was best for himself. I could see the deep misery and unhappiness in his eyes, and I grieved for the poor child, as I grieve now. But I trusted his maturity. You must understand that I have encountered this kind of problem many times before, and I have found that boys in Jamie's position, if they are intelligent, are very often unusually self-reliant and clear-sighted about their own difficulties, and it doesn't do to interfere with them any more than can be helped. Gentle understanding, being there when they call upon you, that is almost all one can do in many cases, as in Jamie's.

"I might even have allowed him to continue with his absenteeism for another few weeks, perhaps even to the end of this term, though I should undoubtedly have pressed him to allow me to help him in more practical ways. He inspired me with that much confidence as to his ability to keep control, to keep it all in balance, and to take care of himself.

"Now, however, I think I must step in; and I think I must have your help, because something else has come to light which makes the whole thing a lot more serious."

"Well? Are you ready to help me?" he pressed. They straightened a little in their chairs, looked at each other and both nodded.

"Then tell me: has Jamie ever mentioned to you - to either of you - anyone by the name of Christopher?"

They looked blankly at each other. "No, he's never mentioned anyone of that name to me," said his mother. "No, I'm sure he hasn't got a friend of that name. I would have remembered, because we almost called *him* Christopher. After my brother..." She dried up. Lane looked at the father.

"No, I've never heard him mention the name. No, I'm sure of it. Why?"

"How much do you know about homosexuality?" he asked.

For a moment there was a stunned silence. Lane could feel the horror spiralling round the big airy room, up to the lofty, carved ceiling and down again, circling round the three of them, like incense round a pentangle.

"No doubt you're aware," Lane went on, "that schools

18

such as this have always been associated with homosexuality. In the main, the association has been somewhat unfair. It undoubtedly exists, always has, always will. You can't keep hundreds of healthy young males who are all either just at or just approaching the full flowering of their own sexuality, or just beginning to enjoy it, and not expect them to find some outlet for it. In addition, and far more relevant, in fact, if people were but aware of it, those boys are also just discovering the blossoming of something else. That is their *romantic* sensibility.

"Boys are very romantic creatures, you know. That isn't understood as well as it ought to be, not least because this country is at once obsessed about sex and repressed about emotion, at least among boys. But boys, when both their sexual and their emotional - their romantic - personae first flower... well, the effect is overwhelming. They cast about for *objects* to lavish all this emotion and sexuality upon. A few have girlfriends. The overwhelming majority don't. We're beginning, some centuries behind most civilised countries, to accept that it isn't the end of civilisation to allow the sexes to be together at this time in their lives. We're beginning to allow girls into schools such as this. At this one, we have girls in the sixth form. Which is all very well for the sixth form boys, but not much use to a boy of any other form.

"So we have a certain incidence of homosexuality. Most of it is entirely harmless - it takes the form of emotional attachments between close friends, hero-worship, and many other small things which are, in the main, beneficial and innocuous. There is also a certain amount of overt sexual attachment. We know about it, we know how far to let it go, and we know how to deal with it. Some of our boys, undoubtedly, are homosexual and will remain so when they leave us. The most we can do for those is to be properly understanding and supportive when they discover that they are not and will not be as most of their friends are, and do what we can to prepare them for the difficulties they will face later on, outside our protective walls."

Dr Lane paused to light himself another cigarette. He

offered the box to the Pottens, and this time they both accepted. They were, he thought, and hoped, beginning to look a little calmer as his voice droned gently in the room.

"They, however, are a minority," he resumed. "Then there is what has been called 'institutional' homosexuality. This is quite simply the name applied when people who are not normally homosexual turn to homosexual behaviour when, and because, there is no other outlet for - as I have described in the case of a school such as this - burgeoning sexuality and romanticism. You get this kind of homosexual behaviour wherever there are men without women: on board ship, in the armed forces when they are deprived of access to women, in prison. And in schools. Here." He breathed hard, tiring of the sound of his own voice. The two across the desk remained, motionless, waiting for the next word.

***

Jamie walked, quite calmly, across the few feet of sward and into Christopher's arms and buried his face in his shoulder. A few tears squeezed out of the corners of his eyes. He could feel Christopher's heart beating against his cheek. He threw one arm round Christopher's neck, burying his hand in his brown hair and tugging his head down onto his own shoulder. The other arm he clasped as tightly as he could round Christopher's waist. He was trembling violently from his neck to his ankles. Christopher held him firmly but gently, rocking him slightly in his arms, feeling the immense tension vibrating through the whole of his small, neat body. "Jamie, Jamie, my sweet, whatever is it?" he said after a while, but Jamie only made small animal sounds into the breast of his pullover. He held him for a quarter of an hour, feeling Jamie's death grip in his hair and round his waist, and wondering what on earth his parents could have done to him this time.

At last Jamie released him, but only for long enough to slip his hand into Christopher's and lead him to the water's edge. "Caught anything?" Christopher asked. Jamie turned and looked up at him. Christopher examined the small, triangular face, with its heavy mop of dark red hair, the straight nose and the wide-spaced grey eyes and, as always, his throat contracted and his heart felt as if it was swimming up his larynx, at the beauty that he saw and at the incredible chance that had brought the boy to him instead of someone, anyone, else. And, as always, his brain worked overtime, calculating what would happen if anyone ever found out about them. Had he been Dr Lane, the line from Gray about snatching a fearful joy would probably have swum into his mind. Christopher had read Gray, but he was far too engulfed in Jamie's presence, his beauty, the fresh boy's smell of him and his own rapture to think about Gray, or about anything else.

He slipped a canvas bag, much like Jamie's, from his shoulder, and knelt beside it, undoing buckles. "I said, have you had any luck?" he said gently. Jamie looked blank for a moment, then plummeted down beside him, as if he could not bear to be even five feet away from him. Which, in fact, Jamie couldn't, just that morning. "I had a couple of tiddlers," he said, squatting beside Christopher as he opened his bag. He pushed his fingers into Christopher's hair and began stroking it gently. Christopher, feeling the churning in his stomach and the blood-running-cold sensation that intimate physical contact with Jamie always brought on, pulled a heavy blanket from his bag, followed by an old canvas groundsheet. He spread the groundsheet and shook out the blanket and laid it on top. "It's huge," he said, gesturing. "We can cover ourselves in it *and* wrap it round us. And if it rains we can just roll up in it with the groundsheet outside. Will here be okay? Near enough for you to get at your rod if you get a bite?"

"Bugger bites," said Jamie. "I'm not here for the fishing. Not today. I want you today." Christopher sat down hard on his blanket, reflecting in some wonder how adult Jamie could sound at times. It's as if he was the one who was four years

21

older, he thought to himself. He talks like a character in a novel. Probably a woman, who demands that the hero goes to bed with her. "I want you today." He sure as hell doesn't sound like a little fifteen-year-old. And of course, Jamie wasn't a fifteen-year-old boy, he reminded himself. Or at least, not a normal one.

Jamie was tugging at him and already wriggling under the blanket at the same time. Anxious to get me into bed, thought Christopher, and shivered violently. "What's the matter?" asked Jamie, becoming stock-still, instantly aware of the slightest movement or reaction from Christopher. "I dunno," said Christopher. "Just somebody walking over my grave, I suppose." He didn't quite dare tell, not even himself, let alone Jamie, what the thought of being in bed with Jamie did to him. It wouldn't do to let *that* particular beast out of its cage.

He became aware that he had become rapidly and painfully erect. He fidgeted with the front of his trousers, trying to manoeuvre his penis into a less uncomfortable position. Jamie, turning to urge him under the blanket with him, saw him. He looked carefully at the swelling in Christopher's trousers, and smiled. Christopher felt as if he was going to faint, and almost lost the lot in his pants there and then. Jamie blushed slightly. Like everything else he did, he blushed prettily. "Come on, Chris," he said, and Christopher's heart missed another beat. Jamie used Chris very much as a pet name. He never called him by it except when he was especially happy or loving.

Christopher shot under the blanket beside him. "Pongs a bit," said Jamie, not giving a damn if the blanket smelt a bit musty. "Won't do you any harm," Christopher said. "I know," said Jamie, gently. "Now come to me, Chris. Please. I need you." Who's in charge here, thought Christopher, knowing quite well what the answer was. Fifteen-year-old, neat, beautiful Jamie Kieran Potten came into his arms, and bliss came down and enveloped them in a cloud.

"At the moment we have no way of knowing which of these categories Jamie fits, assuming that he fits either," said Dr Lane. "There is no absolute guarantee that he is engaging in any sort of homosexual behaviour. But I must say, I think myself that it's as good as certain that he is, and I think we must ask him, gently but firmly, as soon as we can."

"Why?" demanded David Potten truculently. "Yes. Have you really got anything to go on?" put in his wife.

"Of course I've got something to go on," he said slowly. "It would have been outrageous behaviour on my part to worry you like this without strong evidence. You see, Jamie had a secret hide-away here, at the school. It looks as if he used it for storing anything that he didn't want discovered at home. I'm afraid we had to use some pretty underhand methods to find it. Methods I'm not particularly proud of."

"God damn it all," burst out the father suddenly. "What could be more important than getting hold of whatever's at the bottom of this?"

"Quite so, Mr Potten. That was the view we took also, otherwise we should never have resorted to such methods. I'm afraid I had to use a fair amount of threats against his form-mates, including the only boy with whom he is close, and, what's worse, a certain amount of deception, to winkle it out of him. We eventually found these..."

He opened a drawer in the desk, and took out a large filing wallet, which he emptied on the desk top. He sorted the items out and began passing them across to the Pottens one by one. "This paperback book: *Fielding Gray*. It's a novel by Simon Raven - not, in my judgment, a suitable book for fifteen-year-old boys, though a most accomplished writer. The theme of this particular novel is a passionate, and, in passing, tragic, love affair between two public schoolboys. One of them being named Christopher. You will note that several passages are marked in Jamie's hand, with romantic allusions to *his own* Christopher - even, here and there, with crosses. Denoting kisses, one assumes. Now that need not mean anything at all. Mere adolescent romanticism, very probably, if it were taken on its own. Schoolboy crush on some senior boy. Or perhaps a calf-love affair with some junior or contemporary. However..."

He sifted among the papers again, and passed over a sheaf of paper torn from a school exercise book. "These are some verses Jamie has been writing. Some of them are on general themes - fishing, the countryside and the like. There are some - ah - somewhat unflattering ideas about his home life, which I should not, perhaps, mention. Many of these poems are very good, as it happens. He has a considerable talent. But the significant ones are the half dozen written to Christopher. They are passionate. They are, unquestionably, genuine love poems. And frankly, they are so explicit as to leave little doubt in any reader's mind that they relate to actual incidents that Jamie has experienced with this Christopher. I think it would be sensible if you didn't dwell on them for the moment." He drew the sheets back and put them with the paperback.

"There is more. This," he said, showing them a cheap spiral-bound pocket notebook, "is a diary, begun at the beginning of last term. It recounts in great detail - in a detail that becomes more passionate and explicit as the entries proceed - every meeting he has had with Christopher. It describes how they first met. What they talked about. It seems that for much of the time they did very little *but* talk. Boys will do that, especially when a true and deep friendship is formed, as is undoubtedly the case here. But it also describes Jamie's feelings towards this boy. It seems that he is about nineteen, a student, or, more precisely, waiting to take up his place at university. He presumably lives locally; but the diary gives no address. It makes no mention of which university he will attend, his surname or, in fact, any details at all that would help us to identify the boy. I don't think this is accidental," he went on after a pause. "I think this demonstrates well how sharp-witted he is. The substance is here, all right. But, powerfully - overwhelmingly, I believe - in love as he is, he has carefully avoided mentioning any of the vital particulars that could identify this boy. Knowing

24

Jamie's intelligence I have no doubt that he knows exactly what view would be taken by others, by you, by society at large, if this affair were to be exposed; and knowing also his character, I have equally little doubt that it is Christopher of whom he is thinking. He's being protective, and acting with a wisdom beyond his years.

"As I say, the diary goes on to recount Jamie's feelings for this Christopher, in the most graphic detail. It details his - ah - fantasies... he makes it quite clear that they were masturbation fantasies - of sexual intimacy with Christopher. But much more powerfully it describes, with the clarity that his exceptional honesty and his considerable writing ability combine to produce, his overwhelming *love* for the boy. It is clear to me that Jamie took the lead in all of this. I think Jamie fell in love with Christopher, who at first at any rate regarded it as a chance acquaintance with an engaging, intelligent younger boy - a boy whom he could converse with, as I read this, as an equal, despite the four-year gap in their ages.

"Then, gradually, as their meetings became more frequent - which I think, must have contributed largely to the increasing absenteeism from school - Jamie's feelings communicate themselves to the older boy. At first he is, it seems from this, horrified. But those feelings are very quickly supplanted by the realisation, so powerful that he cannot do otherwise than confront it, that he reciprocates the feeling. There we have it: Jamie has revealed that he is in love with Christopher. Christopher, though at first dumbfounded, rapidly perceives that he is in love with Jamie.

"And then the physical intimacy begins, and that, too, is all described in vivid detail. It is better that you don't read it, I think, for the moment at least. But I can reassure you that so far, at least, it appears strongly that it has never gone beyond kissing, caressing and petting, up to mutual masturbation. And that, of course, would be that, if we could feel that it was going to rest there. Virtually all boys indulge in that, many of them for several years. Many men do it, even those who ultimately turn out not to be homosexual. Even with the age gap here, one would not feel too worried. It could be dealt with by a warning from us.

25

"Unfortunately, although the boy Christopher would, it seems, be happy with that for the foreseeable future at least, Jamie is far from happy. Jamie, I'm afraid, wants it to go much, much further. He says so, quite unequivocally, and in the most explicit language possible. The last entry in this diary is dated Tuesday of last week. This is Wednesday. That gives us seven school days since the final entry. Jamie has been absent on four of them: all this week and one day of last. I don't think we can doubt that he has seen Christopher on some, probably all, of those days. Personally I have no doubt of it."

He could see, from the expressions that were chasing each other over their faces, that they didn't doubt it either. Mrs Potten pulled herself together first. "What, er, conclusions do you draw from all this?" she asked. "And more to the point, what the hell do we *do* about it?" asked her husband. "I'll find out who this Christopher is, I know that, and break every bone in his body. But what about James?"

"Quite," said Dr Lane. "What about Jamie? Let me urge caution on you in the first place, Mr Potten. You won't do Jamie, or Jamie's cause, any good whatever, by finding this boy and half killing him. That would, in my judgment, probably be more perfectly calculated than any other single act to drive Jamie into his arms. I think also that you must be prepared for the result that you will find least palatable of all *anyway*." He hesitated, reached for a cigarette, put it back, then took it and lit it after all. "You asked, Mrs Potten, what conclusions I drew from all this."

"Yes. I think I know, but I'd like to hear your own conclusions. I think you're on James's side and I respect your judgments."

"Thank you, Mrs Potten. You're right, I am, entirely, on Jamie's side. Well, the conclusion I draw is that Jamie is, in all probability, a true homosexual." He glanced sternly at David Potten, who was flushing angrily, eyes bulging, and beginning to rise with a furious expostulation. Mrs Potten leaned across and pushed him hard back into his seat. "Shut *up* David, and listen."

"I conclude second that the other boy Christopher is

26

probably likewise, though less assured of himself than Jamie. Third, I conclude that Jamie has been greatly aided in reaching this most critical conclusion about himself partly by the comparatively liberal climate of opinion these days, but mostly by the exceptional strength of his own character. He is, and for many, many years has been, very much a lone wolf. He is an almost totally solitary boy, and such boys almost invariably have strong character. They can often tend to be obsessive characters, but in Jamie's case, as I've said earlier today, I don't think that is so. He is almost certainly a neurotic, but he is a strongly controlled and self-possessed one. Frankly, I doubt if he is the kind who will ever come to a great deal of harm in the world... provided, that is, that no one makes life deliberately any more difficult for him than they can help." He looked significantly at David Potten.

"Finally, I conclude that unless we take action very quickly, Jamie has every intention of turning this - ah - relationship into a full-scale sexual affair. It is already a full-scale love affair, and given the reciprocal love that the other boy clearly entertains for Jamie, I doubt very much indeed if his will-power can be expected to hold out against Jamie's, which I suspect is considerably the stronger of the two in the first place.

"It is entirely possible - given the strength of the will involved here - that Jamie and Christopher may end up having this full sexual affair in due course anyway. They can be restrained until they are 21. But that entails the law, and the law finds it very difficult to penetrate private individuals' bedrooms. I'm afraid that if Jamie decides he wants to sleep, or live, with Christopher, he will find it easy to do the moment he leaves your house - which he is legally entitled to do without let or hindrance, I believe, at the age of seventeen."

"He'll do it over my dead bloody body," snapped his father. "I'll see him in hell without a penny before I let him shack up with some dirty little queer."

"Please, Mr Potten," said Lane mildly, "have a little sense. I told you that Jamie has been greatly aided in being able to make this most difficult and traumatic of conclusions about himself by the strength of his own character. How do you think he has come by that great strength? Mr Potten, it is largely due to you. When you come to read these poems, this diary - if Jamie ever allows you to read them, which I should doubt - you will see what you ought to have seen with blinding clarity, if you had had any eyes to spare for your son: that the formation of this tough, this incredibly tough character; this devastating capacity for honesty with himself, this furious integrity, this immense will-power and moral fibre, so uncommon - it's almost unnatural in a boy of fifteen years - is almost entirely the product of the overwhelming resentment he feels towards you, his parents. Do you really think he'd care what you thought of him if he decided to sleep with this boy? Do you really think he gives a damn for all your money? No, sir. I'm afraid cutting him off without a shilling won't work. It's far less likely to be effective nowadays anyway, and with a boy like yours? There's not a chance of it. In any case," he said wearily, "is that really the proper way to help your son?" He halted abruptly and then said, suddenly sounding immensely tired, "I am sick to death of the sound of my own drone. Would you like a drink? I could use a very large one myself."

Their expressions alone told him the answer before their almost yelped response. He went to a large wall cupboard, unlocked it and took out three heavy crystal tumblers. "Scotch do? Right." He poured three very large whiskies.

***

While his parents were being ushered back to their car, in a state of anger and confusion more easily imagined than described, Jamie was easing himself out of Christopher's arms and pushing back the blanket. He stripped it off his lover and stood over him, smiling down on him and feeling as if the love in him was endless. He bent to undo the laces of his trainers, kicked them off and peeled off his sweatshirt and his jeans very quickly. He stood over Christopher triumphantly, wearing nothing but dark blue, surprisingly well-filled underpants. His erection was strong enough to push them clear away from his brown, flat stomach. He grinned, which made him look much more like a fifteen-year-old boy, and mimicked a stripper's bump and grind motions as he eased the pants down slightly. Then, with a quick movement he stripped them off, kicked them down his legs and twirled them with a flick of one foot into the branches of one of the sallows that ringed their little haven.

Christopher said a prayer to a god he did not believe in. Then he decided the only thing he trusted any longer was this moment, this utterly secluded greensward and the beautiful object of his love who was at this moment dropping onto his knees beside him. I'll always love him, he thought. I can't believe it won't all end in disaster, but I can't resist him, and I can't stand up to him. He's the stronger of us two, I must do what he asks. Christopher stripped off his clothes. Jamie fell on him with hoots of joy, and they rolled naked together on the heavy, musty-smelling old blanket. Jamie flung his arms round the older, considerably bigger boy and held him clasped as tightly as he could. He rolled him onto his back and lay on top of him, his legs straddling Christopher's belly.

"I love you, Chris," he said softly, smiling the smile again. "I'll always love you, and never love anyone else like this." This was too much for Christopher, who looked at his beauty and his youngness, and thought his heart would break, not knowing how Jamie had felt that his would break a few hours earlier that day as he set up his rod. His eyes filled with tears, for the beauty of it all and the dread foreboding that nothing could last, least of all anything pure and unstained and beautiful like this. He reached out to pull Jamie down to his lips.

Oh, dear God, thought Christopher, this can't be happening. Life's not that kind. But the thought was gone before it had properly formed. "I love you, J," he whispered. And then, without any conscious thought, he slid round in Jamie's embrace. "Make love to me," he murmured. As he said it many barriers slid back. All the conditioning that had made him timid, the worldly conventions that had bound him with fears for himself and even more for Jamie, disintegrated in a splintering burst of bright light. I'm yours now, he thought. For better or worse, richer or poorer or whatever the hell... he turned onto his stomach and raised himself, offering himself to his beloved.

Afterwards they lay for some time naked on the blanket, close but hardly touching. Each was too occupied with his own thoughts and emotions for talk. After a few minutes they simultaneously became aware of the chill in the air, and wrapped themselves in the blanket, and it was natural then to wrap themselves in each other also. It was a half hour before either was ready to speak. Then Christopher nibbled gently on Jamie's ear and murmured, "How was it, Jamie? Was it... was it all right for you?"

Jamie kissed him, but gave no answer for so long that Christopher began to go cold with dread that something had been wrong. Perhaps he should have resisted. Perhaps this was the end of it all, before it had properly begun. The thought that he might be in danger of losing what he had barely begun to possess sent his mind into black, deep waters. He was eerily detached, as if he was able to feel each succeeding thought as it separated itself from the central mass of his mind, to examine it in the strange, sub-lit detachment where he felt himself floating.

He wondered what form of words Jamie would find to tell him that it was over, that it had been wrong, a mistake, that they would not see each other again. The possibilities swam into the light like protozoa swimming into the lit circle on a microscope slide. He was trembling. He had a strange sensation that he could feel his nerves, individually inside him. Time stood still. He felt as if he had been dipped, like a chrysanthemum, in liquid helium, his whole personality ready to shatter at the tinkle of a bell. When Jamie spoke he heard it from the same remote distance of detachment. "It hurt a bit at first," he said conversationally, "but after the first few moments it was... I don't know... I just thought it

30

was the nicest feeling I'd ever known. I wanted it to go on and on and never stop. I felt as if you really belonged to me." And then, with a tinge of anxiety in his voice, he went on, "Was it all right for you, Chris? Was I all right for you?"

Christopher lay for a moment feeling the warmth ebb back into him as he circled back to time and place. What he felt could have been expressed in no known language, so he simply turned to face Jamie, who saw his answer in his eyes. He gathered the younger boy to him, passion rising rapidly, and felt Jamie respond. Afterwards they washed themselves in the freezing lake, then dressed, huddled in each other's arms under their blanket, and slept.

It was dusk when they were awakened by a lash of cold rain across their faces. They packed their things in the bags hurriedly and began to scramble through the alders. Then they remembered Jamie's rod, still lying in its rest where they had forgotten it, and had to go back and dismantle it. When it was back in its case and they were just about to set off again Christopher suddenly muttered to himself and reached into the back pocket of his Levi's. "Here," he said, passing Jamie a small envelope. "You said you wanted a photograph of me, so I got one. It's not much of a picture, I'm afraid," he added after a pause, "just one I took in the passport booth in Woolworths. I could get you a proper studio job, if you'd like it, but will that do for now?"

Jamie took the passport-size photograph from the envelope and peered at it in the gathering gloom. Christopher's heart-shaped face looked out with a half-smile that made him look younger and vulnerable. It was in indifferent colour, which made his heavy brown hair look black and his pale face look even paler. But the large brown eyes were clear, with brilliant spots in them - from the flash in the booth, Jamie thought. And the mouth was curved in an expression that Jamie knew well and loved. He put the picture to his lips and kissed it softly. "Were you thinking about me when you took it?" he asked seriously. "Of course I was," said Christopher. "What else could I have been thinking of?"

"Oh, well, it's just that you're smiling just like you do

31

sometimes. When we've just... after we've been kissing or something. And when you first saw me this morning." He peered at the photograph again, having to squint now, looked up and said, "You look beautiful, Christopher. It's a lovely photo. Thank you." He kissed it again, then put both arms round Christopher's neck and kissed him, carefully, on the lips, then on each cheek, on the tip of his nose, and finally on each eyelid. "Thank you, dear Chris. I'll keep it on me always. Then I can look at you, and kiss you, whenever I want." He seized Christopher's hand and pulled him towards the trees.

They walked the two miles of towpath back to the outskirts of the town, blessing the darkness, for it allowed them to go hand-in-hand. Each was profoundly conscious that every moment of contact, even holding hands, was a precious moment before they had to go back to a normality that loomed over them like the shadow of a gallows. The hours before they could meet again extended into a nameless and immeasurable future.

They parted under a stone bridge. Jamie had to climb a stile and cross fields to his parents' farm. Christopher had to cross the bridge and walk under streetlights into town. The nearest lights were already close enough to cast a faint illumination onto the towpath, but under the bridge it was dark enough that no one could have seen them from five yards as they held each other in a fierce hug. They kissed for a minute. Then Christopher muttered that they had to go. "Shall I go there tomorrow?" he asked. "You'll have to go to school some time, you know."

Jamie groaned. "I know. I'm going to be in trouble. But it was worth it," he breathed. He giggled suddenly, and mischievously put his hand between Christopher's legs and squeezed him gently. "Do you love me, Chris? Tell me it's real. You do really love me, don't you?" Christopher answered as lovers have done as long as people have loved, with a fierce whisper in his lover's ear.

"I'm glad you're here, Chris," said Jamie sadly. "I wanted someone to love me. You're the first one who has." He kissed him again, quickly. "Go there tomorrow," he said quickly, "but if I'm not there by ten, you'll know I can't make it. I've got trouble coming. You know." He turned to go, but immediately turned back. He took Christopher in his arms again and kissed him, a brief, hot kiss, then pressed his face against Christopher's and muttered, "Don't worry. I'll see you soon. I can't not see you." Christopher felt warm tears on his cheek. And then, in a moment, Jamie pulled himself free and was gone.

Jamie walked home quickly at first, more and more slowly as he neared the house. When the lights of the farmhouse appeared in the distance his feet dragged until he was hardly moving at all. He swallowed hard and forced himself on, wondering what was going to happen to him.

Christopher trudged through the suburban streets to his home, his feelings churning between the golden afterglow of the day's happenings and nagging tugs of concern for Jamie. He had sat quietly listening for more than enough hours, during their early meetings, murmuring such comfort and consolation as he could think of to say, to have a fair idea what sort of reception awaited his young lover when he got home, and, deeply though he respected Jamie's ability to look after himself - for he acknowledged, with the candour love can sustain, that Jamie was in truth a deal more grown up and capable than he was himself - he feared for him. Even so, these fears could not keep out the golden glow of what he knew had been the happiest day of his life. Between the glow and the fears the mile walk to his home went unnoticed, and he forgot all about his own dark premonitions until he found himself standing on the front doorstep. The lights and the noise of a television brought him precipitately to earth. He felt for his key in a black shroud of mingled dejection and fear.

He let himself in, and walked straight into his mother, coming from the kitchen with a handful of knives and forks. "Hallo, Chris," she said, smiling at him. Then she saw his face and, dumping the cutlery on the telephone table, ran to him. "Chris, dear, whatever's the matter? You look as if

33

you've been ill." She looked closely at him. "Chris, you've been crying!" she said in alarm. "What is it?"

"Nothing, Mum," he said, gulping miserably. "It's nothing. Please..." He looked so wretched that she put her arms round him, something she hadn't done since he was a little boy. He stayed limply in her arms for a moment, then shook himself free. He would not have allowed the thought to come into his head if he had known such thoughts could exist, but he couldn't help it: the feeling of arms round him brought a hellish cocktail of blissful recollection of the last arms that had been round him, the pain of separation that lovers specialise in, and the trepidations he had for his future, unspecified but none the less grim for that, that he couldn't bear his mother's embrace. When immediately there came alongside these confused emotions a cold douche of guilt for comparing his mother's embrace with Jamie's, it was more than he could bear. He wriggled free and gazed at her in anguish for a moment. "Please, Mum, don't say anything to the others," he muttered, and bolted upstairs to his room, leaving her rooted to the spot in horrified amazement. After a moment she followed him softly upstairs and found him sprawled face down on his bed.

"Do you want to talk about it, whatever it is?" she asked him, sitting carefully out of contact with him on the foot of the bed. "I... no, Mum, I c-can't," he said, half-turning his face to her. "I can't," he repeated, his voice getting a little stronger. "I... I'd like to, but I can't. Not yet."

"All right, dear. Of course you don't have to. You know you can talk to me any time if you feel you want to. I don't want to pry..."

"I know you don't, Mum," he said. He turned to face her, and gave her a watery smile. "I know you're the last person in the world to do that. It's just... just something I can't really talk about yet."

She smiled fondly at him. "I understand, dear. Tell me about it when you're ready, if you like. Would you like me to go?" She didn't wait for an answer, but patted him once, very quickly, on his leg, and went to the door. There she turned and smiled reassuringly at him. "We'll be having dinner in a few minutes. Would you like me to leave yours out for the time being?"

"No, Mum. No, thanks. I'll be all right. I'll be down in a minute or two and say hallo to Dad. Is Neil in?"

"Yes, he's busy with his homework. He'll be out soon, anxious to bore you to death telling you about the goal he scored today. Now, you are sure you're all right, dear?"

"Yes, Mum, I'm okay. Honestly. I'll just go and have a splash and I'll be down." She smiled at him again and left him. Downstairs she went to her husband, who was sprawled comfortably in his armchair watching the news. "That Chris?" he said, his face brightening. Chris has always been his favourite, she thought. He tries his hardest not to show it, but I know it, and Neil does too. He's very fond of Neil, but he worships Chris. Look how his face lights up when he thinks he's home. "Yes, dear, he's just gone upstairs to wash and change," she said. "And Bob, when he comes down, please *don't* ask him what the matter is."

"Why? What...?" her husband said, alarm signals immediately showing in his face. "Is there something the matter?"

"Yes and no," she said practically. "He's just come in looking as if he's dead and gone to his own funeral. I think he's in love, Bob. And that means that he won't - emphatically he *won't*, Bob, thank you for barging in in your hob-nail boots where angels fear to tread, asking him what's the matter with him. You just talk your usual sweet nothings to him about football or whatever nonsense there is on the news, and carefully don't notice when he goes into a trance all of a sudden. Tread warily, Bob. I remember that expression very well. You used to have it on your face every time we said good night when you were courting me."

Her husband laughed. "Then I know what he's going through. Poor old Chrissie." He jumped up and gave her a quick hug. "Don't worry, Audrey. I won't do square dances on his poor old exposed nerve ends. I'm not so ancient that I can't remember what it's like the first time. It was bad enough with you, and you were the twentieth."

"You beast," she said, pummelling him in the chest. Then she gave him a quick peck, smiled fondly at him and went out leaving him laughing. "Ha!" he snorted. "In love at last. By jove, Neil'll give him hell when he finds out. Poor old Chrissie. I wonder what she's like."

***

The reception that met Jamie Potten when he walked in through the farmhouse kitchen was worse than his worst forebodings. The kitchen was empty when he arrived, but his footsteps had been heard as he crossed it and walked to the living room. He opened the heavy oak door and walked into a menacing, deafening silence. His mother was seated in a deep leather armchair, and was laying a book on the floor beside it as he entered. His father was sitting at the great oaken dining table that occupied one end of the immense room, with innumerable papers strewn round him, writing in an account book of some kind. As soon as Jamie walked in he laid down his pen, closed the book with a slam, and sat back, staring directly at him with a cold, contemptuous look on his face that Jamie, for all his self-possession, found unnerving, almost frightening.

"Hello, James," said his mother quietly. He looked across at her. There were dark smudges under her eyes, and he was quick to notice that although she didn't look downright hostile as his father did, she certainly wasn't looking very welcoming. Jamie, who had stopped expecting anything much in the way of affection from either parent before he was out of short trousers, nonetheless felt a chill run through him at this reception. This was something special. He steeled himself as best he could, swallowed, hoping they would not notice it and, forcing as bright a note as he could manage into his voice, said, "Hello, Mother. Hello, Father."

36

The silence continued for several very long seconds. Finally his father spoke, in a cold, quiet voice that was as nasty as anything Jamie had ever heard. "So you've put your uniform on again, then." Jamie went cold. They had found out. There was nothing much he could say, so he said nothing. "I'm talking to you, boy," his father said, still ominously quiet. "I said, you've got your school clothes on again. Have you got a tongue in your head?"

"Yes, Father, I've got my uniform on," he said obediently, and waited.

"Where have you been?"

Jamie hesitated. He hadn't prepared for this moment, though he was far too bright not to have known that it must come some time or other. His father unwittingly came to his aid. "Don't insult me and your mother by giving us some pack of lies about being at school. Where have you been?"

"I wasn't going to say I'd been at school," he said. "I'm quite intelligent enough to realise you know I haven't..."

"Don't you stand there and tell me how intelligent you are, you despicable little tyke," said his father, beginning to raise his voice for the first time. "I asked you a straight question, and by God you'll give me a straight answer, or I'll whip it out of you. Where have you been - today *and* all the other days?"

Jamie paused. Every second he could gain was time to think and to recover his composure. He thought he had armoured himself so successfully against his parents that they were no longer able to disconcert him. That, he now realised, had been an error. But his usual self-possession was coming back with each second of time he could buy. "Actually, I've been fishing," he said at last.

"Fishing," said his father, very softly again. "Actually, he's been fishing, Annabel." He swung round to face Jamie again. "A fine occupation. Fishing. Yes. What do I pay per year in fees for your very fancy schooling, James? Do you know?" James had a good idea. There was again nothing to be said, so he said nothing, but walked to the nearest armchair and sat down.

"Stand up," said Mr Potten softly. "I haven't given you permission to sit down." Jamie hesitated, then looked at his mother, but she, after barely catching his eye, looked away at nothing. His leather briefcase containing his schoolbooks, which had been hidden with his uniform in a disused outbuilding at the far side of the farm all day, he dropped into the chair. Then he returned to the point near the door where he had been before.

"That's better," said his father, looking almost disappointed at being obeyed meekly like this. "It's time to get a few things straight in this household, and one of them is that *I* am the householder, and *you* are a fifteen-year-old schoolboy, who goes to a very flash school with a pretty badge on its pretty blazer and cap, by courtesy of your father's paying - what is it? I was just looking it up - yes, here it is: six thousand, four hundred and eighty pounds per annum. Plus extras which come to a further - let me see - yes, a further two thousand, one hundred and forty-seven pounds and thirty-six pence, to date. That's over the two and a half years you've been there, so shall we say a round figure of - what? - a shade over seven thousand three hundred each year, I work it out at. What do you think of that, James?"

"What am I supposed to think?" asked James.

"You are asking me to tell you what you're supposed to think? Surely not. The gifted schoolboy prodigy, asking his mere father for advice in matters of the intellect? No, I can't believe that. I'm not the intellectual in the family, am I, after all? I'm only the bloody fool that pays the bills. No, boy, you tell *me* what *you* think of those figures I've just given you. Seven thousand three hundred a year, plus loose change."

He waited with a look of savage enjoyment on his face, mingled with something else, which Jamie, for all his experience in assessing his volatile parent's moods and expressions, could not quite place. It was, in fact, disgust; but Jamie could not be expected to recognise that, because for all the indifference and preoccupation with themselves and their differences that his parents had shown him since his infancy, they had always been, at least, proud of him and his attainments. If he was not a child yearning for affection, he was at least something for which they might legitimately take the credit, an achievement of their own, worthy of boasting about over the bridge table or among cronies at the Golden Hind Hotel where his parents took their Sunday lunchtime drink.

After a long pause Jamie said, "I don't know what I'm supposed to think
someone's education. I quite like the school, but I don't know if it's worth that much. You're a businessman, so I expect you'll be able to assess that sort of thing better than me. Have you decided I'm too expensive to run?"

"James, James, my boy, I've decided all sorts of things today, and you'll hear of them in due course, but meanwhile you'll keep a civil tongue. I'm not going to pay thousands of pounds out on an education that you seem to think a trifle as light as air *and* sit here in my own house - *my* house, James, remember that - and take sarcasm and insolence from a bit of a kid like you." There was a bitter, scathing tone of real dislike in his voice now. It unsettled Jamie anew.

"All right, Dad," he said eventually. "So I've been fishing. I played truant. But that's not the end of the world, is..."

"You shut your mouth, you little *shit*!" roared his father, unable to keep at a simmer any longer. "You shut your dirty little fucking mouth - by God, I wonder where *that's* been today..." This really puzzled Jamie, and he began to feel really worried. He wasn't sure what the last cryptic reference meant, but it sounded perilous. He forced his attention back to the gathering tirade. ."..and listen to what I've got to say.

"Today, your mother and I were dragged from our proper business to go to your fancy school. There we had to sit like a couple of delinquent children and listen to a lecture from that prissy, clever-clever, superior... *ponce* of a headmaster of yours telling us - telling me, your own father - how much better he understood and sympathised with you and your little ways than we did. He told us a lot about you, oh yes, he did, James. He told us all about how exceptionally intelligent you are" - his mouth twisted and he affected an

39

ugly imitation of Dr Lane's dry, patrician accent. "He told us all about your wonderful qualities of self-possession - 'almost unnatural in a fifteen-year-old'; he told us about all manner of unnatural things.

"He was also kind enough to tell us that he thought that *we* were two world-class shitbags. He generously told us that the problems you were going through were *our* fault. Yes, James - no, I'm sorry, my dear, precious, 'exceptionally intelligent', sensitive, gifted son, I should have remembered, you're *Jamie* to your *friends*, aren't you? 'Jamie'." He mimicked the headmaster's voice again to say the name, and made it sound like an obscenity.

"Well, Jamie, the good doctor told us all about your attendance record. It seems that I pay a year's fees to your posh school, and you for your part condescend to put in about a term and a half's attendance. But does your headmaster haul you in front of him and thrash you within an inch of your worthless life, as any schoolmaster worth his salt would? Does he my backside. No, your headmaster calls you in and lays you on a psychiatrist's couch and asks the little man what the matter is." The flush was rising dangerously up his neck and cheeks now, and his eyes were bulging with suppressed fury and, Jamie thought, malice.

"And the little man dutifully obliges the amateur psychiatrist, and tells him a lot of private business of his poor old parents, and the good doctor sends him on his way with a matey pat on the head. And then calls the parents in and spends hours telling us how the son of our loins is so upset by our behaviour - *our* behaviour, I ask you - that he can't possibly concentrate on trifles like his work that I pay a small fortune for, or his games that cost another small fortune over and above in kit, because he's too upset. My Christ, you've really pulled the wool over that superior bastard's eyes, haven't you? I'll hand that much to you, boy, you've made a monkey out of that high-falutin graven image."

Jamie opened his mouth to speak. "There's no need for you to speak," his father snapped. "You're listening this time. It's me speaking, not some intellectual arsehole that you can twist round your little finger with your snivelling lies and your whining, wheedling slanders and your fancy intellectualising. I bet you never knew your old dad knew big words like these, eh? Not the fucking old business-wallah at home who sweats in trade to pay the accounts. Well listen and be educated, my pretty son. There are other sorts of education than the sort lofty intelligences like the good doctor hand out to their more 'exceptionally gifted' charges.

"I had to grovel to that bastard, James, my pretty boy. I had to grovel to him, and promise him faithfully that I would be kind and understanding to you when you eventually condescended to show up. I had to grovel because it was the only way I could see of escaping. I thought if I didn't promise him everything he wanted we'd probably still be there now. Come to that, there were moments there when he almost had me believing the psychologist's claptrap he was spewing out. But I've had time to think about it since then, and let me tell you, boy, there's going to be no loving kindness for you here, no sympathy and understanding..."

"There never was any of that," shouted Jamie, who promptly cursed himself for having raised his voice.

"No? No?" sneered his father. "You need loving kindness like a fish needs a bicycle. You need a boot up your arse and a punch in the mouth when you open it too wide, and I might just be the man to give it to you. Now tell me, who's Christopher?"

The tone of his voice as he uttered the name was positively ferocious, and this tone, combined with the heart-stopping mention of the name at all, took Jamie so utterly aback that he physically staggered. His face went a sickly fish-belly white and his mouth hung open. His father leered at him revoltingly.

"Ah-*hah*!" he crowed. "*That's* set the little man back on his heels a little, hasn't it? HASN'T IT?" he roared suddenly at his wife, who had shrunk back into her chair as the pitiless tirade had progressed. She started violently when he bellowed at her, but said nothing, just hanging her head.

"Your mother, my pretty boy, has nothing to say to me.

She doesn't like me very much, your mother."

"I don't blame her," roared Jamie, suddenly furious. "You're a bastard and a tyrant and a filthy, foul-mouth-ed...pervert. You leave a trail of slime wherever you go like a slug, and you pollute and wither everything you come into contact with. I *fucking* well HATE you. I've hated you for as long as I can remember. You talk about how much money you're spending on me, but I'd've swopped it all for one day feeling as though I had a decent father like all the others. They talk about their fathers and the things they've done with them, and when they ask me I invent lies for them, because I'm too ashamed to admit that I've got a father who wouldn't tell me the time and hasn't had a minute to spare for me since the day he fucked me into my mother's belly. You're not human. I hate the fucking sight of you, and there's another of your fuckings back for you. And don't you *dare* to talk about Christopher to me. You're not fit to speak his name."

He said the last of this in a high-pitched yelp. Tears were streaming down his face, from rage and shock more than from chagrin. He felt that he had lost every vestige of whatever dignity he had ever possessed, had sunk as low as it was possible for a person to fall. He choked on a vast sob, and bolted for the door. But his father was too quick for him. Moving with a speed astonishing in so heavy and bulky a man he leapt from his chair, shot across the room and seized Jamie by the hair just as he got the door open.

Hauling him back by his hair with one hand, he grabbed a handful of the seat of Jamie's trousers with the other and hurled him backwards into the centre of the room. There was a shriek from the far side of the room, and Annabel Potten rocketed out of her chair, driven at last by simple fear for her child into some kind of spirit. "David! NO! Don't you *dare* touch him. You *shan't* touch him!" she howled, and with that she rushed to where Jamie was picking himself up, eyes distended with fear, but with an ugly set to his mouth. She stood over him, between him and the advancing, looming bulk of her enraged husband.

"Get out of my fucking way, you evil cow," he screamed at her, and, too possessed with rage to count what he was doing, swept a brawny forearm towards her to brush her aside. If the blow had landed on the side of her head where it was aimed it would have done her grave damage, but she flung an arm up and deflected it. Even so it hit her arm with sufficient force to knock her off her feet, and she crashed down beside Jamie on the carpet. As she fell her head hit one of the huge, bulbous legs of the great Victorian dining table a glancing blow. She shrieked at the impact, and immediately gasped as she hit the floor, all the breath knocked out of her. Jamie bounded up from the floor and shot a desperate look round the room, seeking something he could use as a weapon.

The sudden eruption of violence, however, had some effect on David Potten, bringing him some of the way back to his senses. He halted in his menacing advance on the other two and stood, swaying a little from side to side. His eyes were bulging out of their sockets, his hair was standing out from his head and his face was a livid purplish red. He stood for some moments, sucking in gulps of breath. Then he subsided, almost visibly, like a toad after it has puffed itself up for combat, and stamped back to the table. He dragged a chair from under it with such force that the edge of the seat smashed against the underside of the top, crashed it down and dropped onto it like a sack of coal. There he sat for some minutes, breathing heavily, with his eyes fixed on Jamie and a look of loathing and disgust written all over his face.

Jamie had helped his mother to her feet. "Are you all right, Mother?" he asked. She nodded, still breathless, and a little dazed by the blow to her head. Jamie helped her back to the chair she had been sitting in. Then he moved to a position by the heavy oak sideboard. There were bottles and some ornaments on it that he thought might be usable as weapons if he was attacked again. He leaned on it to recover his breath, watching his father warily. After what seemed like an eternity, David Potten spoke.

"Get this into your head, you vile, revolting, disgusting

little fucking *queer*. You needn't think anything's changed because I let you go. You've got a lot coming to you, and you're going to get it, all of it, with interest, before you're much older. Your headmaster told us all about your little games with this Christopher. And something else for you to think about, too. I'm going to find out who this Christopher is, and I'm going to tear him apart. I don't give a fuck if I do time for it, it'll be worth that, because I'll at least have the satisfaction of knowing that he's in hospital. While he's in there having his bones set he won't be shit-stabbing you, my fine fellow. And if I'm in prison, I shan't have the responsibility for paying for you to play hookey from school to let a fairy ream your arsehole out for thirty quid of my money a day. Oh yes, my pretty little fairy of a son, it'll be a *pleasure* to have fifteen three-minute rounds with your little friend."

"You're sick, Dad," said Jamie, very quietly. "I'm sorry for some of what I said just now. I feel sorry for you. Sorry you can't understand anybody who isn't just like you. I expect most people who know you feel sorry for you. That crowd of hypocrites you play bridge with, coming round here and guzzling your booze and sucking up to you because of your money, they probably despise you, or feel sorry for you. That's your trouble, I see that now. You're so used to people sucking up to you for your money that you can't understand it when someone's indifferent to it. That's why you'll never understand me. I'll have to go now, of course. I don't know where I'll go, but I can't stay here. We've said too much to each other that we shan't be able to forgive. I'd better go now." Stifling another sob, he moved towards the door.

His father immediately jumped up and bore down on him. "You're going fucking *nowhere*," he roared, and aimed a heavy punch at Jamie's head. The boy ducked under it, but he was not quick enough, and it caught him heavily on the shoulder. He staggered back against the sideboard, and his father, who had risen instantaneously straight back to boiling point, moved in to follow up his blow with another. Jamie, desperate and terrified, swept a hand along the sideboard seeking something to defend himself with. His clutching hand found something cold and heavy. He snatched it up and, as his father, completely out of control of himself now, towered over him, he swept it sideways as hard as he could. It struck David Potten full on the side of the face with a soggy splat, and stopped him in his tracks. He stood for a moment, swaying, and looking at Jamie with a slightly puzzled expression in his eyes. Then they lost their focus and he fell with a gentle thud to the carpet, where he lay making a slight snoring sound and dribbling from the corner of his mouth.

Jamie looked down at what he had done, and felt nothing. He was vaguely aware of a terrible relief at being out of immediate danger, but other than that he was too numb with accumulated shock and emotional overload to feel anything. He swayed a little, and leaned on the sideboard. The only thought in his mind was to get away. He ran jerkily from the room, and never even remembered his mother, sitting slightly concussed in her corner chair.

The door slammed behind him, and that roused her from her daze. "James. My James. Jamie!" she sobbed quietly. "What have we done to you? What have we done to ourselves?" She got up and went groggily over to where her husband lay. He was beginning to come round. She looked at the great bruise along the side of his jaw, across his cheek and over his temple. Then she found a brass candlestick on the floor where Jamie had dropped it. It had been straight and about eighteen inches in length. Now it was bent to an obtuse angle from the force of Jamie's blow. She rose unsteadily to her feet and stood it on the sideboard. Then she tottered across to the telephone to call the doctor.

Jamie ran up to his room. He dragged a canvas holdall from under his bed and stuffed it with clothes. When he had what he thought would be enough for a few days, he grabbed his torch off the window sill and a couple of books. The whole operation took a minute and a half, and then he was taking the stairs three at a time. He shot through the kitchen and raced across the farm to his disused outbuilding. For a few moments he thought of sleeping there, but quickly decided it was not safe to stay anywhere near home. He added the clothes he had been wearing that day to the contents of the holdall and set off, walking aimlessly but more or less in the direction of the town. Suddenly a thought came into his mind, and almost jolted the breath out of him. How, he wondered, could he have forgotten? Christopher. If he could only talk to him they would be able to work out what to do.

Jamie loved Christopher for almost numberless reasons, and in many ways. Sexually and physically he loved him. Jamie knew what he was, and he knew that Christopher was also. That was how they were made and there was nothing more to be said. But he loved him on other and far deeper levels than that. Christopher was the only person who had ever loved him, or treated him with love. He was also the only person in Jamie's short but interesting life who had been identifiably kind to him on anything more than an impersonal level. He was the only person who had ever been willing to sit and listen to Jamie without interrupting and, having allowed Jamie to say his piece, to offer a considered judgment, or advice, or admit that he didn't know, or just ruffle his hair and give some kindness or consolation. He was the only person in Jamie's experience who had been willing, indeed glad, simply to be there when needed. They had sat together for hours and hardly said a word, but in a deep and comforting companionship. At other times they had talked as if they had unfathomed wells of subjects to talk about and things to say about them. It made, in the end, little difference. Christopher was there, and he had never let him down. Jamie made up his mind.

And, as soon as he made it up, he promptly changed it. It would never do to invade Christopher like this, late at night, half out of his mind with everything, with unresolved problems at home that were beyond a boy's competence even to think about solving; with more trouble, of an unknowable nature, facing him on the school front. School. He would, he supposed, have to go tomorrow. Though judging by the insistent theme of his father's outburst that evening it seemed highly problematic that he would remain at school much

46

longer, it was nevertheless a problem in the short term.

No, he couldn't possibly take that kind of burden to Christopher now. Not to mention Christopher's parents, his family. Jamie only knew one family, so he had limited standards to judge by. He took it for granted that Christopher's people knew no more about their son than his had done. He could conceive intellectually of a kind of family that wouldn't react as his had reacted to things; but he had nothing in his pack of experience to enable him to imagine how such a family would seem or be. He opted for safety. He would have to go somewhere else.

And in a moment he found his answer. Only a moment ago he had supposed that he would have to go to school tomorrow. Why not give himself the advantage of a little advance notice of the kind of reception he was going to receive? Dr Lane had told him in the strongest terms that he was to take any problems to him without a second thought. Dr Lane lived with his wife, a friendly woman with soft grey eyes and a cheerful affection for the boys, in the headmaster's house, across the cricket field from the school. Why not? thought Jamie. He thought about it for a few yards more, probing the idea for hidden snags. Then he nodded to himself, and set off at a more purposeful pace for school.

***

"All right then, Annabel," muttered the doctor. He leaned awkwardly over the small table in the hall on which the telephone extension sat and scribbled a prescription. "It's Librium, 10 mil. No more than four a day, mind. They're powerful, and they can be habituative." He slipped his raincoat over his shoulders, and prepared to dash to his car through the downpour that had just started. As Annabel Potten held the door open for him he hesitated on the threshold. He took a step out into the portico, then turned

47

back to her with a very uneasy expression on his face.

"Look here, Annabel, I don't like this at all. I know you've had your problems in the past. God knows, I ought to, I've given you enough scrips for that bloody poison over the years. But I really don't like this. I've never known you two to go for each other like this before. I'm not sure I oughtn't to..." He trailed into silence.

"It's all right, Harold, really, it's all right," said Annabel Potten, too quickly, and speaking in a low, urgent tone. "We've had a terrible fight, and I had to defend myself, but I can control David, honestly, I promise you. Please don't do any... please don't make things worse," she ended in a flat tone of finality. "It wouldn't do any good, and it might do a lot of harm. More harm than you could possibly realise. I can handle him, I promise you. I just need something for my nerves."

The doctor looked very hard at her for a moment and began to say something, but thought better of it and turned for his car again. "All right, Annabel, I'll take your word for it this time. I wish I knew whether I'm doing the right thing." He still hesitated, looking tired and worried. "You give me your word that it's all over and you can take care of it?"

"Yes, yes, yes, Harold. It's over and I can deal with it. Please believe me. It was only a flaming row, and we've had enough of them, as you know. This one was just worse than usual. Now please go. I hate to be like this, but I've got to talk to David."

He shrugged. "All right. David's not really badly hurt, as I told you, but he must have rest. And for God's sake don't let him near the Scotch bottle. And the same goes for you. Take two of those capsules I gave you. Now, you take care of yourself. Good night." He stared hard at her in a last moment's indecision, shrugged again, then ran through the rain to his car.

Annabel Potten watched the tail lights disappear round the gatepost and listened until the sound of his car had died away in the lane before closing the door. Then she sagged against the doorpost and began to summon up her strength to go back to her husband. She was already half-regretting her urgent dismissal of the doctor for, despite her assurances to him, she was not at all confident of her ability to control David. She had always in the past found one or other of the weapons a woman can call on adequate when he had been in one of his volcanic moods, but this time he had gone far beyond anything she had seen before. The thought flashed painfully through her head that she was, for the first time, genuinely afraid of him.

She pressed her elegant hands to her temples and gathered what there was to gather of her resources. She was feeling sick, weak and tired, just at the moment when she felt sure that she was about to need all her strength. However, there was no help for it. She walked shakily back to the living room.

David Potten was lying sprawled in a deep armchair, his head heavily bandaged. The first thing she saw was a large glass on the small table beside him. "David!" she ejaculated in dismay. "You mustn't. Harold said you *mustn't* drink. What is it? Scotch?" She took a step towards him with a hand outstretched to take the glass. He snatched it from the table and drained it.

"Don't you bloody well tell me what I can do and can't do," he snarled. "And don't tell me what that smarmy bastard Holdsworth said either. I'll decide whether I have a drink or not, and what it is." He heaved himself upright in the chair, got rather groggily to his feet and went to the sideboard. His wife stood uncertainly where she was near the door and watched as he poured himself another very large measure. She noted with relief that it was at least from the brandy decanter that he helped himself. She supposed it was probably better for him than whisky. Thoughts ran sluggishly through her mind. She had hoped vaguely that somehow his being hurt might have done something to dampen his temper a little. That hope now fizzled out. A grey wash of despair passed over, almost paralysing her.

Potten was holding the brass candlestick with which Jamie had struck him, looking with an oddly detached air at the great kink in it made by the blow. He turned towards her, drinking deeply as he did so. His left eye was hugely swollen and the eye itself had completely closed. It looked as if a purplish-black billiard ball with a livid blue slit across its equator was squeezing itself out of his head. Annabel Potten felt her gorge rise, and swallowed desperately to keep it down. "I never thought that little bastard had the spunk in him to do it," her husband mused. "Little bastard. Ha! First time I've ever been laid out in my life, you know." She cringed against the door. This soft, murmuring tone was more terrifying than all his normal bluster.

"Ha!" he muttered again. "Imagine that. First time in my life I've ever been knocked cold, and it's by a little milksop of a queer. A bit of a kid, and my own pup at that. Well, well. I wonder what the guys at the club, or in the Golden Hind would say about *that*." And, to her astonishment and dismay, he threw back his head and bellowed with laughter. Not, she saw with gathering consternation, any kind of laughter that she had ever heard. There was nothing but horror in it. It seized him in a paroxysm. He roared and gasped and spluttered with it, and eventually leaned over the big oak sideboard, helpless, cackling with this unnatural, sour mirth.

Eventually he got control of himself and straightened up. He drained his glass and refilled it. "David," she said feebly, "Harold said..."

"I told you before," he said, still chuckling at intervals, "I don't give a *shit* what Harold said. I don't give a shit what you say. If I want a drink in my own house, I shall have one, without asking anybody's permission, especially yours. That's just one of the things you're going to learn before you're much older. You and that son of yours. He's got his to come yet, when he comes down from his room. If he's got the guts to come down. He's probably locked himself in and hidden under the bed with his teddy bear. But there's plenty of time. There are going to be some changes, Annabel Faulkner." He managed to make her maiden name sound like a discharge of spittle. "There's going to be a *lot* of changes round here. Now I'm going to bed. I'll go along with Harold that far. Off to bed to recover from injuries inflicted on me by your greasy little poofter of a son. I'll see you tomorrow."

"He's your son as well," his wife said with a brief spark of her own anger. She immediately regretted saying anything at all. In his present strange condition he was too unpredictable to take risks with. But there was no explosion. He turned the livid eye on her again, still with the menacing half-amused expression on his face, and said softly, "Yes. My son. I wonder." He stepped towards her and the door, and despite herself she flinched. He saw the movement and a broad smile flitted across his face.

Her movement drew his eyes to one side as he tramped towards the door. "Hallo, what's this?" he muttered, and stooped to pick something from the floor. It looked like a scrap of paper, an inch or so square. He stared at it for some moments, then turned it over, and she saw that it was a photograph of someone's head and shoulders. "Well, well," he said, again softly. "Well, well, well. So this is the beloved." He held the picture close to her eyes. She had a chance to take in a pale, youthful face with a shaggy mop of dark hair, then he flicked it round in his fingers. On the back she read, "To my darling Jamie, with all my love. C."

"Christopher," he said, almost lovingly. "How nice to meet you." He moved his wife, quite gently, to one side and went out, still looking intently at Christopher's face. She stood motionless, hearing his heavy footsteps going up the stairs, then moving along the passage to Jamie's room. The door opened and closed. "James!" she heard him shout, "James!" The steps came back along the passage and down the stairs. She still had not moved when the door opened. Potten poked his head round the door. "I just thought you'd like to know," he said in a mock-solicitous tone, "your brave son has decided that discretion is the better part of valour." She just stared at him, unable to speak. "He's gone, Annabel. He is no longer among us." He grinned unpleasantly at her. "I just thought you'd like to know."

The door closed and the sound of his footsteps faded as he

went upstairs once more. Annabel Potten walked slowly to the great bay window that looked out over the drive and stood gazing silently at the reflection of the brightly lit room fragmenting and coalescing in the rain streaming down the panes. As she began silently to cry, the telephone rang.

***

Edith Lane came soundlessly into the living room and set her tray on the coffee table. She poured weak tea into a small bone china cup for herself, and into another cup, as thin but the size and roughly the shape of a conch shell for her husband. He took half a dozen sips, grunting with pleasure. "How is our waif of the night?" he asked.

"Fast asleep," she said, her eyes gleaming with a hint of a tear. "He insisted on having a shower. Said he'd been fishing and hadn't had a chance to get himself washed. The poor little mite. He was more worried about soiling our sheets than he was about himself. I embarrassed him, I'm afraid."

"Eh? How's that?"

"I thought he was already in bed when I took him some tea, and walked in as he was just getting in. He blushed like a traffic light. He sleeps naked," she added, unnecessarily.

"I dare say you set his mind at rest," he observed drily.

"I told him he'd got nothing I hadn't seen before, and he had enough spirit in him to give me a smile, bless his heart. He was asleep in a few seconds, as soon as he'd drunk his tea. He's at the end of his tether, the poor child. But John, he's got the most beautiful smile. I could fall in love with someone who smiled like that myself. It's no wonder he's got that poor boy captivated."

"Hmmm. 'That poor boy' is going to be a problem. Jamie's mother says her husband is still breathing wrath and likely to go in search of this Christopher to tear him apart. My God, I don't like all this. It's quite the nastiest situation I've encountered, in all my years dealing with boys." He lay back and stared into vacancy for a while. "The father is an atrocious man. Blustering, of course, but not *all* bluster like most of that kind. This one's got a real streak of viciousness in him, and not far below the surface, either. The boy is clearly terrified of him and so, by the sound of her on the telephone, is the wife. I think the other boy is in real danger. Which means that he's somehow got to be protected. Warned, at any rate."

"Did you get his name out of Jamie?" asked his wife.

"No. I asked him, casually in passing, but he's far too quick for such things, even when he's just about dropping from shock and exhaustion. And I didn't feel that I could press him in his condition. We'll have to know, of course, but it can wait till tomorrow."

"You won't allow him to attend classes tomorrow, will you, John?" she asked anxiously. "I really don't think..."

"Good Lord, no, of course not. No, he needs at least a couple of days to get over the dreadful business this evening." He sat in thought for a while. "You know, Edith, he really is very strong. He'll be formidable when he's older. Look at what he's gone through today - and I don't think he's told us all of it, by any means. There has, I think, been some kind of crisis between him and the boy Christopher. He very carefully skirted round all mention of the boy that he could avoid, but every time he mentioned his name an expression came over his face... I don't know... one feels rather self-conscious about using such terms, but really, Edith, he looked... *radiant*. It was as if the sun had come out, right here in the room..."

"I know, dear," she said. "I've seen his smile. Well... he's a very lucky young man." She picked up the tray and took it out, leaving her husband staring after her. He jumped out of his chair and followed her into the kitchen. "Edith, what do you mean by that? He's *not* lucky at all. We can't for a moment allow this... this liaison to continue..."

"Oh? And how are we to go about stopping it? We can curtail some of its murkier aspects, but how do you propose

53

to prevent them from meeting? You can't imprison Jamie, and there's little you can do about the other boy, short of bringing the police into it - and you're not proposing to do anything as foolish as *that*, I trust."

"No, no, no, of course I'm not. But we must warn the other boy; tell his parents what has been going on and make sure they take the necessary action. You sound as if you think they will continue with this relationship, but that's preposterous. It will end in disaster."

"And what of Jamie the while? Why, you said yourself you told the poor child's dreadful parents this morning that it was quite probable the relationship would continue."

"Yes, yes, but that was this morning, before all this had taken place. Since then he's had some sort of... of... apotheosis with his Christopher, he's been abused and assaulted by his father while his mother looked on and more or less let it happen, he's cracked his father's head open, and he's run away from home, with his mother thanking God he's done so. She admitted as much, in so many words, when I spoke to her on the phone just now. She practically had hysterics when I made the merest hint about taking him back there. Now he's in temporary digs with us, and his father's just as likely to go rampaging off tomorrow, armed with this photograph, bent on committing murder. That's quite enough to be going on with, I'd say. The last thing we want is for the whole damned confection to be topped off by any resumption of this relationship. The position is too damned complicated as it is, Edith."

He paused for breath, and his wife moved quietly to his side and stroked his grey head. "John, dear, you forget one thing, and, just like a man, you pick the most important thing of the lot." He looked down at her in some mystification. "What am I omitting, then?" he demanded.

"As I said, dear, the most critical factor of all," she said placidly. "He *loves* this boy. That's the cause of the whole thing. Every single one of the events that you've just catalogued happened because of that one thing. He did it all for love of this Christopher. And it's my belief that he'd go

54

through it all again, if he had to. No, John, the most important thing is not putting any sort of stop to the relationship, but to try to put a stop to Jamie's father before he does something catastrophic. Now, let's go to bed. And in the morning you go into school, and leave Jamie to me." With that she started for the stairs, and after a moment or two he followed her, still troubled but, because he had immense faith in her wisdom, somewhat comforted.

***

By the time Jamie woke the next morning his headmaster had already taken morning assembly and was guiding the classical sixth form a little distractedly through the intricacies of Plato's *Symposium*. "Very appropriate," he had commented to his wife as he rose from breakfast.

It was a cheerless day, with tattered clouds in a myriad shades of grey racing swiftly, low across the sky. Jamie blinked at the unfamiliar bedroom, then remembered where he was. He bounded out of bed, washed, and was half-dressed when Mrs Lane, who had heard movements, came in with a mug of tea, being careful to tap on the door first this time. He sat on the bed, bare to the waist, and drank it, as she hovered, wondering if he was in a mood for company. To her surprise he was quietly polite and even cheerful, and chattered quite happily to her while he drank the tea. Once or twice his attention wandered far away and he tailed off into silence, but she tactfully avoided noticing, and the moments passed.

She told him that he was not to go into school, and could do as he pleased with the day. He smiled his dazzling smile at her and, as it had the night before, it sent a brief but quite tangible shiver through her; she was glad that Jamie had turned to pull a clean sweatshirt over his head. He rummaged in his holdall, found his trainers, and followed her downstairs.

She sat with him while he ate bacon and eggs, wanting to find out more about him. She had never paid him any particular attention when he had been just another boy's face among seven hundred. Now, she realised with something of a shock, she was fascinated, wanted to find out everything about him. While she watched him eat and plied him with tea, he talked about fishing. She asked him about the books she had seen in his bag, and he talked readily and intelligently about his favourite books and authors. They talked about what was in the paper that morning, and about football when he looked at the mid-week results. Not once did he mention Christopher, or the situation in which he had become embroiled. She was filled with admiration, not unmingled with astonishment at such resilience in such a pass. She took great care he didn't see her observe his eyes straying, every minute or two, to the kitchen clock.

"Can I really do what I like, Mrs Lane?" he asked when he had finished. "Of course you can, dear," she said. "What would you like to do? I've got things planned, so I'm afraid you'll be left very much to your own devices. But you can have the run of John's bookshelves, if your taste runs to Sophocles, Livy and Milton. Or there's the video. I don't know what there is, but you might find something you fancy. Or I can show you how to work the record player, though we've only got classical music."

"I like classical music, thank you," he said demurely, "but what I was wondering was, would it be all right if I went for a walk?"

"Well, of course you can. Will you be back for lunch?" she asked casually, but watching him closely. "Thanks very much, but I don't usually eat much then. Especially after a smashing breakfast. Would it be all right if I sort of just stayed out till I'm tired?"

"Yes, my dear, if you wish, you do as you please. But do try to be back before it's dark, won't you. We... er, we have things to discuss, you know that, don't you?"

His face fell for a split second, but he was quick to recover.

"I'll be back in the afternoon," he promised. He made her an oddly formal little bow, thanked her politely for giving him breakfast, and was gone.

You artful little devil, she thought as she rose from the table. Her mind held an image, Cheshire cat-like, of his smile as he scampered out of the kitchen door. She experienced a sudden flash of memory, almost infinitesimally brief, yet so poignant and dislocating she felt momentarily almost faint, of how it had felt to be young. It was over before she could identify it, and she was left with just a sharp, coppery taste in her mouth and a wild, fathomless feeling of some great but indefinable loss. Then it was gone. She sighed. She thought she was beginning to fall in love with him herself.

***

Annabel Potten woke late in the guest room, from a sleepless night tossing and turning, with a dry mouth and a whisky-and-dalmane hangover. The house was silent. She threw on a dressing gown and hurried to Jamie's room, remembering only as she saw that the bed had not been slept in that he was at his headmaster's house, out of harm's way. The terrible events of the day before began to eddy back to her. She went on to her own bedroom. The covers had been flung back and left. She looked through the rest of the house, finding it empty.

She went downstairs and made toast and coffee. She took a small nibble out of the toast, gagged on it, and threw it in the bin, took a sip of coffee and tipped the rest down the sink. She washed quickly, then wandered about the house for a long time. Eventually she went to the garage, where she found her husband's car gone. She got into her Porsche, sat and thought for a minute, and roared off down the drive.

As Annabel Potten was driving, much too fast for the state of her head, to cry on the shoulder of a friend some miles out of the town, her husband, meanwhile, was striking oil at his first attempt. "Jesus Christ, David, what the hell's happened to you?" asked the landlord of the Golden Hind, his eyes bulging at Potten's damaged face. "Been five rounds with Tyson?"

"Got into a scrap with a couple of louts last night," said Potten. "Caught 'em trying to break into the car, and had a go."

"Good man," said the landlord. "Let me buy you a drink. Too bloody much of that sort of thing happening these days. You reported it to the police, I suppose?"

"No, not worth bothering them. It was too dark to see much, and I only got close enough to land one punch, then they hit me with something and ran for it. The police are too busy to do much good even when they've got a suspect, let alone when it could've been any one of thousands of kids. Cheers."

They drank for half an hour in the empty saloon, chatting idly of one thing and another. Potten bought himself a pint and the landlord accepted a Pils. "Bit early, but a bloke who's prepared to have a go's worth celebrating," he said. "Cheers." They chatted on until Potten, affecting to remember something suddenly, thrust his hand into his jacket pocket. "By the way, Len, you don't happen to know who this is, by any chance, do you?" He held the photograph of Christopher up for the man to look at. Len reached out to take it from him, but he turned slightly, drawing it out of the man's reach. Len squinted at it. "Mmmm, yeah, I think... Let's have a look." He leaned forward, squinting. "Y...yes, I'm sure of it, that's Bob Rowe's son - Chris, I think his name is. He's been in here once or twice with Bob. You know Bob?"

"No, no," said Potten casually, though internally he was

quivering with elation. He slipped the photograph back into his pocket. "No, I just wondered who it was. It was on the floor outside, in your foyer."

"Oh. Can't think what it can've been doing there. Want me to keep it and give it to Bob next time he's in?"

David Potten would not for the world have allowed the photograph, with its damning inscription on the back, to have fallen into anyone's hands. But he cast about furiously in his mind for a way to retain it when Len's suggestion, so awkward for him, was on the face of it so obviously sensible. Anyone, he knew, would think it was the obvious thing to do and hand the picture over. His mind raced, and rapidly found a solution.

"Sure. Good idea," he said, still casual. He made no move to produce the photograph again, but swigged his pint and ordered another, waving expansively at Len's glass. Len provided refills for both and took Potten's money. Potten took a pull at his pint, then said "Got to go and see Mao Tse-Tung about a music lesson," and sauntered to the gents'. There he locked himself in the cubicle and sat for a quarter of an hour, mentally hugging himself in glee.

When he got back to the bar Len's attention had been distracted by a couple of customers, and by the time he returned to resume his chat with Potten the photograph had gone clean out of his head. "Your son may be 'exceptionally intelligent'," he told himself under his breath as he strolled out half an hour later, "but you're not so bloody dumb yourself, David, old mate." He headed straight for the Post Office, where he shut himself in a telephone booth and consulted the local directory.

***

Christopher had reached Jamie's swim before it was properly light that morning. He was still in a state of profound

59

emotional turmoil. There was shock, trepidation, euphoria and the fear that it might be snatched from him and, most of all, there was the shattering realisation of both Jamie's love for him and his for Jamie. He had hardly slept, or at least that was how it seemed. He had risen and dressed long before anyone else was stirring, and slipped out of the house while it was still dark.

Christopher watched the first grey light trickle along the horizon and soak its way gradually up the sky like grey ink into indigo blotting paper as he swung along the towpath, enjoying the chilly, gusty wind blowing a little rain and occasional leaves into his face. There had been just enough light for him to negotiate the passage under the hawthorns without impaling himself too painfully, and he enjoyed a pleasant cold shower forcing his way through the alders. Once through he shook himself like a wet dog and unpacked his old groundsheet and blanket. He rolled himself up in them and lay comfortably on his back by the water's edge, watching the light seep westward across the sky.

The profound silence amplified the occasional plop as a fish jumped, the lap of the wavelets beside him and the wind as it hissed softly in the reeds and soughed in the alders, the old trees creaking in reply. A hedgehog trundled across the little sward of grass to the lake's edge, lapped a little water and trundled back to the cover of the trees, passing three feet from his face. He started in his cocoon as a duck quacked somewhere nearby, smiled to himself and settled again. A sallow leaf drifted down and landed on his nose. He blew at it and then had to wriggle a hand free to shift it from his eye. He had never felt more tranquil, yet wide awake.

He was woken from a deep sleep by Jamie, swearing as he lost his footing among the slippery hazel roots and descending most of the twelve-foot bank in one crashing jump. Trying to shoot out of the blanket too quickly he tied himself up, and was still frantically trying to extricate himself from a tangled knot of blanket and canvas when Jamie, who had heard his struggles, slipped through the trees and ran to him. He struggled to his feet just in time to catch Jamie as he flew into his arms, almost knocking him flat again. The next thing he knew was Jamie, holding him in a clinch so tight that he had trouble getting his breath, sobbing into his breast as if his heart was breaking.

He stood, puzzled and frightened, caressing Jamie's hair and murmuring to him; he tried to ask him what was wrong, but Jamie only wept. He could feel the boy's whole body trembling violently, each great sob heaving its way up and breaking and being overhauled by the next. He murmured soothing noises to him and wondered if the paroxysm was ever going to stop. It was fully half an hour before he felt the tension begin to ebb gradually from the boy, and the tears slackened. He somehow managed to prise Jamie off him for a few moments and pull him down to the blanket. He wrapped them in it and suffered Jamie to wind himself round him again. They lay for an unknown period in silence, simple physical contact easing some more of the tension and pain out of Jamie until, at last, he began to speak.

When he had got it all out, now blurting too quickly and tripping over his tongue, now faltering and sometimes dissolving into brief bouts of sobbing, Christopher lay for a while, thinking. He was, he admitted to himself, very scared. By any interpretation, and whatever allowances one made for Jamie's possibly exaggerating in his fear and hysteria, Potten senior sounded a formidable man. Christopher was by no means a weakling or a milksop and he was least of all a coward; but he certainly wasn't a fighting man, and against a man of the size, strength and power of David Potten, as described by his son, he reckoned he had no earthly chance of escaping injury. On the other hand, he was quite decided that he was not going to run away from the thing.

"Wh...what can you do but keep out of his way?" asked Jamie tremulously, blinking at him through wet eyelashes and looking, Christopher thought, heart-breakingly appealing. He smiled down at him and kissed him on the nose. "Well, I don't know, love, but what I do know is that I can't just keep out of his way. Why, I'd never be able to walk down the street without wondering if the big bloke

61

walking towards me was your father and getting ready to break my jaw when he got level with me. He sounds pretty obsessive. It might fester in him for years, and I'd never have any peace of mind. No, love, I've got to face it out somehow."

"He... he's terribly strong," said Jamie. "And he's... he's... I think he's a bit mad," he said, whispering the dread word. "I've seen him in all sorts of baits, but I've never seen him anything like he was yesterday. He was doing all sorts of strange things, laughing when there was no cause and so on. And one minute he'd be bawling his lungs out at me, and the next he was silky and..." He groped for the right words. "Next minute he'd be, sort of, sinister and menacing, and all the time he'd got these blazing eyes. He looked at me as if he *hated* me, Christopher. As if I was... well, as if I was just some sort of *filth*. He called me that - amongst other things. I've never heard anything sound as horrible. It was *really* nasty.

"I didn't think I was frightened of him. I mean, I haven't liked him for years, but I never thought he'd ever actually do anything to harm me. But yesterday, you know, I thought once or twice he was going to kill me. I really think he's mad, Christopher. And I don't think you should go near him. He'll hurt you, Chris, and I couldn't bear that. I'd kill him if he hurt you. I don't know how, but I would. But that wouldn't help you."

"All right, now, Jamie. Hush now, and we'll think it out between us. I promise you I won't put myself in any danger. If it looks as if I'm likely to get badly hurt I'll run for it. But I don't think he'd go completely off his head and do me any serious damage in public. Now just settle down with me, and let's think." And Jamie, starved all his life of someone to trust, and trusting Christopher implicitly, obediently curled up in Christopher's arms, nestled his head against Christopher's neck, and began to feel better for having found one constant in an uncertain world.

Christopher, conscious that for once his masterful younger lover was not feeling masterful at all, putting him in charge, held him close and gave himself to thoughts which were

62

unpleasant to say the least. Morning drifted into afternoon. In the afternoon they made love, first gently and tenderly, then passionately and at length with a desperation that flowed from the imminent parting. Jamie got hysterical again as the time approached when he would have to set off back to the headmaster's house, and pleaded desperately with Christopher to let him stay longer; but Christopher gently but firmly made him wash and dress.

"You can't break your word to them," he said, striving to hide his own deep distress. "They've been wonderful to you, and you can't play ducks and drakes with them. You *must* go back, and be back when you said you would. You must see that Jamie." Jamie did, and eventually he allowed himself to be led through the trees and back along the towpath. They held hands as long as they dared. When they reached the bridge where they had parted the night before they at least had the comfort of going the same way for a while longer. "I'm going to call this the Bridge of Sighs," said Christopher sadly as they crossed it. "Why?" asked Jamie, to his surprise. Christopher explained, and Jamie gave him a damp edition of his devastating smile. Soon after that they parted, and went to their homes deeper in love than ever, and deeper still in pain.

***

Edith Lane had not been thirty years the wife of a schoolmaster for nothing. She had ministered to countless thousands of boys in all their diversity of needs, and was an expert reader of signs. Her heart went out to Jamie when he sidled waif-like into the kitchen. "Hallo, dear," she said cheerfully. Ignoring his watery attempt at a smile she sat him down and quickly produced an enormous mug of tea. She sat next to him and sipped her own tea, pretending not to notice his downcast head. After a few minutes she ruffled his hair and ordered him, kindly but in a voice that brooked no refusal, to drink his before it got cold. He slowly lifted his head and, although she was half torn apart by the grief in his face, she chattered cheerfully and inconsequentially until, eventually, with a feeling of considerable triumph, she extracted a reluctant smile from him. Soon she made him laugh, and the evening's cure was begun.

Having hauled him out of the depths she worked on him assiduously until he was well towards his normal self. Judging her moment with the utmost care, she waited for a lull in the chatter. Then, catching his eye and holding it she allowed her face to straighten and said, very gently and quietly, "Have you told him?" He looked faintly startled, but she gave him no time to reflect. "I mean Christopher. You've seen him today, of course. What I want to know is, have you warned him about your father? It's very important, don't you think?"

"Oh, yes, terribly important," he said, and then sat back, his eyes widening as he realised what had been said. "You knew?" he said, gazing at her. "Knew, dear? Knew what?" she replied, poker faced.

"You knew I'd seen Christopher."

This was too much for her. She sat back in her chair, threw back her head and went into peals of laughter. "Jamie, my dear boy, I've been sitting here for the last half hour gently probing with a pin to winkle you out of your shell, and it has been written all over your face, in capital letters, if not in neon strip lighting, that you've been with Christopher. Of course I knew. I've just been biding my time to make sure that you warned him of the danger he's in. Because he is in some danger, isn't he?"

Jamie's face darkened with worry. "Yes, Ma'am, he is. My father's violent. I didn't realise how bad it was until yesterday, but he would have hurt me badly if I hadn't got out of the way. I was lucky. And he said…" He broke down, and for a moment looked close to tears, but he rallied. "He said he was going to find Christopher and break every bone in his body. I had to get warning to him. Didn't I, Mrs

Lane?"

"Why, of course you did. You did quite right." She took his mug and refilled it. "There you are dear. Now then, we've got an hour or so before my husband gets back. He's supervising the play until about six-thirty this evening. I'm sure you know that he is as much on your side as I am, and we both want nothing but to do what's right for you. But I wondered if you might like to talk to me about Christopher. It's sometimes easier for men to talk to a woman about this sort of thing. You don't have to tell me anything, you know that too, I hope. But if you would like to get things off your chest, I think you'll find it may be a relief. You haven't been able to talk about things much, have you?" she added, glancing shrewdly at him.

"No, Ma'am, I've never had anybody to talk to," he mumbled. "Until Christopher. I can tell him anything. But I... I'd like to tell you about him, if you really..."

"Come on then, dear. Let's go in the other room. It's a bit more comfortable than this."

When Dr Lane walked in, exhausted from his exertions with the school dramatic society and *Twelfth Night*, he found Jamie in full flood. His wife was a very good listener, and, with a little judicious prompting here and there, she had extracted virtually the whole story from him. He had still withheld Christopher's surname and address, and she did not press him for these details, feeling that everything she heard was privileged. She had no intention of breaching Jamie's hard-won and very shaky trust. Dr Lane quietly left the room and didn't return.

***

David Potten pulled his BMW on to the kerb directly opposite the Rowe family's house and switched off the lights. He lit a cigarette and opened the window to release the smoke, but took care to keep the glowing end out of sight below the level of the glass. There were very few people about in the quiet street of smallish semi-detached houses, but there were several lights on in the Rowes' house. He sat there, smoking cigarette after cigarette, for almost three hours and saw hardly a soul.

He was thinking about giving it up as a bad job and driving back for a late pint in the Golden Hind when a light went out upstairs in the house he was watching. A few moments later another went on just inside the front door. The door opened, and a man came down the short path and began walking up the street past Potten's car.

There was a streetlight thirty yards ahead. As the man approached it Potten drew away from the kerb and, with his lights still off, pulled alongside him. Under the lamp he saw that the man was in his middle forties, slim but well built. He thought he could detect some resemblance to the face in his photograph, but it was too slight for certainty. From the darkness of the car he called, "Excuse me, are you Bob Rowe?" The man halted in surprise. "Yes, that's..." He got no further, as Potten slammed his foot on the accelerator and the car roared off. Before Rowe had gathered his wits enough to note the colour, size or shape of the darkened car it had disappeared round a bend in the street. He mused for a moment, then shrugged, dismissing the incident as a prank, and continued on his way to the local pub.

David Potten entered the Golden Hind, in time for his late pint after all, feeling very pleased with himself. He had not felt ready to go stalking his prey yet, for, half demented though he was with rage, resentment and the paranoia that was taking hold of him, he could still think coherently enough to realise that even a chance blow in the area of his injuries could be disastrous. But he had established beyond doubt that he had the right address, and spied out the land. He drank his whisky and chatted to Len the landlord in a high humour.

***

Christopher Rowe watched a bit of television and five minutes after the set was switched off he couldn't have said what he had been watching. He toyed with his dinner and answered absently when anyone spoke to him, while the rest of his family grinned at each other. Eventually he went upstairs. He had some preparatory work that he wanted to get finished before he took his place at university in a couple of months' time. But the associations kept reminding him that he would be moving over a hundred miles away. Jamie and he had talked about it briefly in an abstract way, but it was so large a lion in their path that by common consent they had since avoided the subject, marking it as something to be dealt with when it had to be but not before. All the same, the words persisted in swimming wildly before his eyes. He gave it up.

Throwing himself on the bed he lay with his hands behind his head, considering the options facing him. He thought they reduced themselves to two. He could tell his parents the entire story and seek their advice and protection; or he could simply wait for Potten to make his assault, fight as best he could and do his utmost to see that he escaped without serious injury. Privately he had already made up his mind to follow this course.

He had subjected himself to a rigorous cross-examination, asking himself if he was afraid to tell his parents and merely putting off the dreaded moment. He concluded that he was willing to tell them, but not yet ready. The situation with Jamie was too complicated; then Neil was in the throes of examinations at school and he didn't want to be the cause of any further distraction. He wasn't at all sure that Neil was distractable, but he liked his brother, and wasn't willing to take the chance. Making a mental promise that as soon as some sort of stability had been secured for Jamie he would talk to his parents, he lay and agonised. He admitted to

67

himself that he was quite badly scared, but he felt a little happier at having come to a decision. He was courageous enough to choose the best of a range of options of which all were bad and most were verging on the frightful. He turned his thoughts to where he could always find solace, and daydreamed of Jamie. Downstairs his brother Neil was tormenting his mother with accounts of the things he planned to say to Chris about being in love, until she cuffed him in exasperation and he fled, hooting gleefully, from the kitchen.

Jamie was excused school again the following day, and took some work that Dr Lane had set him down to the swim. He and Christopher spent a calmer day. They lay in rather brighter weather and went through the schoolwork together. Jamie, who was knowledgeable about wildlife, pointed out to Christopher, who was not, seven species of duck, four of geese and two of grebe on the lake. They made love peacefully. But of course much of their time was devoted to discussion of current affairs, in the course of which Christopher told Jamie of the odd incident last night, which his father had recounted when he returned from his drink. Jamie's eyes widened. "It could've been my dad," he said in alarm.

"It could have been," assented Christopher. "But I don't see how he can possibly have known where to come. You've never said anything, have you?" Jamie's face showed his distress. "No, Christopher, I've never said a *word* to anyone that might give you away, honestly. I *promise* I..."

Christopher drew him closely into his arms. "Jamie, my darling, of course I know you haven't. I know you wouldn't. I only wondered if maybe you'd let it slip out without realising it. I wouldn't blame you in the least if you had with the pressure you've been under lately. I don't suppose it can have been your old man at all. As I say, I just can't think how he would know where to come."

"I can," said Jamie, in great distress. "I've just remembered. You know the day you gave me the photograph of you? The day before yesterday? Well, when I got home I changed into uniform. I always used to do that, so they'd think I'd been at school. And when I changed I transferred your picture into my school bags, so I could have it with me. I was going to keep it under my pillow, so I could look at you when I got up, and kiss you and so on. Only in the fight with dad he grabbed me by the seat of my trousers and sort of chucked me about. And when I got to the head's house after the fight I found the back pocket half hanging off. He must've torn it off when he grabbed me, and your picture must've fallen on the floor. Oh, God, Chris, I'm sorry, I'm sorry. I didn't mean..."

"Of course you didn't mean it," murmured Christopher, stroking his hair. "How could you have helped it? It doesn't matter."

"But he must have asked people who it was in the photo," Jamie gulped miserably. "He must've read what you wrote to me on the back. And when I got to the head's I found the trousers torn and forgot all about your photo. Oh, Chris, how could I?"

"Forget it. I'll get you another photograph, a better one this time, and write something better on it for you. I'm not ashamed of what I wrote. I'm *proud* of what I said to you. I'm proud of loving you, and proudest of all that it was me you came to, when you could have had so much better..."

"I'd never find anyone better than you, Chris," said Jamie, burrowing against Christopher and nestling his head against his stomach.

"You could have anyone you wanted, I think, Jamie," said Christopher seriously. "I shall never want anyone but you," was the muffled reply from his lap.

"Well, I hope not," said Christopher, quivering. "But I owe it to you to see this business with your dad through. Once it's over and your situation's been settled properly, I'll talk to my parents. They'll be a bit shocked, I should think, but I don't think they'll turn on me." His face darkened in anxiety as he imagined the scene. "At least," he amended, "I'm *pretty* sure they won't."

"I just think you're pretty," said Jamie, and grinned up at

him lasciviously for a moment before sobering again.

They fell silent, both occupied with thoughts of their own. Jamie wondered about Christopher's family, while Christopher's mind persisted in unreeling various pictures of the confrontation with David Potten, and he drew no comfort from any of them.

Jamie sat up abruptly after a long silence. "Christopher," he asked without preamble, "will we live together one day? When this is all over, I mean?"

The question was so unexpected that it jolted Christopher out of his brown study. He looked at Jamie, first with eyebrows raised in surprise, then with great tenderness. "I suppose so," he said after a few moments' thought. "I hope so. Would you want to?"

Jamie looked quizzically at him, then raised his eyes skywards. "Honestly Christopher, you do ask some *asinine* questions. Of *course* I shall. I'd like to now," he said more slowly. "I don't suppose we can do that, can we?"

Christopher looked at him and gave vent to a little bark of laughter. "I don't quite think so," he said. "I haven't got a job, and I've got three years of university to do. I don't really think they'd think I was a fit and proper person to give custody of you to, do you? I'd have to see you off to school every morning before I went off to lectures." He laughed again, and suddenly succumbed to a giggling fit.

"I don't know," said Jamie, looking dreamily into space. "I could look after the home. Get your dinner, and make sandwiches for you to take with you, and do the washing and things." He looked so seriously at Christopher as he said it that Christopher collapsed into giggling again. Jamie promptly caught the infection, and they fell onto their old blanket and rolled together in peals of laughter, healing and cleansing. They carried on the game, imagining duties for each other and tumbling from one fit of laughter into another, until they subsided weakly into each other's arms.

***

Over the next couple of weeks their lives began to return to some sort of normality. Jamie returned to school, and had to possess his soul in such patience as he could muster until he could escape into Christopher's arms in the evenings. The Lanes quickly came to enjoy the presence of a lively youth in their house for the first time since their own son had left home ten years before.

Dr Lane took to holding long conversations with Jamie as the evenings drew in, and quickly conceived a profound respect for the boy's mind. He found himself talking to him for much of the time as an equal, and often had to remind himself that he was talking to a fifteen-year-old when he had to retrace an argument to explain something to Jamie. Edith Lane for her part loved the boy unequivocally as if he was her own, and spoiled him as dreadfully as her husband allowed her to get away with. "You'll be giving him a swollen head," he complained from time to time. "He'll expect preferential treatment in school."

"He won't, John," she retorted. "He's not the kind of boy to get swollen-headed, and you know that as well as I do. Besides, who are you to talk about spoiling him and preferential treatment? You treat him like a favourite undergraduate yourself. I've heard the discussions you have with him. If you come to that there's more than a little of the favourite uncle about it, too."

One evening in a lull in a discussion Jamie became absorbed in reflections of his own. Dr Lane wisely did not interrupt his thoughts, but waited to see what they brought forth. When he emerged Jamie asked seriously, "Do you think I'll be able to stay with you for very long, sir? Or will they take me away soon?" Edith, who was coming into the room with tea, moving silently as usual, almost choked behind the door to hear his voice, flattened into a dead tone by anxiety. Her husband, who had been wondering when such a question would come, pursed his lips and hesitated before answering.

"I *think*," he said slowly, "that you are safe for quite some time. Clearly a time will come when some firm decision will have to be taken about your future. But, for the moment, I think we can safely say that you will be able to stay with us for some time yet - probably some weeks, at least." He hesitated for a long interval before going on. Jamie sat on the floor, as he preferred, and watched him anxiously. Edith touched him gently on the shoulder and indicated his mug beside him. "I'm not quite sure how to go about asking you, Jamie," Dr Lane eventually resumed, "but, do you miss your parents?"

"No, sir," replied Jamie promptly. "I hated my father. At the end particularly, but I realised after we'd had the fight that I'd hated him for a long time before then too. He's a bully and a tyrant, and he never had the time of day for me. Or for mother, either. But she deserved no better, sir. She doesn't care about me either, does she? I mean, *she* knows I'm here, doesn't she? She could have come to see me, but she's never even rung me up. I don't suppose she even misses me." He stopped speaking, and a variety of expressions chased each other across his face, ending with a grim look of resolution which sat unhappily on his young features.

"Well, sir, I don't specially blame her for not missing me. We never used to have much to say to each other - no more than dad and I did, really. So I'm not missing *her*, am I sir?" But Dr Lane noticed that he instinctively looked across to Edith for support. He shook his head sharply, as if in dismissal of an unworthy notion. "No, if I'm to be truthful, I haven't even thought about them since I came to you that night all that time ago..."

"Two weeks, and a day or two," put in Dr Lane gravely, carefully waiting for a pause so as not to interrupt Jamie's flow.

"Well it may only be a fortnight, but it seems a jolly sight more to me, sir."

"You're happy here with us, Jamie?" Lane asked quietly.

"Oh, *yes*. Of course I am. You must know I am, sir." Once again there was the appealing glance at Mrs Lane. She smiled encouragingly, and trembled inside.

"Yes, I thought so. I was sure you were, in fact, but one should ask these things from time to time. It precludes complacency. Now, Jamie, I've been waiting until you raised this subject, as I knew you must sooner or later, to tell you something, upon which I should like your comments. You haven't known this, but I must tell you that your mother has spoken to me on the telephone several times; and after the last call she has sent me a cheque to cover our expenses in caring for you. It is, I may say, for a very large sum. I have the cheque, but I have as yet done nothing with it. What are your thoughts on that, please, Jamie?"

"It proves what I said, I think," the boy responded without hesitation. "She'll feel better about things if she can send money. That's them all over, sir. They hardly think about anything except money. They'll think that by sending you a lot of money they'll have made everything better. I expect they'll try to make out that nothing ever happened, now it's all been greased over with a fat cheque. Can I ask you something, sir?"

"Of course."

"I bet it was for a thousand, sir. I know how they think," he said bitterly. "They'll have sat there deciding they owe you for my keep, and one of them'll have said a figure. 'That'll cover it', whoever it is will say. And I can just hear them at it, holding a bloody auction over me. I'm sorry, sir," he added as he noticed what he had said.

"Never mind," said the head gently. "I confess myself horrified, but humbled also, to see a boy of your tender years brought to such a pitch of cynicism, but I cannot, I fear, disagree too much with your assessments. However, there is more that you don't yet know."

"May I say something, please?"

"Of course. What is it?"

"I'm not trying to be clever, sir, but somebody I read about said that a cynic is a name an idealist gives a realist. I can't remember who it was, but I think I'm a realist, not a cynic, sir."

Dr Lane almost smiled, but decided it was not appropriate. "Are you sure you know the difference, Jamie?"

"John, don't patronise him," murmured his wife from her armchair.

"I shouldn't dream of it, my dear. But when one sees the words in use in the adult world and realises from the percentage of solecisms how many men old enough to be Jamie's grandfather lack any notion of the distinction, I think it's a fair question to ask. I think it's a distinction that one ought to know. Do you agree, Jamie?"

"Yes, sir, and I think I know the difference."

"Very well, then, Jamie. How would you define a cynic?" He looked keenly at the boy as he waited for an answer, and Edith could see that the real purpose of the discussion was in danger of being forgotten in the pleasure of academic exploration. She had heard several discussions of this kind in the short time in which Jamie had enlivened their house and their lives. She waited, intensely curious to see how Jamie dealt with a fairly fast ball.

"I'd say a cynic is someone so hard-bitten that he's never willing to credit *anybody* with honourable motives, sir," he said almost without pausing to think about it. Dr Lane raised his eyebrows. "Mmmm. Very good, Jamie. Very good indeed. I don't know that I could improve on that."

"Yes, sir. And that's not what I'm doing, is it? I mean, I'm only not crediting people with honourable motives that I know haven't got any, aren't I? If you see what I mean, sir."

"I see perfectly, Jamie, and I don't think I can find fault with your logic; though I might in one of my more critical moments find one or two with the syntax of the last..."

"John," said his wife in a warning tone. "I'm sorry, my dear. Carried away. Very well, Jamie. I said that there is more for me to tell you. We must postpone further investigation of the cynic to a more suitable moment. So, then, you don't feel any sense of loss by your - ah - estrangement from your parents?"

"None at all, sir. I've seen things in my mother that I don't like one bit. And I'm just scared of father. I think since this blew up he'd like to kill me. I thought he was going to, when we - you know, sir." The sidelong glance at Mrs Lane again.

"And you feel inclined to believe also that your parents for their part are feeling no great sense of missing you?"

"As I said, sir, I don't think they'll be missing me at all, unless father's wishing I was there so he can take all - all that business out of me."

"Dear, oh dear. What a state of affairs. Still, I find myself forced to agree with you. Now, then. Your mother is not for the moment living at home. Does that surprise you?"

"Not at all. I think she's probably as frightened as I am. Has she gone to live with Angela? Mrs Turnbull, that is? She lives at Howley Bend."

"Yes, she gave an address there, and I believe the name she mentioned was a Mrs Turnbull."

"I thought so. She helped Angela through her divorce years ago. I expect Angela will help her through hers now. She'll enjoy that. She's always hated the sight of my dad. She refused to come to our house. She said she wouldn't be able to stop herself hitting father with a croquet mallet." He giggled, and suddenly looked like a small boy. "She told me that once, sir, when mother took me to see her. I liked her. She's very jolly, and drinks a lot. But she - er - she doesn't like men much."

"She sounds positively formidable," said Dr Lane, greatly amused by Jamie's description. "And if I may say so an admirably succinct - ah - encapsulation of a character. Have you ever thought about a career as a writer? I think you'd have them fighting for tickets to your latest West End smash."

"I want to be a writer, sir. It's the only thing I've ever wanted to do."

"Hmmm. We must give that some thought some time. But back to your mother. When she last spoke to me on the telephone, she suggested that you must be running short of clothes, and that there must be other things of yours that you're missing. She stated most emphatically that she did not feel it would be, well, safe, I'm afraid is how she put it, for you to venture back to your home, so she offered to go there herself and bring your things over here in the car. That was, in fact, when the redoubtable Mrs Turnbull's name was mentioned. I gather that she would be a member of the, ah, foraging party. What thoughts does this information prompt, Jamie?"

"It proves what I said, sir, doesn't it? She doesn't want me to get hurt, and she's as scared of dad as I am. But she doesn't want me with her. She's quite happy for me to be with you as long as you let me stay." He paused for several seconds. "So am I, sir. It's the first time I've ever had anybody at home I can talk to, or be with and feel... well, feel at home, sir. I always used to dread going home, and now I'm quite glad to. I've never felt..." he paused, groping for the word, "... relaxed, sir. That's what I feel here. Please let me stay."

Looking across at his wife Lane saw that her eyes had filled with tears, and suddenly became aware of a lump forming in his own throat. He hastily pulled out his handkerchief and blew his nose vigorously. Faced with such an appeal there was only one answer to be made. He was scarcely conscious that he was making a decision of great magnitude as he made up his mind. "Of course you will stay, Jamie, for as long as you like. There will be all manner of arrangements to be made, but no doubt we'll be able to cross those bridges as we reach them."

There was a loud sniffle from across the room, startling Lane and Jamie equally. Edith, unable to keep it in any longer, gave a loud sob and came to Jamie. He stood up and suffered himself to be embraced. After a moment she released him and looked embarrassed. "I'm sorry," she said with a vigorous snuffle, and busied herself gathering Lane's cup and Jamie's mug. Jamie, recovering with his usual rapidity from the bolt of happiness that had just jolted him from head to toe, looked up at the two of them and, at last, they saw the smile that Christopher saw.

***

Annabel Potten was quite happy in her own way. She had settled down after a series of heavy sessions with her friend Angela in various pleasant inns and hotels round and about, each followed by a drive back to Howley Bend in the Porsche which Angela Turnbull made with her eyes shut. "I don't want to die," she had commented when she rose, shaking, from the little car after one particularly hair-raising journey, "but if I've got to lay down my life for a friend, at least I don't want to see it bloody well coming. For Christ's sake let's get in," she had added quickly, "I need a sodding great drink. I think I lost most of what we've had on the way back!"

By now, though, their excursions were more for pleasure than for therapy, and Annabel was enjoying life more than she could remember for years. She had done what she conceived to be her duty by Jamie by sending the Lanes the sum of money which they thought very large but which was a trifle to her, she being worth at least as much as her husband, and, having thus silenced her conscience she more or less dismissed him from mind.

Indeed, one thing that Dr Lane had not thought fit to tell Jamie was that on each of the occasions when she had telephoned he had asked her if she wished to speak to her son, and each time she had declined, negligently dismissing the idea with some phrase about 'not wanting to upset him.' Lane had accepted that as best he could, and she hardly gave Jamie a thought nowadays, as Jamie himself had accurately surmised.

"Come on, Ange," said Annabel as, five miles away, Edith Lane, eyes still glistening, handed Jamie a refill of tea, "let's go and see Don and the gang at Steeple Wynton. I feel like drinking bubbly tonight. Let's buy a magnum."

"Suits me," said Angela Turnbull. "Two magnums?"

"Let's buy a *case*" cried Annabel. "I want this to be a night to remember."

77

"If it's anything like the last time we went to the Magpie," muttered her friend, "it'll more likely be a night we'll have forgotten by the time we wake up tomorrow afternoon."

"I don't care whether *we* remember it," said Annabel. "It's that bastard of a husband of mine that I want to remember it. I want him to remember tonight as the night I broke the bloody bank. I found our joint Access card this afternoon. This one's on dear David. We'll have *two* cases. I hope they've got something bloody expensive."

***

David Potten was also enjoying life more than he had done for a long time. The absence of his wife and son he regarded as a blessing in so far as he thought about it at all. He got the wife of one of his employees to come in and keep house for him every day, and spent his free time with cronies in the Golden Hind and various other pubs, or playing bridge or snooker at his club; calmly waiting for his injuries to heal over, biding his time, as paranoia bound him ever more tightly in its toils, for the moment when he would avenge himself for the devastating hurt that had been inflicted on him.

None of the cronies he drank with noticed anything unusual about him, and all would have been without exception dumbfounded had they been told, but his personality was rapidly disintegrating - indeed, he was very close to being quite mad. He concealed beneath the facade of normality a single purpose, deadly, clearly and steadily held in the sights, and utterly single-minded.

The very occasional moments when his attention drifted into some remote region and his eyes lost their focus, his friends put down to the understandable distress of a man whose wife had run off, taking his son with her, which was the story they had all been fed. His friends naturally sympathised, bought him lots of drinks, and confided to him that they had always thought she was a chancer and that he was well out of it. Only one or two, such as Harold Holdsworth, the doctor, knew a little more than the official version, and they sensibly kept their own counsel. Harold alone knew where Annabel was, and he kept that item especially to himself.

Meanwhile, every evening when he returned home and every morning when he rose, Potten inspected his face to see how much the great bruises had faded. On Thursday, two weeks and a day after the fight in which Jamie had inflicted the wound to his head and, unknowingly, a far more serious wound to his psyche, David Potten looked in the glass and saw that he was pretty well healed. The bruising was still visible, but only from fairly close. Although there was still a sizeable dark patch below his left eye, the eye itself was now down to its normal size, and hardly bloodshot at all.

Early that evening he made his move.

TWO

PC John Cook sat bored at the wheel of the car thinking, for the twentieth time since they'd booked on duty four hours earlier, that when he had impulsively sent off for application forms to join the police four years before he had been, temporarily but calamitously, out of his mind. 'What in the name of sanity was I thinking about?' he asked himself. 'Why did I think this would be interesting? Why did I decide to go ahead when they accepted me? Why the hell am I *still* in it now?' And, most of all, he asked himself, also for the twentieth time that late turn, 'Is anything, *ever*, going to happen tonight, before I leap out of this bloody machine, tear off all my clothes and run down the High Street, gibbering maniacally and assaulting passers-by?'

He lapsed into a reverie about the things he would like to do if he once made up his mind to put his papers in. Half his mind was still watchful, half an eye remained on duty, watching without any interest but with a certain professional attention, in case some motorist did something that could justify their pulling him to give him a flea in his ear, or even, perhaps, to book him for something, give them something to do and so make half an hour pass like half an hour, instead of half a decade. In the passenger seat his partner, PC Stuart Paget, slept peacefully.

Their companionable silence was suddenly shattered by

the squawk of the radio. "Any unit, vicinity of Cross Oak Gardens, deal with a disturbance, over?" Paget was immediately awake, slipping his seat belt on and picking up the hand-mike in the same movement, as Cook started the engine and switched on the lights.

"Control from Tango Two," said Paget into the microphone as Cook swung the car round in a tight three-point turn and began speeding down the road, "we're just round the corner and on way. What's the SP?"

"Thanks, Tango Two," came the metallic voice of the radio man at the station, "it's a disturbance outside number nine, that's number nine, Cross Oak Gardens, informant a Mrs Howard at number six. She's apparently opposite number nine. All we have is several men fighting. Don't know how many. I'll get some back-up units to assist."

They rocketed round corners and along darkening residential streets, the revolving blue light above them illuminating their faces eerily every few seconds in the darkness of the car. The radio man was audible above the scream of their tyres, calling for any other units available to assist them in dealing with a fracas involving an unknown number of people. Their boredom was nothing more than a memory as the adrenalin jetted through them, faster and faster as they approached the scene of the unknown incident. Within ninety seconds of receiving the call they careered round a last right-angle bend and into Cross Oak Gardens.

As they roared along the street their headlights picked out a chaotic scene ahead of them. Already beginning to assess what was happening even as they slowed up, they saw that two men were fighting fiercely on the footway, with another, smaller and younger, getting to his feet from the gutter. As they screeched to a halt a woman shot out from a garden gate and hurled herself on one of the combatants, throwing her arms round his neck and hauling him backwards with such violence that although the man was twice her size he was jerked away from the other man. The scream of their tyres and the sudden glare of their lights stopped the action dead, and the four people all froze, eyes turned towards them in alarm. The two PCs came fast out of their car and moved in.

Cook walked rapidly to the woman, now standing, wild-eyed and panting, beside the man she had attacked. He was a big, powerfully-built man, standing with chest heaving, eyes bulging, and despite having a number of superficial injuries he was clearly about to launch himself at the other man as Cook approached. Cook, who, despite the man's size, was inches taller and considerably larger, stepped into his path and shoved a big hairy hand into his chest. "You stay where you are, pal," he snapped. The woman came quickly to his side, gasping something he couldn't hear, but recognised as relief and gratitude for his arrival.

Paget meanwhile was restraining the other, smaller of the two fighters. The third man, who at closer quarters was only a boy, picked himself up and went to the woman and began to comfort her. "Right, then," said Paget, taking command as senior PC, "now someone will tell us what's been going on. You stay where you are," he added, glaring at his man. He crossed to his partner. "I'll take my man to the car. You talk to the big bloke here." Cook nodded, and began to shepherd his man away from the others. The boy had his arms round the woman and was speaking softly to her, comforting her as best he could. The PCs looked quickly at them and decided that they posed no threat to anyone and could be left where they were.

"Wait for a moment," said Paget, gently pushing his man against the side of the car. He reached in through the open driver's window, fished out the radio mike, and used it to call the station to cancel any additional units that might be on the way to the scene. "Okay, Stu," squawked the radio. "Duty Officer will give you a look in shortly, though," it added a moment later. Paget returned the mike and turned back to his man. "Right, then. What happened? First of all, are you hurt?"

"I... I've got a few bruises," muttered the man quietly, "but I don't think there's anything to worry about. I'm sorry, officer, but it wasn't my fault. This... this... maniac came here tonight and attacked us. My son first, and then me. I don't know why, or who he is, or anything..." He trailed into silence, panting still as he recovered his breath from the brawl. "Right. Sit in the car for a minute," said Paget. They got in, and Paget extracted a notebook from his pocket.

"Right, then. Let's start with names, can we?"

"Rowe," said the man. "Robert Rowe."

"Address?"

"Eh? Oh, well, here. Nine, Cross Oak Gardens. We live here. That's my wife and my son. My elder son, Christopher."

"And the other man? You say you don't know him?"

"I've never seen him before in my life, as far as I know. He just arrived and attacked my son."

"Why should he do that?"

"I tell you, officer, I haven't the slightest idea. I don't know anything about him." He paused, beginning to regain his composure. "Let me tell you what happened."

"Yes, do that, please," said Paget quietly.

Rowe gathered breath and said "There was a ring on the doorbell. About - God, I don't know, it seems like hours - it must have been about a quarter of an hour ago, I suppose. Yes, about that. We'd just finished dinner, and the bell rang."

"Who'd finished dinner, please? All three of you?"

"And Neil - my younger son. We were just finishing, and the bell rang. Chris was nearest, and went to answer it. We heard a man's voice, yelling something. Then there was a tremendous crash and I heard Chris cry out. I ran out and saw this man standing over Chris, he was right inside the hallway - inside my house," he went on, his voice rising in anger. "Cool down," said Paget in soothing tones. "Just stick to what happened."

"Well, of course, I assumed he must've hit Chris. Chris was sprawling on the floor, he'd fallen against the telephone table and knocked it over. He... he had blood all over his face. He was as white as a sheet, and he looked utterly shocked. He was trying to get up, and the man was standing over him, shouting something. I've no idea what he was saying. All this happened very fast, you understand."

"I understand, sir," said Paget. "So what did you do?"

"Well, of course, I ran at the man and hit him. Hit him very hard, and he sort of staggered back and fell over the doormat, and fell outside. I slammed the door and yelled at Audrey - my wife - to phone the police. She came out, don't suppose she heard me, saw Chris and practically passed out. I had a look at Chris, and he seemed to be all right. He'd got a badly split lip, but nothing desperate. Then this maniac started kicking the front door. I suppose he was kicking it, it sounded like it. So I opened it and - well, we started fighting, and it just sort of... well, you know, we went up and down the path and ended up outside. Chris came out to help me, I suppose, though I didn't notice at the time, and then you arrived."

PC Paget switched on the interior light and looked closely at the man. "Hmmm, you don't seem too badly damaged, Mr Rowe," he said. "I'm blessed if I know what to make of this. People don't just attack perfect strangers in their own homes like this. Not people like him, anyway. He looks respectable enough, from what little I saw of him, doesn't he?"

"Well, I don't know," said Rowe, looking puzzled himself. "But, yes, he certainly didn't look like some young... well, tearaway. I didn't have much of a chance to look at him closely, but I'd say he was middle-aged. Honestly, officer, I can't begin to explain it. I take it you'll arrest him, will you?"

Paget hesitated, with professional reticence, but said "I think we'll be taking him in for questioning, Mr Rowe - assuming what he says bears out what you've told me," he added, peering closely at Rowe as he spoke. Rowe's face lightened in a relief so obviously unaffected that Paget made an immediate mental note that the man was almost certainly telling the truth. "Okay, sir," he said, "Let's have your full details, then I'll go and see how my colleague's getting on with the other man. Full name, and your occupation, please."

"Robert Anthony Rowe. I work for a building society. Assistant manager at the Abbey National. Here - the High Street branch." Paget noted the details and got out of the car.

"Sit tight here, Mr Rowe, if you will, please. I'd like you to come to the station with us." Rowe nodded, anger, confusion and the onset of concern about his bruises competing for precedence on his face. Paget left him in the car and walked across to where Cook had the other man firmly pressed into the privet hedge surrounding a garden beneath a streetlight. He drew his partner a little distance away from the man, who still held himself, bunched and tense, as if still ready to fly back into violent action. The two policemen eyed him alertly as they talked.

"You got anything out of him?" asked Paget. "Nothing very coherent," said Cook. "It's a pretty rum thing. He's got some sort of bee in his bonnet about the boy - name of Christopher something. It sounds as if he's got some cause for it, too. I can't get a lot of sense out of him, but from what little I can gather, it seems as if the boy's been interfering with his son. He came round here to sort him out. It *sounds* as if the kid opened the door to him and he went berserk and laid him out, and then the kid's father seems to have come blasting out and laid *him* out, and it went on from there."

Paget's face darkened. "Ahh. Now we're getting somewhere, then. That all tallies with what the kid's father's told me. The father seems a decent enough bloke. He says the man rang the bell, the son answered it and the next thing they knew the big bloke had smacked him one. Dad comes chasing out and wades in, and there we go." He paused in thought for some moments. "This is beginning to sound very nasty. If the son's been messing about with chummy here's son I can't say as I blame him for going after him. I must say, I don't think the boy's father knows anything about that. He says he doesn't know the bloke from a hole in the wall and hasn't got a clue why he came round here like a maniac, and I believe him. He couldn't be that good an actor."

He paused again, and made up his mind. "Come on, John. We can't sort this out out here in the road. We'll take the lot of 'em in for questioning. Tell you what, you keep an eye on chummy here. Better caution him, to be on the safe side. Common assault'll do for the time being. We can always make it up to ABH or whatever later on. I've told the father he's got to come in to make a statement. And we'll have to have the boy in as well. It looks as if he might be at the bottom of all this."

"Specially if he's been at the bottom of chummy's kid," Cook murmured, for his partner's ears only. Paget half-smothered a giggle and advanced on the burly man leaning in the hedge. "You got a car here?" he asked roughly. "Yes," said the man. He still sounded furious, and he was wholly uncowed by the sight of uniforms. "The BMW - over there." He indicated a dark blue car a few yards up the street. "Right. John, we'll need a driver to take it in. Or are you willing to leave it locked and parked here?" he asked the owner. "Leave it here, or do what you fucking well like with it," snapped the man. "I don't give a sod what you do with it."

Paget shrugged. "Okay. Give me your keys, then. We'll leave it here. No skin off my nose." He waited while the man fished in his pocket and took his keys. Then he trudged to the BMW and locked it, returned and handed the keys back to their owner. Leaving him in the hedge under the eye of his bulky partner he went back to Mr Rowe in the police car, signing to him to get out.

"We've arrested the man, Mr Rowe," he said, noting the plain signs of relief in the man's face. "Now, we've got to take him to the police station in this car, and obviously we can't have you or anyone else with him. So what I'd like you to do, if you will, please, is to come to the station - with your son and your wife, please. You got a car?"

"Yes. Now?" was all Rowe said.

"Yes, now, sir, please. Right away. Did your other son - er, Neil - have anything to do with this?"

"No, officer," said Rowe, "nothing at all. I shoved him back inside and made him stay in the house. He never even got out of the living room."

"Is he old enough to be left here?"

"I... well, he's fourteen, nearly fifteen. But I don't like to leave him here on his own. He'll be worried out of his mind."

"Okay, sir. Bring him with you. We can sit him down

somewhere with someone to talk to him. Ah!" he added, as a car swept up beside him. A policeman with two pips on each shoulder emerged. "Evening, guv," said Paget. "Can you give us a hand?"

"Course," said the newcomer. "What've you got?" Paget drew him aside. "It looks complicated, and nasty," he said in an undertone, and rapidly sketched out what they had established. The inspector looked grim. "Child molesting. Christ, it's a while since I've had one of *those* to deal with. Right, what do you want to do?"

"Cookie and I'll have to take the other bloke in, so I was going to get the Rowes - that's the boy and his parents, and a younger brother they don't want to leave alone in the house, poor little sod - to come in under their own steam. But I'd rather they didn't have a chance to talk too much, so if you can pack four of 'em into your motor, Guv..."

"Quite right, Stuart," said the inspector. "Round 'em up."

"One other thing, guv," said Paget. "I haven't said anything to Rowe about what chummy's alleged, and we haven't spoken to the boy at all, or the wife. I thought it would only cause chaos if we brought *that* out, out here in the street. The father hasn't got an inkling, I'm sure of that. You reckon that was right?"

"Too true I do," muttered the inspector. "I think the less said about it the better until we get them apart. I'll give the CID a shout while you're rounding 'em up." He slid back behind the wheel of his car.

A few minutes later the Rowe family were squashed into the inspector's car and speeding back to the police station behind the other car, driven by Paget. David Potten was in the back with a very vigilant Cook squeezed in beside him. All that was left outside the Rowes' darkened house was the locked BMW and a spot or two of blood on the pavement. Half a dozen curtains were at last allowed to drop back, half a dozen televisions ignored as the neighbours discussed the evening's excitement.

***

"We want to know. Where is he living?" asked the uniformed inspector who had brought Christopher and his family to the station. Christopher sat on the edge of an upright chair in a dreary, distempered room and shook his head doggedly. "I won't have him dragged into this," he muttered into his lap, choking back the tears that tried continually to break out again.

The inspector sat, frustrated, for a moment. Then he leaned forward and, putting his fingers under Christopher's chin, jolted his head upright. His fingertips left livid marks on the soft flesh under his jaw. Christopher flinched in fear, and he immediately dropped his head once more. The police officer did the same again. Christopher sat staring at him bleakly, but had enough sense not to drop his head again. "Now," said the inspector in a concentrated tone, "you are going to tell me where he is, if I have to sit here and ask you all bloody night. Do you understand what I'm saying to you, you slimy, child-molesting, shitty little faggot?"

Christopher's eyes blazed momentarily at him, then his face sagged into the weary, hopeless expression it had borne ever since the devastating moment when he had realised that they were going to make his relationship with Jamie an issue. "I won't tell you anything to bring him into it," he said dully, feeling his bowels churn and contract with fear as the inspector shifted in his seat. "I've told you a dozen times, I never molested him. I never molested anyone in my life. We were..." His voice faded, and his face twisted in misery. He felt a wave of despair flow over him, knowing that he would never be able to make the man see his point of view, that his mind was closed. "It's no good trying to tell you anything about us," he eventually mumbled. "You wouldn't begin to understand..."

The inspector's faced twitched. He seized Christopher by the shoulders, hauling him up, and slammed him against the wall of the room. Christopher cringed into the corner, surprised into a sharp yelp of hurt as his head smacked against the dusty wall. The officer looked at him with an expression of scalding, and genuine, contempt and disgust. Then, suddenly, his features lost all expression whatever, and he was surveying him as if he was nothing human at all, merely an object.

Without violence he took a step towards Christopher, who cringed again. The man halted. "You don't need to cringe and snivel in the corner like that, you despicable little worm," he said, rather wearily, and with only a suspicion of a return of the sneer. "There's a limit to how much I can do to something like you. Not that I wouldn't like to beat you to a pile of shit on the floor and rub your snout in your own dirt, because I would, as well you know. I've got kids of my own the age of this little fancy boy of yours, and I'd like to do to you what any decent, normal bloke would want to do. But you've no need to worry. If I kick seven shades of shit out of you I'll end up in court myself, and I wouldn't do that for all the satisfaction I'd get out of it. But don't kid your slimy self that I don't understand. I understand people like you only too well, and you won't do yourself any favours by putting on superior college-boy airs and telling decent people what they do or don't understand. Now sit down."

He shot out a hand, grabbed Christopher painfully by the throat and slung him roughly, but not very violently, back onto the chair. Christopher, wondering if the nightmare would ever end, summoned up what was left of his courage and looked up at him. "Now, let's try again," the man said with soft menace. I've heard them say that in films, Christopher found himself thinking. Before he could stop himself he emitted a small, strangled giggle. The inspector's eyes bulged, and he started towards the small, huddled figure on the chipped and battered chair. The reflex sound died on the spot, and the boy's eyes grew huge with terror. Something in that expression halted the police officer in his tracks, and his face almost softened for a fraction of an instant. "You'd better tell me," he said, suddenly sounding weary and, Christopher sensed, a little defeated. "I want to know where the boy is, and I also want to know *exactly* what it is you've been getting up to with him." Christopher dug deep and found a shred more courage.

"I never did a thing with him that he didn't want me to do. I didn't even do what I did until he begged me to do it," he said. "He *wanted* me to do everything I did, I keep telling you. But I'm not going to have him dragged into this and frightened and bullied by you. He's... he's... He's had all this from his father, and any more of it from you would break him. He'd go and..." He stumbled into silence, unable to utter the worst fears that haunted him - in fact, they were so unformulated that he had no real idea of what it was that he dreaded. He was vaguely conscious that as he strove to protect Jamie his own courage rallied just a little: there was the beginning of a belief that somehow he could find the fortitude to endure a little more if he had to.

At that psychological moment there was a tap on the door. The inspector clicked his tongue in irritation and swung round as a police constable entered the room. Christopher felt an overwhelming gratitude to the man. He vaguely recognised him as the enormous officer who had arrived in the street outside his home where his and Jamie's fathers had been fighting - where he himself, he recollected with a sudden sharp taste of shame in his mouth, had been promptly knocked out of the game by the first heavy swing of David Potten's fist.

Never suspecting that he had come as the answer to a prayer the PC said something quietly to the inspector, and Christopher had survived the first round. "Look after this piece of dirt for me, Cookie," he said, with a brief glance of scalding dislike at Christopher, and went out. Christopher shot a frightened glance under his eyelashes at the PC, wondering if there was yet worse to come, but the man looked back at him with nothing whatsoever in his face, then busied himself rolling an astonishingly thin cigarette out of a battered Golden Virginia tin. He smoked it, leaning against the door, his giant bulk blocking it from side to side, and hardly looked at Christopher.

After a few minutes of very empty silence that was broken only when the constable exhaled a stream of smoke Christopher ventured to speak - as much to see what would happen as anything else. "Will he be coming back, please?" he asked. The PC took a moment to turn from contemplating the end of his microscopic cigarette and glanced indolently at him. His face was completely neutral. "No idea," he said, and resumed his examination of his fag; then, unexpectedly, he spoke again. "No, I don't suppose he will, as it happens. He's had to relieve the Station Off... someone who's gone off duty early." He looked down at the scared boy and, still expressionless, added, "The CID'll be down to talk to you in a bit." He went back to his cigarette and from then on ignored Christopher completely. Christopher sat and prepared himself for whatever might be coming as best he could.

***

Detective Sergeant Richard Bly rose to his feet and looked down at Christopher's face. Although the boy looked even paler than normal and his face was streaked with tears, he had rallied quite well, and seemed fairly self-possessed. "I'll have to lock you up for a bit, son," he said, kindly enough. "You won't think about doing anything silly, now will you? There'll be someone watching you." Christopher shook his head. "I shan't hang myself," he muttered. "You haven't left me much to do it with, have you?"

The detective, a thin, balding man with a big moustache, nodded to himself and moved to the door. "Would you like something to read?" he asked. Christopher blinked at him gratefully. "I wouldn't mind, if you've got anything," he said. "If it's no trouble."

"No trouble at all, son," said the man. He locked the heavy door behind him.

Two hours earlier, when he had first taken over from the inspector, the detective had taken him to another small, dingy room, indistinguishable from the first one except that it had an eight-inch square of armoured glass in the door. There he had taken all his possessions off him, and made him give up his belt and even the laces from his trainers. The things had all been put into a big brown envelope, which he had had to sign across the flaps. Then the man had started the questioning. There had been none of the violence or the insults that the inspector had used, none of the hatred, not even any dislike or contempt. Just quiet, methodical questioning, the same questions often repeated but coming from different angles, inexorable and in a way hypnotic.

Bly was, at least, not cruel. At one point he had said "Okay, time for a break. Wanna cuppa?" Christopher had practically broken down in tears then. Bly had popped his head out of the door and spoken to someone, and a few minutes later a uniformed PC had appeared with two large mugs of strong brown tea. Christopher drank his as if it was nectar, not even noticing that it was stewed and that it had sugar, which he didn't take. "Smoke?" said Bly, offering him a packet of Marlboro. Christopher declined but thanked him gratefully. Bly sat in silence while he smoked one himself. Then the tea-break was over and the questioning had begun again. "All right, then, Christopher. Now tell me, what *exactly* did you do...?"

***

"...I see. And what did you do *then*?"

"...let's get this quite clear. You say you made love. How, exactly? Yes, I mean, what did you *do*?"

"...Yes, I'm sorry, Christopher, but I have got to know. I'd much rather not, believe me, but..."

"*Ah*. Let's be quite sure about this. You're telling me that you had full intercourse with him? *Anal* intercourse, you mean? Yes. You with him, or him with you? Yes, I'm afraid so. *Both*? So, then, he penetrated you? I see. And then you penetrated him. Thank you..."

***

After Bly had gone Christopher sat with his head in his hands for a few minutes. Then he got up and went to peer through the thick glass in the door, already beginning to feel panic rising. He tried to squint up and down the passage, looking for the person who was apparently watching him, but could see nothing but a few feet of institutional cream and brown painted corridor. He stood there for an incalculable period. Three or four times in as many minutes he looked at his wrist, forgetting that his watch was in the brown envelope with the few other things he had had on him.

After what seemed to him like an almost interminable wait he heard the iron door of the cell passage open and slam, a heavy bolt drawn and the detective sergeant's footsteps approaching. Christopher moved away from the door and stood, ghost-like, in the corner of the bare little cubicle. A key was turned in the lock and Bly came in. "Not much about to read," he said apologetically. "Got you what I could find. Not many university types round this place, I'm afraid. Still, you won't be here all that much longer, with a bit of luck." He dropped a couple of magazines on the bench and went back to the door.

"Sir... er, officer," said Christopher desperately as he opened the door. Bly turned back and looked at him interrogatively. "Yes? What is it?"

"What's going to happen to me, please?" asked Christopher. "I've been here for hours, and I haven't seen anyone yet - I mean, apart from you and the other policeman. Are my parents still here? Is the other man still here, and is he going to be prosecuted? I mean, I still don't know what's going to happen to me, or... or... or anything - at least," he added, "not for certain. I don't know why you're keeping me here..." He trailed into silence. He had a good idea what was going to happen next, but could hardly bring himself to contemplate it, or to utter the words. He held out his hands towards the detective in a plaintive gesture of supplication. "I mean, can't you at least tell me what you're going to do to me?"

Bly shut the door and came back towards him. "Siddown," he said, pushing Christopher gently towards the bench that ran along one side of the room. He sat down beside Christopher and looked levelly into his eyes. "I don't know that you really need me to tell you that you're in a fair bit of trouble, son." Christopher nodded miserably, his eyes large with fear and strain. "I'll tell you as much as I can, though," resumed the detective. "Thanks," muttered Christopher, meaning it.

"We've interviewed your parents, who tell us exactly the same as you have. You must know perfectly well why the man caused all the disturbance, don't you?"

"Well, I... he's Jamie's father..." began the boy. "Exactly," said Bly. "And a nasty piece of work he seems if ever there was one." Christopher's face brightened immediately. Bly saw it and hastened to dispel any rising optimism. "Yes, son, I can tell a shithouse when I interview one. But you'd better not feel encouraged by that. I mean, don't think that my opinion of him makes the trouble you're in any less, because it doesn't, and it can't." He paused to let that sink in, then continued. "There was - there is - a clear case against him - Potten, that is - of common assault on you and on your father. Maybe actual bodily harm on your father, we might've been able to swing it. But your father's declined to prefer charges, so we've let him go."

"You've let him go?" said Christopher, amazed.

"Oh yes. No complainant, no charges. Nothing we can do about it."

"But... but, what about *me*?" spluttered Christopher, his

expression turning from amazement to outrage. "I'd have charged him."

"Christopher, do yourself a favour," said the detective. He laid a large, bony hand on Christopher's arm and gently pushed him back onto the bench, from which he was beginning to rise angrily. "You ain't gonna be charging *anybody*. And it'll be a lot better for you that way, too. Believe me." He paused again, looking carefully at Christopher as his excitement subsided. "You're not going to carry much conviction as a victim, boy, and the sooner you realise that the better. Low profile's the operative words for you."

"What's going to happen, then?" asked Christopher desperately. "Just tell me what's going to *happen*. And my parents - and Neil. What about Neil? He's nothing to do with all this, nothing to do with it at all." His desperation, mingled with panic, mounted again fast.

"All right, Christopher. I'll tell you as much as I can." Bly brushed his moustache with the back of his hand, choosing his words carefully. "Your parents are still here. Your brother's been taken home by a policewoman, who will stay with him until your parents get home. They'll be here until we let you go..."

He broke off hastily, seeing the clouds on Christopher's face beginning to clear rapidly. "Don't get too excited," he said gruffly. "We'll be letting you go this evening - in an hour or so. But we'll only be bailing you." Once again he paused to let the significance of his last words sink in. "We're going to have to charge you, Christopher. Didn't you realise that?"

"N..n..no," stammered Christopher weakly. He slumped back against the wall, his eyes widening as horrified realisation fell on him.

Bly's face softened a little. "You didn't realise, then," he said gently. "We've got to charge you. It's a serious offence."

"But what offence?" asked Christopher, struggling to hold back tears. "I never did anything he didn't want..."

"I'm afraid that's not the point, son. It's an offence, still a pretty serious one. It can carry life imprisonment..." Mentally cursing himself for a fool, he shot an arm round Christopher, who had almost fallen off the bench, and hauled him back to a sitting position. "I'm sorry, son," he said quickly. "You won't be getting life, or anything like it. You won't be going to prison at all," he added, crossing his fingers as he said it. Christopher rallied. "Go on, then," he said, dully. "What are you going to charge me with?"

"Can't say for certain," said Bly, wishing he had said nothing at all. "It'll be something under the Sexual Offences Act. We're bringing the other boy in - at least, we will be as soon as we find out where he is." He looked sharply at Christopher. "You know where he is, don't you?"

Christopher gazed at him in horror. "Bring Jamie in?" he said in a low, hopeless voice. "But I kept saying to that other man, it'll kill him," he wailed. He turned to the detective in sudden animation. "You can't bring him into it," he said urgently. "You *can't*. After everything else he's had to go through, that would just about *kill* him. To be dragged into a police station and grilled like you've been grilling me, and then court and... and... and whatever else..." He lapsed into a silence. Bly could almost smell the fear and horror coming off him. He reeked of it.

"The boy's father doesn't know where he is," Bly eventually said, quietly, in an attempt to convey something of calm to the boy. "He doesn't seem to care very much, either, come to that," he added. "He wasn't even sure of the whereabouts of his wife, though he seems to think she's gone to stay with a woman friend for a while. He's given us a list of half a dozen, and we're trying to raise her, to find out through her where the boy is. Unless, that is, you care to save us a bit of time. It might do you a bit of good," he added, a little hesitantly. Christopher looked at him with bitter contempt. "I see," he said, with more spirit than he had shown up to that moment, "I turn Jamie in, and you put a word in for me at court, that's it, isn't it? I've seen that on the television."

"We'll find him before long, son," said Bly evenly. "The only difference is that if you tell us now and save a bit of time, we'll get him here early enough that he can be out of

96

here this evening, and so, for that matter, will *you*. But if you don't want to tell us, well, as I say, we'll find him. You might as well make it as easy as you can on yourself - and on him." He sat back and waited. Christopher's face twitched for a moment as he struggled with himself. "What will you do to him?" he asked after a long pause.

"That I can't say, son. It rather depends on what he has to say." He hesitated. "What do *you* think he'll say?"

"He'll say the same as I've told you," said Christopher, with such simple certainty that the detective, hardened as he was to hearing every known species and degree of lying from people frightened, people defiant and people, generally, doing their utmost to lie themselves out of trouble, believed him without a suspicion of doubt. "He'll tell you that I love him, and that I'd do anything to keep him from being hurt. And he'll tell you that he loves me too, and that I never - not once - did anything that he didn't want me to do. If he tells you anything other than that it'll be to protect me. He'd never lie for any other reason - not about us, anyway."

Bly wrinkled his nose in thought, mingled with some distaste. "Hmmm. Well, that might make a difference - *if* he comes across with it as you seem sure he will," he said slowly. Christopher looked at him with the same bitter expression as before. "Might make a difference to what?" he asked acidly. "To you, son. If he swears all that you say he'll swear, it might make a difference to the charge. Not that I can promise that," he added hastily, "but it just might reduce it to a lower charge." He looked hopefully at Christopher. Christopher sat in thought. Then he surrendered. "Oh, well, you'll find him soon enough, I suppose," he said. "He's staying at his headmaster's house, at the school. He went there looking for help after he had a fight with his father. He couldn't think of anywhere else to go. But they've been very good to him. He's told me. It's the first proper home he's ever had..." Christopher burst into tears.

"Thank you, Christopher," the detective said after watching him for a moment, hunched and shaking with sobbing on the drab bench seat. "I'll have him collected right

away, and we'll have you out of here as soon as we can.
I'll…" he hesitated. "I don't like qu… your kind much," he
said, inconsequentially, "but you seem like a decent enough
lad otherwise. And your people seem all right. I'll see if
there's anything I can do." He stood and left the room
quickly, as if escaping from an unpleasant smell, as
Christopher perceived it.

**

For Jamie, the nightmare now began. Ten minutes after
Christopher had told Bly his whereabouts a uniformed
policewoman rang the doorbell at the headmaster's house
and spoke with the Lanes for several minutes. They both
attempted to insist that they accompany the boy to the police
station, and were politely but distantly told that they would
be asked to make statements later, and that they would be
requested to go to the station at the appropriate moment.
And now, if they would fetch the boy, please… It was, as
Lane commented later to Edith, the first time he had been
shouted down *sotto voce*.

A few minutes later Jamie had been fetched from his room,
where he was dealing with his evening preparation, by Edith
Lane, fighting not to show tears that were trying to escape.
His eyes grew huge with anxiety as she told him the
fragments that she had learned. The mere fact that it involved
Christopher and that he was in some kind of trouble was
enough to frighten him into a panic, and she had to work
hard for several minutes to suppress his incipient hysteria.
However, she managed to soothe him, assuring him that he
would be back with them soon, and that whatever it was
would be capable of being dealt with. As she took his hand
and led him to the door of the room she could feel him
trembling.

He glared at the policewoman waiting by the front door,

and she flinched slightly, taken aback at such a depth of ferocity in so boyish a face. After that one glance at her his face set into a frozen self-possession. He turned back to Edith, put his arms round her neck and kissed her cheek. "Please don't cry," he said to her softly, seeing her tears now coming freely, and the policewoman thought it sounded more as if he was the adult and she the child needing comforting. "I'll make it all right." He looked at Dr Lane, who had now appeared in the hallway, and from some deep part of him found a smile. Lane found that he was struggling against tears himself. They went out into the drive where a police car waited with a constable at the wheel. Jamie was put into the back, the policewoman slipped in beside him, and the car moved off.

"My God, he's got some pluck, that boy," muttered Lane as the rear lights disappeared. "He practically vaporized that poor girl."

His wife clutched him and put her head on his shoulder. "Oh, John, what are we to do?" she sobbed. "We can't just sit here and wait, and do nothing. We should be with him."

Lane stared out into the darkness, wondering what to do. He too felt that they should be as near to Jamie as possible. But he also believed in taking what people said seriously. "The policewoman was firm," he eventually said. "She was quite definite that we shouldn't be allowed to be with Jamie." His wife's head shot off his shoulder and she looked grimly at him. In the light from the porch he saw clearly that the distress and grief had been wiped from her face and supplanted by a look of determination. "That policewoman," she snapped, "has no right to tell us whether we may or may not be with our child..." She broke off, her mouth a hard line. "Yes, our child, for the time being. He's our responsibility, and he hasn't got another soul in the world who gives a damn about him - he's ours for now, John - and that bloody little madam of a policewoman has no business telling you and me what we ought or ought not to be doing for him. At a moment like this, of all times, we're supposed to leave him - to desert him and leave him to their tender mercies. I'll do no such thing, and neither will you. Get the car."

She stalked into the house. John Lane, who had seen her in such a frame of mind no more than two or three times in all the thirty-five years he had known and loved her, never thought for a moment to disobey. She was for the most part a pliant and gentle woman, secure enough in her placid temperament and her own separate personality to have no need to strike poses. Feeling no need to demonstrate her equality in their partnership, she was quite content to allow him an apparently dominant role, making the decisions and, generally, happy to follow where he led. The couple of occasions when she had behaved like that, however, he had known quite instinctively that there would be no argument. The other times had all concerned the welfare of their own children, and, he thought to himself as he changed into his shoes and got the car out of the garage, he couldn't disagree with her about Jamie. He might not be theirs for long but at that moment he was theirs or he was nobody's. He left the car with its engine running in the drive and went in to fetch his jacket.

***

At about the same moment Angela Turnbull was staring at her friend and temporary house-guest in alarm. The bell had chimed and Annabel had answered it. There had been voices, which had faded, and she had heard the door of her little-used dining room closing. A few minutes later the voices had been raised somewhat. A door had opened and closed, violently. Then the front door had opened, and there had been the sound of a car starting up and moving away, followed by a tremendous slam of the front door. Now Annabel had swept back into the room, in a positive fury.

."That bastard!" cried Annabel Potten. "That absolute, bloody *bastard*!" She stood in the middle of the room, clenching and unclenching her hands by her sides, almost spitting as she uttered the words. "I'll *kill* him." She whirled round and marched across to the neat little bar in the corner, almost sweeping occasional tables and standard lamps down as she went. She seized a glass, which happened to be a brandy balloon, sloshed a huge measure of whisky into it and drank half of it, all in the same motion.

"Annabel, whatever's happened?" she said. Her voice seemed to rouse the other woman from a trance. She swung round on her and glared furiously down at her. Angela observed that her knuckles were white round the big glass. "Careful with that, my dear," she said quickly, "those glasses cost fifty quid apiece. Now calm down a bit, and tell me what's happened. Was that David?"

Annabel looked down at her glass, as if surprised to find it in her hand, and relaxed her fierce grip on it a little. She opened her mouth, but whatever emotion had her in its grip had her so tight that she could not speak for a moment. She went for a short walk round the room instead, draining her glass en route and coming to rest by the bar to pour herself another one. This seemed to calm her, and she walked more slowly back and sat down beside her friend. "It wasn't David," she eventually said. Her voice sounded as if it was being filtered through ground glass. "Not in person. No, it was an envoy. The police." Her voice rose. "He sent the *police* to find me."

"The police?" queried Angela. "Whatever's happened now, then?"

"Oh, nothing very much," said Annabel bitterly. "That stupid, crass, block-headed imbecile of a husband of mine's only gone and got himself arrested. That's all." She took a long pull on her drink and sat, breathing heavily and staring into vacancy. Her friend waited for her to go on in her own time.

"The great big dummy," she eventually spat out. "He's *only* been round to this other boy's house, this Christopher's, beaten him up and his father as well, from what I could gather, and been arrested for assault and battery or grievous bodily harm or some bloody thing or other. Then they've started asking questions, and it's all come out into the open about those two having this ridiculous adolescent love affair. They've charged the other kid with seducing him - it seems they're going to throw him in the tower and chuck the key away, and bloody good riddance to him, as far as it goes. Now they want to interview James as well, with a view to possible charges against *him*. They want me to go to the police station and make a statement, about my own son. That was a policeman wanting to know where he was living. Dear God!"

Angela Turnbull sat, slightly stunned. "Jesus Christ," she breathed softly. "What a mess. The poor kid. We'll have to see him right away. You didn't tell the copper where he was, I suppose?" She looked at her friend's face and saw the answer there. "You *didn't*, did you?" she said, in dawning horror. "Christ, you *did*. Annabel, what in God's name possessed you? You could have given him a breathing space, so we could get to him first..."

Annabel Potten remained sitting, staring into the middle of the room, while Angela tapped her foot and looked at her impatiently. Suddenly, as if she had just thought of something original, Annabel looked round at her and said, "It'll be all over the papers, you know. That bloody awful local rag will think it's their birthday. Can you *imagine* what this will do us? I shan't be able to show my face. God, what a thing to do."

Angela gazed at her friend in something approaching amazement. "Are you more worried about your local reputation, or what they're doing to your unfortunate child?" she said acidly. But she was a practical and masterful woman, and saw immediately that there was nothing in talking but waste of precious minutes. "Come on," she snapped. "Drink that quickly and we'll get going. We might just be in time to stop them from interrogating the kid around the kidneys. I'll drive - you've had enough to melt their bloody breathaliser. Come on," she said again, "move, woman. You and your bloody husband have done enough damage between you.

Now it's time to see if we can put some of it right."

"I wonder if David's still there," murmured Annabel, even as she obediently finished her drink and got up to go. "You can leave him to me, if he is," said Angela tartly. "All this situation needs to turn it into a full-scale diplomatic incident is for you and him to have a punch-up on the bloody police station doorstep. "I'll send *him* packing. Now come on, let's go."

***

The 'incident' had already reached impressive proportions when the two women ran breathlessly into the front office of the station. The inspector, who was now Station Officer for that night, was speaking to a tall, grey-haired and authoritative man in his fifties as they arrived, while at the same time attempting to deal with a very angry woman who kept interrupting with imperious demands that he allow her to do the talking. Three pairs of eyes turned on the newcomers. "Ah, you've arrived. And not before time," snapped the woman. This," she said, turning back to the inspector, "is the boy's mother."

Annabel looked at them, and suddenly flushed. She opened her mouth, then closed it again. Angela Turnbull took in the couple in one rapid glance, and took charge. "You're the boy's headmaster?" she enquired. "Doctor... "

"Lane, madam," said Lane coolly. "And you will be Mrs Turnbull, no doubt. Thank you for coming so promptly. One gathers that officers were dispatched to find Jamie's whereabouts from Mrs Potten. All quite unnecessary, I find, since the other wretched boy had already told them where he could be found. Under pressure, or the spurious promise of some favour that has not, in fact, been forthcoming, it appears."

"That's not true," put in the inspector sharply. "Now, all

103

of you, please calm yourselves. The officer in charge of the case will come down shortly and speak to you in turn. Now, if you'd all just take seats in the interview room, I'll tell you the moment there's anything to tell." He sighed, and indicated a door beside the counter. Reluctantly they filed in and sat awkwardly round it in an electric silence.

***

Detective Sergeant Bly finished talking and looked at Robert and Audrey Rowe expectantly. He thought they had taken it all too calmly, and waited apprehensively to see what form the explosion, when it came, took. It didn't come. After he completed his outline of the facts, which was succinct but nonetheless lengthy, they sat looking at him for a long moment. Then they looked at each other. The father, he noted, was showing some distress. The mother seemed very calm. She was the first to speak, and her voice, too, was level and apparently normal. Delayed shock? Bly wondered to himself.

"So our son is to be charged with a serious offence, then, sergeant?" she said.

"I'm afraid so, ma'am," he replied, feeling increasingly uncomfortable. This was the last reaction he had expected. He waited.

"Will he be convicted?" she asked. "I don't think there's any doubt of it, ma'am," Bly said. "He'll plead guilty, I should think. He's admitted everything to us, and made a statement. The other boy confirms what he's said in every detail. We'll be bailing your son out to you very shortly, after he's charged. He'll have to appear at the local magistrates' court. Then they'll commit him to appear for trial at the Crown Court. If he pleads guilty it'll all be over and done with very quickly."

"And what'll happen to him, assuming he pleads guilty?"

104

Robert Rowe spoke for the first time since Bly's outline of the evening's events. His face was a little haggard, but his voice too was even. The effort of holding himself in was more visible in him than in his wife.

"I can't tell you for sure," admitted Bly. "I wish I could, but this is a very rare offence - or at least, we don't get many cases round here. I've been here fifteen years and this is the first of this kind I've had to deal with. I can tell you what the maximum possible sentence is..." He hesitated. They sat forward, expectantly. "Before I do tell you that," he said "I would ask you not to get agitated. I told your boy himself this and he practically passed out on me. You can take it from me that he won't receive the maximum, or anything like it. So long as you realise that..." They nodded. "Go on," muttered Rowe.

"It can carry, in these circumstances, life imprisonment. That's one reason why it must be tried at the Crown Court."

Robert Rowe drew in his breath with a hiss. His wife sat bolt upright, eyes wide and her mouth trembling. "They wouldn't..."

"No, ma'am, they won't do that," the detective said unhappily. "I can't promise you much, but I can promise you that much. They won't send him to prison at all, I shouldn't think. If they do, it'll be for a very short term, it'll be youth custody, which isn't as bad as prison, and it would almost certainly be suspended. As I say, I doubt..."

He fell silent, watching the misery pass across their faces. "He's of exemplary character up to now, Mr and Mrs Rowe," he resumed, trying to offer them some comfort. "Also, the other boy has fully admitted that he was a consenting party, indeed he was the prime mover in the whole affair. He wants to tell the court that it was all his fault, that he pushed your son into it against his will." He mused for a while, rubbing his moustache. "He's lying, in part at least. Your son admits that he was a fully consenting and instigating party. But in the circumstances, with the younger boy insisting on taking his part of it, I very much doubt if Christopher will get anything much more than a suspended sentence, maybe even a con-dis - a conditional discharge," he elaborated, seeing their blank looks. "He's a game little sod - sorry, ma'am, shouldn't've used that expression. But he's got a lot of guts, this kid. I wish..." He left the thought unspoken.

The telephone on his desk rang, shattering the quiet and making them all jump. Bly picked it up. There was a squawk from the other end. "Yeah. Oh, right. Okay."

"Governor's been raked out of bed. He's coming up to see me now," he said, replacing the receiver.

"Who's the governor?" asked Rowe.

"Superintendent, sir. In charge of this station. He's what we call the late senior. He gets called out if anything big crops up. This is big, for us. Here he is," he said, as the double doors into the CID office opened. A welcome draught of cold air blew into the stuffy office, followed by a big, florid man with sandy hair. He was wearing civilian slacks and an orange sports jacket, with a thin tie that had obviously been tied in a hurry, the knot loose and somewhere under his right ear. He came in and surveyed the three of them. Bly stood up and introduced him. "Superintendent Goodfellow, Mr and Mrs Rowe. These are the parents of the older boy, guv. I've been explaining what'll be happening."

"How d'ye do," the new arrival said perfunctorily, in a broad Scottish accent. He hardly looked at them as he said it, and was already walking Bly to the far end of the big open-plan office before the words were properly out of his mouth. They sat and watched as he and Bly perched themselves on two desks. Then they waited for twenty minutes while the two men went into a huddle. Bly was doing most of the talking. At one point he got up off the desk and came back towards them, but it was only to fetch a heavy legal-looking book from where he had been sitting while he talked to them. As he picked it up from the desk, his back turned to the superintendent he raised his eyes at them and mouthed "Not long now" to them. "He's quite a nice man, really," whispered Audrey Rowe to her husband. He grimaced, shrugged and went back into a private contemplation of his own.

Eventually the two policemen came back to the Rowes. "I gather ye've no complaints about the way Detective Sergeant Bly has been dealing with the case?" the superintendent said brusquely. It wasn't really a question.

"It's not exactly a case to us, Mr - ah - Goodfellow," said Audrey Rowe. "This is our son you're dealing with, and we're desperately worried..."

"Aye, aye, of course. But ye're happy with the way Sergeant Bly is handling it."

"Mr Bly has been very kind," said Robert Rowe. "As far as it goes, we have no complaint to make. But we are terribly worried, as my wife just said, and we don't yet know what will happen to Christopher. We don't even know precisely what he's going to be charged with. As far as I can see, the other boy was the..."

"There's no going to be any charge just now," said Goodfellow, swinging round towards the double doors leading to the stairs, on his way.

"What?" cried Audrey Rowe. She leapt from her chair, the first tears of relief already gushing, and ran after Goodfellow's burly figure. She reached him as he was half-way through the doors and clutched his arm. "You mean you're going to let him go?" she said, eyes shining.

Goodfellow swung round on her and let the door go. "Bly'll be telling you about it. I said we aren't charging him *just now*, and I normally say what I mean." He stared at them irritably for a moment, then appeared to notice Mrs Rowe's face, tearful but now also utterly confused, and his face softened just a little. "Madam, my home is thirty-one and a half miles from here. I'm now going to return to it. That makes a drive of sixty-three miles, to come in here and point out an elementary matter of law to my officers, any one of whom ought to have known it without having to drag me from my bed. Sergeant Bly will explain. Good night to ye." He strode heavily to the doors and they heard his footsteps receding down the stairs.

The Rowes turned to Bly, who was looking mildly embarrassed. "He's not the most polished governor we've ever had. Good copper," he excused. The Rowes made similar snorting sounds simultaneously. "What did he mean, Mr Bly?" asked Robert Rowe.

"I'm afraid he was having a dig at me," said Bly, pulling a wry face. "He was quite right, as a matter of fact." He broke off, musing to himself for a moment. "There *is* a point of law that I failed to notice. I'd've seen it later on, but... well, that's my problem.

"Now, I'm a bit hesitant about mentioning this, because I don't want to raise any false expectations in you..." He broke off, seeing hope instantly flaring into life on their faces.

"There may - I emphasize, there *may* be - some hope for you." He sat and watched them for a moment. "But please, don't let yourselves get too optimistic about it... what Mr Goodfellow meant was that there is another step to be gone through." Once more he paused. "Please, tell us, what is it?" pleaded Audrey Rowe, looking beseechingly at him.

"Well, as he said, we shan't actually be charging your son tonight, Mrs Rowe. We'll be letting him go as soon as I've talked to you. That'll be in a few minutes now. The reason for the delay is that nobody remembered enough of his training to recall that in these circumstances, where the parties both consented to the acts and are under 21 years of age, no proceedings may be taken without the consent of the Director of Public Prosecutions.

"What that means is that for now we're going to bail Christopher out. Nothing to that, just straight bail in his own recognisance of fifty pounds. That means simply that he'll forfeit that sum if he doesn't observe the conditions - mainly that he come back here when we tell him to. That'll be a week or ten days, I guess, when the Director's had a chance to see the papers and make his decision."

"And we'll know then if Chris is to be..." Robert Rowe choked suddenly.

"Yes, Mr Rowe, you'll know then," said Bly gently. "You'll know as soon as we can tell you. We shan't keep you worrying a moment longer than we can help. Now, let's get you downstairs and see your boy."

He looked keenly at them for a moment. "One thing. You'll be on your son's side in all this, will you? I mean," he said, seeing their puzzled expressions, "the other poor kid seems to have a pretty strange pair of parents. The father doesn't seem to give a damn if the boy lives or dies, and the mother's only interested in whether it gets her name in the paper. The only people who seem to care a curse about him are the headmaster of his school and his wife. He's living with them for the moment, and lucky he is, by the look of things. I'm pretty sure I know how you'll react to your boy, but he'll be needing all the support he can get just now." Once again he peered closely at them. "I just thought I'd better be sure," he said awkwardly, seeing their indignant looks. "Of course I can see what kind of parents you are. But..." He let it go. "Come on, let's get you downstairs and on your way home."

"You've no need to worry, Mr Bly," said Robert Rowe slowly, a dawning respect and even liking for the scrawny detective beginning to form. "We've both been shocked by what we've heard - we had no idea that there was anything... that Chris was... as he is, and it's come as a great shock. But we're with him, of course. I don't pretend to understand what can have made him like this, or brought it on, but obviously we shall stand by him, whatever happens. Whatever happens," he repeated to himself, under his breath.

He stood up and gave his wife a hand up also. He turned to Bly and said, "Thank you for being so considerate, Mr Bly." Bly stuck out a hand. "Nothing to that, Mr Rowe," he replied, a little awkwardly, rubbing his moustache. "I hope it all turns out right for you. In any case, I'll be seeing you in a week or so's time, when the DPP's made his decision. I'll keep my fingers crossed for you."

The Rowes looked at him as he began to shepherd them to the stairs. "Would you be willing to tell me, Mr Bly," said Robert Rowe, "how you feel about Christopher, you personally? I can't help feeling you seem to be a bit on his side in all this."

Bly stopped by the doors and looked candidly at him and

thought for a moment. Choosing his words carefully, he said "I've got nothing against gay people in general. You learn not to make too many judgments in this job, and in the main I don't think they do anybody any harm, except maybe themselves. I feel sorry for them, and I'm bloody glad I'm not that way myself, or my own son. But when young children are involved it's a different ball game, and I've nothing but hatred and contempt. Normally I'd say this other kid was a child, but I've seen him, talked to him, and he's not like any fifteen-year-old kid I've come across. There's people out there wearing coppers' uniforms less - less adult. I must admit, it's made me think a good deal about this affair, and I think..."

There was a long pause. Then, reluctantly, he went on, "I'm not sure that your boy is *altogether*... ah... blameworthy. That's not to say I condone what he's been getting up to with the boy. He shouldn't have meddled with him, he shouldn't have allowed himself to be tempted, whatever the boy's maturity, however forceful he may be. The law's cast iron on this, and so it should be, in my opinion. But...there is one other thing about Christopher..."

They waited anxiously. "Yes," prompted Rowe.

"I liked him," said Bly, with a slight air of confession. "I'll say that. I liked him." They went downstairs.

***

"You do understand the conditions of this bail - you understand what it all implies?" asked the inspector frigidly. Christopher, white-faced and haggard, nodded silently. The inspector looked at his parents. "You're quite clear about all this? Particularly that he must have no contact with the Potten boy whatsoever?"

"Of course not," said Rowe. "We wouldn't want him to see the boy anymore, anyway."

"Very well. Then that's all, and you can go," said the inspector impersonally. He nodded dismissively at Christopher, who rose slowly from the chair across the table in the charge room. He turned and took a couple of steps towards his parents. He looked dazed and slightly sick. His father took him, very gently, by the arm. "Come on, my dear," he said softly, and steered him through the door, into the front office and out of the police station. Bly was standing at the top of the steps down into the street, looking out into the night. He seemed to rouse himself from a trance as the three of them made to pass him. "Good night," he murmured as they went down the steps into the street. As they passed him they just heard him add "Good luck." Christopher passed him like a spectre, not seeing or hearing anything.

***

"You don't care much about him, do you?" said Angela Turnbull to Annabel, glancing curiously at her friend out of the corner of her eye as she ran the car into her garage.

"What makes you say that?" asked Annabel Potten. Angela halted the car, switched off the engine and turned to look at Annabel. "What makes me think that?" she said in mystification. "You need to ask that, after what I've seen tonight?" She got out of the car and locked it, talking in an everyday tone as she did so. "Tonight so far you've bitched about David - well, I don't blame you for that. You've told me how terrified you are about getting into the local paper. Okay, I can imagine how you'd feel. You've heard this frightful horror story about James and everything that's happened tonight. You've been called out in the night to the police station, where you calmly made a statement to them telling them that you hardly know what your own son's been up to but that what you do know confirms what they've found out from David and his lunatic antics. And then you

111

not only practically give your son away to that headmaster and his wife, but you refuse even to see the poor little sod. He's in the *police station*, Annabel. He's been dragged away from home - well, it amounts to home for him now, poor little mite - when it's damn near his bedtime, he's been locked up, interrogated, most likely bullied or pressurised, had to make a statement incriminating the person he thinks he's in love with, and then his mother turns up and refuses to see him. Refuses. Christ, even the copper that took me in to see the poor little devil told lies and made excuses for you. Not that they cut any ice with James. He's seen right through you, and lucky for him he has."

"What did he say, then?" asked Annabel as they let themselves into the house.

"Nothing very much," replied Angela. "He just said that he'd sort it out for himself. He said he wasn't surprised that you didn't want to see him, but he said to tell you he's all right where he is, and you're not to worry. I think he was being sarcastic. I hope he was."

"Are you turning òn me, then, Ange?" asked Annabel, looking a little anxious.

"Me? No, I shan't turn on you. There's been a damn sight too much of people turning their backs on people in this whole shabby affair, and I'm not going to start learning from the examples I've seen about me. No, I shan't turn on you. You're welcome here with me for as long as you like. But I'm not going to try to make you feel better, or happier than you ought to be by lying to you about what I think of you. And frankly, Annabel, I don't think much of you right now. I think you've treated that poor child of yours like a leper, at the critical moment when he needed help and sympathy and people round him to love him and no strings attached.

"I wouldn't expect that rotten hound of a husband of yours to offer him anything in the way of love or anything else. He's no good and never was, as I told you long before you married him. But I thought you'd have done something to stand by him, at least at a time like this, when he's up to his neck in trouble."

112

Annabel sighed. "I didn't interfere, Ange, but don't be too hard on me. I didn't expect you to understand... I just hoped you might."

"What *are* you talking about?" asked her friend, in something suspiciously close to a snort.

"I said, I didn't interfere. Don't you see, Ange? If I had seen him tonight, if I see him at all until this thing's over, that's what it will be - interfering. Because he's not mine any more. Did you see how they looked every time they spoke of him? I mean the Lanes. They love him, in ways I never could. I couldn't love anything enough to make me look like that when I talked of it.

"James? I quite liked him, once he'd got old enough to be a person, he was quite amusing company now and then. But I could never love him, not as most people seem able to love their children - or at least, claim they do. I'm not capable of the emotion, and that's that. I don't deserve James, and the Lanes do, and that's the way it is. Now for God's sake let's have a drink." And she helped herself liberally. Angela took a smaller drink and sat sipping it reflectively. You think you know someone, she thought, and then, out of a clear blue sky, something drops on you like a thunderbolt, and you realise you never really knew them at all...

Annabel had two more stiff drinks and went to bed. For a long time after she had gone her friend remained sitting and sipping on the sofa, seeing again the tormented, determined, and most of all *sad* grey eyes looking up at her from under a dark red fringe in the grimy little interview room. There had been a moment when something she had said had brought a smile. It had been a faint one, struggling for life in a sea of circumstances, but it had been a smile, and it had lit up the dingy little room like a flare. Most of all, she thought, topping up her glass at the bar, it was his courage she admired. That smile, in such a setting, in such a predicament. If Annabel Potten, sleeping like the dead and snoring faintly, had suspected the kind of thoughts her friend was entertaining downstairs she might have slept less easily.

***

"How is he?" asked Dr Lane anxiously as his wife came back into the room.

"He's sleeping, at least," she said wearily. "John, I think we might have some - oh, you've already made some, I see."

"Of course, my dear," he said, pouring tea into a cup he had ready for her. She sat down heavily beside him and sipped the tea appreciatively.

"It's been a desperate day," he murmured, scratching the back of her neck gently.

"I suppose it was always likely that something dreadful might come of the poor boy's infatuation with that wretched Christopher, but, oh dear, oh dear, John, I never feared that it might be anything as awful as this..." She trailed off, depression settling heavily over her. Her husband pursed his lips. "I agree, Edith, except that if we're to be truthful about it, it's rather the reverse, isn't it?"

"How d'you mean?"

"Well, if we're honest, it's that wretched Christopher who's been infatuated with Jamie, is it not?"

"It doesn't make a lot of difference, does it?" she demanded.

"Well, it may make quite a lot," he replied mildly. "If the unfortunate boy is charged with some offence of indecency with Jamie, and Jamie insists on claiming responsibility, well, Christopher may be let down comparatively lightly, but Jamie... well, Jamie may find that he's volunteered for some kind of punishment himself."

"But, John, that policeman said that Jamie wouldn't be involved at all. He said..."

"I know what he said, dear. That juvenile procedure and all the other jargon he spouted at us. Yes, it seems that Jamie would never be put through the ordeal of a court appearance - unless he can somehow insist on testifying as a witness..." She would have spoken, but he continued speaking, "I know

114

the detective officer said that the boy would plead guilty and that therefore there would be no necessity or occasion for Jamie to appear. But we have to face the fact that Jamie *wants* to appear - nay, he *demands* it. We have to face the fact also that he is a quite extraordinarily self-willed and determined boy, as well as being, as we know, just as extraordinarily intelligent. That means that he knows what his proposed course of action may entail, and he is quite capable of circumventing any attempts to frustrate him in putting it into effect. What I'm wondering, though, is whether, in fact, we have any right to make any such attempt."

He lit a cigarette and retreated into his own thoughts, sipping absently at his tea until he noticed that the cup was empty. "More tea?" he asked, pouring for himself. She gave him her cup.

"As you know," he resumed, "when I first discovered the true extent of this Christopher business - good Lord, it seems like months ago, yet it's only a couple of weeks - I was clear that the only possible way to proceed was to halt it then and there and ensure that Jamie saw no more of this boy. I've since had a good many second thoughts."

He looked round to see her regarding him in surprise. "Oh, I don't mean that I've changed my mind about letting Jamie carry on seeing the boy. Of course that's quite out of the question. But I know Jamie a very great deal better now than I did then. I know at first hand the qualities of strength and steadfastness he has. That's a good old-fashioned word one doesn't have many occasions to use nowadays. Steadfastness. But it does very accurately describe our Jamie, don't you think?"

"I think I see what you mean," she mused. "You mean that we would be wrong to do anything, even if it was in Jamie's own interests, if it came between him and this steadfastness?"

"Exactly, my dear. I don't think Jamie would forgive anyone who came between him and his loyalties - which are, like so many other things about him, developed to a remarkable degree for one his age. Now think, Edith, where do Jamie's loyalties lie at the moment?" He read the answer in her face and nodded. "Exactly. To Christopher. He conceives, rightly or wrongly, that he has got Christopher into this plight. I think he's wrong, I think Christopher has got himself almost entirely to blame, if only by being quite disgracefully weak and irresponsible. But does Jamie - will Jamie - see it that way? You tell me, Edith."

She sat for a long time in thought, the light from the fire flickering on her shadowed face. Finally she said slowly, "He won't see it that way for some time, I don't think. Not until he's got Christopher out of his system."

"I think you're quite right," he said approvingly, rather as he might commend a suggestion from one of the sixth form for a translation of a difficult line in Thucydides. "And he won't, in my judgment, begin to get Christopher out of his system as long as he feels a powerful sense of guilt about him. That's where he's truly exceptional, Edith. He feels *responsible* for the boy. He's years younger than Christopher; but that's only years. If maturity was all, I could make him Head Boy tomorrow. But now to the heart of it: he not only *feels* responsible for Christopher, he intends to *take* that responsibility. There's not one man in a thousand that's man enough to do that. Responsibility is an old-fashioned virtue, not at all fashionable today. But he has it."

"John, are you sure you're not over-crediting him just a little?" Edith asked him carefully. "You're making him into almost some kind of Messiah, perhaps?"

"No, dear, I'm sure I'm not. I remember that countless boys not two years older than Jamie lied about their age to go to the Somme. They took responsibility for whole troops of men, and they managed the burden. He *could*, you know, have evaded all responsibility, in any one of a dozen ways, by a couple of words, tonight. He didn't. And I ask you: can you imagine his face if either of us had suggested to him that he should avail himself of any of them? Can you?

"Quite so," he said softly when she made no answer. "You can. So can I. Next point: is he, in all truth, wrong to feel this responsibility?"

She waited for him to go on. He said nothing. "Is that a rhetorical question?" she eventually said.

"No, my dear, it's not. The answer is clear, to me at least. He's right. He *is* responsible. And there's our conclusion. We must allow him to shoulder it, and help him to bear it in whatever ways we are able. Even..."

She sat upright as an ominous note entered his voice. "Even," he continued slowly, "if it means that Christopher is not banished from his life at the earliest possible moment." He raised a hand in a polite gesture to her to allow him to conclude. "We have to accept that possibility, Edith, however little we like it - and I don't like it at all, any more now than I did two weeks ago when I didn't know a hundredth part of what I know now. But If Jamie decides that Christopher is not to be banished, we may well find ourselves having to accept it as a fact."

"You may be right," his wife replied. She put a hand on his arm and gripped it hard. "But I'm not going to stand by and see him do anything to endanger himself. He's our boy, now, John, my love. We've been told so tonight, as plainly as any words could tell us. The mother is plainly no use at all, and the father is worse than useless, positively - well, demonic was the word I was going to use. Neither appears to have the slightest interest in whether the poor child lives, dies or begs for his living. That friend of the mother, Mrs Turnbull, was the only person there who gave the slightest sign of having Jamie's own interests at heart - apart from the detective, what was his name, Fry?"

"Bly."

"Yes, that was it, Bly. Well, apart from him, and he seemed a human enough man, all things considered, Mrs Turnbull alone seemed to be thinking about someone other than herself. I caught the tail-end of a couple of glances she threw in that woman's direction, and I shouldn't want anyone to look at me like that. As long as Jamie's in no danger, as long as he's not put at any risk, or allowed to put himself at risk, I think you're right. We'll simply have to play the thing by ear and help him however we can. Would you mind making more tea, dear? Just one more cup, and then we must go to bed. I've got a splitting headache, and you've got to be up in less than five hours."

"Do you think he'll sleep all right?" he asked her, heading for the kitchen. "He will tonight," she said, beginning to sound a little drowsy. "I dissolved a whole mogadon in his chocolate. The poor mite was out cold in ten minutes."

***

"What are we to do?" asked Audrey Rowe of her husband.

"What about?" he riposted. "About him being qu... being hom... being - Christ, I don't even know what word to use. I've never had to discuss it except in bar-room jokes. I suppose we're going to have to start using 'gay', are we?"

"Bob, my darling, what earthly difference does it make what word we use? He's still the same Christopher. Still the same Chris."

"But that's just the point," he expostulated, "he's *not* the same Chris. At least, he's never *been* the Chrissie I thought he was. That's the point, surely. Why didn't he *tell* us?"

"Oh, Bob, don't be naive. How would you go about telling anybody? Especially your parents. He loves us - especially you. No, there's no need to bother. I've always known there was something special between him and you, and I've never been in the least bit jealous. Most boys are closer to their mothers - Neil is. Chris was always different. He loves me, but he worships you - just like you worship him. He's still *that* Chris. There's just something rather..." she groped for the word. "Something rather distasteful about him - which *we* find distasteful, that is - that we're going to have to come to terms with, that's all. But he *is* the same Chris. He's always been like this. Now he's told us, because he hadn't got a choice about it, and we're going to have to accept it, because we haven't got any choice about that, either."

He reached for her along the sofa. She saw as she came into his arms that his eyes were glistening with tears. I haven't seen Bob cry for twenty years, she thought, and set about comforting him. It was fortunate that things had not gone very far when they heard sounds of someone coming down the stairs. She flew out of his arms and began rapidly buttoning her blouse, her fingers fumbling with the buttons in her haste. They sat apart, at opposite ends of the sofa, like teenagers disturbed by parents returning unexpectedly early. The door handle turned and Neil walked in, rubbing his eyes a little blearily.

"Hallo," he said. "I went to bed, it got so late. That policewoman drank some of your whisky, Dad. I said she could. Then she went to sleep, and I left her to it."

"Good for you, Neil," said his father. "The question now is, why aren't you still in bed?"

"Oh, Dad, I woke up, and I couldn't stay there. What's the matter with Chris? He's in his room, isn't he? I heard him. Mum, I think he's crying."

"Oh, God!" she blurted, and shot from the room. Neil looked after her, then turned to his father. He was an engaging boy of fourteen, freckled, nice-looking in a nondescript way, not always spotless, and possessed of an impish sense of humour. Now his face was very serious. "Has something terrible happened to Chris, Dad?" he asked, his real anxiety showing clearly.

"N..." Robert Rowe hesitated. "Not terrible, perhaps, Neil. But something pretty bad. Can it wait till the morning?"

"I wouldn't sleep, Dad, you know I couldn't, not not knowing. I'm not tired, honestly. You'd better tell me," he said in an oddly grown-up voice, and his father had an eerie feeling that he was hearing Neil in twenty years, as he might then be speaking to his own children. My grandchildren. I shan't have any by Chris, he thought involuntarily. He shivered slightly, as if someone had walked over his grave. "You'd better wait till your mother gets back from Chrissie," he said, a little gruffly. Neil nodded simply, and sat down to wait.

Audrey returned after a few minutes, distressed. "He's all right," she muttered, answering two anxious faces. "I've given him something to make him sleep, poor darling. As for you, Neil, out you go. Bed," she said imperiously. "Oh, *Mum*," he said urgently.

She began to shoo him towards the door, helping him with a slap on his pyjama-striped bottom. "I told him to stay, love," said Robert, a little apprehensively. She raised her eyebrows. "Oh?"

"He's worried about what's happened to Chrissie, and I said he ought to know, if it's going to keep him up worrying about it. I said he'd have to wait until you got back."

Her expression softened. "All right, Neil. You'll have to know, and sooner rather than later. Bob, can we have a drink?" And, at about the same moment as Dr Lane, a mile and a half away across the town, was making a last pot of tea, Bob Rowe went to the sideboard and poured two large drinks, eyeing the damage done to his scotch by the babysitting policewoman, and firmly refusing his younger son's pleas to have just a *little* scotch in his dry ginger.

"So what's all the mystery, Dad?" asked Neil seriously when they were all settled. His father paused long before he answered, wondering what was the best form of words to use to explain something that would be, he was certain, wholly out of his son's ken. He decided in the end that the best way was the simplest and most direct.

"Neil, old fellow, this is going to be a bit of a shock. Your brother is not quite like most of us. He's... well, the point is, he's - er - *gay*."

There was a moment's echoing silence, in which the two parents' apprehension gathered and swirled in the room. It was broken by Neil, who spoke in a transparently genuine tone of puzzled surprise. "Is that *all*?" he said.

***

The only telephone available to the boys at Jamie's school was in the foyer, just inside the great main entrance. Jamie sidled up to it during his morning break the following day, trying to look in all directions at once, ready to vanish through the door into the front drive if anyone, and especially Dr Lane, appeared. No one was about. He was trembling all over, and could feel his heart pounding, as he cautiously lifted the receiver and dialled Christopher's number. Christopher's mother answered. Jamie gently put the receiver back in its cradle and swore virulently under his breath as he fled into the drive and made his way circuitously back to the quadrangle. There he wandered, solitary and pining for the briefest sound of the beloved voice until the bell summoned him to the next period.

There was no time during the remainder of that day when he was not conscious of being watched. Dr Lane had no specific idea what Jamie might do. The two boys had been given no chance to come face to face throughout their ordeal at the police station the previous night, and Lane knew that Christopher would have been given the same orders to make no attempt at contact as he himself had had to give Jamie; but, knowing the intensity of their feelings for each other, he had a suspicion that the boy might be harbouring some notion of absenting himself in order to try to meet Christopher. Therefore, giving no reasons beyond saying that the boy had extreme problems in his home life, he had issued quiet instructions to the entire staff to keep Jamie under discreet observation until further notice.

"If he does anything at all untoward," he had concluded at that morning's staff meeting, "I don't want him approached, unless he appears to be actually leaving the premises. But I do want anything - absolutely anything - odd reported to me *immediately*. Interrupt me whatever I may be doing at the time. And report to me alone." The staff looked at each other and speculated among themselves afterwards, but they asked no questions as they left the common room to take their places on the platform for assembly. Afterwards

Lane assembled the prefects in their den and issued the same instructions to them.

In consequence his use of the telephone in the morning break was seen and reported, but no other action was taken. When the prefect who had noticed the incident informed him Dr Lane wondered briefly whether to summon Jamie and tax him with it, but decided that it would be unfair to put the boy in a position in which he would in all probability feel compelled to tell lies. Lane knew that he was a truthful boy, who would be reluctant to lie, especially, he thought, to him; but he had no doubt that where anything to do with Christopher was concerned he would lie without hesitation if he had to, and cope with his conscience later. So he filed the information away and awaited events.

Jamie thus passed the day, frustrated, oppressed with a great burden of anxiety for his friend and half out of his mind with pining for him and, increasingly, angry. He had become extremely fond of the Lanes, and he was more than mature enough to realise the debt of gratitude he owed them. But his sense of logic was too much at odds with his emotions for him to be altogether rational, and as the day passed his feelings of anger and bitterness intensified. In class he was preoccupied, answering absently and often failing even to hear when he was addressed. The masters, with their chief's sulphurous warnings about upsetting him in mind and, in any case, seeing the grief and distraction clearly in his face and his demeanour, considerately avoided noticing.

Back in the schoolmaster's house that evening the telephone was out of the question, for Edith requested him, kindly but in terms that brooked no argument whatever, as soon as he got in from afternoon school, that he must on no account try to make contact with Christopher. "I know you miss him dreadfully, dear," she said, feeling an intense pity at his woebegone expression, "but you really must be obedient about this. It would get you and all of us into the most awful trouble. And Christopher too, for that matter. Perhaps him most of all." She put an arm round his shoulders and gently stroked his hair and neck; but he wriggled angrily out of her embrace and fled, half crying, to his room, where he went through the motions of attending to his preparation. Masturbating a couple of times during the evening gave him some small relief as he day-dreamed of Christopher, naked and beautiful on the old blanket in the fishing place. But he had to come back to the grim reality of the present, and the consolation was short-lived.

The Lanes were especially kind and indulgent when he emerged for dinner, keeping up one-sided conversation and trying to ignore his distraction, but they were relieved when he announced that he didn't feel very well and would have an early night. Soon after that the Lanes also, tired and suffering emotional overload from the traumas and very late hours of the previous night, went to bed themselves and quickly fell into the deep sleep of exhaustion.

Jamie lay sleepless until he heard the grandmother clock in the hall downstairs striking two in the morning, when he judged it safe at last to put into effect the plan that had been dimly shaping itself in his mind from the moment he realised he was not going to be allowed to make contact by phone. Slipping out of bed, he went to the wardrobe and groped in the darkness for his holdall. He found the tee-shirt, jeans, pullover, trainers and torch that he had stowed there and dressed silently and rapidly. Then he eased the bedroom door open and crept downstairs. His heart palpitated when he kicked the telephone table in the hall, and he had to endure few minutes' delay while he listened with his heart in his mouth, sitting on the stairs listening for movement from upstairs, in case the slight thump and scraping sounds had been heard.

When he was sure it was safe, he groped his way into the kitchen. Once he had the door pushed to he felt safe to switch on his torch, and this got him without mishap to the back door of the house. With infinite care he drew back the bolt, turned the key and eased the door open, remembering at the last moment to switch off the torch lest the slightest glimmer of light might be seen from above. He slipped through the door and then took an age to ease the door closed again, pulling it tight against the jamb before letting the tongue ever so slowly back into its socket. Trembling and sweating hard from fear of being caught breaking out, he stood for a minute or two to calm himself. Then, keeping to the shadows, he moved silently and cautiously into the trees that lined the approach to the house. It took him several minutes to gain the cover of the trees and the darkness. Only when he was closer to the gates than to the house did he venture to put on his torch. Then he ran.

***

Christopher sat up in bed, instantly wide awake. He had hardly slept, and when he had dropped off it was only into a fitful doze, induced more by exhaustion than by normal need to sleep. The sound that had roused him had been almost infinitesimally small, but it had been enough in his state to bring him to complete wakefulness. He sat, wondering what it could have been, and after a few seconds it was repeated as a handful of earth made a soft pattering sound against his window pane. His heart contracted and he went cold. There was only one person who could possibly be trying to wake him in the middle of the night in such a stealthy manner. (Jamie, in the time-honoured way of lovers, had early on demanded to know which curtains hid the room his beloved slept in.) He felt for the cord above the head of his bed and switched on the light, then instantly shut it off again, to show that he had heard. Then he got out and padded silently to the window and opened it, feeling his blood go cold when it made a slight creak.

He looked down into the back garden. There was no moon, but the stars were casting a faint glimmer of light by which he could just make out a figure and a pale blur of a face. For a fraction of a second a torch shone, then was instantly extinguished. His heart raced. He slipped into his clothes as

124

quickly as he could in silence, then crept downstairs, taking very much the same meticulous pains to keep silent as Jamie had done half an hour earlier. In the hall he felt in his pocket for his front door key, then slipped round the house to the back.

Jamie was waiting for him at the corner of the building. They fell into each other's arms and held one another, crushing the breath out of each other, making no sound but saying an infinity of things by the mere desperation of their embrace.

After several minutes had fled by, Christopher whispered into Jamie's ear. "Come on, we've got to get away from the house. You shouldn't have come here, you know that. We'd get into frightful trouble."

"I had to come, Chris," whispered Jamie.

"Come on," hissed Christopher. He disengaged himself from Jamie's arms and took his hand. He led him to the bottom of the garden. "There's a shed," he whispered. Jamie curled his fingers round Christopher's hand and followed him trustingly. Christopher halted where a patch of deeper blackness stood against the faint star-shimmer, and fumbled with a latch. There was a faint creak and a groan, and Christopher bundled Jamie hastily into an even deeper darkness. It smelt faintly of earth, must and old sacks.

He drew the door to after them, and then said softly "You can put your torch on now. There's no windows." Jamie switched it on, and shone it somewhere to one side of Christopher's face. He looked lovingly for a few moments on the familiar face, pale and haggard from torment and lack of sleep. Then he flashed the beam about, found a shelf behind him and laid the torch on it, and hurled himself into Christopher's arms once more. "Oh, Chris," he breathed.

It was a very long embrace, but eventually Christopher prised Jamie away. "We've got to talk," he said in an urgent whisper. Jamie put an arm round his waist. "As long as I can still hold you," he said.

"Look," whispered Christopher. "You mustn't come here again like this. You do realise that, don't you?"

Jamie whimpered. "Do you mean," he gulped, "do you mean that I can't... can't see you again?"

"Not for a bit," said Christopher, though his heart turned to lead as he said it. "You know it'll get us into terrible trouble - even more trouble than we're in already. Well, I'm in, anyway..."

"Oh, God, Chris," moaned Jamie softly, "please don't be angry with me. I couldn't bear not to see you. I won't get you into trouble, I promise. I promise..." His voice began to rise hysterically.

"Shh, quiet, for Christ's sake," breathed Christopher, with the beginnings of panic in his voice also. "Jamie, my darling, I'm not angry. I know how you've felt. It's breaking my heart too, but we've got to sort things out first. I'm in awful trouble. You know that."

Jamie clutched him. "You don't love me any more, Chris," he said, bleakly in the darkness.

"Of course I love you, Jamie, my sweetheart," Christopher said desperately. He put his arms round Jamie, but he pulled himself free, panting and sobbing, and turned towards the door of the shed. "You don't love me, I know you don't..." He began to scramble at the door.

Christopher seized him and hauled him roughly back. "Jamie, I love you, more than ever. Please, please believe me." He threw his arms round him again, and this time Jamie allowed him to hold him. But the vibrancy had all gone from him, and he felt passive and unresponding. Christopher kissed him, but he turned his face to one side, and the kisses found only a cheek, streaming with silent tears. Christopher, frantic, stroked the back of his head and neck, and they stood like that for minutes. At last, to Christopher's unspeakable relief, he felt a small beginning of response. "Jamie, my dearest," he said in anguish, "I love you, I do love you. More than ever, I promise you. Please don't desert me, I couldn't bear that. Not now, when I need you more than I ever did."

Jamie stirred in his arms, and Christopher felt a kiss on his cheek. He thought that nothing would ever be such a relief in his life again, not if he was snatched back from the brink of death itself. He buried himself in Jamie's hair and kissed the top of his head. The same small kiss came again on his cheek, then another, and then a cascade of them. More time passed.

After a while they sorted out some sacks and sat down, twining their legs together and cuddling as best they could in a sitting position in the cramped space they had. When the first flood of passion had ebbed a little they began to talk. Christopher, in terror of frightening Jamie into another abyss of panic, whispered urgently to him, saying that they mustn't meet in such circumstances. "It's just too risky, for both of us. If they found out we'd even spoken on the phone they might... they might do anything. They might take you away, I don't know, make you a ward of court or something. God knows what they can do."

"But what can we do?" pleaded Jamie. "I'll die if I can't see you. I'll kill myself. I couldn't bear it."

They talked themselves round in circles for some time. Then Christopher had an inspiration. "Jamie, my darling, listen to me," he said softly, stroking Jamie's hair. "Will you promise to listen, and not interrupt, if I say something?"

"All right," said Jamie, taking a still fiercer grip round Christopher's waist.

"My love," said Christopher. "The police have sent the papers about us away to somebody. The Director of Prosecutions. He has to decide whether I'm going to be charged with... with... with some horrible offence, making us out to be something obscene. Anyway, I shan't know for a week or ten days if I'm being prosecuted at all. But whether I am or not, they're going to stop us seeing each other. You can bet your life on that. They think there's something filthy about us. They don't understand, and they never will, they don't even want to." He paused, gathering his thoughts. Jamie started to speak, then remembered his promise and waited.

"Now, Jamie," Christopher continued, "whatever happens, I'll have to go to university in a little while - unless... unless..." He left the unthinkable possibility of prison unspoken, sagely guessing that the mere mention of it would be likely to send Jamie into a paroxysm of hysteria from which he would be unable to bring him back. "I'll have to go to university," he repeated. "So we'd have had to be apart in a few weeks, anyway.

"Now, then, they may be able to stop us seeing each other, an injunction or some legal trick of some sort. But they can't stop us writing to each other, and we'll be able to speak on the phone sometimes, once the dust's settled. But between now and whenever it *has* settled, you must promise me that you won't try to come here, or see me like this again. You *must*. No, don't butt in yet. Let me finish. Please," he pleaded. Jamie hugged him tighter, but obediently stayed quiet.

"Now, my dearest," Christopher continued, "I want to make you a promise, if you'll make me one."

He paused. Jamie blurted out, "I'll promise you anything, if you won't make me go away, or not see you..."

"Let me make my promise," urged Christopher. "It's this. One day, quite soon, we'll live together. We'll be with each other all the time. I want that more than anything in the world. I'll marry you, Jamie." He paused again. He heard a sudden hiss of breath and a single, loud, hiccupping sob from Jamie in the pitch darkness, but there was no other sound. He rushed on. "It's possible. I've read of it happening in the papers. If you can find someone sympathetic, gay people can actually get married. If you'd like that, I'd do it. If you still want to be with me, if you haven't forgotten about me if we have to be apart for a while..."

Jamie, unable to control himself, threw himself on him and sobbed "Forget you? I'll *never*..."

"Shhhh!" hissed Christopher violently. "Keep your voice down."

"I'll *never* do that, Chris. You know I'd never do that. Tell me you believe me," he said in a fierce whisper.

"Of course I believe you," said Christopher soberly. "I think we're meant to be with each other. If I didn't I wouldn't be saying all this. But the thing is, it will take time. We'll be together the moment it's safe for us to be, not an instant later. But if it takes time, please, Jamie, my darling, you've got to be strong. You're incredibly strong - far stronger than me. Please, please, be strong now."

He fell silent. Jamie said nothing for a while. Then he muttered "How long do you think it'll be?"

"I don't know," said Christopher, bleakly. "I just don't know. Months, maybe. It would probably be a year..."

Jamie started to cry again, the tears hot and fierce against Christopher's face. "I couldn't wait a year, Chris, I couldn't. It would kill me not to see you for a year..." he burst out. Christopher soothed him, stroking his hair. "You could wait that long if you *knew*, Jamie. If you *knew* we'd be together at the end of it, couldn't you?"

Jamie thought about it, his body heaving gently against Christopher's. "I... I suppose I *could*, if I *knew*..." he said, sounding like a little boy. Christopher breathed a deep sigh. His heartfelt relief was mingled with an awareness that he had been less than honest with the person who meant more to him, he felt, than life. He knew that it could be more than a year; but he told himself in the darkness of his heart that the deception was worth it to keep Jamie on an even keel. After all, he told himself, it might only be a year, perhaps not even that, before we can work out some way of getting together. Maybe we could go abroad... He snuffed out that fantasy before it had a chance to live, and brought himself sharply back to the present.

"But all that will be for nothing," he said, despising himself for exerting anything resembling leverage on Jamie but knowing he had to do it anyway, "if we get caught together now. So you must promise me, in return, Jamie. You must promise me you'll leave it to me to work out when we can see each other next, and how. You *must*."

Jamie thought for a second. "All right, Chris," he said, docilely. "I promise. I couldn't bear it if I was the one to get you into any more trouble." They half-sat, half-lay together, cuddling awkwardly. After a while Christopher murmured "You'll have to be getting back. We must've been here for over an hour. Jamie squirmed round to see his watch in the dim glow of the torch. The battery was dying perceptibly. "It's five to four," he said, in sudden alarm. "I'll *have* to go soon." There was a pause. Each of them was listening to the sound of the other's breathing. Then Jamie said, "You'll write to me, Chris? They can't stop you writing, you said so yourself."

"Every day, if you like," said Christopher simply. "Every day," repeated Jamie. And then, "I'll go soon, Chris. But there is one thing..."

"Yes. What is it?" asked Christopher. Some premonition of what was coming made his heart miss, and a breath got lost in his throat. "Do it with me, Chris," said Jamie in a small voice. "Make love to me. Here. Just so I can remember this last time." Christopher choked a little. "We'll have to stand up," he muttered thickly.

***

They kissed goodbye, a long, desperate embrace, in the shadow of Christopher's house. Jamie slipped silently through the garden gate and into the street. He halted just before going out of sight behind the next-door hedge and turned. Christopher moved into the slightly lesser shadow of the starlight and waved. Jamie flicked his torch on and shone it for a second on Christopher, standing by his front door. He wagged his fingers for a second, and then he was gone. Christopher, with a heart as heavy as stone, and with feelings that could not have been expressed, let himself stealthily in and crept up to bed.

With identical feelings Jamie fled through the streets. He had enough sense left to remember caution as he slipped into the house and up to his room. He stripped and hid his clothes, dusty and grimy from the floor of the potting shed, in the holdall. Then, as the grandmother clock chimed the quarter-hour after five, he tumbled disconsolately into bed. His body still felt faintly flushed and tingling from love-making, and he thought he could smell a trace of Christopher's body about himself. He hurled himself over onto his belly and, overcome with unassuageable grief and loss, sobbed into his pillow as if his heart would break.

***

Two days later Jamie was toying with his breakfast when the mail slapped onto the doormat. Edith went out and returned with a sheaf of letters. Jamie watched her intently. "Two bills," she said, tossing two envelopes to one side. "Telephone and electricity. One for me - that's from Denise. Two for you;" she handed him two letters. "And one for you, Jamie." Jamie rose from his seat too eagerly, and had to be slapped on the back as a mouthful of egg went down the wrong way. When he stopped spluttering his face was brighter than they had seen it in days. He snatched at the letter eagerly, remembered his manners and apologised. Edith smiled fondly at him, but looked a little anxiously at her husband.

Jamie, catching the glance and interpreting it accurately, immediately looked fearful, defensive and a shade furtive all at once. Lane paused in the act of slitting open the first of his two letters and raised his eyebrows. "Christopher, I suppose?" he said, glancing at his wife interrogatively. She spread her hands in a gesture of uncertainty. They both looked at Jamie. He gave them a trapped look, then nodded. "Yes, sir," he said. Then, with a rush, "they can't stop him *writing* to me, can they, sir? Surely they wouldn't object to writing? They couldn't be that cruel?"

Lane pursed his lips in perplexity. "I don't know that 'they' would necessarily regard it as cruel, Jamie," he said, "but I think if 'they' knew he was writing to you they would object fairly strongly. I think they certainly could stop it, and probably would..."

"But, sir," he burst out, "that's not fair..."

Lane considered for some time, with Jamie watching him like a cat stalking a sparrow. Eventually he half-smiled. "It's not fair," he mused as if to himself. "The *cri de coeur* of abused children and oppressed youth down all the ages of man. No, Jamie, I'm inclined to agree in this case. It's not fair. Open your letter, and I hope there will be something in it to cheer you up."

"After all," he said to his wife, "no one will ever know that he's received the odd letter, unless we choose to tell anyone. And since the letter is here, it would be unkind to withold it. No, I don't see that any harm can come of it. I'll add only one rider to that, Jamie. If this letter, or any other you may receive from your friend, should cause you any distress or interfere with your work, or your health, or in any way bring difficulties in its wake, then it will stop, there and then, without argument and with no appeal. That is final. Understood?"

"Yes, sir. Oh, thank you," babbled Jamie. "May I get up and read it, please?" He was almost out of his chair before he had finished asking. He received a magisterial but more or less benevolent nod. Almost without pausing as he passed Dr Lane in his headlong rush for the door he bent and planted a hasty, rather clumsy kiss on his headmaster's cheek. Before Lane, utterly taken aback, could move or open his mouth, Jamie was half-way up the stairs.

There was a moment's rather stunned silence in the breakfast room. Then Lane, with a strange expression on his face, murmured,"He keeps finding surprises for us, doesn't he?"

"John," said Edith, "it's not so *very* unusual for a fifteen-year-old boy to make an elementary gesture of affection towards his guardian. Especially when the guardian is very kind to him, and has just done perhaps the greatest kindness the boy has received for some long time."

He looked sharply at her, surprised to hear a lecture from

132

her, only to see that she was smiling broadly, almost laughing. "It was the right thing to do, John. *I* couldn't have stopped him reading his letter. Did you see his face?"

"Yes, I did. That's why I decided as I did. The point is that he's generally so adult for his age that it comes always as something of a shock to be reminded that he is only fifteen. Bless my soul, it's a long time since I've been kissed by an affectionate son." He sat back and mused.

"You've forgotten your own letters," she reminded him. "Eh? Oh, yes, of course." He completed opening the first blue envelope. It contained a brief scribbled note and a cheque. He passed it over to his wife. "From Jamie's mother. A further instalment. Generous, would you say?" he said, a little sardonically.

"I doubt if she knows the meaning of the word, let alone how it feels," she said, unusually acidly for her. "Still, since she's got no feeling or affection for the child, her money, I suppose, is the only thing she can give. I'll pay it in this morning."

Lane had opened the other, and was staring at it with raised eyebrows. "Mmm. This is a little mysterious. What do you make of this one?" He handed it to her. On expensive, deckle-edged Swiss writing paper was a short note in a strong, clear hand. Edith murmured it aloud to herself as she read it:

Dear Dr and Mrs Lane,

It is imperative that I come to talk to you as soon as possible about something of importance to both of us - you know what I am referring to. I shall be at home to receive a telephone call on the above number at all times over the next two days, and I should be grateful if you would call as soon as possible. Please believe me, it is very urgent, or I would not trouble you.

Yours sincerely, Angela Turnbull.

"You'd better ring her this morning," she said without

133

hesitation. "I wonder what's behind this."

"I'll ring her from the school," he said. He looked at his watch, and jumped slightly. "And it's high time I was *at* school," he added. He rose, gulped the last of his tea and went hurriedly into the hall, where he met Jamie, coming downstairs. Lane gave him a quick, searching glance, and was very glad he had decided as he had over the letter. Jamie's face was alight. Like it was a week or so ago, he thought. "Come along, my boy," he said, with a slightly crusty smile.

Edith watched the two of them walking to the school together, Jamie's slight, graceful form trotting beside her husband's tall, slightly stooping one, dark red hair bobbing a foot below Lane's windblown grey, the turning of their heads indicating animated conversation. "I wonder if that Christopher knows what power he's got," she muttered to herself. "I wonder if he has any idea..."

***

"Mrs Turnbull?"

"Speaking. Is that Dr Lane?"

"It is, madam."

"Oh, good," she said. There was relief clearly marked in her voice. "Good. You've had my letter then. I hoped it would get to you today."

"Yes, Mrs Turnbull, it came this morning. I confess, I'm a little mystified, but I took you at your word that it was urgent."

"Yes, yes, it is. But I can't discuss it over the phone. Please, can I come to see you?"

"Yes, of course you may. When would you like to come?"

"Any time it suits you, but the sooner the better, Dr Lane. Only one thing. I don't want James to see me with you, or coming to see you. He'd be bound to know it was to do with him, and he's got quite enough on his plate, without worrying himself silly wondering what it's about."

Lane hesitated before replying. "Mrs Turnbull, I believe you have Jamie's interests at heart..."

"I certainly have," she said forcefully. "Unlike some people I could name. Yes, I feel desperately sorry for the poor little beggar, and I've got hold of something very nasty that's about to crawl out of its woodwork and make more trouble for him, if we don't do something about it and pretty damn quick at that. Where d'you think we should meet? I can see you any time today, or this evening, or tomorrow - whenever you like. You say where and when, I'll be there."

"Very well, madam. It would perhaps be best if you didn't come to the school, since you don't want to risk Jamie's seeing you. But I can see you at my house, if that would suit you. It's within the school precincts; but it is very strictly out of bounds to the pupils, which, of course, includes Jamie during school hours. And you needn't pass within sight of any of the school buildings if you come in by the side entrance. It's on the Steeple Wynton road. Do you know it - I assume you'd come by car?"

"I know it, Dr Lane, and it'll do fine. What time?"

"One moment, please. I'm taking the upper sixth for a double period, until 9.50. I have no other teaching periods all day. The administration can take care of itself. My secretary knows the drill better than I do, in any case. I suspect that she only tolerates my occasional interferences on sufferance. Shall we say ten-thirty - on second thoughts, eleven o'clock, if I may. There are one or two things..."

"Right. Eleven o'clock it is. I'll see you then. Thanks, Dr Lane. Goodbye." And she rang off. Lane started to scribble a note of the appointment on his daily book, then obliterated it. He sat for a while, scratching the side of his nose with the end of his pencil, curious and a little alarmed. He was roused from his meditation by the bustling entry of his secretary. "Oh, I beg your pardon, Dr Lane, I thought you were in class," she said, surprised at finding him there.

"Good Lord!" he exclaimed. "I am. Or rather, I should be."

He snatched up his case and hurried out, a little flustered. He was ten minutes late for Sophocles, something almost unprecedented, but much to the satisfaction of the waiting upper sixth.

***

Jamie had run up to his room and opened his letter carefully to the point of reverence, unwilling to inflict the slightest unnecessary hurt on an envelope that had been licked by his lover. He had read it twice since, surreptitiously under his desk in the first periods. Now, in morning break, he sat in the end cubicle of the middle school boys' lavatories and read it again.

Along with Christopher's letter he had found another, smaller envelope, which Christopher referred to in a postscript. Jamie had been eaten alive by curiosity to know what it contained, but he had taken so long lovingly reading the letter that he'd had no time to open this other before it had been time to leave with Dr Lane for school. In class the temptation to open it under the cover of the desk had been great; but the thought of discovery and the inevitable confiscation had been unbearable enough to deter him. Now he imposed a pleasurably masochistic torture on himself by reading the letter once more.

He had almost dreaded the moment of reading this first letter, fearing it would serve more than anything else to rub in the stark fact that it was a substitute for its sender. But in the event it had cheered Jamie more than he could have believed possible.

It was a long letter, in Christopher's untidy scrawl. Jamie loved his handwriting, not only because it belonged to Christopher but because it was so like him, and so unlike his own handwriting. Jamie's was small, neat and firm, like Jamie himself. Christopher's was like his hair, wayward,

136

tending to fly about in all directions at once, yet oddly pretty.

Jamie kissed the letter, and read it slowly and carefully. It was chatty in parts, though Jamie, with his deep intuitive empathy for Christopher, sensed that those parts were somewhat forced for Jamie's benefit. But it was equally clear to him that Christopher was trying his hardest to rally his forces, with some success. He was able to talk about the possibilities of his being charged, even the possible sentences. He swore that he'd be able to bear anything 'they' might hurl at him, provided only that Jamie kept faith with him.

But mostly, it was a declaration of love. Every sentence held some signal of its author's love, or some private reference that only Jamie would understand, some reminder of something they had said, something they had once laughed about. In places it was a very sexy letter, which had left Jamie painfully and pleasurably swollen for much of the morning.

"*Did you know,*" Christopher wrote after one passage, "*that it's illegal to send obscene material through the post? Well it is, so that's something else they could charge me with, if they got hold of this...to give their dirty minds something to get excited about.*" Then he had gone back to being deliciously indelicate about Jamie, who read it and writhed with pleasure and for a little while forgot the troubles of the moment and their separation, though that slouching monster was never far below the surface of his mind.

Jamie came to another paragraph that had made his heart swell.

You can write to me. I've told my people I'm going to write to you, and after some huffing and puffing they've agreed to keep quiet about letters. They're terrified about it being a breach of the bail conditions and all that balls, in case I get clobbered extra hard. But they can't do much about it, unless they want to turn me in. So write to me, dear Jamie. It will help to keep me going. As long as I know I can look forward to a letter from you, I'll have something to keep fighting for, whatever the bastards do to me.

Best of all were the final paragraphs. Simple yet enormous, they exposed by their very simplicity all Christopher's vulnerability, a fragile net of a few words that had to carry the whole of Jamie's world:

One day, soon I hope, we'll look back on all this horror and wonder how the hell we could be so upset by it. It still looks pretty terrifying to me right now, but sometime we shall see it for the silly, pathetic, petty little hiccup it is. Meanwhile, I think about you all the time. So, unitl tomorrow, all my love, all of it for you, always. Your own Chris.

Last came the mysterious postscript: "*P.S. Two small things for you. One's something I promised you ages ago - well, it seems like ages, anyway. Think about the other in bed tonight. Love you, C. XXX*" Jamie controlled his feelings and found further pleasurable self-torment by fishing for his pocket knife and forcing himself to slit it open carefully.

Enclosed he found a postcard-sized photograph. It was of a far higher quality than the one that Jamie had lost with such disastrous consequences on the night of his estrangement from his home and, as he regarded it now, from his entire life up to that point. Christopher, he thought, looked at his most beautiful. His large brown eyes were soft, his mop of long brown hair was for once in its place, and his wide mouth was slightly curved in a half-smile. On the back Christopher had written, carefully so the impression did not show through on the photograph, "To my dearest Jamie, with all my love, from Chris." Jamie's heart ached.

The other enclosure was a folded square of white tissue paper. When Jamie unfolded it he found that it was blank except for a large, irregular yellowish stain. Jamie looked at it blankly for a moment. Then the penny dropped. He grinned at first, but then the poignancy of it struck him with full force, and his grin softened to a gentle, reminiscent smile, and his eyes filled with tears. "Oh, Chris," he whispered to himself, and immediately cocked his head, fearful that someone might have heard, but there was no sound from outside his little cubicle.

He sniffed the tissue delicately; pressed it against his cheek; then he kissed it, refolded it and replaced it with the letter in its envelope. Then he kissed the photograph, replaced that too, and finally the envelope itself. Then he slid it carefully into the side pocket of his blazer, flushed the lavatory for cover and reluctantly headed for his next class.

***

"Thanks," said Angela Turnbull as Lane set coffees down on a small table between their chairs. "D'you mind if I smoke?"

"Not at all. I'll join you." He fetched an ashtray, accepted a cigarette and sat down. "Now, please put me out of my misery."

"It's about James, of course," she said. "Or rather, it's about his parents. You know Annabel's staying with me for the moment. Well, now they're getting divorced, and it's likely to be pretty squalid. As far as that's concerned I can't say I'm bothered. Couldn't happen to two nicer people, is my attitude..."

"I understood that you and Mrs Potten were close friends," Lane interjected.

She wrinkled her nose. "I'm a friend, and I *would* have said a close one," she said thoughtfully. "But I've seen a lot of things lately that have shaken me a good deal. She was good to me when I went through a bad time a few years ago, and I owe her something. And... I won't say I don't like her. She's good company, on one level. I've enjoyed having her with me. It's not much fun living on your own. Better than living with a class one bastard, if you'll pardon my French, but not much fun all the same. But it's quite possible to like someone without having much time for them, wouldn't you agree?"

"Of course," assented Lane. "The likable reprobate is a constant character throughout lit... But never mind that. Please continue."

139

"Well, as I say, I've seen a lot that I haven't much liked in the last little while. Most of it to do with that unfortunate child of theirs. Well, it's going to get worse, and I think you must know what's going to happen. You and your wife seem to be the only people who give a damn about the poor kid.

"Annabel had a visit from David the night before last. He hadn't known where she was until that business at the police station. Not that it would have taken him long to find her if he'd really set out to. She hasn't got that many friends locally, and he knew she'd helped me with my own divorce. I think mainly he didn't give a damn where she was, as long as she was out of his hair. They've really gone a very, very long way apart over the last few weeks. I think they were already, in fact, but hadn't realised. Or maybe it was less trouble to just drift along and gradually go their own ways than to make the break.

"But, of course, everything that's happened lately has made it impossible. Annabel's told me about the fight David had with James - plucky kid, taking a great brute like David on like that, I must say. And now this police business, and possibly a court case, with the papers having a sacrificial orgy over it - well, David doesn't seem to care one way or the other. All he seems to be keen on is crucifying James - some warped sort of revenge, as far as I can see. I've never understood it - your own son, a child of fifteen, but there it is. But the night before last I had a very long talk with Annabel about the whole business, and a lot of things have become a lot clearer." She drank some coffee and lit another cigarette.

"I'd better start at the beginning. As I said, David came to talk to her the other night. I wouldn't have let him in. I've never had any time for him. I don't like loud-mouthed bullies, and that's all there is to David Potten. But he was quite calm and peaceable, and swore that he only wanted to sit and discuss things in a civilised manner, so I thought, well, it had to happen sometime and somewhere, so it might as well be where I could pick up the pieces afterwards if he started on her. I also thought it might be safer if I was somewhere on the scene to call the police if he started getting violent - he's a violent man, Dr Lane..."

"I've had some acquaintance with the man, Mrs Turnbull, and I formed the same impression," he said quietly, "quite apart from what I've heard from Jamie. Go on."

"Right. Well, they talked for two hours, without raising their voices. It was all pretty evil and bitter. I know, because I was eavesdropping outside the door of the room I put them in." She gave him a brief, wan half-smile. "I'm not ashamed to admit that, because I wanted to pick up anything I could that might concern James. The way those two operate I reckoned I was the only one in the house who would have *his* interests in mind - that was the other reason I decided to give that bugger houseroom, in fact."

She paused to drink, and lit another cigarette. Lane accepted one, and said, "So what does all this amount to, for Jamie, Mrs Turnbull? I should like to say, incidentally, that I think you have acted most properly, indeed laudably. I don't think there is anything to be remotely ashamed of in listening in to this conversation. And I am glad to find someone else who cares about Jamie sufficiently to act on his behalf. So, the more information you can provide me with, the better equipped we shall be to deal with whatever unpleasantness his parents can devise for the boy."

"The long and the short of it, Dr Lane, is that they're both going to do a bunk. In separate directions, of course. And in the process, they're both going to wash their hands of James. To hear them talking the other night, you'd'd've thought the poor little beggar didn't exist. And of course, when you're dealing with parents like his, well, he doesn't.

"I don't know where David's going to go, and I don't care. The farther away the better. But I do know that Annabel's laying plans to clear off to Switzerland - she's got a lot of money there - and from there to South Africa. Why anyone should want to go to *that* benighted, miserable hole God alone knows, but I gather she's got friends there. The reason for all this is that she can see pretty clearly that the papers are going to have a field day when this case comes up - if it

141

does. And if it doesn't, their divorce would be manna from heaven for the local rag, when *that* comes to court. So Annabel's going to do what comes naturally. She's going to run for it - leaving anybody and everybody holding the baby - in this case, *you* holding a fifteen-year-old baby."

Lane sat with his lips pursed. Angela watched him closely, a little afraid. When the silence became unbearable she ventured a question. "What will you do, Dr Lane? You and your wife? You're all he's got now."

He sat for a further minute in silence. Then he said, quietly and a little grimly, "We took Jamie in like a waif, Mrs Turnbull. We did that when he was *in extremis*, because there was no possible alternative. Since then, however, we have come to love him... my wife, I know, loves him as if he were her own, and I feel much the same. His mother has sent us money - generous sums of money - I take it as a sop to her conscience, since she appears to have little feeling for the boy." He paused, and sighed heavily. "Should your prediction as to her intentions prove accurate, we should undoubtedly continue to care for him for as long as he needed us, supposing that we were allowed to do so. We should be able to do that whether or not his mother were to continue to contribute to his maintenance. If both parents are planning to disappear, I imagine that they must also intend to take their money with them, and therefore to desert Jamie altogether. I must say, I should expect no better of them, judging by my own limited acquaintance of them. In such circumstances, it would not be beyond us to stand *in loco parentis*."

Angela bounded out of her chair and clapped her hands. "I *knew* you'd be a brick!" she exclaimed. "I knew you'd be the one person to be relied on. Okay, Dr Lane," she went on more quietly, dropping back onto the edge of her chair and looking intently at him. "I sat up with Annabel half the night after I found out what was afoot, trying to persuade her that she owed someone something. I got nowhere, as you might expect. So what I'm really here to tell you is this: if she does run out on the poor kid, and you need any help, you can

142

come to me for anything I'm good for. Which is mostly money. Because here's the next blow.

"David is going to withdraw him from this school. That's the first thing he thought of, and he'd've done it already if the fees for this term weren't paid already. So you can take it from me that the kid'll be taken out in the near future. Annabel might have coughed up for him, if she hadn't been so busy working out how to get as much of David's money away with her, along with her own. I had a long session with her the other night, in the course of which I told her pretty explicitly what I thought of her. I'm doing my best to persuade her to lay out a decent amount for the boy, whatever she's planning to do on her own account; but I'm not having a lot of luck so far, apart from the bit she unbelted and sent you yesterday...

"So, what I want you to know, Dr Lane, is that *if* David tries to do the dirty on James and withdraw him, and *if* Annabel runs for it before I can browbeat her into doing something decent for once in her worthless life - which I shall do my bloody damnedest to do - if that happens, Dr Lane, well, I screwed a pretty fair settlement out of my old man when I divorced him. He wasn't exactly a billionaire, but he was pretty well britched, and I got a fair slice of it - enough to see me out even if I had to subsidise Annabel's drinking for longer than I intend to." She suddenly sank into her armchair, and all the energy seemed to run out of her. She lay back for a moment, as if regrouping. Finally she said, quietly, "If you're ever in want of the kid's fees, or if you need money for anything to do with him, call me. I'll send you a blank cheque by the next post." She lay back again, seeming drained.

Dr Lane sat back and smoked his cigarette in silence for some time, marvelling at what he had just heard. He had not known quite what to expect, but he had never expected a munificent offer, let alone one made in the throwaway fashion in which Angela had finally made it - almost as if it was an impulse that she felt slightly ashamed of. Finally, he leaned forward and put a hand on her expensively-tailored shoulder. "Mrs Turnbull, I thank you, most profoundly and sincerely. Jamie would be most moved to know that he has such staunch and selfless friends..."

"Don't you go telling him anything about all this," she yelped. "I don't want him being grateful..."

"I shall say nothing whatsoever, Mrs Turnbull," Lane said quietly, "unless you permit me to do so. But you can't prevent me from being grateful. If I may ask it of you, please do what you can to persuade Jamie's mother that she owes him some kind of duty. She may thank you for it at some time later on. But if - if she does as you suspect she is planning to do, well, probably there is nothing lost, after all. And now, may I get you another coffee, perhaps?"

"You'll be wanting to get back to your school," she said softly from the depths of her chair. "But I suppose you couldn't run to a drink, could you?"

"Would you like a scotch?" he said, smiling slowly. "I think I should rather like a small one myself."

"You couldn't make it a large one for me, I suppose?" she said.

***

The next few days brought a gradual and much-needed calm. Jamie, with the resilience of his youth, began to settle down a little. Christopher's letters arrived each morning, and Jamie would give a shy little smile as he carried them off to his room. The Lanes, still not completely sure they weren't playing with fire, would grimace at each other, but generally they were pleased with the way he had accepted the state of affairs.

A few days after his conversation with Angela Turnbull, Lane received a telephone call from her to say she thought Annabel was about to make her move. But she also said that she had hopes of convincing her of her obligations to her son.

"I don't know whether I've brought it home to her or not," she said, "but I hope I've tweaked her conscience enough to get a few bob out of her. There won't be anything else, like affection, or a sense of responsibility, because she's not made that way. But we may be able to lay something down for the kid. I'll keep working on her.

"Meanwhile, David's cleared off. We had a smarmy lawyer here yesterday, wanting to talk about putting the farm on the market. Annabel was half-cut, so I had to stand in for her. I managed to get enough sense out of her to tell him that he could do what he liked so long as she got her half - it's in joint names, much to my surprise. I shouldn't've thought he was the kind to share anything, but then, she may well have put up some of the money when they bought it. I haven't been able to get any details about that sort of thing out of her. I'll keep you posted." Dr Lane found that he was beginning to look forward to her calls, finding her sardonic, bluff manner engaging.

Every morning Jamie and Dr Lane would set off across the field to the school, chatting amiably, and each morning Edith thought she saw a little more normality enter into Jamie's manner. In the evenings he worked at his preparation, and they resumed the pleasant conversations they had got into the habit of enjoying soon after Jamie had first come to them - so long ago, as it seemed to them, though in reality it was no more than a month or two. Dr Lane found himself once again appreciating the boy's quick wit and intelligence, and enjoyed throwing out lines of enquiry for him to follow, looking forward to the results the following evening. Edith hoped it was not a fool's paradise.

One morning, ten days after Angela Turnbull's visit, two things happened. Jamie carried his precious letter off to his room as usual. The Lanes, also as usual, glanced at each other, still not sure that they were doing the right thing by permitting the letters. Yet, as one or other of them had remarked on several occasions, they seemed to be doing no harm; rather a great deal to reconcile Jamie to the fact that he was not able to see his friend. This time however, only a minute or two after disappearing upstairs with the letter, Jamie came back into the breakfast room with distress written all over his face.

"Jamie, darling, what is it?" asked Edith, suspecting strongly that she could guess what was in the letter that day. "It's... it's Christopher," he said in a small, frightened voice. "He's... they... he's got to go to the police station, this morning. They're going to charge him with... with..." His head dropped, he went to her as she rose from her chair, buried his head on her shoulder, and burst into tears.

THREE

"Come in here, Christopher," said Detective Sergeant Bly. He took Christopher's arm and steered him with a kind of gruff gentleness into the charge room. He sat Christopher down in an upright chair in front of a deal table, then went quickly out to the front office to speak to Bob and Audrey Rowe. "It won't take very long, Mr and Mrs Rowe," he said, quite kindly. "I'll come out and speak to you again shortly. Explain the charge, and the procedure, and so on. Get him charged now - better to get it over and done with." He turned to the man standing with the Rowes. "Morning, Mr Hope-Thomson. You representing Christopher?" The man greeted him affably and nodded. "Want to be with him while he's charged?"

"Yes, please," said the man. He turned and smiled reassuringly to the anxious parents, and followed Bly into the charge room. "How d'you feel, Christopher?" Bly asked, looking closely at the boy's pale face.

"I'm not too bad," said Christopher, unable to keep a tremble out of his voice, but doing his best to remain calm and not, Bly thought, making too bad a job of it. Bly sat on the edge of the table and drummed with his fingertips impatiently, waiting for the Station Officer. The solicitor leaned negligently against the wall to one side. After a minute or two a uniformed inspector came in. "'Lo, Dick," he said, and Bly murmured, "Mornin', Alan." The inspector nodded civilly towards the solicitor, seated himself across the table from Christopher and dumped a heavy book and a fat bundle of forms in front of him. "Right, let's get on with it," he said to no one in particular.

In front of him was a blackened, battered clip-board, which looked as if it had been gnawed by mice at the corners. Fastened to it was a large white form, with a yellow copy underneath it and a pink one beneath that. The inspector smoothed the forms flat and took a ballpoint pen from the breast pocket of his uniform jacket. "Right then," he said, looking at Christopher for the first time, "you're Christopher Martin Rowe?"

"Yes," said Christopher.

"All right, then, Mr Rowe, you are charged that on one or more dates between the fourth and the tenth of last month, you committed buggery with a male person under the age of twenty-one years, namely James Potten, you yourself also being under the age of twenty-one years, contrary to section 12, sub-section 1 of the Sexual Offences Act, 1956, as amended by the Sexual Offences Act, 1967. Do you understand the charge?"

"Yes," said Christopher quietly.

"Very well, then. I must caution you that you are not obliged to say anything in answer to this charge, but that anything you do say will be taken down in writing, and may be given in evidence." The inspector laid down his pen and glanced expressionlessly across the table at Christopher. After a few seconds he picked his pen up again and murmured, "Nothing said" to himself as he wrote in another section of the big white form. He filled in several boxes, ending by scrawling a large, flamboyant signature at the foot. When he had finished writing he laid the pen down and looked across at Christopher again. "Okay," he said, not unkindly. "You understand what all this means?"

"Yes," muttered Christopher again.

"Right. Well, DS Bly and Mr Hope-Thomson here will talk to you and your parents before you go. You will appear before the magistrates, here in Oldacre, the day after tomorrow, at ten a.m. This offence is triable on indictment - you know what that means?" Christopher looked mutely across at him, not trusting himself to speak. The inspector stared at him for a moment. "It means that you can only be tried by a judge and jury, at the Crown Court. You have to appear before the magistrates for committal for trial. They can't try you themselves," he went on, again speaking quite kindly. "They hear the evidence and decide if there's a case for you to answer. DS Bly and your solicitor will explain it all to you." He glanced up at the detective for confirmation, and Bly nodded at Christopher.

"Right then. For now, I'm bailing you to appear at the magistrates' court on Thursday, ten o'clock in the morning, in the same sum as before, namely fifty pounds in your own recognisance. You know what *that* means?"

"Yeah, Alan, he knows what that means," put in Bly. "Come on, Christopher. I want to talk to you and your parents. That it, Al?" The inspector nodded. Bly took Christopher by the elbow and led him out into the front office, with the solicitor following them. From there he propelled Christopher into the small interview room beside the counter. He motioned Christopher's parents, huddled miserably in the far corner of the counter, to go into the room through the other door. He sat Christopher down, then emerged into the front office again in search of an extra chair. Taking it into the little room, he sat in it back-to-front, resting his bony arms on the back-rest, and surveyed the three scared, unhappy people in front of him. "Right, then," he said. "I'd better explain what happens next."

***

149

"I've got to go and see his solicitor," said Jamie, quietly and without a hint of emotion. Edith thought she had not seen him this self-possessed for weeks. The pressure's on, she thought, and he's responding to it. She remembered her husband remarking that boys not two years older than Jamie had gone to the front in the first world war, and thought to herself that she could see Jamie doing just such a thing. She looked at her husband's face, assessing what he was going to do.

Lane, for his part, glanced across at her, raising his eyebrows questioningly. She hesitated, then made up her mind, and nodded.

"Very well, then, Jamie," he said, seeming to make up his own mind suddenly. "Edith will take you in to see the man this morning, if he's free. Will you ring him, Edith?"

"Yes, John, of course. I don't suppose he'll get to his office before nine, do you? No, well, I'll ring him just after that, and take Jamie in as soon as he can see him. Do you want him to come into school afterwards, or if the man isn't available?"

Lane wrinkled his brow in thought. "If he can't see Jamie at all, yes." He turned to Jamie. "Will you be able to manage school, Jamie? From second period?"

"Yes sir," said Jamie calmly.

Lane looked hard at him, but could not read his expression. "All right, then come into the second period, if you get back by then. Otherwise, come in this afternoon." He looked searchingly at the boy once again. "You're sure you're up to this, Jamie?"

"Oh, yes, sir. I must speak to the man. I must say what I can for Chris," he said, quietly but with such an adult air of determination that both Lanes saw at the same moment that he would not be dissuaded, even if they had proposed any such thing.

"Very well," said Dr Lane. "Well. I must be gone." He rose and headed for the door. "There is one other thing, sir," said Jamie, respectfully but with the same very adult intonation in his voice. "Yes, my dear boy," said Lane, turning and looking down at his small, set face.

"May I have my diary, sir, please," he asked. "I should like to show it to the man. It will prove that Christopher never did anything that I didn't ask him to do. Then they'll never be able to do anything to him, will they?"

Lane felt his heart go out to the boy. He stood before him, small, neat, pale-faced but exuding an unbending, iron will. "If maturity was all, I could make him Head Boy tomorrow," he recollected himself saying some time in the very recent past. He stood for a moment in thought. Then, making up his mind once again, he nodded brusquely. "Very well, Jamie. I don't know if I'm being altogether wise, still less whether you are. But I think we must give you your head in this matter, my boy. I'll send someone across with it the moment I get to school."

He came back into the room and drew Jamie's slender form to him, squeezing his shoulders in a brief, and uncommon, gesture of affection. "Goodbye for the moment, Jamie, my dear boy. And good luck." He went into the hall and picked up his case. Jamie watched him crossing the field for a few moments before dropping back into his chair at the kitchen table and sinking his head into his hands in deep thought. Edith left him alone for a long time. Eventually she touched him gently on the shoulder. "Would you like some more tea, dear?" she asked softly. To her utter amazement, he looked up and bestowed on her, for almost the first time, his beautiful smile at full voltage. "Yes, please," he said, brightly. While she was still trying to assess the significance of it he said, as if reading her thoughts, "It's better than waiting on tenterhooks, isn't it? If I go and tell them it was all my doing, they can't possibly blame Chris, can they?"

She felt herself close to tears, and could not look him in the face. "I hope not, dear," she said very quietly. "I hope not."

***

Edith Lane pulled up on a double yellow line and looked about for traffic wardens as Jamie scrambled out, clutching his diary. "There you are, dear," she said. "Now, are you absolutely sure you wouldn't like me to come in with you?" For a moment he looked a little forlorn, and she thought he was about to change his mind and permit her to go with him, but his face quickly cleared and returned to the expression of slightly blank determination that he had worn all morning. "No, thank you very much all the same, though," he said, and in a moment he was out of sight among the morning shoppers. Edith sighed and put the car into gear.

Jamie climbed a flight of stairs in an antiseptic-smelling building off the High Street. The carpets were a dull light green that reminded him of the powdered paint of the noxious shade known as terre verte used in the school art room. He got to the first floor, pushed through some steel and glass double doors and into a reception area, and approached a desk where a girl was clacking at a huge document in a typewriter. "Yes, what can I do for you?" she said, looking up without ceasing from her ferocious assault on the machine.

"I've got an appointment with Mr Hope-Thomson, please, miss," he said, smiling at her. She stopped typing abruptly, becoming the second to fall to his smile that morning. "What's your name, please?"

"Potten, miss. Jamie Potten."

"Will you have a seat," she said, waving at a deep sofa in dark green leather. Jamie dropped into a corner of the sofa and watched her carefully as she picked up a telephone. "Mr Hope-Thomson? There's a young man in reception to see you. Says he's got an appointment. Oh, right." She put the receiver down and looked at him with interest. "He'll be down straight away," she said, smiling at him. "He says you're his star witness." Jamie grinned, pleased.

A few moments later a door opened across the reception area and an angular man with wild, thinning blond hair and fierce gold-rimmed glasses came across to Jamie. "Jamie Potten?" he said pleasantly, extending a hand. Jamie heaved himself with some effort out of his floor-level seat and shook the hand with cool aplomb. "How d'you do, sir," he said.

"How d'you do yourself, Jamie," said the man, smiling a thin smile at the boy's grown-up air. "It's very good of you to come. Please come with me." He courteously gestured to Jamie to precede him through the door from which he had emerged and Jamie went through, feeling the receptionist's eyes on him. The clacking of the typewriter resumed as the door closed behind the two of them. Hope-Thomson showed him to a large, airy office. It was lined on two sides with leather-bound and gold-blocked books. A large grey steel safe occupied half a third wall, and the office was dominated by a huge desk covered mountainously with tottering piles of dog-eared papers, folders, books, three telephones and an intercom. Have a seat, Jamie, please," he said, sliding into a swivel chair across the expanse of desk. He pressed a switch on the intercom, and the reception girl's voice came on instantly.

"Yes, Mr Hope-Thomson?"

"No calls for one hour, please, Brenda," he said. "Right, sir," came the crackled reply.

He swept several of the piles of papers to either side to make room for his elbows, propped them on the desk and looked keenly, but with considerable respect, straight at Jamie. "Now, then. How do you think you can help us?"

Jamie swallowed hard, feeling suddenly very nervous, but quickly pulled himself together. "I'd like to tell you all about Christopher Rowe and me," he said.

***

The clerk to the Oldacre justices was a slender and attractive girl with long, straight blonde hair and large blue eyes. She stood up, drawing admiring glances from the three or four policemen, two local journalists and half a dozen citizens with nothing better to do who were sitting on the hard wooden benches for the public. "Christopher Martin Rowe," she said in a pleasant, conversational tone that accorded ill with the words she addressed to the pale young man in the dock, "you are charged that on one or more dates between the fourth and the tenth of last month you did commit an act or acts of buggery with a male person under the age of twenty-one years. To that charge do you plead guilty or not guilty?"

"Guilty," said Christopher, barely audible in the small, modern courtroom.

The chairman leaned forward from his chair behind the slightly elevated bench and murmured to the clerk, "What did he say?"

"He pleads guilty," murmured the clerk back to him. She turned back to Christopher again. "Will you speak up a little, please. The magistrates must hear you." Christopher, who was doing his best to control the trembling that was threatening to turn his legs to rubber underneath him, said nothing, wiped a damp film of sweat from his forehead with the upper part of his sleeve, and fidgeted with the knot of his unaccustomed tie. "You may sit down," said the clerk, seeing that he was about ready to fall down. Christopher sat down hard, rocking the flimsy little dock.

The clerk stood up, having to stand on tip-toe to lean across the Bench, whispering for some time to the chairman. When she sat down the chairman looked sternly at Christopher. He was a bulky man in his fifties, a local general practitioner with no bedside manner. He was known for being a hard sentencer, and he surveyed Christopher with evident dislike. "You understand, Rowe, that this charge may be heard only by a judge at the Crown Court?" Christopher said, slightly more audibly, "Yes, sir."

"Stand up when you speak to the Bench," said the clerk, and Christopher struggled in confusion to his feet. "Do you understand what that means, Rowe?" asked the chairman. "You have pleaded guilty to this... to this charge here before us, but you must be remanded to the Crown Court for sentence."

"I understand that, sir," said Christopher, his voice becoming a little stronger as he got used to the surroundings and the ordeal. "Does the defence wish to say anything?" asked the chairman gruffly. "Not at this time, sir," said Hope-Thomson smoothly, "except that we ask for bail on the same terms as the police bail hitherto."

The chairman turned his eyes and his heavy black-rimmed spectacles on the wispy little sandy-haired man representing the Crown Prosecution Service. "Does the Crown have any objections?" he asked, his tone clearly suggesting that he would have rather liked it if the Crown had. "No objections, your worship," said the man. "We request that the conditions include the stipulation that the accused make no attempt to make contact with the patient involved in the offence."

"Humph!" said the chairman, as if cheated of his prey. "Order granted. Bail in the same terms as before." He glared at Christopher. "You heard that, Rowe, and understand what it means? If you try to make any sort of contact with the victim of your offences, you'll be brought back before this court and answer for your conduct."

Christopher, who had sat down, got to his feet again. "I understand," he said. It was clearly audible to everyone in court that his voice had suddenly become stronger, and one or two of the police officers and journalists turned to look at him with a slight quickening of interest. The more observant of the two reporters noticed immediately that his bearing had, equally suddenly, become much more upright, and his eyes were no longer fixed on a point a couple of feet in front of the dock, but looking directly at the chairman. He had a little more colour in his face, and, more than anything else, his expression now registered anger. The journalist nudged his colleague. "Kid's beginning to show a bit of spirit," he whispered, and made a note on his pad.

The chairman saw the slight movement out of the corner of his eye and turned towards the two reporters in their box. "I suppose I don't have to remind you gentlemen that the name of the - ah -" he leaned forward and beckoned the clerk to lean across. They whispered briefly, then he sat back again. "Yes, the *patient*, as the law strangely chooses to refer to the other boy involved in the unnatural acts that are the substance of the charge, may not be identified in any way." The reporters nodded as he turned back towards the front of the court. "Very well, remanded to the next session of the Crown Court. Let him stand down." He looked straight through Christopher as if he was a hole in the air.

Christopher flushed, and slipped gratefully out of the dock. Hope-Thomson came round from his place and hurried him through a door into the passage that led to the gaoler's and other court officials' offices at the rear of the building. "Okay, we're over the worst of it," he murmured to Christopher as they went down the corridor. "I'd say we're fortunate in not being tried here. That doctor would've volunteered for the Bloody Assize." Christopher managed a faint, grateful grin. "He didn't take much of a liking to me, did he?" he said, gulping slightly in his relief at the end of his ordeal.

"You won't find that people who commit your kind of offence are very popular anywhere," said Hope-Thomson drily. Christopher looked sharply at him, looking for condemnation, but the man's face was neutral. Christopher swallowed and asked the question he had been trying to pluck up the courage to ask throughout his meetings with the solicitor. "What do you think I'll get?"

Hope-Thomson glanced at him, ran a hand through his straying hair and thought as they entered an office and leaned on a counter. "Hard to say," he said. "Depends in part on which judge you get. Personally, I should say we're likely to get a term of probation. With the mitigation we can produce, coupled with your previous good character, I'd say it's as good as a certainty that you won't receive any custodial sentence." He rubbed his chin. "Yes, I'm inclined to the view that you'll most likely receive something like probation for, oh, I don't know, probably two years, I'd guess. Or possiblty a conditional discharge. You know what that means?"

"I think so," said Christopher, not liking the sound of it

much, but glad to be reassured once again about the impossibility of prison.

"It means that you have been discharged without any actual penalty - that they are taking into account the fact that you haven't got any previous convictions, your youth and the mitigation - especially that provided by the other boy. The sting in the tail is that if you commit any other criminal offence, but especially another of a similar kind to this one, during the period of suspension, you'll be brought back before the court and some sentence will *then* be imposed for this offence, on top of anything you may get for whatever other offence you commit."

"I shan't be committing *any* other offences," said Christopher fervently. "I shan't ride my bike without lights after this."

"I don't think we need worry too much about that," said Hope-Thomson with the trace of a grin. A court official finished dealing with another solicitor and client and turned to the two of them. Hope-Thomson dealt rapidly with the matter of Christopher's bail, and five minutes later delivered the boy to his parents, waiting in great distress outside the building. On Hope-Thomson's instructions they had slipped out by a rear entrance, through which he and Christopher now followed them.

"With a bit of luck we may just evade the photographers," he muttered to Christopher as he hustled him down an alley to the street. He was right, and they walked quickly to put a quarter of a mile between themselves and the court building.

"What happens now?" asked Robert Rowe.

"Could we go somewhere for a drink, Dad, please," asked Christopher. "Somewhere away from here."

"Er, well, yes, all right, I suppose we could," said his father doubtfully. He looked at the solicitor. "Will you come with us, Mr Hope-Thomson?" he asked. "I'd like to go into what happens next in a bit more detail."

Hope-Thomson consulted his watch. "I don't see why not," he said. "I haven't got any appointments until two, and I can understand Christopher's needing a drink. I should

157

think you could perhaps do with one yourselves." They looked gratefully at him. "You drove here, I suppose?" said Rowe. The solicitor shook his head. "I walked from the office. How about the Cherry Tree?" he suggested. "It's a pleasant enough place, and it's on my way back. It's only a short walk from here." They walked together towards the High Street, where Hope-Thomson turned down a narrow passage, then ducked into a door into a pleasant, dimly-lit inn.

Robert Rowe went to the bar while the others ensconced themselves in a far corner, and came back with a pint of bitter for Christopher, whiskies for himself and his wife and half of lager for Hope-Thomson. He sat for a quarter of an hour repeating in substance what he had told Christopher in the court passage. Then Audrey Rowe voiced the dread that loomed most fearsomely in their minds. "What about the papers?" she said, tremulously. "Will Chris's name be in the papers?"

Hope-Thomson looked round and saw three pairs of eyes focussed intently on him. He hesitated, steeling himself to give them the answer they were least hoping to hear. "I'm afraid it will," he said eventually. There was a hiss as all three of them expelled the breath they had unconsciously been holding at once. "Oh, *God!*" moaned Audrey. Christopher's head dropped, and he looked up from under his eyelashes, unable to meet the eyes of his parents for shame at bringing this on them.

"Is there any chance at all that they won't report the case?" asked Robert Rowe, showing in his face that he knew the answer before he spoke.

"Not a hope, I shouldn't think, I'm afraid," said Hope-Thomson gently. "No, it's too unusual a story. I doubt if there's been more than one charge of buggery in that court in the fifteen years I've been practising in the town. They can't miss a story like this. I fear that you'll be under a certain amount of pressure. Indeed, if it's at all possible for you, I should recommend that you try to be away for a while, until the dust settles a little. Christopher, in particular, will, I'm afraid, very probably be subjected to a lot of harassment -

there may well be hate mail, possibly worse." He looked round at them, sympathising as he saw the horrified looks dawning on their faces.

Christopher groaned aloud, tears glistening in his eyes. "Oh, my *God*," he said softly, wagging his head from side to side in anguish. "I never meant to bring all this down on you all."

"There, there, dear," said his mother, with an effort. She moved closer to him and put an arm firmly round his shoulders. "Of course you didn't mean to. You couldn't possibly have known. You're not to worry about it."

"I can't help worrying, Mum, how can I," he wailed, then abruptly lowered his voice, looking fearfully round. But there was hardly anyone else in the bar, and none of the few other drinkers had taken any apparent notice. "What about poor Neil?" he said, in deepening misery. "Can they take it out on Neil? And what about his school. He'll go through hell, there, won't he?" He looked instinctively to Hope-Thomson as he said it.

The lawyer looked sadly at him. "I'm afraid in cases such as this it usually happens that everyone connected with the person suffers. It's grossly unjust and unfair, of course, but it's part of the price of a free press. So they tell us, anyway." He patted Christopher on the arm. "The only thing you can do is be as strong as possible, bear it with what fortitude you can, and ignore it as far as possible. They'll eventually tire of it, and other stories will come up. The hate mail can be dealt with up to a point. The post office are usually quite helpful; you may well have to have your telephone number changed. You're not ex-directory, I suppose?" They shook their heads. "Yes, well, that I think you should do straight away. I don't suppose I have to go into unpleasant detail about the sort of thing you're likely to have said about you, Christopher." Christopher shook his head in despair. "I've already been called most of them, I should think," he said, snuffling, "by some of the police."

"As I said," Hope-Thomson continued impersonally, "I should try to get Christopher away, at least. Perhaps to relations?" They looked dismally at each other. "Don't know that there's anyone he can go to," muttered Bob Rowe gloomily. "He's got to report to the police here every other day until the Crown Court hearing."

"That could be arranged," said Hope-Thomson. "He can arrange with the police to report to another station, anywhere else. It doesn't matter where. I'll see to that, if you'll let me know where he's going to be." They looked gratefully at him. "For the rest," he continued, "I think you must do your best to prepare your younger son for something of an ordeal, at school in particular. Talk to his headmaster. If necessary, ring me and I'll make bloodcurdling threats as to what will happen if the boy is victimised. Though in point of fact I suspect you may find that schoolchildren turn out to be remarkably tolerant - much more so than many of the pillars of the adult community. It has been my experience that young people are far less horrified by minor sexual peccadilloes than their elders and alleged betters. They are generally much more willing to live and let live. He'll simply have to be as prepared as he can be, and wait and see."

"Do you really regard this as a *minor* peccadillo, then?" asked Bob Rowe, looking up at the lawyer a fraction more cheerfully.

Hope-Thomson looked levelly at him, rubbing his chin. "I can't say I regard it as earth-shatteringly serious if two sexually mature youths perform acts together discreetly, with each other's whole-hearted consent," he said slowly. "If the other boy in this case were other than he is, I might well feel entirely differently. But the Potten boy is a remarkable specimen. I've had the advantage of meeting him. He's made a statement, which he insisted on making entirely unaided by me, except for occasionally seeking my advice as to how he might most effectively emphasize the entirely voluntary nature of his involvement. You might ask Christopher to tell you something of the boy, if you haven't already."

"We never really wanted to hear about him," confessed Audrey Rowe. "All we could feel about him was a bitter hatred for getting Chris into this terrible mess."

160

"And all of us, for that matter," put in her husband.

"Mmm. I suspect that Christopher didn't subscribe?" suggested Hope-Thomson. Christopher gave him a damp and grateful blink.

"Well, n-no," said his mother, "he didn't. We put that down to simple loyalty. But you can't expect us to feel very kindly towards him, when he's got us all into this terrible trouble. Hate mail," she breathed with horror.

"Well, I understand your feelings, but I suspect that if you could see his statement for the judge you would see that the loyalty is on both sides," he said.

"Can I see it?" begged Christopher. "Please?"

"I'd rather you didn't, please, Christopher," said the solicitor. "I don't want there to appear to have been any suspicion of collusion when it's read to the judge. The less you obviously know about its contents, the better the effect should be." Christopher's face fell in disappointment.

Hope-Thomson went to the bar and fetched drinks. "No," he said as he sat down, "I don't really think this amounts to much, in the special circumstances - the character of the other boy being the special circumstances. Unfortunately the law lags behind what we may agree to call enlightened opinion - as it frequently does, especially in matters of private morality. Regrettable, but a fact with which we have to live, pending reform - which, in this particular area of morality, seems highly improbable in the foreseeable future. I'm sorry, Mr and Mrs Rowe, and sorrier still for you, Christopher, but you're going to have a pretty rough time over the next few weeks, and you're going to have to get over it as best you can."

They finished their drinks in a dismal silence, and left the pub.

***

Christopher's brother Neil saw the group of men gathered round his front gate as he turned into Cross Oak Gardens on his way home from school. He walked towards the house in growing puzzlement, wondering what they could possibly be finding so interesting about the neat front gate and the low golden privet hedge of his front garden. It was only as he got very close and saw the cameras that he connected them with his brother's case, which he knew had been heard that morning, though he knew nothing at all of what had happened.

Neil edged his way through the half a dozen men and tried to get to the gate. "Hey!" cried one of the men. "It's the brother. Here, you," he said rudely to Neil, and grabbed him by the sleeve of his blazer. Neil, who was very fond of his brother indeed, and was in all things robust and uncomplicated, swung round on him. "Leave my jacket alone," he snapped, and jerked his arm away. "What do you think about your brother's case?" asked another man. "Mind your own business," snapped Neil once more, and tried to push past them and get to the gate.

"You'll have to talk to us, boy," grinned a burly photographer, snapping busily with his Nikon. Another reporter pulled at Neil from behind, this time grabbing his collar. Neil, who was a big and well-built boy for fourteen, swung round once again, glaring furiously at his assailant. "Come on, lad, you can tell us what you think about it," said the man, smiling ingratiatingly.

Neil stopped struggling to get free, and the ferocious scowl on his face was suddenly replaced by a mischievous schoolboy grin. "I'll tell you what I think," he said, sweetly. "Yes?" they chorused, crowding in on him. "I think you're a bunch of wankers," he said. "Now fuck off." And, picking his spot with great care, he kicked the man who had seized his collar very hard indeed on the projecting bone of his ankle. The man howled an oath and fell against the other men behind him, who all promptly fell all over the pavement, roaring with laughter, giving Neil just the split second he needed. He wriggled through them like an eel and fled,

162

cackling, up the path. He slammed the gate behind him and laughed joyously as he saw it crash heavily into the shins of another reporter who was trying to follow him, and then was gone, round the house, and hammering on the locked back door.

***

Jamie read that evening's edition of the local newspaper in gathering horror. "Look!" he wailed to the Lanes, who stood looking over his shoulder, his own dismay reflected in their faces. "They're crucifying him," he said in a low, desolate voice. "The poor, poor boy," said Edith Lane.

"Well, he had to expect something of the sort," said her husband, but he put a friendly arm round Jamie's shoulders to soften the effect of his words. He had a sudden idea. "Would you like to go out for dinner somewhere?" he asked the boy. Jamie twisted round under his arm and gave him a watery smile. "Oh, yes, *please*," he said. "Could we?"

***

"Look at this," said Annabel Potten to Angela Turnbull, thrusting the same paper at her. "I'd never thought about their not printing his name." She laughed aloud, unable to contain her delight.

"They're making a human sacrifice of the poor kid," observed Angela, wrinkling her nose in disgust as she scanned the front page. There was a picture of Christopher being hustled through the front door of an anonymous-looking suburban house, with his parents trying to conceal his face with their bodies. All that could be seen of him was part of a cheek and a smudge of dark hair. Another picture showed Neil, glaring into the camera, and yet another showed him scudding round the corner of the house. It also showed clearly the drawn curtains in all the windows. The address was given in full. "Just so every crank and self-appointed Mary Whitehouse in the bloody district knows how to find him and make his life a misery, and his family's as well," she snorted. As she said it she was suddenly struck by what her friend had said. "And all you can do is stand there crowing about how they haven't been able to print *your* name as well. Don't you give a *damn* about *anybody* but yourself, Annabel? Can you imagine what that poor kid's going through? Or what your own child would be going through at this moment if they'd been allowed to print his name?"

"I couldn't care bloody less what this Christopher goes through," snapped Annabel. "He's the one who started all this off, perverting James with his filthy ways."

"Get away with you," jeered Angela, past all patience. Her voice was crackling with anger and contempt. "You never gave a *sod* about what the boy got up to. If you'd kept a proper eye on him none of this would have happened. But you left the poor little blighter to his own devices, and you'd be doing so this minute if they hadn't had the infernal bad luck to fall foul of that ogre of a husband of yours and he hadn't been certifiable bloody lunatic enough to bring it all into the open, going round on his insane crusade trying to half-kill this boy." She opened her mouth to say more, but snapped it shut in a tight, angry line. "Get me a drink, Annabel, for Christ's sake," she said eventually. "A large one." And Annabel, utterly taken aback by the ferocity and contempt in her friend's face and voice, meekly went to the bar and did as she was bidden.

***

Robert Rowe telephoned Hope-Thomson the following morning from his office to inform him that Christopher might travel to London as soon as the agreement of the police had been secured, to stay with his grandparents until his appearance at Crown Court was imminent. "I haven't told them everything," he said in answer to the solicitor's query, "just that he's in some unspecified trouble and would appreciate a change of air. I tried to give the impression that he's had some sort of nervous breakdown - overwork and so on, I implied - and they're going to be very tactful."

"Good," said Hope-Thomson. "Very good indeed. I'll square it with the police right away, and ring you back within the hour if I can. How's it been?"

"Well, not too bad, really," said Rowe. "We had a gaggle of newspapermen outside yesterday, making a bloody nuisance of themselves, but there was no-one there this morning. Neil had a bit of an altercation with them, and kicked one of them on the shins. You may have read about it in the local rag last night. I was proud of him."

"I did, and so was I," said Hope-Thomson. "How is it in other ways?"

"Well, again, nowhere near as bad as we feared, so far at least," replied Rowe. "I've had sympathetic ostracism, as you might say, here in the office. Neil rang me in his morning break earlier this morning from school, and apparently the kids are being pretty decent about it - just as you said they would be. He's had a bit of ragging about his brother being a nancy boy, but I gather that most of the attention has been on his kicking that bloody reporter. It seems to have made him into something of a hero." He chuckled.

Hope-Thomson echoed the laugh. "Ha! Can't be too much wrong with the younger generation if they think someone who kicks a reporter is a hero," he said. "So it's not too hard so far."

"Not so far," agreed Rowe. "Chrissie's pretty cut up still, of course. He blames himself dreadfully for bringing all this on us, and he's very unhappy. I'll tell you something else, though, which has made me sit up and take notice..."

"Yes?" said the lawyer curiously. "What's that?"

"Well, he seems to be pining for his young friend. He really does seem to be missing him more than anything else. I really was astonished by that. I mean, when you think that it was that boy who got him into all this, well, you'd have thought he would be the last person in the world he'd want to even think about, wouldn't you?"

"Tell me, Mr Rowe," said Hope-Thomson drily, "does your wife share your surprise?"

"Er, well... as a matter of fact, she doesn't," said Rowe in a puzzled tone. "As a matter of fact she seems to think it's the most natural thing of all. She was actually talking in terms of possibly engineering a meeting for them somehow. Of course, I squashed that one flat as soon as she raised it. I rather lost my temper with her, actually," he confessed a little sheepishly. "But really, can you imagine such a thing, only five minutes after he's been warned like he was in court yesterday?"

"I quite agree with you, Mr Rowe," observed Hope-Thomson "it would be the depths of foolishness to attempt to connive at or merely to countenance any such defiance of an order of the court; but frankly I'm not in the least surprised that your wife felt as she did. I'm inclined to agree with her. You have to understand something quite fundamental to this case, Mr Rowe - something which you perhaps haven't fully grasped yet. Something which possibly the boy's mother may have found it easier to adjust to and comprehend than you have."

"What's that, then?" asked Rowe, mystified.

"Quite simply this, Mr Rowe," said the quiet, smooth voice at the other end of the line. "These two boys are not just infatuated with each other. I've had a chance to gain some quite intimate understanding of both of them, as opposed to just one of them, and I'm satisfied that this is not simply an adolescent crush. They love each other. Just as you and I might love our wives, and may have loved them when we were courting them, as people of our age used to put it. They are in love, Mr Rowe. That is the only possible explanation for the quite extraordinary devotion and loyalty they have consistently shown each other, and are still showing each other now. I have myself have had a message from the younger boy this morning, made, if I'm not mistaken, in his morning break at school. I haven't yet made up my mind whether I can pass it on, but it has come. And as a model of dispassionate - and yet, on the other hand, passionate - loyalty and devotion to a loved one, it could hardly be surpassed.

"The Potten boy is interested, in that he is desperately concerned, about Christopher's well-being. He is tortured by guilt and self-reproach for having, as he believes, been largely responsible for his friend's catastrophe, and he is anxious to do anything and everything within his power to save him from any further hurt. Since he perceives that every moment of suffering for the rest of your family is another moment's suffering for Christopher, he feels a second burden of guilt on that account.

"Frankly, Mr Rowe, I confess myself shaken by what I have seen of these two boys. Shaken and, I may say, somewhat moved. Their concern for each other seems genuinely to negate their concern for themselves. This case is in many ways outside the normal rules for dealing with such things." He fell silent, and waited for a reaction from the worried father at the other end.

Rowe was silent for some time. "Well," he said at length, "I must say, I'm very surprised at what you say. I wouldn't have thought two boys of this age would have been capable of this kind of emotion. In any case, I don't find it at all easy to understand this homosexuality aspect. I mean, you could have knocked me down with a feather when I found out that Chrissie was... was... that way inclined... but to have you telling me that there's something - well, almost as if there's something *noble* about it, as if this Potten boy is some sort of a *hero* - well, it's pretty hard to take, if you're in my position."

"If you want my opinion, Mr Rowe," said Hope-Thomson after a pause, "I think you might have searched for quite a long time before you found a better word than 'noble' for what I've seen in this case. And, if I may make one further suggestion..." There was a long pause. Then he continued, "Look, I most certainly shouldn't be suggesting any such thing. As a solicitor I'm first of all an officer of the court, and what I'm about to venture, very tentatively, to suggest, is in direct defiance of the very court of which I am an officer. But, Mr Rowe, if Christopher seems to be getting desperate in his desire to make contact with his friend, well, there must be no possible question of their meeting in person; but if there happened to be no one about in the vicinity of the telephone some time before the boy goes to his grandparents... well, Mr Rowe, if I were you, I think I might possibly develop cloth ears just for a few minutes..."

There was an even longer pause before the precise voice continued. "That was, very emphatically, off the record, Mr Rowe. It was tantamount to a contempt of court on my part, even to countenance such a thing. If I were ever challenged about it I should, of course, deny that I ever made mention of it. But, honestly, I suspect that in the extremely unusual circumstances prevailing in this case, the good that even a brief few words on the telephone might do would out-standingly outweigh any possible risk - provided only that the boy was fully aware of the risk, it would be so minimised thereby as to be negligible; and I have no doubt that both boys are far too intelligent not to be aware of the need for total secrecy. And now, Mr Rowe, I'll talk to the local police for you."

"Why... well, thank you Mr Hope-Thomson. You've given me a lot to think about. I don't know... Well, anyway, you've been very kind. Thank you, and goodbye."

"I've been a very naughty solicitor, Mr Rowe - quite naughty enough for one day. Goodbye." He rang off, leaving a very astonished Robert Rowe indeed sitting back in his office and doing a lot of revision of his ideas.

***

The first time the Lanes' telephone rang that evening Edith happened to be walking past, and picked it up on the first ring. There was a whirr on the line before she had finished giving the number, and it went dead. The second time Dr Lane went, and the same thing happened. He stood looking at the receiver in his hand. "Hmph," he muttered, "must be faulty," and he made a mental note to ring the engineers from the school the next morning. The third time Christopher's luck was in, for Jamie was passing when it rang. He picked it up and gave the number. When the familiar, loved voice came through he almost fell down in mingled wonder, fear and joy. "Jamie! For Christ's sake don't say anything," said Christopher urgently at the other end, before he had a chance to open his mouth. "Just say the number, as if you can't hear anything," said Christopher, speaking very quickly and quietly. "I've only got half a minute. If you can ring me in your morning break tomorrow, I'll be by the phone. We'll have about ten minutes. If you can't, too bad. But for God's sake don't let anyone know. Bye, my darling. Love you."

Jamie cast a frantic look about him. The door to the living room was closed, and the Lanes were listening to Mozart on the record player. "Love you too," he hissed in a desperate whisper into the mouthpiece. "I heard," said Christopher hurriedly. "Must go. Bye, sweet." There was a click. Jamie stood, half-stunned. Then he pulled himself together and went on his way into the living room. "Who was that?" asked Edith. "Dunno," said Jamie, not feeling happy about lying but, knowing he had to lie, lying smoothly, pulling a face. "I just got a lot of clicks and whirrs, and then someone saying hello."

"I think there must be a fault on the line or on our receiver," commented Dr Lane from his armchair. "That's three times in the last hour it's done that. I'll ring them in the morning and have them check the line." He went back to his book. Jamie picked up his books, slipped out and went to his room. The hours set aside for his preparation passed like seconds as he sat hugging himself joyfully. He went down with a light heart for his chocolate drink, and could hardly wait to get to bed, where he lay plotting his strategy for the following morning, until his joyous thoughts of Christopher sent his hand down his body and he found relief in dreams.

The next morning Jamie carefully left a book that he knew he would need in the period after break concealed beneath his bed. He was down early, picking up the post on his way to the breakfast room. He handed the letters to Dr Lane, who rifled through them and immediately spotted the now familiar blue Swiss stationery and the firm hand of Angela Turnbull. He immediately laid the others down and opened it. Inside there was a cheque signed by Annabel Potten for five thousand pounds. With it was a quickly scribbled note from Angela: "She's done her bunk. I managed to get this out of her - her last bow - I don't think we'll be seeing her again. Will ring you at school this AM. If you can't be there to receive it, NTW, but hope to be able to talk briefly. Yrs, AT."

"She goes in for lots of initials," he murmured to himself.

"What did you say, dear?" asked Edith.

"Eh? Oh, nothing. Just muttering to myself. Tell me, have you any idea what NTW stands for?" Edith raised her eyebrows and looked enquiringly at the letter in his hand. He handed it over, with a warning half-glance at Jamie, who, however, was still immersed in his own thoughts. She scanned the letter quickly, drew the cheque half-way out of the envelope and drew her breath in sharply when she saw the sum. She slipped it instantly out of sight again. "NTW?" she murmured to herself. "Oh, yes, of course - it means 'not to worry'." They chuckled in unison. "NTW this AM it is then," said Lane. "This means that I'll have to remain at the school over break to await the call. I shan't be able to get back to meet the telephone people, assuming I can extract a promise from them to come at a set time. Will you be here, Edith?"

"No, dear, I've got a committee meeting at ten o'clock which will go on most of the morning." Jamie had by this time pricked up his ears. He could have hugged himself, to see everything being made easy for him. He wouldn't even have to tell any lies.

"Oh, well," said Lane, a little crossly. "I'll have to leave the telephone until the afternoon." He clicked his tongue in mild annoyance, and forgot it.

***

At the end of the second period Jamie made his way to the master's dais and asked permission from his form master to return home for a book he had somehow managed to mislay. He covered the quarter of a mile as if on the cinder track, though retaining enough circumspection to make sure he kept out of sight of the headmaster's study windows. He let himself in with the front door key they had given him, and leaned against the wall beside the telephone for a moment or two to get his breath back. Then, as soon as he was breathing half-normally, he dialled Christopher's number. The receiver was picked up before the first ring was half-complete. "Hallo," said a low, non-committal voice.

"Chris! Chris, it's me," he said, so excited and strained that it came out in a strangled squeak. "Jamie," came back softly down the line. "Jamie, my *dear*. How are you?" It was a commonplace enquiry, but the tone of love and concern in which Christopher asked made Jamie's head swim. "Oh, God, Chris, I miss you. How are *you*?"

"Missing you, my darling. Things are pretty rough, but not as bad as we thought they might be. You saw the paper the other day, after my case at the magistrates' court?"

"Yes, Chris, my darling," breathed Jamie. "I nearly died. All that terrible trouble, and all my fault…"

"Don't talk like that, Jamie. It wasn't your fault, or mine or anybody's. It was just the way things are for - for people like us. The law's a mockery, for people like you and me. But never mind the bloody law. We've only got a few minutes.

171

Jamie, my dearest, I know it'll be very difficult for you. Probably impossible. But would you like to see me once more before... before - before the Crown Court hearing?"

Jamie's heart swam up his throat and he felt as if he was suffocating on it. He choked for a moment before he could answer. "See you? Oh, Chris, I'd do *anything*. Anything. But how..."

"Quick, then, get a pen and something to write on." Jamie crossed to the kitchen in three bounds and was back with a pencil and a scrap of paper in seconds. "I'm here, Chris."

"Okay. But for Christ's sake don't let anyone find the paper, because if I'm caught even talking to you on the phone they'll lock me up, so they said at court. One of the conditions of my bail," he commented bitterly.

"All right, Chris, but be quick," said Jamie, glancing frantically at his watch. "I've got to go in five minutes. I won't let them see it."

"Right. Take this number down, then. That's my grand-parents' home, in London. I'm going to stay with them for about three weeks. To get me out of the way of cranks and poison-pen letters until my case comes up. I'm going tomorrow. Now, I haven't got it all worked out yet, but I've thought of a way we could have a day together. It would give us a chance to sort things out, and to talk about everything that's happened. Can't say any more right now, but if we can fix a time for you to ring that number, I'll have the details worked out. I'll work them out on the train down. When can you ring, do you know? Can you set a time?"

"I can usually get to a phone in break - that's now," he said, his mind racing against the clock. "Would that do?"

"Yes, love, that's fine. Tomorrow? No, make it the next day. That okay?"

"Yes, yes, yes, Chris. I'll do it, whatever I have to do to fix it up." Jamie looked at his watch again and saw with a groan that he would have to go back in a minute's time. "Chris, I've got to go," he said, and Christopher's chest contracted as he heard the loneliness and sadness in his young voice. "All right, then, Jamie. But we'll see each other for a few hours, at least, soon, now. And Jamie..."

"Yes," said Jamie breathlessly, fidgeting in his anxiety but utterly unable to put the telephone down before his beloved.

"We'll belong to each other soon, then," said Christopher. "Goodbye, my sweet Jamie. I love you, more than ever. I'm yours now, you realise that, don't you?"

"Oh, Chris, of course I do. I love you."

"Good. And goodbye," Christopher said; and, sensing the difficulty Jamie was having at the other end, considerately solved the problem by putting the receiver down. Jamie shot upstairs and collected the planted book, slipped out of the house, looked cautiously round, and scudded back to the school with a heart too full for words.

***

That morning Dr Lane held a lengthy conversation with Angela Turnbull on the telephone, then sat for longer debating with himself how best to bring Jamie abreast of the latest and least creditable behaviour of his parents. In the afternoon he took a call from the telephone engineer's department which gave him further food for thought. In the evening he left school earlier than usual and cornered Jamie before he went to his room to do his prep. "Jamie, I want to talk to you," he said, quite gently, but watching the boy closely. Jamie, despite himself, looked guilty. Lane drew him into the living room and sat him down on the sofa beside him.

"There are several things that we must discuss," Lane opened gently. "First, though, I must ask you something, and I want a truthful answer. I know you are a truthful boy, but I know also that there are some things - one thing, at any rate - on which I can't absolutely trust you. Don't take that too hard," he added quickly, seeing Jamie's face crumple. "I understand how difficult life is for you at the moment. But

173

you must realise that if we are to help you - we who want nothing more than to be able to do so - we must have complete truthfulness between you and me. Now I must ask you: have you been seeing Christopher?" He bestowed his sternest headmasterly gaze on Jamie, who sat looking very small and wretched beside him.

He answered promptly, however. "No, sir. I haven't seen him for... for ages, sir."

"But you have spoken to him, haven't you, Jamie?" asked Lane, looking a little less sombre. Jamie thought rapidly, but quickly decided that lying was too risky an undertaking. He had become very fond of the Lanes, and already behaved towards them as if they were the parents he had never had. But he was also more than a little in awe of his headmaster. He was too frightened to lie to him; in addition he felt that the adult affairs in which he was embroiled were simply too complicated for him to fathom any more. He told the truth. "Yes, sir," he said unhappily. "He rang me up, and I've rung him once." He sat looking utterly defeated.

Lane's face softened in pity for the boy, who seemed at times so astonishingly adult for his years and yet at others looked so much like the boy he was. Lane thought for a while. "I won't ask you to give me details of this," he said at length. "I think perhaps that may remain private. But I must ask this of you, Jamie. In fact, I must command it. You must not do this again. Not once more. I pass over the fact that it was deceitful of you, my boy, because I can understand how you feel at present. But..." A steely note of command entered his voice, "I must have your word, to me, as your headmaster as well as, de facto, your guardian for the time being, that you will on no account whatever make any further contact with Christopher without my express permission - which, Jamie, I'm afraid I shall be unlikely to give. Very unlikely." Jamie lowered his head in misery.

Lane felt his heart throb at the dejection and shame in the boy's face. His voice softened a tone. "Jamie, look at me." Jamie did so. "You must promise me this, Jamie. There simply isn't any alternative. It will be found out, of that you

174

may be quite assured, and it will simply make a mountainous amount of trouble for everyone involved in this business. For you, for us, and certainly for Christopher. Did you think of that?" Jamie's drooping head and the tears dropping silently into his lap told Lane that he hadn't - or that, if he had, he had thrust the thought from him. He hardened his heart and went relentlessly on. "And, Jamie, you must believe me, if trouble of *that* kind accrues, it may well be impossible for you to stay here."

That brought Jamie's head up. He blinked up at Lane, aghast, and even though he was certain of the rightness of what he was doing Lane felt a sharp pang of self-dislike pass through him. He forced himself to retain the headmasterly bearing and went on, "So, for your own good, Jamie, and for that of your friend, if for nobody else's, you *must* refrain from *all* further contact with Christopher; and I must have your firm promise on that, with no exceptions allowed. Is that clear?" He sat, striving to keep his expression stern, and waited for his answer.

Jamie raised his head again and looked at him through his tears. "I... Yes, sir. I promise," he gulped.

Lane offered up a silent prayer of thanks, and at last allowed his face to soften to show his own feelings. He moved closer to the boy and put an arm gently round his shoulders. He could feel Jamie shaking, and held him tighter. "Jamie, my dear boy, Edith and I have... We have come to feel very fon..." He hesitated before the unaccustomed expression of emotion towards one of the hundreds of boys in his care, then looked down at Jamie's tear-stained face and dismissed his diffidence. "We have, I mean, come to love you, Jamie," he said softly, "as if you were our own.

"We have also," he went on more strongly, on more accustomed ground now, "formed a very profound respect for you. We truly have your own well-being at heart in this, Jamie. Perhaps you can't see it quite like that at this moment; but we want only what is best for you. But, please believe me, Jamie - I speak as your friend, not as your headmaster - you won't be serving your own or anyone else's interests by being deceitful, in something as grave as this. That's why I had to have your promise. Unless we can rely on you implicitly to behave sensibly and not to do anything foolish, we shall be grossly handicapped in all our efforts to help you." He fell silent, a little appalled by the suffering he saw in Jamie's face. He squeezed the boy's shoulders again, recoiling from the other things he had to discuss with him. "Would you like some tea?" he asked Jamie on an impulse. Jamie glanced up and nodded, unable for the moment to speak. Lane squeezed him again and went out to the kitchen in some relief.

When he returned with the tea he looked down kindly on Jamie and said gently, "There are other things that we must talk of, as well, Jamie. One of them is your mother." Jamie looked more steadily at him, blinking at him damply. "I'm afraid the news is not very good on that front, either," said Lane, steeling himself. Jamie looked enquiringly. "I'm afraid that she has gone away, for a while," said Lane, seeking to soften the impact and deciding that a little blurring of the truth was legitimate in a good cause.

"She's gone away for good, hasn't she?" said Jamie, with the faintest ghost of a smile. "You've no need to worry about that, sir. I had her worked out a long time ago. I know she doesn't care about me, and I know she wouldn't stay around to see this trouble through. She's not the kind," he said seriously, without any trace of emotion. He shrugged. "She never really cared where I was, what I did, or anything about me, sir. I thought she'd be off. She's been rowing with Angela - with Mrs Turnbull. I know. I could see that from Angela's face when she came to see me at the police station the other night. And when Mother didn't come to see me there at all, I knew I wouldn't see her again. Angela made excuses for her - she said she was too upset. But I knew it was just excuses. People have been making excuses for her since I was little. I don't care where she is, and I'd rather you didn't tell me, sir, if you know." He looked, with a trace of defiance, at Lane, and waited.

"Well, Jamie, since you take so adult a view, I don't see

any point in trying to deceive you," murmured Lane. "Especially having just lectured you on deceitfulness," he added wryly. "I won't pretend that my opinion differs very greatly from your own on this, and I'm thankful that you can take the news so well. However, there *is* a somewhat brighter side to this. You may not know it, but you have a friend, and a very staunch one, I think, in Mrs Turnbull..." Jamie gave him a damp smile. "Oh, I knew that, sir. She's always liked me. She used to tease mother about it. Said she'd kidnap me if Mother and... and Dad didn't..."

He trailed off, his lip quivering. Lane's throat contracted. Jamie sat for a while, drinking his tea and recovering his composure. "I know Angela will be on my side, sir," said Jamie eventually. "It's... it's nice to have a few friends..."

"Have some more tea," said Lane, feeling ineffectual. He went to make further supplies. When he came back he was surprised to see that the boy had pulled himself rapidly together. "I won't blub any more, sir," he said with an attempt at brightness. "I think I know who my friends are."

"Good boy," said Lane. "Now, I don't like to have to talk about painful things any more than can be helped, but I must tell you what the position is..."

"There is just one thing," said Jamie, and Lane stopped speaking immediately, seeing the urgency in his face. "Yes, my dear boy, what is it?"

"It's... it's a favour. Something I must ask you. I *must*, sir. I won't lie to you any more, sir. Never. But I couldn't lie to Christopher, either. You do see that,. don't you? I *couldn't*. Not lie to him, or do anything - deceitful - sir, could I?" Lane nodded, having a good idea of what was coming. He motioned the boy to continue. "You know we've been talking on the phone," said Jamie hesitantly. Lane nodded again. "That night, when you thought the phone here was out of order... well, sir, it wasn't... It... it was Christopher, trying to get in touch with me to give me his new number," said Jamie, mentally crossing his fingers. It's not exactly lying, he told himself, swallowing hard, it's just not telling him quite everything that's happened. Lane nodded a third time. "I'd already worked that out for myself, Jamie," he said, "but I'm pleased with you for telling me the truth about it unprompted. Now what is it that you want to ask?"

"Well, I've arranged to ring him once more, sir. I can't do that, now I've promised you, but, well... now that I *have* promised, may I just phone him this once? Please, sir, may I? Only to tell him that I can't do it again, and why. I promise I won't try to talk to him again until you say I can, sir. But I couldn't just leave him waiting and wondering why I hadn't... I *couldn't* do that. It would be too unkind. I couldn't bear to think of him wondering if I was ill, or in trouble..." He tailed off, watching Lane's face in mingled eagerness and apprehension. "Nobody would ever know," he pleaded anxiously.

Lane's expression grew stern again, but he said nothing for several minutes. Jamie watched him with his heart in his mouth. Eventually Lane's face cleared and he nodded briskly to himself, making up his mind. "When are you due to make this call?" he asked, "and where from?"

"Tomorrow, sir," blurted Jamie, his words tumbling over each other in his anxiety. "From here."

Lane nodded again. "Very well, Jamie. I can understand your feelings. I shall put you on your honour. You may speak to him just for a few minutes, to tell him that I have put you on trust not to try any such thing again until everything is resolved." Jamie's face lit up, but Lane had not finished. "However, Jamie, I can't permit you to do this entirely on your own. I think you will understand that, even if you don't like it especially much." Some of the light went out from the young face before him, replaced by a look curiously adult and speculative. "I shall be there myself, Jamie. In matters in which Christopher is concerned, you are not, I think, entirely your own master. I shall be beside you as you speak to him. Once you have conveyed the substance of what I have outlined, then I will leave you for a few moments, and no more - you understand that, Jamie? - I see that you do. Then, as I say, I will leave you for a few moments, so that you may make your farewells as best you can; and when I judge that you have had time enough to do so, then that will be that. You understand?"

"Yes, thank you sir," said Jamie. The light was still there: he looked rather like a puppy with a new and unfamiliarly-shaped bone. "Thank you *ever* so much, sir." The relief and happiness in his face, though modified, were so genuine that Lane's misgivings dissolved. "Now, then, Jamie, as I said, we must talk of other things."

***

Jamie fought against sleep until he heard the grandmother clock downstairs strike eleven. He slid out of bed and found his underpants and a tee shirt. He sat on his bed in the darkness, thinking of Christopher and stroking himself to counter his impatience, until the clock had chimed the first quarter and then the half-hour. Then, judging that it was safe, he flitted noiselessly downstairs, listened hard for a full minute more, and then lifted the telephone and dialled.

It was a long shot, with no possibility of second chances, but his luck was in. Christopher answered after only a couple of rings. "Chris," Jamie breathed, "it's me." He was speaking hardly loud enough to be audible, but he heard Christopher's sharp intake of breath at the other end, and knew that he had heard. "I can't say anything tomorrow. They've found out. It'll just be hello and goodbye. Ring you as soon as I get a chance. Wait for me. Love you." He listened anxiously. Christopher breathed his answer so faintly that Jamie had to strain to hear the words. "Okay. Love you. Bye." There was a click. Satisfied, Jamie replaced the receiver, taking infinite pains to make no sound. There was a loud ding, however, and he almost gasped. He sagged against the wall, listening in terror, but there was no sound. He gave it a full minute, then slipped silently, a half-naked shadow, back to his room.

***

Dr Lane left the sixth-form room when the bell rang for break the next morning and proceeded majestically to Jamie's classroom. He almost collided in the doorway with a boy bolting for the quadrangle to enjoy his maximum minutes of leisure. The boy skidded to a halt, saw who it was and wished he was somewhere else. "Oh! I... I'm terribly sorry, sir," he stammered, "I was..."

"This is a school corridor, Patterson," said Lane mildly, "not a bear garden. Look where you're going, and try to behave with a certain amount of decorum, if that's not asking too much."

"Yes, sir. No, sir. That is, yes, sir," said the boy. Looking fearfully up at the headmaster and seeing that he was dismissed, he edged round Lane and walked off down the corridor almost on tip-toe, hardly breathing until he was out of sight. Lane walked into the room. "Oh! Headmaster!" ejaculated the young master in charge, halting in the middle of packing up his books. "Form! Attention!" he rapped. Everyone stopped what they were doing in mid-movement. Books were suspended above desks into which they had been about to be pitched. Sweets and strips of prohibited chewing gum were dropped hastily back into blazer pockets, or even more hastily swallowed. There was a gurgle, instantly suppressed, from some unfortunate whose boiled sweet had gone down the wrong way. Lane's face relaxed into a slightly forbidding smile at that. The atmosphere eased, only a little, but perceptibly. "Can I help you, headmaster?" asked the master, a little nervously, wondering what had brought the majestic presence to his room.

"Carry on, Mr Surtees, carry on," Lane said, motioning the master to continue gathering his papers. "The form may dismiss." The master, almost as glad to be dismissed as the boy Patterson had been, watched from under his eyebrows as Lane glanced round the room until his eye fell on Jamie, who was disposing his books in his desk at the back of the room, his eyes, like everyone else's, remaining watchfully on the headmaster. Lane crooked his finger to Jamie, who lowered the lid of his desk and came to the front. "Come with me," said Lane quietly, and with a further courteous gesture to the master he swept from the room, his gown billowing behind him in the doorway. Jamie trotted after him, leaving the boys in a subdued hubbub of speculation. The master, aware that Jamie was the headmaster's ward, took it that it must be a private matter and breathed a little more easily, glad that the visit did not at any rate betoken any sins of omission or commission on the part of his form.

Pacing sedately across the field to the house, Lane observed the spring in the boy's step. At the front door he fished for his key. Jamie, hopping from foot to foot in his efforts to contain his eagerness, looked up at him. Lane, despite himself, smiled somewhat crustily at him, and received a smile in return which almost melted him. He let Jamie in and the boy half-ran to the telephone and dialled.

"Hello. Chris. Yes, it's me," said Jamie, and Lane perceived that the awkwardness that his presence had occasioned Jamie could not wholly dampen the boy's delight in speaking to Christopher. It was visible in his face, half-turned away from Lane, and a good deal more audible in his voice. Half-way through the first sentence, Lane saw clearly, the boy had almost forgotten his existence. For some minutes Jamie indulged in small talk, occasionally suppressing some endearment half-uttered. Once he half-turned, as if to remind Lane that he was eavesdropping on a very intimate conversation. Lane took the point, and retreated through the front door and out into the drive until he was out of earshot. Jamie saw the move and appreciated it. Craning his neck to see exactly how far distant Lane was, he hissed urgently, "I'll ring you as soon as I can, Chris, darling. Can we still see each other like you said?"

"For Christ's sake, be careful, Jamie," said Christopher urgently. "Yes, I'm working on it. Ring me early next week, if you can. Okay?"

"Okay," hissed Jamie. "I must go, Chris, he'll want to take me back to school now. Tell me you love me, please tell me."

"Of course I love you," said Christopher, suddenly becoming placid. "We'll be together soon, you and I. I won't keep you now, though. Goodbye for now. Love you."

"Bye, Chris, my dear. Love you," Jamie just had time to blurt out, and there was the fateful click on the line as Christopher replaced his receiver. Jamie leaned on the wall beside the telephone table and savoured the beloved voice and the final words for a while. Then he made his way out into the drive and smiled shyly up at Dr Lane. "Finished, sir," he said in a subdued tone. With Lane not altogether happy about having aided and abetted the boys in breaching the conditions of Christopher's bail, and Jamie cast down by the reflection that he would only be able to speak to his lover with the greatest difficulty for the foreseeable future, it was a subdued and somewhat dejected pair who returned to the school in time for third period.

***

Over the next two weeks Lane adopted a deliberate policy of keeping Jamie heavily overworked at school, on the legitimate grounds that he had missed so much of the syllabus in his frequent absences earlier in the term that he needed badly to catch up. His real intention was to keep Jamie so fully occupied that he had neither the time to fret over his enforced separation from his friend nor any opportunity to try to make contact with him. In both he was largely successful. Jamie did manage to hold three brief, furtive conversations on the telephone, but they were miserable affairs, characterised by fearful glances over his shoulder, and neither of the boys was able to derive much joy from them.

In the last Christopher began to tell Jamie that he had

worked out his plan for their meeting, but Jamie cut him off almost before he had begun. "I can't come, dear Chris," he said miserably. "They watch me all the time, and if I asked for permission to go anywhere they'd smell a rat straight-away. And they're loading me up with so much extra work I hardly have time to watch the telly or anything." He chattered miserably on about his tribulations for a few minutes more, until the whole conversation became so dismal that they were both rather relieved when Jamie spotted the Lanes returning from their trip into town and had to make a hasty farewell. He hung up and bolted to his room safely before they got in. That night two equally depressed and lonely boys masturbated themselves to sleep, a hundred and fifty miles apart. After that only their frequent letters gave them any solace.

Then, taking them both by surprise, Christopher was called home with the news that the Crown Court sitting was to begin, with his case called for the first day. They had both by now reached the point of suspense in which even knowing the worst would be something of a relief, they would at least have slightly better opportunities for occasional secret meetings. In a way they were both almost relieved.

***

"May I go, sir?" pleaded Jamie, the day before the hearing. "I couldn't bear to have him in the court all alone, without me there to... well, sir, at least I could *smile* at him, so he'd know he wasn't all alone, that he hadn't been deserted. *Please* let me go." His voice had taken on a tone it often took lately, brittle, cracking with tension, and very un-boyish.

Lane thought it over during the morning. At lunch time he went home. "What do you think, dear?" he asked his wife. She pondered the question for some minutes. "Mmmm," she said slowly. "I'd be inclined to allow him to go, on two conditions. First, I certainly don't think you should allow him to go alone. He's not altogether rational where Christopher's concerned, and there's no telling what he might do if there was no one to keep an eye on him. The second condition is that the other boy's family have no objections. I really don't think he ought to go if it's going to cause them a lot of additional distress. They must be suffering torments as it is, poor people."

"I think that's very wise," he said, appreciatively. "Perhaps I'd better telephone them."

"I think it might be a better idea to telephone the boy's lawyer, dear. Jamie knows who it is - he visited him, if you recall, to make that statement in support of the poor boy." Lane nodded, and returned to school feeling a lot happier. In his study he summoned Jamie, who came hot-foot, all the accumulated tension and anxiety of the past weeks written all over him. When Lane merely asked him for the name of Christopher's solicitor his face sagged in disappointment. "Cheer up, Jamie," said Lane, "I'll give you my decision very shortly. You may wait outside if you wish. Go and sit in the secretary's office. She'll make you a cup of coffee." Jamie went out, and proceeded to irritate the headmaster's secretary immensely by fidgeting constantly in her office while she tried to type the day's correspondence.

"Mr Hope-Thomson? Ah, good morning. My name is Lane. I understand that you are representing a young man, Christopher Rowe, who is appearing in court tomorrow morning. Yes, I am indeed connected with the case, in an oblique fashion. Perhaps I may explain my problem..."

The buzzer on the intercom sounded quietly in the secretary's office, but it might have been an explosion, from its effect on Jamie, who shot out of his seat as if he had been galvanised. He stood, trembling slightly, watching the woman hawkishly as she depressed the switch. "Will you send the boy in to me now, please," came Lane's voice, rasping metallically in the machine. Jamie was on his way before she had flicked the switch back. He almost ran back into Lane's study, remembering just in time to tap on the door before entering. He scrutinised Lane's face anxiously, but found no clues there. Lane motioned him to sit down.

"I'm afraid..." he began. Jamie's heart sank, and his face crumpled in anguish. "Don't jump to conclusions, my boy," said Lane, touched by the grief he saw sketching itself across his countenance. "All I was going to say was that I'm afraid I can't give you a definite answer for a little while. I've spoken to Mr Hope-Thomson, and he shares my uncertainty. We feel that the only proper course is to speak to the family and ask them if they have any objection to your presence in court. If they have, that ends the matter - I'm sure you will see that their wishes should be paramount..."

"But, sir," the boy burst out, "that's not fair. It's all because of me that Christopher's in trouble in the first place. Surely..."

"That, Jamie, is precisely the point. Personally I cannot agree with you - I don't think it was entirely your fault, I think Christopher himself is at least as much to blame for his present difficulties as you, probably more so. But that is by the way. What is important is that his family have tended to regard you as the - ah - as the villain of the piece, and they don't feel very well-disposed towards you. I imagine you can understand that."

"Yes, sir," mumbled Jamie. "But what I was going to say is that surely it's Christopher who should decide whether *he* wants me to be there. He's the one who's in trouble, sir, isn't he?"

"It would greatly advance our cause, Jamie," Lane rebuked him mildly, "if you would not keep anticipating me." Jamie muttered an apology and hung his head.

"That was the point that I was coming to," said Lane, a little sharply. "And Mr Hope-Thomson has very kindly said that he will himself find out precisely that information for me. He is speaking to the family, probably at this minute. He tells me that he will make a point of asking them to ascertain Christopher's wishes in the matter, and he will, he says, urge them to treat his wishes as paramount." He paused to let that sink in, then went on, "You've made a friend in Mr Hope-Thomson, Jamie. You seem to have made a very favourable impression there." Jamie's face had brightened as quickly as it had fallen. He waited expectantly for Lane's next words.

"It means another wait for you, Jamie, but Mr Hope-Thomson suggested that he would probably be able to ring me back within a short while. However, since there is no guarantee that he will be able to make contact with the family immediately, you had better return to your..." The telephone rang. Jamie jumped out of his skin, and even Lane started slightly, infected by the almost palpable tension coming off the boy like smoke. He gave himself a moment, then lifted the receiver. "Dr Lane," he said into it. Jamie twisted his fingers in his lap and strained his ears vainly in an effort to hear what was said at the other end. He listened in a torment of apprehension to the end of the conversation that he could hear.

"Yes... yes... I see... quite so... yes.. yes... I understand... yes... yes, I have him with me at this moment... yes... I'll tell him... and thank *you* Mr Hope-Thomson. I'm exceedingly grateful to you, you have been most kind. It's very good of you to take so much trouble. Yes... quite. Thank you again. Goodbye." He replaced the receiver and sat for a moment looking levelly at Jamie, who sat on the edge of his chair, eyes wide with agonised anticipation. Lane's face softened into something very close to a smile.

"Well, Jamie," he said gently, "your instincts were correct. Hope-Thomson was able to speak to Christopher's father immmediately. He was at home, discussing matters with his son, so they were able to consult him there and then. Christopher wishes you to be there, as I dare say you could have predicted," he added with a trace of irony, which was wholly lost on Jamie, who was almost bouncing up and down on the edge of his chair.

"There is one strict proviso," continued Lane, stilling Jamie with a gesture. Jamie immediately froze, listening intently. "Mr Hope-Thomson has already been doing his best to dispel

186

the family's understandable hostility towards yourself - with some success, it would seem. He also recommended that they should encourage Christopher to talk more about you to them, and that he has apparently done. The result is that much of their initial feeling tow⁻ :ds you has been modified. On the other hand, you arᴄ still, I think equally understandably, not popular in that quarter. They have agreed to Christopher's urgent entreaties that you be allowed to be in court. But this is on the strict understanding that you remain unobtrusively in the public gallery, that you are accompanied, and that you remain silent, and make no attempt to approach either Christopher or any of the family at any stage whatsoever.

"I have decided that I myself shall accompany you to the hearing..."

"Oh, good," said Jamie spontaneously. Lane gave a slight smile of gratification. "Thank you very much, sir. It's very kind of you."

"As I said, I shall come with you, and I shall be responsible for ensuring that you adhere to the family's requests implicitly. You must not - you *must* not, Jamie - do anything to make things even more difficult and unpleasant for them than they are already. That is clear?" Jamie nodded soberly. "Yes, sir."

Lane looked keenly at him, but saw nothing in his face but a sober, earnest gravity. His evident happiness at being allowed to attend the hearing was now betrayed only by a faint upward curve of the corners of his mouth. "Very well, then, Jamie," said Lane with a faint sigh. "We'll leave after assembly tomorrow morning." He stood up and came round the desk. Jamie rose also and prepared to leave the study. Lane walked with him to the door.

As Jamie put his hand on the knob, Lane rested a hand on his shoulder. "I know how unpleasant this has all been for you, my boy," he said. "Try to keep your chin up. Mr Hope-Thomson said that it is in the last degree improbable that Christopher will suffer any terribly serious punishment, and he said most urgently that emotional demonstrations

187

from you in the court would be most unhelpful - such a thing would, indeed, be the worst thing that could possibly happen. So bear up, my boy, and remember it's nearly over now." Very briefly he ruffled Jamie's hair. "Now go back to your form-room," he said, becoming a headmaster once more. Jamie looked up at him and gave him a quick, shy little smile and was gone.

Lane sighed again, glanced at his watch, and walked across to the wall-cupboard where he kept his visitor's bottle of whisky.

FOUR

The next morning Lane, with a scrubbed and immaculately blazered Jamie at his side, crossed the foyer of the Court house to where a fat, middle-aged police constable was pinning some papers to a large green baize covered notice board. "Excuse me, officer," he said courteously. The man half-turned and mumbled something unintelligible through a hedge of long pins with bright plastic heads stuck in his mouth. Jamie giggled, despite the sombreness of his feelings, and even Lane's face twitched. The officer finished his operations with the papers and disgorged the remaining pins into his hand. He glanced down at Jamie and grinned at him. "What can I do for you?" he asked.

"Could you direct me to the public area of the Court, please?" asked Lane.

"Straight through there," said the man, gesturing towards a heavy, leather-padded door across the foyer. "Public seats are just inside the door, on the left as you go in."

"Thank you," said Lane. "I wonder if you may also be able to give me some indication of when the case in which we are interested may be expected to come on."

"Try, sir," said the man. "What case is it?"

"The boy's name is Christopher Rowe," said Lane quietly. The officer turned back to the sheets he had been pinning up. "Rowe," he muttered to himself. "Yeah, here it is." His eyebrows rose. "Ah. The buggery. Don't get many of *them* round here." He swung round and surveyed the two of them with narrowed eyes. "This the victim, by any chance?" he asked, looking very sharply at Jamie. "You realise it's a guilty plea, don't you?" He stared at Lane, with a degree of chill, almost hostility, entering his voice and his face.

Lane replied, equally quietly, "Yes, he is the other boy involved in the case. Why do you ask?"

"Well, since it's a plea, there won't be any requirement for anyone to give evidence. I shouldn't have thought it would be necessary to drag the kid along..." He fell silent, continuing to subject Lane to the same severe scrutiny. After a moment, a little impressed by Lane's unruffled demeanour, he added, "I suppose it's no concern of mine, but I'm a little surprised, if you don't mind my saying so. You his father?"

Lane studied the man for a few seconds. "I am his headmaster, and also his guardian," he said coolly. "And I understand your taking the attitude you do, but you are not fully *au fait* with the case, I suspect. The boy is here at his own request - I might say, his own demand. I am here to look after him and, if possible, to ensure that he does not allow the proceedings to distress him unavoidably." He returned the constable's gaze and waited. The man gave him a further appraising stare, then shrugged. "Well, sir, I hope you know what you're doing."

"Perfectly well, thank you, officer," said Lane icily. "Now, perhaps you can give me some idea of when the case is likely to be heard?"

The man shrugged slightly once again, and said, "You're second in the guilty pleas list." He consulted the notice for a minute. "Hmm," he murmured to himself, "yes, that shouldn't take long." He turned back to Lane. "The one in front of you won't take all that long. It's old Pennington today - that's the judge. He doesn't hang about if he can help it. Give it, maybe say, half an hour. Yeah, I'd say about ten-thirty. You'll be on then or soon after."

"Thank you," said Lane, and he took Jamie by the shoulder

and led him to the door the man had indicated. The door swung soundlessly back, and the constable watched them curiously as they went into the courtroom. Inside Lane steered Jamie towards the rearmost bench and directed him to sit down at the end, right beside the door. Both of them looked around curiously, each a little surprised at how small and unmajestically fitted the room was.

At the far end was a raised platform running the width of the room, panelled in front in some light, honey-coloured wood. Above it they could see the high backs of three chairs of antique design in anomalous dark wood, and above the central and most ornately carved of these was a relief of the royal arms. This and a scarlet curtain round some alcove at one end of the wall behind the chairs were almost the only splashes of colour relieving the pine-wood monotony.

Around the remaining parts of the room were various booths and boxes of different shapes and sizes. In one of them a nondescript-looking man in early middle age, wearing a dark suit and a blue-striped shirt with a plain white collar, was sorting a mass of papers. A yellowing, moth-eaten looking wig was hung askew on the corner of the box he sat in. He took no notice of them. "A barrister," murmured Lane to Jamie, seeing him looking at the man with interest. He glanced at his watch. "Jamie," he said in a low voice, "we're very early. Would you like to go and have a coffee?"

Jamie had never been in a court before - nor, for that matter, had Lane - and his interest in the surroundings had enabled him to forget for a moment that he was feeling sick and trembly with apprehension. Lane's enquiry reminded him of the fact. "N-no, thank you, sir," he muttered, looking greenish. Lane stared hard at him. "Are you sure you want to go on with this, Jamie, my boy?" he asked, feeling slightly infected by Jamie's tension himself. "If you're not feeling well..."

Jamie shook his head, gulped and swallowed hard. "I... I'll be all right, sir. Honestly. I don't feel too good, but I've got to stay. I've *got* to," he repeated, fiercely. "I couldn't let Chris think I'd deserted." Lane looked hard at him once more, but saw the determination in his face, and nodded. "Of course," he said simply.

He left Jamie to recover for a few minutes, then, in an attempt to take his mind off his feelings, began pointing to the various boxes, guessing from their size what their functions might be. "You know, Jamie, I'd never thought of this before, but we ought to give some elementary instruction in English law at school. Here am I, a headmaster of nearly twenty years' standing, and I'm having to guess which box is which in a perfectly ordinary courtroom. Ignorance of the law is no defence, Jamie, yet how many of our boys - or any other schoolboys, for that matter, possess the most elementary knowledge of their own country's legal system? Hardly one in a thousand, I'd suspect. I must look into that." He pulled a small diary from his inside pocket and made a note. Jamie looked a little better, and Lane, encouraged, talked to him until a few people began to come in and occupy various positions round the room.

By a few minutes to ten the room was fairly full. The man with the papers had transferred his scruffy wig from the corner post of the box to the back of his head, where it sat crookedly, looking scruffier than ever above his neat clothes. He had also put on an equally scruffy black gown. Jamie thought he looked terrifying. There were other barristers in the same part of the room. Some of them looked hardly older than Christopher, he thought, and immediately began to feel sick with fear once more. He swallowed several times, set his teeth and took a determined interest in the other people, all of whom seemed to be men in dark suits. His own royal blue blazer was the only bit of variety in the room.

At ten o'clock the red curtain was suddenly swept aside and yet another dark-suited man stepped through it. "Court rise," he called in an incongruously loud bellow, making Jamie jump. He held the curtain back deferentially, and the judge stepped through. He was a small, slender man of about Dr Lane's age, with sharp features, not unkindly looking, and horn-rimmed glasses, but Jamie hardly saw his face at all in his first sight of the scarlet robe with its ermine trim and black sash. His wig was even dirtier than that of the middle-aged barrister. The barrister, Jamie thought, glancing back and forth between him and the judge, was the merest beginner in looking terrifying. Jamie trembled at the thought of Christopher having to face so fearsome a vision.

The first case was called. Jamie found it very difficult to follow. Someone called something loudly, and several more people filed into the room. Various people uttered unintelligible jargon, mostly addressing the judge. "Charge of burglary, my lord," said someone, and a slim, ordinary-looking man of about twenty-five was brought in between two prison officers. He was steered into another box, facing the judge. Jamie goggled at him. He had never thought consciously what a burglar looked like. Seeing one for the first time he felt a twinge of disappointment that he looked so utterly indistinguishable from any other young man.

The case was over in twenty minutes. Jamie had understood almost nothing of what had taken place, and Dr Lane, who had been watching with a fascination little less than Jamie's own, had gathered very little more. Everything seemed to happen extremely quickly, and few of the voices could be heard clearly at the back of the room. In the end everyone was silent and the judge spoke for almost the first time. Jamie was a little surprised to hear that, though he was perhaps better-spoken than the average person, he had an ordinary, human voice. His voice *could* be heard at the back. He asked the young man if he had anything to say, and a lawyer spoke briefly and, apparently, from the little they could hear, intensely to the judge. The judge heard him without any apparent emotion, and he sat down.

"John Mason, you have pleaded guilty to three counts of burglary with intent to steal. I don't intend to waste much time on you. You are a feckless, reckless young man and you clearly have no scruple about following a path of crime whatsoever. You are a professional criminal - not a very successful one, to judge by your record, which for a man of your age is appalling - but a professional never the less. As such I take it that you regard a prison sentence as just another occupational hazard. It has been urged in your behalf that you never resort to violence, and that you never carry any kind of weapon. Well, I take that into account. If you did so, no doubt the charges against you would have been of aggravated burglary, and the sentence of this court would have been a lot heavier. As it is, you will go to prison for five years." The judge made a small motion with his hand, and the prison officers escorted the young man out of the room. Jamie shut his eyes, feeling sick with fear.

A door swung, and Jamie opened his eyes in time to see Christopher enter through the door by which the burglar had left, with Hope-Thomson beside him. His face, normally pale, was a greenish, fish-belly white, and there were deep black circles under his eyes. Jamie's heart throbbed, and his stomach heaved violently. He fought all his feelings down, and was glad he had done so, for Christopher's eyes, darting round the room, lit on him, and for a fraction of a second a little brightness flashed across his face. He was directed into the dock and stood there, even more youthful than its late occupant. Jamie could clearly see that he was trembling all over. There was more mumbling from dark-suited men. Then, to Jamie's dismay, the barrister with the yellow wig stood up and began to speak. Apart from the judge, he was the first person whose voice had carried clearly to the back. Lane looked sharply down at Jamie, and kept a close eye on the boy as the barrister addressed the judge.

Speaking in a rather sneering, high-pitched voice, he described the details of the meetings between Christopher and Jamie, at first in general terms, and then dwelling on "the beginnings of intimacy, at first, it is believed, M'lud, of a purely affectionate nature. It soon developed, however, M'lud, into something far more than affectionate, and far less than pure. It is not certain, M'lud, when precisely this - ah - this affair took on an overtly sexual aspect, but certain it is that it did so, and very quickly. There is no doubt that it did so at the instigation of the prisoner. The fault, in other words, M'lud, was entirely his. The other boy was the blameless dupe and victim of an older and more sophisticated man."

Jamie began, unconsciously, to rise from the bench, and his mouth opened. "I…" he began to say, but Lane, who had been watching him very closely, was ready for just such a thing. He threw his arm round Jamie's shoulders, forcing him back into his seat and at the same instant clamping his hand over Jamie's mouth. Jamie's eyes swivelled up towards him, and Lane felt a wave of great pity. The boy looked like a terrified animal. He squirmed briefly in Lane's vice-like hold, then subsided.

Lane glanced rapidly round the room, and was vastly relieved to see that no one seemed to have noticed. He thought he had acted so fast that Jamie's anguished squeak of protest had been strangled before anyone could hear, and breathed silent thanks. Hardening his heart, he glared ferociously at Jamie and mouthed "Silence" at him. Some of the fear ebbed out of the boy's eyes, and he nodded his head. Lane released him and bent to whisper urgently in his ear. Jamie, white-faced, looked guiltily up at him and nodded once more. They turned their attention back to the barrister, who was still recounting the details, as far as they were known, of the sexual encounters between the boys.

"…at least two occasions when full sexual intercourse, *per anum*, M'lud, took place. Those are also admitted in Rowe's statement to the police, and they are the substance of the charges of buggery to which he has pleaded guilty." He paused and looked down at his bundle of papers, rifled through them and turned to a general description of Christopher's character, home life and biography. After fifteen minutes of continuous speech he sat down. The judge looked neutrally round the room. He looked at Christopher with no more expression that he gave anyone else, but Lane had a faint and uneasy impression that his gaze did rest on himself and Jamie for rather longer than it rested anywhere else. All he said, however, was, "Yes. Thank you, Mr Raeburn. Yes, Mr Compton?"

At this another barrister rose to his feet. Jamie saw that he was much younger than the other man, with a much whiter, neater wig and gown. Jamie's heart sank. It rose, however, when the young man started to speak. He spoke quite clearly, and to Jamie's incomprehension did not appear at all nervous.

"My lord," he said, "my client has pleaded guilty to the charges, as he was quite properly advised to do. His statement to the local police was made entirely voluntarily, and we accept it without question. Indeed, My lord, I'm told that he made a favourable impression on the police officer in charge of the case, Detective Sergeant Bly. He gave every impression of being positively anxious to be helpful to the police." He paused, but the judge only murmured, "Go on, Mr Compton."

"If your lordship pleases," said Compton suavely. Jamie decided he trusted him. "My lord, the impression that my client made particularly vividly on Detective Sergeant Bly was that he was most anxious that he do nothing whatever to the detriment of the other boy in the case, James Potten." The judge looked sharply up, raising his eyebrows. "You say he wished to do nothing to the other boy's detriment, Mr Compton. Hadn't he already done that, and done a great deal? Isn't that what he's pleaded guilty to?" Jamie's spirits plummeted so far down that a swathe of blackness passed in front of his eyes. A moment later they rose with equal rapidity as the young barrister dealt with the judge's interjection.

"With respect, my lord, there is a great deal more to it than that. My learned friend has stated, with the total certainty that rightly belongs only to the realm of fact, that my client was the prime mover in all that occurred between him and the boy Potten. He has stated, quite categorically, that my client was entirely responsible for the affair between the two boys, entirely responsible for initiating the sexual dimension of the affair. I emphasise, my lord, my learned friend has stated all that as if it were fact."

"I heard him say so quite well myself, Mr Compton," said the judge drily, and Jamie's heart sank once more, only to rise yet again with Compton's next words.

"If your lordship pleases. But, my lord, my learned friend

was wrong to say so. That, with respect, is the point." He stopped speaking and rummaged for a long moment among a bundle of papers beside him. The judge watched him, with, Jamie thought in a further bout of despair, gathering irritation on his face. Just as the tension was becoming unbearable to him, Compton straightened, and held aloft a sheaf of paper. Jamie's heart did a small somersault as he saw that the top sheet was covered with his own distinctive handwriting. He swallowed desperately, trying to force down the large lump that had formed in his throat and was threatening to choke him.

"This, my lord," said Compton easily, "is a statement. Or rather, to be more precise, my lord, it is an affidavit, made and signed before a solicitor." He paused once more, then, just as the judge's mouth was opening, he continued. "It is the affidavit, my lord, of James Kieran Potten." There was a hiss of breath from somewhere in the court, he could not say precisely where.

"It is dated the twentieth of last month, my lord. It is in James Potten's own hand, and it is signed by him. With your consent, my lord, I wish to read it in its entirety to the court." The judge looked at him speculatively. Even from the back of the room Jamie and Lane could see that there was a look of interest on his face that had been absent before. Jamie looked towards the dock; and a few moments later, as if by some telepathy, Christopher looked round at him and gave him a valiant effort at a smile. It almost melted Jamie's heart. Dr Lane also, in that moment, forgot the nagging core of resentment towards Christopher and felt a wave of pity wash over him.

"Very well, Mr Compton," the judge was saying. "Read the affidavit, if you please."

"Thank you, my lord," said Compton. He held the sheaf of sheets up before him and, in a clear, carrying voice, began to read.

"My name is James Kieran Potten, and I am fifteen years and eight months old. I am the son of David and Annabel Potten, of

197

Highwater Farm, Coopersfield Road, Oldacre, but because my parents are separated and getting divorced I am living with my headmaster and his wife, Dr and Mrs Lane, at the school house of Oldacre School, where I am a day pupil. They are very kind to me, treating me as if I were their own son, and I am very happy with them, much happier than I have been with my own parents for as long as I can remember.

I am making this statement in the presence of Mr Frank Hope-Thomson, solicitor. I have sworn an oath to tell the truth, and I am doing so voluntarily and willingly. I am of sound mind and memory.

I am homosexual. I discovered this entirely on my own, and have known it for several years. No one has ever tried to influence me in coming to this conclusion about myself. I fully understand what the word homosexual means, and what being homosexual myself involves. I have had occasional sexual relationships with other boys at school, but only with boys who were willing to share them. I have no interest in girls, and am attracted only to boys. None of my relationships with other boys has ever gone beyond masturbating with them, until the last few weeks.

At the time I write this I am the lover of a man, Christopher Rowe, of 9 Cross Oak Gardens, Oldacre, who has been charged with a criminal offence as a result of his affair with me. I have known him for about six months. We met by chance and became friends. When we first met I was very unhappy and lonely because of difficulties I was having with my parents, though these difficulties were nothing to do with my homosexuality, which my parents did not know about at the time. The difficulties were caused mainly by the fact that my parents' marriage was breaking up. They argued and fought constantly, and seemed to me to be coming to hate each other. They both seemed to have little time for me, and no affection for me. I felt that I was unloved, and often felt that in fact they disliked me as much as each other. I believe they both blamed me for being the cause of their breaking up, though I have since come to believe that this would have happened anyway, and that it cannot have been my fault.

I was unhappy at home and not very happy at school, where I found it very difficult to concentrate on work, because of the problems at home. I could not talk to anyone at school about it, though I now think I was wrong not to have gone to the headmaster, Dr Lane, who I am sure would have helped me. But since I did not realise this, I kept it bottled up, until I met Christopher Rowe.

From the first time we met I found I could talk to Christopher and tell him about my problems. He listened to what I said and understood how I felt. He was very sympathetic, and I found it a great comfort to have someone to listen.

One day about a month after we first met my parents had a particularly vicious fight. It started in the evening just after I had gone to bed. I could hear them screaming at each other for hours, and cried myself to sleep, which I did often. When I woke up the next morning it was still going on, or had started again, I do not know which. I was so upset by this that I could not face going to school, so I played truant and went to find Christopher. He did not have a job, as he was waiting to go to University in October of this year. He was upset to see me in the state I was in, and we walked for several hours in the country, while he listened to my troubles.

After walking for several miles we sat down in a spinney. I cried on Christopher's shoulder, and he put his arm round me. It seemed quite a natural thing to do, and I enjoyed it. This was the first time I felt strongly physically attracted to Christopher. Before I had felt this, but it was submerged by my main feeling towards him, which was emotional - I was deeply grateful to him for befriending me, and for just being a sympathetic friend who would let me talk to him without interrupting and try to give me advice about how to bear the troubles I had at home. But on the occasion I am describing I felt, for the first time, very strongly sexually attracted to him. I did nothing about it, because I was frightened that if I told him about it he might be disgusted or think I was sick. I thought that if he hated homosexual people like me he would never have anything more to do with me, and I could not bear the thought of losing my only friend. I never mentioned being aroused on this occasion, and as far as I know he never realised.

After that we began to meet more frequently - up till then we had met about once or twice a week, but after this time we met almost every evening, and I spent almost the whole of every weekend with him. He seemed to be very fond of me, and he never seemed to notice *that I was only fifteen, while he was nineteen.*

I was often very upset and distressed in those weeks, and Christopher sometimes put an arm round me to console me. But I also started putting mine round him, simply because I wanted to touch him. He never once touched me sexually, or mentioned it in words, though I wanted him to very much by this time. I decided to make my own feelings plain, and looked for a chance to do it in such a way that I could back away if he seemed to dislike it.

One Saturday we were out walking and got caught in a storm. We sheltered under some bushes in the woods off the Steeple Wynton road, and we had to huddle together to keep as dry as we could. I was sexually aroused, though I do not think Christopher realised it at the time. Later on the sun came out and it became very hot. I took off my shirt and trousers to hang them on the bushes to dry out, and Christopher saw that I was aroused then. I started to take his shirt off, but he stopped me. I thought at first that he was disgusted, but quickly saw that he was only frightened, though I do not know if it was from fear of being found or because he thought it would be wrong to undress with me.

I wanted him so badly that I decided to take the initiative, so I touched him sexually."

Compton lifted his eyes from the manuscript and commented "My lord, at this point the boy has inserted a caret mark and indicated a parenthesis on the back of this page of the statement. It reads, my lord, as follows:

"Mr Hope-Thomson has asked me to insert this after completing this statement. I broke off here and asked him if I had to say exactly what I did, and he told me that I had to. I would rather not have described it, because I feel it is very private. But he has told me that it is necessary if I am to help Christopher, so I am doing it willingly."

"That parenthesis is signed by the boy, my lord, and initialled by Mr Hope-Thomson." The judge, who had been following the statement attentively, nodded. "Go on, Mr Compton, please," he said.

"My lord, the next section of the statement is extremely

sexually explicit. It is couched in - er, medical English, I suppose would be the nearest description. At least, it is in distinctly non-erotic terms. One may suspect that possibly the learned solicitor may have had some influence on that, though the boy clearly has a vocabulary and articulacy far beyond that of the average boy of his age. Does your lordship wish me to read this explicit section aloud in court, or would you prefer to read it silently in your own copy, my lord?"

"I think we're adult enough not to be prudish about a small amount of sexually explicit material, Mr Compton," said the judge, looking a little nettled.

"With respect, I wasn't suggesting that your lordship was likely to be shocked," said Compton. "I was thinking more about the sensibilities of the boy who wrote the document. He has stated in the preceding paragraphs that he felt some offence at the notion of making public something that he clearly regards as exceptionally intimate. I wonder if we might perhaps decently spare his feelings, my lord. I understand that he is in court, my lord."

"Oh," said the judge. He lifted his eyes to Jamie and gave him a hard, concentrated scrutiny. Jamie coloured, and squirmed uneasily under his gaze. After a few seconds the judge looked back to the barrister. "Yes. I see. Very well, Mr Compton, we'll pass over the next section. Will you indicate where you wish to continue reading from, please?"

"Certainly, my lord. I'm very greatly obliged to your lordship. If you will read from page three of your copy, beginning of the second paragraph, to the end of the second paragraph of page five, my lord, I will continue from that point."

"Thank you," said the judge. There was a silence while he read the next section. "Very well, Mr Compton, please go on," he said after a minute or two, glancing up with distaste clearly written on his face.

"If your lordship pleases. The statement continues:

"Afterwards I asked Christopher if he had liked what we had done, and he said he had. He was blushing a lot, and seemed

201

uncomfortable, but I could see that he had enjoyed it as much as I had. Later on we carried on walking for several hours, and after a time he told me we should not have done what we had done. I said there was nothing wrong with it, but he said that I was too young to do it with him. I said I had done it with others, but he said it was different with people at school with me. I did not say any more at the time, because it seemed to be distressing him, but I knew I wanted to do it again, and that he was the only person I was willing to do it with. I knew I had fallen in love with him.

After that day we did the same thing again many times, in various places, though we never went further than we had that time. I asked Christopher if he still thought we should not do this, but he said that if I was quite sure I wanted to he had decided that I was right, and there was nothing wrong in it.

I was in love with him, and I still am. I felt that it was perfectly proper for people who love each other to do what we did, and I wanted very much to go further, and in the end we did. In August, when we had known each other for about five months, I asked him to make love to me properly, and…"

"My lord," said Compton, breaking off once more, "there follows a further detailed account of further sexual activity between the boys, this time describing the full acts of copulation that are the subject of the charges in the case. May I make the same suggestion as before, for similar reasons, my lord?"

"Yes, Mr Compton. I see where you've reached. How far do I go this time?"

"To the end of the first paragraph on the final page, if you would, please, my lord." The judge nodded and silence fell again. "All right, Mr Compton. Finish reading the remainder, please," he grunted.

"Very good, my lord. That concludes the history of the boys' relationship. The final paragraphs constitute a statement of the boy Potten's views. They read:

"All the above account is true, and I have described it willingly. In all the time I have known Christopher Rowe he has never once

done or said anything to force or persuade me to have any sexual contact with him whatsoever. I have made the first move every time anything has happened. The whole thing was at my instigation and without my forcing the issue I do not think we would have ever had sex at all.

I do not regret anything I have done with Christopher, because I love him, I know he loves me in return, and I think it is quite right for people who love each other to do everything we did. I did not know it was illegal to do what we did, and I do not believe Christopher knew either. If it is illegal I believe that the law is foolish and unjust. If we were not homosexuals it would not have been illegal, and I think it is grossly unfair that what is legal for others should be illegal for us, since we feel exactly the same things as they do."

"My lord," put in Compton, "the boy is of course wrong to say that these acts would have been legal for hetero-sexuals, since he is as yet still under sixteen..."

"I haven't forgotten quite *all* my law since my appointment to the bench, Mr Compton, though I'm aware that the bar think we take a course in forgetting as much as we can," interrupted the judge with a thin smile. "I can still, by a titanic effort of memory, *just* recall some of the provisions of the Act..." He let the sentence peter out. Compton bowed slightly. "Of course, my lord, I do apologise. Shall I continue?"

"Please do, Mr Compton."

"Thank you, my lord." Compton raised the statement once more. "My lord, he concludes as follows:

"This is a true account of all that has passed between us - the learned solicitor again there, I think, my lord - *and statement of how I feel about Christopher Rowe. I most earnestly beg that the court take what I have said here into account when it considers Christopher's case, and I hereby plead for clemency. If he receives a heavy sentence it will ruin not just his life and those of his family, but also mine."*

203

"My lord, that is the affidavit. It is dated a few days ago and signed James Kieran Potten. It is witnessed by a Mr Adrian Waller, who is employed by the learned solicitor as an articled clerk, and countersigned by the learned solicitor himself, Mr Frank Hope-Thomson.

"My lord, if I may be permitted to say so, I think this is a most material document. Apart from the cogency and articulacy with which it is written, I believe it exhibits a degree of self-awareness and a capacity for dispassionate self-analysis that is astounding in a boy of James Potten's tender years..."

"Really, Mr Compton, I don't like to interrupt you," said the judge gruffly, "but must we have cliches inflicted on us? 'Tender years' is a little more than I can stomach. You'll be talking about 'this day and age' next."

"I'm sorry, my lord, I'll try to avoid them," said Compton, looking very annoyed indeed. "However, I hope you won't hold my crass use of the language against my client.

"My lord, the younger boy in this case admits unequivocally that he was the initiator of every overt sexual act that ever took place between the two boys, and he pleads, most eloquently, I suggest, that in the context - in view, that is, of who they are - there was nothing morally reprehensible about what they got up to. My lord, I fully accept that the law must not be flouted, but I urge you most strongly to follow James Potten's plea in this matter and exercise the greatest degree of clemency possible in sentencing my client. I suggest to you, with the greatest respect, my lord, that there can never have been a case of this kind in which the mitigating circumstances were more clearly marked, more deserving of attention."

The judge made a discreet motion to Compton to pause, and shifted in his chair to flex the muscles of his back and shoulders, stiff from prolonged sitting bent forward to concentrate on the address. Compton stopped speaking and waited politely. "I should like to ask a question or two before you continue with your case, Mr Compton - including one or two which I wish to address to your client himself," the judge said at length. "Do you have any objection to that? I will, if you feel strongly about it, defer my questions until the end of your submission."

"No, I have no objections, my lord," said Compton. "Good," replied the judge. "Then, is the learned solicitor, Mr Hope-Thomson, in court?"

Hope-Thomson rose from his place in the well of the court and bowed slightly to the judge. "Here, my lord."

"Mr Hope-Thomson," said the judge, acknowledging the solicitor, "I'm inclined to agree with learned counsel, this boy's affidavit is a somewhat remarkable document, I wonder if you would object if I ask you a couple of questions."

"Not at all, my lord, of course," said Hope-Thomson.

"Very good. Please don't move. It will be perfectly acceptable for you to answer from the well," said the judge courteously. "Now, perhaps you will tell me, how much assistance did you give the boy in the writing of the statement we have just heard?"

"Very little, my lord," said Hope-Thomson promptly. "At the point where learned counsel indicated, I did, as he said, give a straightforward answer to a question. The boy had scruples about providing a clinical description of acts deeply personal, acts that seemed to him - as they would to anyone, of whatever sexual persuasion, I think - the very essence of privacy. They were also acts that flowed directly and essentially from the deepest of emotions, my lord. I advised him simply that it was unfortunate but that he would have to swallow his scruples and include this material. He accepted that advice at once and without protest."

"Was that all, Mr Hope-Thomson?"

"Not quite, my lord. On a couple of occasions he asked me to help him with minor matters of phrasing. Learned counsel correctly diagnosed one such instance, and there were one or two other points. I should imagine that your lordship will have spotted the odd place in the statement where he uses terms which would not be within the purview of the layman. At such points, it may be taken that I gave the boy a hint as to the best term to employ. Conversely," he added, "there

205

are places in the statement where the boy himself used legal or quasi-legal phrases, evidently imagining that they would be proper. In such cases I elected, on reflection, not to suggest to him that they should be deleted. I felt that the document should as far as possible be in his own words. But my entire contribution amounts to no more than a few superficial pieces of wording. The substance, and ninety-five per cent of the phrasing, is the boy's unaided work."

"Very well, Mr Hope-Thomson. One last question, if I may. Do you, personally, believe that everything the boy has included in that affidavit is the unvarnished truth?"

"Yes, my lord, I do," replied the solicitor simply, and at a nod of thanks from the judge he sat down.

The judge sat for half a minute in a profound silence, looking down at the papers in front of him in thought. Then;

"Christopher Rowe," he said quietly. Christopher took a deep breath and stood up in the dock.

"I shall ask you a few questions, Rowe. You have heard everything that has been said in your defence so far. Have you any comment to make about it yourself? To begin with, about the affidavit sworn by the boy James Potten?"

Christopher hesitated, then glanced over his shoulder at Jamie behind him. Jamie gave him a dazzling smile. The judge, who saw the smile, blinked. "I'm over here," he murmured. Christopher turned quickly back. "It's all true, my lord," he said in a low voice. "But only as far as it goes. He's trying to take it all on himself, and that's *not* true. It simply isn't true," he said, his voice rising. The judge raised his eyebrows, but Christopher rushed on, his words suddenly tumbling over each other. "He's trying to... to make out that he led me on and it was all his doing that we... I mean, well, it was both of us, sir. I mean, my lord. What I'm trying to say is that everything he said in that statement is true, but he isn't to blame, sir. He's trying to protect me, sir, and..."

The judge, seeing his confusion, waited for a moment, then intervened. "But the boy claims in the affidavit that you were reluctant to take part in these sexual antics, at least to begin with," he said. "Are you now saying that he's not telling the truth, that you *weren't* reluctant? Are you impugning his statement?"

Christopher thought for a moment. "I'm not allowing him to take all the responsibility, my lord. I'm only saying that everything he described in the statement is true. I take every bit of the responsibility. It's me that's standing here, and I wouldn't have it otherwise. I mean, I'd rather it was me here than Jamie. And we never did anything I didn't want to do, so I suppose that makes it my responsibility anyway."

"You seem to want it both ways," observed the judge, in a mild tone of voice. "You're telling me that the Potten boy's affidavit - in which he claims total responsibility - is the whole truth, and you're also telling me that *you* accept full responsibility yourself. Which is it?"

"Oh, my lord," repeated Christopher desperately, groping for a form of words to make himself clear, "I'm not doubting his statement at all. From the very first time we - er - did anything, it was always what I wanted. I'm only saying that although I *wanted* to do what we ended up doing, as much as he did, I was frightened..."

"Frightened?" said the judge. "What were you frightened of? Of being found out? Of the fact that you were committing an offence? Frightened of what?"

"None of those," snapped Christopher suddenly, surprising himself. "You're just putting words into my mouth. If you'll let me think I'll be able to say what I mean properly..."

As he forgot his fear and confusion in a healthy burst of frustration and anger he unconsciously straightened and squared his shoulders. Jamie felt his heart lighten for the first time since the judge had begun interrogating Christopher. Even Lane felt a faint impulse to cheer.

Christopher stood leaning on the front of the dock and tried to gather his thoughts, and the judge had enough consideration to leave him alone for a few moments. "*Frightened* was the wrong word, sir - my lord," said Christopher. "I wasn't frightened of being found out or anything. I never gave that a thought. Nor did he. We never thought about that sort of thing. What I meant was that I wasn't *sure*. He said in his statement that I was - I forget what he said, but he meant that I held back, and I did, but only because I wasn't sure he knew his own mind. I wasn't sure he was doing it because he really *wanted* to - because he... because he *loved* me."

He paused for breath, and the judge opened his mouth, but Christopher, his voice rising passionately, rushed on before he could speak. "As soon as I knew, as soon as I was *sure*, I stopped trying to stop him. I just had to know. I had to know he was grown-up enough to know what he was doing, and that it wasn't just a silly kid's crush, or just because he was lonely because of his situation at home. As soon as I *knew* I didn't try to stop him. I didn't even *want* to stop him. So when he says it was all his doing, he's just trying to save me. It *was* my responsibility, if it was anybody's. His too, of course, I'm not denying that, but mine too. I loved him, and I wanted him desperately. It's just that there was nothing - nothing *dirty* about it all, as everybody makes it sound. It was..."

He floundered for the word, and had a moment of inspiration. He became aware that the violent trembling which had afflicted him, threatening at times to take his legs from under him, had ceased altogether. His tongue unglued itself from the roof of his mouth, and he realised suddenly that he didn't care what they did to him any longer. If Jamie could go through *that* for me, he thought to himself, there's nothing I can't put up with for him. "It was *inevitable*, sir," he said, almost shouting the word. And then, as if all the stuffing had been drawn out of him in that one explosive word, he abruptly subsided.

The judge's dry voice dropped into the silence. "Tell me, Rowe. Do you feel any remorse for what you have been doing?"

"Remorse?" queried Christopher, taken by surprise as he strove to gather his forces after his outburst.

"Remorse," snapped the judge. "You're familiar with the

word, I suppose? Do you feel any kind of regret?"

"I feel a lot of regret that I've brought a lot of hatred and trouble down on my family," he said, trying to speak calmly. "I feel a lot of remorse for bringing suffering and anxiety down on Jamie's headmaster and his wife. I feel regret at costing my parents a lot of money, and all the hate mail, and the people cutting them dead in the street. And my brother Neil going through hell at school. And most of all making Jamie - putting Jamie in a position where he felt he had to bring all kinds of things that are completely private and belong only to him and me out into the open, to be read in a roomful of people like some sort of pornography. And, I'm not exactly *happy* to be standing here. It's not very pleasant from where I'm standing."

The judge looked at him irritably. "Are you deliberately misunderstanding me?" he snapped. "You know perfectly well what I mean. Do you feel for one second the slightest sorrow, regret, remorse or whatever you care to call it, for what you *did* with this wretched boy? For practising homosexual acts with him?"

"No," said Christopher in a tone of sudden, utter finality. There was a gasp from the public seats behind him. He looked round and saw his mother biting her hand and his father putting an arm round her shoulders and speaking softly into her ear. The judge looked at him, so surprised by his straight answer that he could think of nothing to say immediately. Christopher saw a chance and took it.

"I can't be expected to be sorry for something that did nothing but good to the only two people whose business it was, and no harm to anyone at all," he said. The words came out in a torrent. A hectic flush suffused his face and neck. "I'm very sorry to have brought all the trouble I spoke of just now on all those innocent people, and I'm very sorry that what Jamie and I did was against the law. That's why I pleaded guilty, because it's against the law. It's a wicked, senseless law, it's inhuman and cruel, but I can't do anything about that. I pleaded guilty..." he repeated, suddenly running out of steam again. He sagged against the dock, grabbing at the rail for support, and waited.

"Very well," said the judge, glancing up at him expressionlessly. "That's all for the moment. You may sit down." Christopher did so, in great relief. As he did so he was able to shoot a quick glance at Jamie, and was comforted by a smile, infinitely tender and full of concern. At the same time Dr Lane gave him a brief, almost imperceptible nod. Christopher caught it and interpreted it as signifying approval. It pleased and cheered him beyond words.

The judge made a note. "Thank you Mr Compton," he said as he finished. "I'm obliged to you for your indulgence. Please continue with your submission."

"If your lordship pleases. My lord, I respectfully submit that the affidavit sworn by my client's friend, James Potten, is a very powerful mitigating factor in this case. I now move on to other mitigating factors. I can deal with those more rapidly.

"I should like to urge strongly on your lordship first of all the fact that the climate in matters of sexual behaviour is considerably more enlightened than in previous times. We have advanced a long way since the days of Oscar Wilde..."

"Not everyone would necessarily claim that that represents an advance, Mr Compton," suggested the judge. Jamie's spirits took another downturn on their yoyo-like course.

"That's true enough, my lord," said Compton in his silkiest tone. "But there is a broad consensus of enlightened opinion that a liberal approach to matters of private morality is, generally, a good thing. It is thus recognised by all shades of medical opinion that homosexuality is neither a disease nor a perversion - at least," he qualified swiftly, seeing the judge preparing to interject, "not a wilful social perversion. It is believed by virtually all experts in the field of sexual psychology that a person's sexual orientation is determined during the first three or four years of life, and that once it is thus determined it is neither possible nor desirable to alter it. In other words, my lord, one's sexuality is not in any meaningful sense 'curable'.

"Many would go further, my lord, and suggest that since

homosexuality is a naturally occurring condition of a minority of people's lives, there is, in effect, nothing requiring a cure. My lord, this condition has now been recognised as a legitimate expression of a person's sexual impulses. The law has it that persons of this deviant sexuality may not gratify it until they reach an age five years greater than that permitted for the heterosexual majority, but..."

The judge interrupted. "Mr Compton, this is not new to me. The fact is that Parliament left the offence to which your client pleads guilty on the statute book. Why was that?"

"My lord, it is not for me to try to fathom the minds of the legislators, but one may hazard that when the law was relaxed it was still believed in some circles that 'cure' or reversal of sexuality was a possibility. I venture to suggest that perhaps Parliament felt at the time that people who grew up to find that they were of this orientation should not seek to fulfil it until a fair time had been granted to see if it was merely temporary. Since that notion is largely discredited..."

"Is it?" asked the judge. "It seems a perfectly proper notion to me."

"As I said, my lord," said Compton, looking cross and, for the first time, a little rattled, "it has been at a discount for some years among virtually all enlightened medical opinion..."

"Are you suggesting that I'm not enlightened?" asked the judge, appearing to be rather enjoying himself.

"With the greatest respect, my lord, I was talking about enlightened *medical* opinion, rather than judicial. I'm sure your lordship's personal credentials in the matter of enlightenment are impeccable." Jamie smothered a giggle, and even Christopher, whose head had dropped lower and lower in the dock over the last exchanges, looked up and managed a faint smile. The judge, by contrast, bestowed a steely glance on Compton, who was apparently engrossed in sorting through his papers. The judge let it pass, however, and Compton continued.

"My lord, in this case, one would surely find it very hard to believe that Potten was remotely likely to become a

211

paid-up heterosexual. I submit that no one reading the statement I read earlier could be in any real doubt that the boy has come to terms with something which he recognises as an integral and immutable part of his personality.

"In the light of that, my lord, I submit most earnestly that, whilst it is not in dispute that the offence has been committed, in present climate of opinion, coupled with the nature of the two participants, it is a technical offence only. In other words, it is a case of *malum prohibitum* rather than one of *malum in se*." He paused, glancing a little anxiously up at the judge, who, however, gave no sign of his thoughts.

"I should like to raise with you next, my lord, the nature of my client himself. Christopher Rowe is nineteen years old. He comes from an excellent family. His parents have been happily married for twenty-three years, and have one other child, a son now aged fourteen. It is a very stable family, all the members of which get on exceptionally well. In the present time, when the divorce rate and numerous other factors all indicate that the family is diminishing in its potency as a social unit, that is itself something that deserves mention. It suggests that my client, if allowed to re-enter his family with the minimum of anguish and the minimum of penalty and the associated stigma, will so much the more rapidly be able to take a full place as a valued member of society.

"My lord, my client's family have been utterly, and admirably, supportive of the boy throughout the terrible ordeal which the past few weeks have been, for all the family, not merely for my client..."

"Have his family suffered?" asked the judge, looking across the court at Christopher's parents, sitting, white, drawn and worried on the edge of the front bench.

"They have indeed, my lord. Since the boy was arrested and the case was reported in the newspapers, they have received a quantity of poison-pen letters of the vilest kind. They have had to have their telephone number changed and made ex-directory. My client's father has had on more than one occasion to paint out obscenities, abuse and threats daubed on the garden gate, the walls of his house, the pavement, the road outside and even on the windows of the office where he works. Both parents have suffered a certain amount of social ostracism in the town, though mercifully most of their acquaintance have been towers of strength to them. The younger son has, inevitably, had problems at his school, though there also, in the main, people have been kind rather than the opposite.

"Then there have been the attentions of the press, who have been the cause of much of the pressure they have been under. On one occasion the younger son was assaulted and jostled by a crowd of pressmen; although one may take a certain satisfaction in reporting that on that occasion he in fact retaliated against the man who assailed him to telling effect. Most of all, though, of course, my lord, the family have had to endure the appalling ordeal of waiting over several weeks worrying about the fate of their beloved son. As Christopher himself said under your lordship's questioning a few minutes ago, the majestic panoply of our profession - of this court, even, with the greatest respect, my lord, of yourself, look very different from his position. It has been, truly, a frightful ordeal for them all, my lord."

"Humph!" grunted the judge. "You tell me the press are to blame for all this, but doesn't everybody with any sort of grievance against anybody these days blame the press? It seems to me that it's your client who should be reproaching himself. If he'd behaved himself none of this would have occurred at all, would it, Mr Compton?"

"My lord, of course if my client had not committed his offence the rest would not have followed. But my client has not so much reproached as tortured himself with the deepest and most agonising remorse throughout the period since his arrest. And with respect, my lord, I cannot take the view that he is to be held responsible for the activities of the press, who published his full address, the place of work of his father, photographs of his parents and even his innocent fourteen-year-old brother and the name of his school. Nor in my respectful submission is my client to blame for the obscenities and other mindless activities of the mentally disordered elements in the local populace. If that view held good, my lord, well, again with the greatest respect, we should be enshrining the idea that any criminal's entire family could properly be held partially responsible for his crimes. I refuse to accept that, my lord." The judge grunted, but he left it at that.

"To continue, my lord, I repeat that my client is a boy with as stable and wholesome a background as any nineteen-year-old boy can possibly be blessed with in this country at this time. They will continue to love him and support him whatever happens. He is due to go to University very soon, in October, to read psychology..."

"Psychology!" ejaculated the judge. "He could have started by making a case study of his own, couldn't he?"

Compton's head shot up and his eyes flashed angrily. "My lord, I must protest at that remark. It was outra... it was most improper, if I may say so with respect."

"Mr Compton," snapped the judge, also angrily, "are you presuming to instruct me in what it is 'proper' for me to observe in my own Court? How dare you?"

"I meant no disrespect, my lord," snapped Compton back at him, his look belying his words. "But I am entitled to make a protest at what I consider to be a gross and unjustifiable slur on my client. Indeed, my lord, it wasn't a slur, it was the merest insult."

The judge stared at him. Then his expression cleared a little. "Very well, Mr Compton, I hear your protest. I myself protest at your own use of the word 'improper'. It's not the sort of word a young member of the bar should get into the habit of directing at judges, if he's wise." He looked witheringly at Compton.

"My lord, if I used an - er - improper word, I apologise. But I don't apologise for making my protest in protection of my client. It's what I'm here for," he said stubbornly. The judge looked hard at him for a long few seconds, then nodded to him. "Go on, Mr Compton."

"As I was saying, my lord," Compton went on, still visibly smouldering, "my client is to go to University very shortly. The University authorities have been acquainted with his present situation, and they have indicated their willingness to keep his place open for him, whatever the decision of the Court may be, stating that they see no reason why it should interfere with his academic career. He intends to seek a practise as a consulting psychologist when he graduates - and since he is a highly intelligent young man, who attained excellent results at school, there is every reason to hope that he may achieve considerable success in his career. I urge you once again, most earnestly, to consider this, and his potential value to society, in passing sentence, my lord."

Compton paused and took a long drink of water. "My lord, there are just two more points I wish to draw to your attention. First, in this case, there is one thing which is conspicuously absent. That is, my lord, any actual *harm* done to any third party. My lord, I mentioned the concept of *malum prohibitum*. This boy's offence was against the law, but it operated against no person's interest. Of course it would be possible to imagine a case in which such actions did operate to some person's detriment, such as where he used his superior age and sophistication to seduce a younger boy who was unwilling, or who was too immature to know his own mind or his own sexuality, into a homosexual liaison.

"*Heterosexual* people, indeed, are being convicted of such things all the time, though the homosexual minority have a notably better record over matters of pederasty than the heterosexual majority, pro rata to numbers. But my lord, I don't think anyone who heard the statement made by the younger boy in this case could suppose for a moment that such was the case here.

"I should go so far as to say that if either of the two boys involved in this affair is possessed of the stronger character, it is the younger one, James Potten. I regard it as inconceivable that anyone, let alone a gentle, compliant and easy-going character such as this lad, would stand an earthly chance of persuading James Potten to do *anything* against his

215

will, let alone something of the magnitude of embarking on a sexual affair." Jamie, flattered, beamed momentarily. Then he looked back to Christopher, sitting hunched in the dock with his head hung almost between his knees, and the smile vanished.

"My final point, my lord, is this. You have a range of sentences available to impose upon my client. But, as I'm quite certain your lordship must realise, there is no sentence that your lordship can pass which will begin to approach in severity the sentence that has already been passed on this boy - which was passed, in fact, before he entered this Court today, before he was committed by the learned magistrates, perhaps before he was even charged. That is, of course, the social consequences of being arrested and subjected to the processes of the law. This perhaps applies more to an offence of this kind than to most. "If many people are far more tolerant nowadays in sexual matters than hitherto, it cannot be gainsaid that homosexuality still provokes in many other people's minds loathing and hostility, and when it creates a relationship such as that between these two boys it inevitably generates a great deal of opprobrium. Of that opprobrium this boy, not yet out of his teens, has already begun to feel the lash; he will feel it with renewed force when he emerges from this court, my lord, when the case is reported. He will, most assuredly, continue to bow beneath that lash for a very long time to come. It is more than probably true to say that, where this town is concerned, my client has indeed already been given a life sentence. I repeat, my lord, that whatever sentence your lordship may see fit to impose, it will be insignificant in comparison with that sentence which he has already begun to serve.

"The plea of this boy then, my lord, this nineteen-year-old who appears before you needing mercy as well as justice, is simply that you hold that in mind. He seeks no special quarter except that which we owe to all young and - in the general sense of the word, of course - innocent people. He is perhaps naive. He has certainly been reckless, misguided and foolish. His views on certain matters which have been

216

adumbrated today may be right, they may be ahead of their time, or they may be perverse and wrong. But he is very young, and he is beginning a mighty and awesome penance. All that remains to me now, my lord, is to urge you once more, with all the force of reason, to look sympathetically on this young life, this intelligent and engaging boy's future value to his society, and to exercise your mercy by awarding the lightest sentence available. Thank you, my lord. That is my submission."

He sat down. Jamie glanced up at Dr Lane by his side with a plea of enquiry on his face. Lane looked kindly down on him, but he didn't smile. Jamie frowned in uncertainty. Lane patted him gently on the shoulder and bent to whisper in his ear. "Try not to expect too much, my boy," he said. "The judge is against him. We'll soon know," he added, as the judge intoned Christopher's name and Christopher rose shakily to his feet.

"Christopher Martin Rowe," said the judge. His face and voice were both quite expressionless. "You have pleaded guilty to a very grave charge. The court has heard your learned counsel offer a plea on your behalf which was eloquent, even passionate, and I trust that you were moved to a due sense of humility hearing it. I confess that I have yet to make up my mind as to the most appropriate sentence to pass on you. Since this case has consumed a very great deal more time than it might have been expected to take, I shall take time to consider how I may best deal with you. The court will therefore adjourn until two o'clock. I trust that you do not need reminding that the conditions of your bail still apply."

Without a further glance at Christopher he rose from his carved chair, shook out the skirts of his scarlet robe, and moved to the curtained exit. The voice bellowed "Court rise" in the same stentorian tones as before, the judge disappeared, and a buzz of voices broke out all over the room.

***

Christopher stepped, still shakily, out of the dock, and was walked quickly across to his parents by Hope-Thomson, who had come round from the well of the court. They perched on the bench beside the Rowes, where they were joined a moment or two later by Compton. The two lawyers conferred in low voices, and Jamie watched as the party left by a door at the far end of the room from where he sat. Christopher contrived to hang back, and as he slipped through the door after the others he glanced quickly back and sketched a white, frightened smile.

Jamie managed to smile back, but it cost him an effort. As soon as Christopher had disappeared from view he turned to Dr Lane. His face was flushed and his eyes were blazing. The whole of his small, compact body was shaking, and Lane thought for a moment that it was with fear or distress. Then, looking more closely, he saw that the boy was possessed with rage. He was so angry that for some time he was unable to speak. When he did speak it was all he could do to force the words out. "The... the old bastard!" he spluttered. Despite the low voice in which he uttered them, there was a concentration of venom in the words which Dr Lane found thoroughly upsetting to hear from the mouth of a boy.

"The old *bastard*!" Jamie said again. He was calmer, and the ferocity was the more frightening for being so quiet and controlled. "He - he did that deliberately," went on Jamie. "He only did it to make Chris suffer on tenterhooks for another hour and a half. Like when they used to hang people and let them down so they could breathe before hanging them again. He's *torturing* him. I'd hang *him*, if I could. I wish I could get to him, sir."

Lane watched him, not sure how to handle him while he was possessed by this passion. Jamie looked up at him, and a lot of the fury went out of his face. "I'm sorry, sir. I didn't mean to burst out like that. But, honestly, he is tormenting

218

Chris, isn't he? You can see it as well, can't you, sir?"

Lane wondered whether to prevaricate in the interests of keeping Jamie's temperature down, but immediately realised that it would be futile. Besides, he felt that there was much in what Jamie said, and that he therefore deserved an honest reply. "I don't think we can say for certain, Jamie," he said thoughtfully. "I'd very much like to feel confident in telling you that it's just prejudice brought about by your feelings for Christopher, but... but... well, I'm afraid I can't. I'm very much afraid you're right. If it is so, then I'm inclined to agree with you. It's quite extraordinarily cruel, to say the least of it." He sat in thought for a minute, while Jamie simmered at his side. "We had better go and have lunch," said Lane. "Are you hungry?"

"Not very, sir, but I expect I could manage something," Jamie said. "Will we go to a pub?"

Lane looked at him in surprise. "Certainly not," he said. "We'll find a restaurant, or a cafe at least. Pub indeed." He looked hard at Jamie as they left the court. "You're quite a lot older than your years in some ways, Jamie, but I hope you don't include pub-haunting among your repertoire of vices," he said. "I'll have something to say about that if you do, my boy."

"Not yet, sir," said Jamie. Lane looked down at him, wondering if it was one of Jamie's jokes, but the boy was walking along with his eyes downcast and seemed to be deep in depression. Lane's brow creased in thought.

***

While Lane and Jamie were looking for a restaurant Christopher was in a pub, sipping bitter with his parents on one side of him and his two lawyers on the other. He was having difficulty in keeping the beer down, and more in giving any attention to the conversation. The party had come to much the same conclusion as Jamie had about the judge's motive in the adjournment. "Can't be anything else, can it?" said Hope-Thomson, glancing at Compton.

"Beats me," replied the barrister. "I've never known anything quite as flagrant. It's bloody wicked of him, if that is it. Perhaps he really can't make up his mind, but…" He let it go. "He's been running it against us all the way, of course," he said after a pause. "You must have realised that," he went on, raising an eyebrow at Christopher and his parents. The three of them nodded glumly in unison.

"I had to tear up half my submission," went on the barrister. "I didn't know much about this judge before today, but as soon as we'd got under way I could see I was going to be up against it. He wouldn't see any point in our favour, and then, of course, he started making sarcastic little cracks. That bloody business about cliches, for instance. And one or two other choice little interventions. I'd've liked to let him have both barrels once or twice, but the trouble with judges like him is that if counsel upsets them they take it out of the client's skin. This old… this one looks as if he'd just be unscrupulous enough to do it, too. So I had to bite my tongue. And, as I say, I had five minutes' worth of purple prose I was going to let him have, if he'd been half-way sympathetic. That all went down the drain, and I had to make do as best I could with the rest of it."

He chatted on for a few minutes, but the rest of the party were too depressed to take any interest. He started talking shop with Hope-Thomson. After a while, however, the atmosphere became too much for Christopher. He waited for a lull in the legal gossip and asked, "What were you going to say, that you had to ditch?"

Compton smiled at him. "I was going to tell the old vulture about a notice board."

"A notice board?" echoed Christopher, looking curious despite his feelings. His parents too looked up and took an interest.

"Oh, well, it's an old tale one hears from time to time in a pub. The story goes that somewhere in a park there stands

220

a notice board, which says simply, 'It is forbidden to throw stones at this notice'." There was laughter from the whole party, and the atmosphere lightened.

"But whatever can that have to do with Christopher?" asked his mother, mystified. Compton looked at his watch. "We've got a little while yet," he said. "It's quite obvious, really, but I was rather proud of it. But I'm afraid the judge wouldn't have appreciated the neatness of my analogy. I was going to say…"

***

Jamie and Lane were already in their seats when Christopher and the others filed back in through the other door. Jamie was pleased to see that although Christopher was still looking tired and washed out, and far from well, he was a little brighter than he had been in the previous session. In fact the legal small-talk had interested him, taking him out of himself for a while. He kissed his mother on the cheek and smiled at her as he said something to her. As he went to resume his place in the dock he smiled quite openly at Jamie, a brave smile that didn't quite make it, but a good attempt. Jamie sent one of his best in return, and turned to Dr Lane. "He's being very brave about it, sir, isn't he?"

"He's doing as well as most boys would in his shoes, I should say," Lane replied. He studied Christopher and pondered deeply, trying to imagine how it must feel to be Jamie or Christopher, wondering what exactly they had found in each other that could exert so unbreakable a hold over them, that they could smile at each other and take a pleasure plain to see at a time like the present. Dr Lane was a wise and learned man, but the thing was outside his understanding. He postponed his reflections as the red curtain was drawn back and the judge was bawled back into

221

court. Everyone rose and sat down again except Christopher, who, at a sign from Hope-Thomson, remained on his feet.

The judge took his time about settling into the big chair, sorting out papers and glancing round him. At length he turned his gaze to Christopher. "Christopher Martin Rowe," he said, quite briskly. "I have given a great deal of thought to how I am to deal with you. My first thought was to impose a custodial sentence." There was an audible sigh from the end of the bench where the Rowes were sitting. Christopher's body writhed slightly and he steadied himself against the back of the dock. Hope-Thomson in the well of the court took off his spectacles and polished them on his handkerchief. Jamie drew in a breath so sharply that he almost choked. Lane swiftly put an arm round his shoulders and held him tightly to his side.

The judge paused, perhaps aware that parts of his audience required a moment to collect themselves, then continued. "It has been suggested by your learned counsel - perhaps I should rather say that it has been delicately hinted - that the offence to which you have pleaded guilty is less than grave. Learned counsel ventured to hint that when persons, even persons as young as the boy Potten..." His eyes flicked up and rested on Jamie's scarlet face for a moment. "...are fully consenting, then acts such as those in which you engaged do not constitute the serious offence that the law proclaims them to be. You yourself, when I gave you a chance to offer your own views, stated that opinion explicitly. I have to tell you, Rowe, that I do not agree.

"Our masters in Parliament thought fit many years ago now to relax the rigour of the law in respect of unnatural offences as committed between consenting adults, and that was Parliament's privilege. They did not see fit to extend the same licence to persons of your age, still less to those of Potten's age. You chose to demonstrate your contempt for Parliament by going ahead with your unnatural practices, and in this room this morning you added to that a similar contempt for the Court.

"I have a note of your actual words here: 'I can't be

expected to be sorry for something that did nothing but good to the only two people whose business it was, and no harm to anyone at all'. That was what you said this morning. Earlier, in answer to my question whether you felt any remorse, after a series of prevarications and, I take it, deliberate misunderstandings of my perfectly simple question, you finally gave me a straight answer. I'm sure it was the true answer. 'No', you said. Well, Rowe, that tells me as much, I think, as I need to know about your state of mind, and I don't propose to waste any more time on you.

"Something else that our masters in Parliament have seen fit to do, in their wisdom, Rowe, is to recommend that someone of your youth ought not to receive a custodial sentence; I must accept their wisdom. The sentence of the court for the vile and unnatural offence to which you plead guilty is, therefore, one of imprisonment for eighteen months, suspended for two years."

This time there was a clearly audible sob from Audrey Rowe, and another from Jamie. Lane squeezed him more tightly still round his shoulders, and watched him very closely, prepared at any moment to run him out into the foyer if he looked likely to be sick, or to make any demonstration. Christopher sagged heavily against the pine planking of the dock and leaned, breathing heavily and trembling so violently that it was visible from the rear of the court. Lane glanced across at the Rowes and saw that the father had his arms round his wife, who was weeping onto his shoulder.

The judge looked round the room before he spoke again. "Rowe, there is more I have to say to you yet. Stand up, please." Christopher did his best to straighten up in the dock, leaning lightly on the front rail. "Your learned solicitor will explain the full implications of the sentence I have just passed on you," went on the judge, "but I shall take it upon myself to offer you a piece of advice myself. You will do well to heed it. The first thing to keep in mind is that if you commit any offence within the two-year period I stipulated, you will be brought back to this court to be dealt with for this offence. That is in addition to whatever sentence you may receive for the other offence.

"I hope it is unnecessary for me to point out to you that this sentence is designed to deter you from committing any offences of any kind; but most of all it is intended as a warning to you that the court will not tolerate any repetition of the grotesque and abhorrent vice of the kind for which you have been sentenced today. If you are found engaging in bestial and unnatural sexual perversion in the next two years, Rowe, you will assuredly find yourself in prison with plenty of time to contemplate your foolishness, not to say your sinfulness.

"Finally, most emphatically of all, I warn you to stay away from the boy James Potten. He is, in my view, as grave a danger to society as you are, if not a worse. Your learned counsel argued persuasively and ably on your behalf that this boy led you into your wicked practices. I myself was not persuaded of that. I take the view that you, as the older boy, had a bounden moral duty to reject his blandishments and inform his parents of the kind of unnatural practices into which he had by some blasphemous pathway managed to stumble. You did not do so, and you have paid the penalty for your insensate weakness, as well as for your perverted nature. None the less, I warn you, he is dangerous, especially for you. So stay away from him at all costs."

Lane, watching Jamie closely throughout this tirade, was becoming very alarmed. Jamie's face was so suffused with scarlet that he looked to be in serious danger of having some kind of seizure, and he was squirming and wriggling to get free from Lane's clamp-like embrace. His eyes were blazing and bulging from his head in such a depth of rage that Lane feared for the boy's health. He bent awkwardly, still holding him down by main force, and whispered in his ear. "Jamie, for God's sake, be still, boy. You'll have to come out of the room with me if you won't be still." This had an immediate effect. Jamie's eyes still gleamed, and his face was still flushed crimson, but his struggles ceased instantly, and he nodded fiercely at Lane, gulping for air. Lane released his grip on him, just resting his arm across the boy's shoulders in case of further mutiny. He bent again, less uncomfortably, and whispered, "You *must* behave yourself. You simply cannot do as you please in this place. Now, can I trust you? Or do I have to take you out?" Jamie nodded mutely at him, then lifted his face. Lane bent, and he whispered "I'm sorry, sir. I'll be all right. It was just those things he said about me and Chris..." Lane nodded at him, immensely relieved.

The judge meanwhile had spotted Christopher's parents. "Are they Rowe's parents?" he asked vaguely in the direction of the counsel seats. Compton nodded. "Let them be brought forward," rustled the judge.

"Dear God," muttered Hope-Thomson in a very low whisper to Compton. "Hasn't he had enough blood for one day, that he wants to have the poor bloody parents' throats as well?" Compton grimaced at him and spread his hands wide. Hope-Thomson got up and hurried across to the Rowes, bringing them back with him and gently pushing them into seats. He himself stood behind them, ready to help them up if necessary.

"Please be seated, Mr and Mrs Rowe," said the judge, switching on a genial, fatherly tone. "I thought I should like a word with you before you leave. I'm afraid it must have been a great ordeal for you to hear such unsavoury accounts of your unfortunate son. But I shall be relinquishing him into your hands very soon, and I think it may be of some assistance if I offer you a couple of suggestions."

"Thank you, my lord," said Robert Rowe. His tone was polite, but sounded as if had issued from the depths of an icebox. Lane, craning his neck to see, observed that Rowe was almost as scarlet in the face as Jamie had been a moment or so before. "Thank you very much, my lord," Rowe repeated, "but I think you've done everything you could for my son. I think we shall be able to take care of him for the future."

The judge looked narrowly at him, but chose to take the words at face value. "I'm sure, from what learned counsel said, that you will," he said, with a benevolent air. "I don't know if your son is a churchgoer, but I suggest that he may find the help he needs to mend his ways in prayer. I hope so. The only other piece of advice I feel bound to offer you is that which I gave your son himself. Keep him away from the other boy, Potten, at all costs. And now, Mr and Mrs Rowe, I entrust your son to you. There are a few formalities, which your solicitor will attend to. I wish you good day."

As the Rowes, speechless, were being gently led from the well by an almost equally dumbstruck Hope-Thomson, there was a sudden sound at the back of the room. Every head turned to the back, to see Lane whispering fiercely to Jamie. The judge looked on with some interest. "Is that the Potten boy?" he asked Compton, who nodded, wondering if there was any limit to the judge's capacity to upset people, or whether he was actually contemplating having the boy brought forward. Compton hoped not, judging that he looked quite likely to hurl himself on the judge and gouge his eyes out. In a moment his fears were all but realised.

"Let the boy's guardian step forward," he said.

Lane froze in disbelief. Then he turned to Jamie and turned on him his steeliest glare. "Jamie. On your *honour*, you will NOT move from this seat," he hissed at him. "I command you, remain here - whatever he says," he added. Jamie shrank back on the bench and nodded dumbly.

Lane stepped forward and entered the well. "You are..." said the judge interrogatively.

"I am Dr John Lane. I am headmaster of Oldacre School. Also the guardian *pro tempore* of James Potten," Lane intoned in his iciest and most headmasterly tone, reserved for quelling only the most troublesome of parents or mutinous of boys.

"Well, Dr Lane," said the judge, deciding to forgo benevolence in favour of a businesslike manner, "you heard what I had to say to the boy Rowe's parents. I am sure you will co-operate to the full by ensuring for your part that your ward is prevented from any further contact with the other boy. I'm sure you will agree with me that it would be most perilous for both of them..." He left the words hanging in the air.

Lane looked steadily at him with his most frigid stare. "My lord," he said, "you may rely implicitly upon my judgment in all matters to do with children and young people. I have many years' experience of attending to their every need, bodily and spiritual, and I am, of course, especially aware of what is good for James Potten. You may rest assured that he will be permitted no contacts with anyone whom I consider to be any kind of threat or hazard to any aspect of his well-being. As to James Potten's future relations with Christopher Rowe, it remains to be seen whether in later years, when they attain the requisite age of consent, they wish to renew the acquaintance. For myself, I shall wait for that time and allow my ward to choose for himself." He shut his lips in a hard line and stood magisterially, gazing levelly at the judge.

The judge flushed. "Am I to credit the evidence of my ears, Dr Lane?" he said. "Do I then take it that if these two boys saw fit to resume their... their practices when they came of age, you would condone it?"

"When they are adults within the meaning set by your masters in Parliament, my lord," said Lane in the same freezing tone, "I shall accord them the freedom of choice that is not in any case mine to withold. I am enlightened, my lord. I bid you good day." And before the astonished judge could say a word to stop him Lane stalked majestically out of the well, to the back, swept Jamie up and went out with his arm round the boy's shoulders. In the courtroom the judge sat looking blankly after the departing pair. The silent cheer that went up from Compton, Hope-Thomson, Christopher, his parents and several others was almost deafening.

**

The moment the padded courtroom door swung to behind them Jamie frisked up and down beside Lane. "You were *great*, sir," he crowed excitedly. "He didn't know which way to turn when you batted him into the middle of next week. I couldn't've done it half as well myself." Lane, who had not been sure whether he ought to show his amusement or register official disapproval, was not quite proof against that, and chuckled. Two policemen who emerged from the other door from the court in time to hear, went out of the foyer grinning. One of them turned and winked at Jamie as he went. "Well, Jamie, I'm not sure I should encourage you in disrespectful attitudes towards venerable members of the judiciary, but if a pair of policemen think it's funny I suppose it counts as some sort of official sanction. And I must say, he was a very unpleasant piece of work."

"He was horrible, sir," said Jamie, soberly. His elation had passed quickly, and he looked serious again. "It is over, isn't it? It really is over?"

"Come and sit down for a few moments," Lane said, and led Jamie to one of the leather benches set in alcoves round the foyer. He sat silent for some minutes, and Jamie waited, not wishing to interrupt his thoughts. "I think you can say that the worst part of it is over, for Christopher, at least," Lane said eventually. "His barrister made much of the difficulties that he's likely to face in future, but I think it's possible that he was exaggerating that a little, for extra effect. He was probably just doing everything he could to persuade the judge to temper justice with mercy..." He sank into thought again.

"I don't think there was any justice there to temper, sir," ventured Jamie after several more minutes had elapsed. "That judge was so... so prejudiced against Chris, he'd made up his mind before it started what he was going to do. He never listened to a word that barrister said. I thought it was a jolly good speech, didn't you?"

"I'm glad to hear somebody thought so," said a voice. They looked up, to see Compton, minus his wig and gown, who had appeared from yet another door in time to hear Jamie's last words. He glanced at his watch, and dropped onto the seat beside Jamie. He dumped a large, shapeless bag, the same royal blue colour as Jamie's blazer, on the floor in front of him. Something hard inside it made a muffled thud. Jamie looked at it with interest. "For my wig, gown, briefs and so forth," said Compton, seeing the look.

"That was a pretty good affidavit," he went on, nodding courteously to Lane over Jamie's head. Lane smiled. "He's got the making of a considerable talent as a writer," he replied, looking down at Jamie. "He intends to be a writer of some kind - I take it that ambition is unchanged, Jamie?"

"It's the only thing I'm interested in being, sir," said Jamie. "Sir, may I ask a question?"

"Of course," said Lane, noticing that the question had been addressed to him for form's sake, but seeing that it was really meant for the barrister. "Sir, why do barristers have blue shirts but white collars, please?"

Compton grinned. It made him look absurdly boyish. Hardly older than Christopher, thought Lane and Jamie simultaneously. "These simple questions are always the unanswerable ones," he said. "As far as I know, it's just part of the uniform."

"Did you really like my statement, sir?" asked Jamie, greatly daring. "I thought it was extremely well constructed," assented Compton. "If you did it without H-T's help as he claimed, I'd say it was pretty remarkable. I've certainly seen opinions prepared by eminent members of my profession that read less fluently."

"Well, there you are, my boy," said Lane, rather proudly. "A feather in your cap, if nothing else has come out of this miserable affair." He turned back to Compton. "I was impressed by your submission, if I may return the compliment," he said gracefully. "I can't claim to have any experience in legal matters, but it seemed to me that you made the best of what I should imagine must have been a virtually impossible job."

Compton grimaced. "There was very little I could do, really, I'm afraid. I didn't know this judge before today. I mean, I'd asked about him, and I hadn't taken much encouragement from what I'd heard, but I never expected him to run it against me from the start like that. I could see from half-way through your boy's affidavit that it was going to go against us. After that I chucked my carefully prepared submission on the fire and improvised. Not that I got any further, but I should think if I'd used my original draft he'd have been reaching for the black cap." He shrugged. "When a judge is against you like that there's not a lot you can do, I'm afraid. You go through the motions and devote most of your mind to spotting things to use in your appeal."

Jamie's eyes widened. "Will he appeal?" he said before he could stop himself. "Sorry, sir," he added, to Lane, realising he had interrupted. Lane nodded. "No, there's no possibility of any appeal in this case," said the barrister. "And in any case, there's no point. He's got away as unscathed as he could have hoped to. I think 18 months is grossly excessive - I would have expected six months at the outside, and so did Frank H-T, but as soon as I saw how the judge was running the case I upped it to a year at least. But the point is, James - it is James, isn't it?"

"Jamie."

"Well, then, the point is, Jamie, that he hasn't actually been sentenced to anything - anything that matters, anyway. At least, you can look at it like that. I mean, he hasn't gone inside, and so long as he keeps his nose clean for two years, he's got nothing to interfere with his life in any way. He doesn't strike me as the type to offend again; so really the only way he's suffered tangibly is in getting himself a criminal record. Not agreeable, but he's free, and he can get on with his life."

"How about..." began Lane, then stopped. "Are we detaining you, Mr Compton? I imagine you have other calls on your time than to sit talking to us."

"No, no, I've got no more cases. Just back to chambers to swot for the next one. I'm being led in a big one next month, and I've got to spend the next three weeks trying to learn a bit about computers. Big computer fraud case. And a big chance for me," he added. The boyish grin appeared again.

"I'm sure you'll seize it with great aplomb," said Lane.

"Judging by the tenacity and ability you showed in there this morning. Courage, too, if I may say so. I was most impressed by the way you held your corner when you thought the judge was exceeding the proper limits."

Compton frowned. "He did more than that," he said. "It was a quite outrageous thing to say, and I nearly used that very word. It would have been a big mistake."

"I noticed," said Lane.

"Well, some people would say I should have swallowed it," Compton said reflectively. "They'd have a point, too, because a judge like that is quite capable of getting his own back by taking it out on the client. But I thought he oughtn't to be allowed to get away with everything. He obviously enjoys riding roughshod over people."

"Well, I certainly share your opinion," murmured Lane. "I wonder if I might ask one more thing." Compton nodded. "Of course."

"You are considerably more knowledgeable than I about such things, Mr Compton. Do you really believe that the boy will suffer greatly in the future from the exposure that this case will bring him? Jamie is worried about it, and I ventured to suggest that you were perhaps exaggerating a trifle for the judge's benefit when you emphasized that aspect of the matter."

"You were quite right, sir," said Compton, and he was pleased to see Jamie's face light up. Then he saw that the boy was looking past him and was clearly no longer aware of his existence. He turned, and saw the Rowes coming out of the court with Hope-Thomson. Christopher was looking across at Jamie. Compton glanced quickly from one to the other and back again, and was a little awed at what he saw. Hope-Thomson said something to Robert Rowe, who spoke to Christopher. Christopher turned to his father and nodded, but his eyes hardly left Jamie for a moment. Meanwhile Hope-Thomson was making his way across to them.

He gave a friendly nod to Jamie, who had spared a moment to glance at him before fixing his eyes on Christopher again. "Dr Lane, how d'you do," Hope-Thomson said. Lane rose to his feet and shook hands. "Off the record, congratulations," said Hope-Thomson, with a slightly conspiratorial smile. "That demolition job on Pennington was worth being in court for."

"Thank you," said Lane. "I've been feeling a little apprehensive since I left the court, wondering whether I ought to have made what I felt so plain, but my small gesture of distaste seems to have received unanimous approbation."

"He asked for that and more, Dr Lane," said the solicitor, "and it was sheer good fortune that you happened to be there to hand him his deserts. He's probably got away with disgraceful behaviour like that hundreds of times, and it's nice to see people like that get their wings clipped just occasionally. Changing the subject slightly," he said, "Michael, are you rushing back to chambers, or have you got time for a quick one? I've just got a few more things to say to the Rowes before they go on their way, and then there was something I wanted to talk to you about."

"I wouldn't mind a pint," said Compton.

"Right. Well, look, Michael, can I see you in a quarter of an hour? Where shall we say - what about the Green Man?" The barrister nodded assent. "Right," said Hope-Thomson. "I'll see you there. Saloon bar. Now, Dr Lane, I wonder if I could draw you aside for just a moment. There's one thing I'd like to discuss with you very briefly." He nodded to Compton, walked away a few paces with Lane, and spoke to him for some minutes, with Lane nodding gravely from time to time. From their glances at Jamie and the Rowes it was evident what they were discussing.

Compton picked up his blue bag and moved away. "Well, goodbye, Jamie Potten," he said as he went. "Good luck with the writing." He noticed the reluctance with which Jamie dragged his gaze away from Christopher, and came back for a moment. "If you'll take a word of advice from a stranger, who doesn't wish either of you any harm, you'll stay away from Christopher Rowe. It can't do either of you anything but damage to see any more of each other, and it could be disastrous for him." He saw the pain in Jamie's eyes as he said it. "You'll get over it, you know," he said gently, "and so will he."

"You don't understand," said Jamie. "But thank you for being so decent. And for trying so hard for Chris. Nobody could have done better." For a moment Compton felt an odd sensation of having spoken to a child and been answered by an adult. Then he said "Well, goobye, then," and went into the street.

"With that bloody Pennington that makes two people today who haven't listened to a word I've said," he commented a few minutes later in the Green Man, handing Hope-Thomson a scotch and soda. "Did you see the way they were looking at each other, those two?" The solicitor nodded gloomily. "Couldn't very well be off seeing it, could you?" he said. "They were practically lighting up the foyer there."

"Do you know, that's exactly how I felt. There's more trouble lying ahead there, if they're not careful - or more likely if others aren't careful of them."

"I had a word with that headmaster," said Hope-Thomson. "He's got his head screwed on the right way. He's desperately fond of the boy, you can see that a mile off, but I'd say if anyone can control that little bugger, he can. The boy's very fond of him, too, of course. That was obvious. But how much it'll weigh against this thing he's got with the other boy... they looked like Nelson Eddy and Jeanette McDonald." Unfortunately he said it as Compton was taking a long pull on his pint of lager. His involuntary snort of laughter hit him before he could get his nose out of his glass, with the result that he inhaled half of it down the wrong way and blew the rest explosively all over Hope-Thomson's suit. When Compton had been thumped on the back, and Hope-Thomson had mopped his suit with his handkerchief, and they had both finished gurgling with laughter, Hope-Thomson raised the subject of the case he wanted to discuss, and they forgot Jamie Potten's and Christopher Rowe's existence.

FIVE

For Christopher and his parents the short drive home was a sad, silent affair. Robert parked outside the house. "I think I'll go into the office for an hour or so," he said. He looked over his shoulder at Christopher in the back of the car. "Unless you'd rather I stayed here," he added. "I took the whole day off. Would you rather I was here, Chris?"

Christopher looked at the strain in his face, the tightness round the eyes and the bags underneath them from lack of sleep and worry. "No, Dad," he said sadly. "I've given you enough trouble to last a lifetime. You'll be better off with a bit of company. I'll be all right." His father smiled at him, but he couldn't conceal the relief in his face.

"Why don't you go for a drink with the people from the office tonight, Bob?" suggested Audrey. "You need a bit of normality for a while, and I've got a lot to talk about to Chris. University and everything."

"I might do that," admitted Rowe. "In fact, I think I'll walk in. I won't have to worry about the car then." He started the engine again, and ran the car into the garage. They got out, and he prepared to set off for the town centre. "Dad," said Christopher quietly. "Yes, Chris?" he replied, turning back.

"Is everything... is it... is it all right at the office for you?"

Rowe came back to him and put his arm round his shoulders. "*Yes*, of course it's all right," he said, very gently. "Of course it's all right." Christopher put his arms round him and hugged him, rubbing his cheek against his father's rougher one. He clung to him without a sound for a long interval. "Poor old Chrissie," murmured Rowe. "My poor Chris." He held his son for a few moments longer, then gently disengaged himself. "Now, you go in and get your mother some tea," he said, briskly now. "Or give her a whacking great scotch, if she'd rather. Have one yourself. I should think you could use one. I'll see you this evening. And Chris..."

"Yes, Dad?"

"Don't worry. It's all over." He turned and walked quickly out of sight. All over, thought Audrey as she found her door key. I wonder if it is.

As she lifted her key to the lock the door swung back. "Why, Neil!" she and Christopher chorused in surprise. "What are you doing here?"

"They let me come home for the afternoon," he said. "It's maths this afternoon, too," he added cheerfully. "Double period." More soberly he went on "they knew it was Chris's case today, and they thought I'd worry about it, so they let me come home to wait for you. How did you get on, Chris?"

"Let's get in, dear," said his mother. "Then we'll tell you about it."

"I got a suspended sentence, Neil," said Christopher as Neil moved aside to let them come in.

"What's that mean?"

"It means I mustn't do anything wrong in the next two years, or I'll be sent to prison, or youth custody, it's called, for this."

"Prison!" cried Neil, shocked into a yelp of surprise. "Can they send you to prison for being gay, Chris?"

"They can if you're my age," said Christopher bitterly. "At least, they can if you do anything about it."

"*Fu-ckin-ell!*"

235

"*Neil*!" said Audrey. "Language!"

"Sorry, Mum. But prison. Just for being... Wow! Wait till I tell Goose and Gander about that."

Audrey and Christopher stared at him. "Goose and Gander?" queried his mother. "Neil, what are you talking about?"

"Williams and Donaldson, Mum. They're in my maths set. The teachers have stopped trying to make them sit where they should be. We call 'em Goose and Gander."

"Neil, *what* are you talking about?" she repeated. "If you're talking about anything." Neil grinned at her and pointed to his brother, who was beginning to laugh. "Chrissie knows what I'm talking about, Mum," he said archly. He made cow eyes and a rosebud mouth, advancing on Christopher in an exaggerated mincing walk, and planted a slobbery kiss on his cheek. Then he grinned horribly at his mother and said, "They're gay, of course". Shaking his head at the slow-wittedness of adults, he seized her handbag, put it over his arm and minced into the kitchen, leaving his mother staring after him in mingled outrage and astonishment, while Christopher sat on the stairs and laughed till he cried.

***

Jamie and Christopher had hardly taken their eyes off each other while they were at opposite ends of the courthouse foyer. Looks passed between them, burdened with affection and desire, passion and concern, but mostly with a great depth of tenderness. Selfish though they were both capable of being, for each other their feelings were real enough, and pure, and they went deeper than anyone close to them had fathomed. Christopher had hoped to be able to snatch a few moments with Jamie as soon as he left the court, but Hope-Thomson had warned him against any such attempt, and his parents had offered him no chance of escaping.

When Hope-Thomson finished conferring with Dr Lane

the two men went back to Jamie on the bench. He stood up, and the solicitor shook his hand gravely, without a trace of condescension. "Goodbye, Jamie," he said. "Keep the writing up. You'll do well, I think. I wish you very well for the future." He said not a word about Christopher, but shook hands with Lane, walked straight back to the Rowes, and accompanied them outside, where he shook hands with them all, wished Christopher well, and left them.

At the door Jamie saw Christopher step back to allow Hope-Thomson to precede him, and immediately shoot a rapid glance back. The instant he saw that Jamie was watching and that Lane's back was to him he turned back to the door. As he did so his hand opened behind him and a crumpled ball of paper dropped to the floor. Christopher was out of sight before it reached there. The whole sequence took only two or three seconds, but Christopher knew Jamie had seen.

A moment later Lane had picked up his coat from the bench and they were half-way to the doors. As they reached them Jamie contrived to trip over his feet and slipped over. He was up again in a second; and by the time Lane was asking him if he was hurt the ball of paper was in the side pocket of his blazer. He transferred it to his trouser pocket on the walk to Lane's car, and within minutes of reaching home he had got it safely hidden in his room, stuffed into the toe of one of his trainers under his bed. Lane was waiting downstairs to talk to him about the day as soon as he had changed, so he did not dare to linger even to uncrumple it. He thought about locking himself in the lavatory and reading it, but decided he wanted to read this unexpected message with plenty of time. He changed into comfortables and went downstairs.

They talked long into the evening, describing every detail of the case for Edith's benefit, with Jamie putting in comments on the bits that had particularly pleased or disgusted him. Edith made an occasional comment but mostly listened in a progressively appalled silence, except for a chuckle at a bravura description by Jamie of her husband's contribution. Then they discussed the implications of it for themselves, and that part of the conversation took several turns that Jamie didn't like at all, though he wisely kept quiet.

"The long and the short of it is, Jamie," said Lane, "that I don't think you can possibly contemplate having any more contact with Christopher at all, for some time to come. I doubt if even the letters can be allowed to continue." Jamie still managed to keep quiet and calm, though his face registered slow pain. He thought the message in his shoe upstairs probably held some kind of answer to this development, which he had more or less expected. After that, he supposed he would have to rely on his own extensive Machiavellian powers to find solutions to problems as they arose. All he was sure of was that he was not going to lose Christopher, or not as easily as everybody seemed to suppose, anyway. He pretended acquiescence, kept his own counsel, and at length was relieved when they called it a night and allowed him to escape to bed.

He retrieved the crumpled ball of paper from his shoe and hopped into bed quickly, strategically placing a couple of magazines to be picked up if either of the Lanes came to say goodnight, as they usually did. Suppressing his impatience, he took care in smoothing out the sheet of lined paper to avoid damaging it, and then read it through. Christopher's wayward writing was even more ragged than usual, showing the haste in which it had been scrawled.

"Dearest J," it read,*"had paper etc ready to write this if I got a chance after the trial just in case I cdnt see you - prison etc. Escaped into lav to write this and have only a min or 2. I'm on lead & collar from now on. No contact with you if they can help it. Dont worry my darling, will write or get messages somehow. Glad it turned out no worse than it did. Wasnt Dr L great. At least Im still at lib. New phone no 665824, but DONT ring me, wait for me - phone out of bounds. Will meet you soon, promise. Jamie, love, whatever happens next few weeks DONT WORRY, DONT PANIC, DONT DO ANYTHING SILLY LIKE CALLING MY HOME. This important - weve both got hard time for next weeks/months. Never forget, nothings changed - nothing at all. Well be together all the*

238

time before too long. Must go now. Try to give this to you, if not screw it up, make sure you see me drop it somewhere - look like litter if you cant pick up. Till I see you will be thinking of you all the time. Love you, Chris."

Jamie read it three times, again not surprised at what the near future seemed likely to hold. Then he kissed it, slipped cautiously out of bed and stowed it in his holdall where he kept everything from Christopher. He got back into bed, put out the light and, exhausted by the emotional strain of the day, fell instantly into a deep sleep.

***

The next day was a Friday, on which day school ended early. Jamie ran home as soon as the bell went, intending to go fishing. He hoped that if Christopher wanted to find him, his fishing place would be the first place he would look. Besides, he had been missing fishing over the last few weeks. All through the worst times when he had been with his parents he had always found solace and relaxation in it, and he realised that he was quite looking forward to putting in an hour or two. As he let himself into the house the telephone rang. He picked it up as he passed, and fishing dropped suddenly and totally out of his mind.

"Jamie, it's me," said Christopher. "Don't talk, just listen. If you can do what I ask, just say 'That's all right'. If you *can't* do it, say 'Okay'. I've *got* to see you. Can you come to the fishing place tonight, midnight if possible? I'll wait anyway if you can't get there till later. Can you do it?"

As he finished speaking Edith came downstairs. "That's quite all right," said Jamie. "Good. Love you," said Christopher hurriedly, and they hung up together. "Hello, Jamie," said Edith. "Who was it?" She looked closely at him.

He gave her his most disarming smile. "Some idiot in a phone box," he said, chuckling convincingly. "First he couldn't get his money in, and then when he did it was a wrong number." He stood aside politely for her to pass him and went upstairs whistling to himself. Well, thought Edith, there can't have been anything Christopher-ish about that call, at least. Jamie, meanwhile, had forgotten there was such a pastime as fishing and was bouncing up and down on his bed, with no idea of the despair into which he was about to be plunged.

Jamie crept out of the house as he had done once before, and ran most of the four miles to the fishing place. When he slithered down the bank and pushed through the trees he found Christopher, rolled up in their old blanket against the cold night air. He ran joyously across and the black shapeless area humped and rose. He dropped and squirmed in with Christopher. It seemed as if epochs had passed since they had last been together like this. Christopher considerately let him get comfortably settled beside him before he spoke. When he did it was like being suddenly dropped into a bath of acid. "Jamie," he said bleakly, "I'm being sent away.

"The thing is, love, they don't trust me very much, and they don't trust you at all. Can't say they're altogether wrong - we're neither of us very trust*worthy*, are we?"

"Huh!" Jamie snorted. "All we want to do is love each other and mind our own fucking business, isn't it?"

"Yes, but never mind that," hushed Christopher. "We haven't got long, and this is going to be our last time together for quite a while. I want it to be something for us to remember, so for Christ's sake let's get the talking out of the bloody way quickly. They're sending me down to my grandparents again, and I've got to stay there until I go up to university in three weeks. They've told the old folks the real truth this time, and I'll be under supervision all the time. I'm not even being given the chance to give them the bloody slip," he added bitterly. "Dad's driving me down there tomorrow afternoon.

"They're really taking this suspended sentence thing seriously. So am I for that matter, but I'd take *some* risks - it's

240

no crime just being with you. But they think it's all your doing. They don't credit me with having enough mind of my own to have a say in it, even. Except Neil - he understands how things really are. But Neil doesn't count, of course. So that's it - no meetings, no phone calls - they'll lock the bloody phone in a safe if they think I've called you on it, and you can bet your life the old couple will've been primed as well. The only thing I can do is write to you. Thank God for..."

"But that's just what you *can't* do," Jamie groaned, and he told him of the latest edict from Lane. "He means it, too, Chris. They're going to come down just as heavy on me as you. Oh, Christ, Chris, what can we do? Could we go abroad, do you think?"

"I've got to do this degree, haven't I? If we're going to live together some time we'll have to have jobs - one of us, anyway - I mean, I'd keep you willingly, though I don't suppose you'd want that. But I must get my degree. I couldn't get a course in a foreign country, and even if I could it'd take years to arrange." And he went swiftly and methodically through all the possibilities he had thought of, demolishing them one after the other. In the end Jamie had to agree. They were doomed to be parted, for a while at least, and there was nothing they could do about it. He moaned, and clutched Christopher silently.

Christopher groped somewhere and the beam of a pen-torch shone briefly on his wristwatch. "It's just gone one," he said. "We've been here an hour already. You can see as plainly as I can that we've got no choice but to do what they dictate. Let's stop talking, for a bit, at least." He started unbuttoning Jamie's shirt.

They lay together afterwards, a little more relaxed. Suddenly Jamie said "There *is* one thing we haven't thought about, you know."

"Whassat?" murmured Christopher, waking from a doze.

"We could kill ourselves. Have a - what do you call it - a pact. I wouldn't care. If I can't have you I don't care if I live or not anyway."

Christopher half-laughed, then thought about the note in

Jamie's voice. "Are you serious?"

"Yes," said Jamie simply, in a matter-of-fact tone. "Why not?"

"Christ almighty, Jamie, you're off your head."

"Yes," he replied. "I think I probably am, a bit, at least. But why not? Do *you* care?"

"Yes, I bloody well do!" he snapped, more sharply than he had ever spoken to Jamie before. "Jesus. I've got fifty years left to me, and you've got more. Even if we had to wait the full five years till you're twenty-one before we could be together we'd have a lifetime. You silly little bugger, what the hell do you think you're on about?"

Jamie sat up. "I... I'm sorry, Chris. Please don't talk to me like that. I only suggested it. I didn't think you could wait five years, or me. So I just thought..."

"Jamie," said Christopher, pulling him back down beside him, "I *can't* wait five years, I only said *if*. I couldn't stay away from you for five whole bloody years, and I know damn well you couldn't wait even as long as I could. But we shan't *have* to wait that long. It won't be a matter of years. This court business will be forgotten about in a little while, the dust'll settle, and we'll be able to work something out. It's only right now that everybody's keeping us under a spotlight. If we can just endure it for a few months, things'll start getting back to normal. Don't forget, you'd have to do without me for ten weeks from October anyway, while I was at university.

"Now stop talking like a silly little boy and come down here. Then we'll go. The longer we stay here tonight the worse it'll be when we *have* to go. The last thing I want to do is have to say goodbye to you in a hurry. If we go soon we'll at least be able to walk back along the towpath slowly."

"I don't bloody well want to say goodbye to you at all," growled Jamie. But he did as he was told, and then they walked slowly and sadly home.

Jamie crept silently into bed at five, and Edith had trouble rousing him at eight for Saturday games. He tottered into breakfast looking washed-out, dull-eyed and depressed. However, he kissed Edith as he usually did and set off for school, at five minutes to nine, after making some odd clatterings in the kitchen. The Lanes exchanged glances. "He hasn't slept well, poor mite," said Edith. "He doesn't look as if he's slept at all," commented her husband.

"He was practically comatose when I went to wake him," she said. "He was overtired after yesterday, I imagine. Perhaps I'll get the doctor to look at him. Some sort of tonic, maybe?"

"Give him a day or two," he advised. "Whatever we think of this affair of his, it's obviously very real to him, and he'll suffer badly for a while. But boys are resilient, and he'll recover fast, I'd say. I'll make sure Matron keeps a watchful eye on him at school."

"I wonder if he's as resilient as some boys," she mused. "He's an obsessive sort of character, John, isn't he? I sometimes get an almost creepy feeling when I talk to him - especially on the odd occasions when he's been depressed. It's like talking to a grown-up, but one with strange gaps in his make-up. He seems to me to be half-way between a true adult and a true teenager."

"He's been robbed, Edith, my dear," said Lane grimly. "There's your gaps."

The telephone rang.

"John, it's Nick Philips, and he says it's urgent," Edith said, coming hurriedly back from taking the call. Lane ran to the hall.

"Headmaster," came the voice of the Saturday duty master, "you asked me to report to you if young Potten acted at all strangely. Well, he has - that is, he hasn't turned up at all. I gave him a few minutes, then I started across to see if he was on his way..."

"Yes, yes," Edith heard him snap. There was an urgent note in his voice that brought her out of her chair. She stepped silently into the hall and watched his back as he stood over the telephone table.

"I didn't see him, so I turned back, and as I turned, Headmaster, I caught a glimpse of someone disappearing into the conker trees up by the lane."

"Was it Potten?" rapped Lane.

"Couldn't see, Headmaster, but I ran up there. No reason for anyone to be heading that way unless they were going over the wall. Well, when I got there there was no-one to be seen, of course - he had too good a start on me. But when I got to the wall - you know the bit they go over when they're..."

"I know it," snapped Lane. "Quickly, now, this may be urgent."

"Yes, sir," said the man, sounding a little wounded. "Well, in the lane just at the point where he would have dropped, I found something odd. It was a packet of Panadol..."

"What?" roared Lane into the receiver, deafening the duty master at the other end, and causing Edith to feel very uneasy indeed.

"Panadol, sir. You know, pain-killers. One of those cards where you press the tablets through the..." But Lane had slammed the receiver down with a crash that overturned a vase of flowers standing beside the instrument on its little table. He dashed into the kitchen. Edith, following him with a great fear growing up round her, found him staring into the large wall cupboard where they kept medicines and first-aid equipment. He turned to her, with fear to match her own spread starkly across his face. "How many pain-killing tablets did we have in here, Edith?" he asked quietly. She felt the blood drain from her face and neck.

"I don't know," she said, thinking rapidly. "Let me think. There was one large box. That had - at least three cards, probably four. They have twelve tablets each. And there were a few aspirins." He looked back into the cupboard. "Are these the aspirins you mean?" he asked, showing her a small bottle. "Yes," she said after a rapid glance.

"Were they the only other pain-killers we had?"

"Yes, I think so - yes, I'm sure that's all we had," she said, nodding to herself as her thoughts raced. Lane suddenly rapped his hand on the work-top and ran past her and through the hall into the living room. He emerged a second later. "The whisky bottle's missing," he said grimly. "Oh, my

God," she breathed. "What now?"

Lane stood for a moment in indecision. "Where would he go?" he said. "Where would he go?"

Edith twisted her hands in anxiety. "Somewhere where he might have met Christopher..." she began.

"That's it!" cried Lane. "Christopher. He'll have gone to Christopher first, whatever happens. Even if he's decided to... to... he wouldn't do anything without at least trying to see Christopher first. Edith, get the car out," he commanded.

"John, darling," she said soothingly, "why not ring the Rowes? They'll..."

"They had their number changed - the furore after the story in the papers. Don't know the new number. Get the car while I ring the doctor."

"But what can you tell him?" she queried logically. "Where can you tell him to go?" He stared at her for a moment. "Yes, I suppose so," he said. "I'll get the car, I'm a faster driver. Get your shoes on," he called over his shoulder, delving in his pocket for his car keys as he disappeared.

Lane, who customarily drove as sedately and majestically as he walked, roared to a halt in Cross Oak Gardens nine minutes after he opened his garage doors. He strode up the short path, with Edith following breathlessly yards behind. He leaned on the bell, rapping on the panels at the same time. Edith looked at her watch. It showed exactly 9:30. Audrey Rowe opened the door as Lane turned to Edith, with the result that he almost rapped her on the jaw, and then almost stumbled into her arms. "Dr Lane!" she ejaculated in astonishment to see him. He presented a disconcerting appearance. He was still in shirtsleeves, and the tail had worked loose and was flapping outside his trousers. His hair was flying wildly about his head like an iron-grey halo. Behind him Edith was in flat shoes and a pair of scruffy black slacks with a hole in one knee, which she used for dusty household or garden jobs, and the top two buttons of her blouse had come undone in her frantic battle to get her seat-belt on as Lane careered round the bends of the Steeple Wynton road into town.

Audrey quelled her initial astonishment in a moment, perceiving that only some kind of emergency could possibly have brought the suave and self-possessed Lanes into public view in such a condition. "What's happened?" she asked sharply.

"Mrs Rowe," he said, striving to speak calmly while he recovered his breath. "I'm terribly sorry to inflict myself on you like this, but it's an emergency - at least, I think it is. Please tell me, do you know where Christopher is?"

"Why, yes, he's here," she said. "Please, what is it, Dr Lane?"

"Is Jamie with him? Please tell me. It's very urgent."

"Jamie? No, he certainly is not," she said, going instantly onto the defensive, her eyes hardening. "Is that boy trying to..."

Christopher appeared in the hallway behind her "What is it, Mum?" he began to ask. Then he caught sight of Lane beyond her, and immediately pushed past her, taking in the Lanes' dishevelled appearance, the car left outside with the driver's door wide open, and his mother's expression, in a single glance. He sized things up in a moment. "Hello, Dr Lane," he said rapidly. "It's Jamie, isn't it? What's happened?" He seemed suddenly to grow in stature, taking over from his mother as by right.

Lane had got his breath back. "Christopher," he said, breathing deeply. "I'm very glad you're here. Please tell me quickly: have you seen Jamie this morning, since just after nine?"

"No, sir," said Christopher immediately, alarm filling his eyes. "Why, sir, what's happened? You can tell me."

"He's disappeared," Lane said. "He left the house for Saturday school this morning at five to nine, as usual. He never got there, but he was seen absconding over a wall - a known place for boys who want to go out of bounds. He's taken with him, we think, a bottle of whisky and an unknown but probably large quantity of tablets."

"Oh, NO! Oh, my *Christ!*" cried Christopher, sagging against the door jamb as if he had been struck. "What in

God's name is he thinking about?"

"I fear the worst, Christopher, and I need your help. I thought at first he might have come here to see you. If he was going to do anything desperate I thought he would try to speak to you first. As he hasn't, can you think of anywhere he would be most likely to go? Think well, I beg you. Time is vital." He looked at his watch. It was 9:40.

"The fishing place," said Christopher without hesitation. "He'd go to the fishing place, I'm sure of it."

"Where is this place, this fishing place?" asked Lane.

"It's at the lake," said Christopher over his shoulder as he retreated into the hall and stooped for his shoes. He came back and knelt on the front step to put them on and tie the laces, talking up to Lane as he did so. "The old gravel pit. Favourite place of Jamie's for fishing, and we used to meet there often. About two miles along the towpath. Three miles from here, about."

"Can I get my car there?"

"No, sir. Can't get anything bigger than a bike along the towpath. You can drive as far as the stone bridge across the canal, then it's bike or on foot."

"Mrs Rowe," said Lane, his composure back, "I know you have no cause to feel kindly disposed towards Jamie, but I must ask you - beg you - to allow me to use Christopher's help. He may, quite literally, make the difference between life and death."

"I couldn't stop him if I wanted to - not that I do," she said. "Look at him." Christopher's face was set, and he looked only to Lane. "I'm younger than you, sir. Run me down to the stone bridge - I'll direct you. I'll get there in ten minutes. You can follow. You can ring for a doctor from here. Mum, get Dad, will you. He can follow me down. Tell him to take my bike. Ambulance can wait by the bridge. I can carry him that far if... if..." He walked fast to Lane's car. "You can go out the way you're facing, sir," he said to Lane over his shoulder. He went round, got in and had his seat-belt on before Lane had reached the vehicle.

On the way Lane glanced across at him, and there was

247

something almost like affection in his look. "If we're right about the location," he said, "you'll never do your friend more service than this. It would take us three times as long to get there, and that might be too late." Christopher gave him a smile of strange serenity. "I'm right about the place, Dr Lane," he said with utter certainty. "And I'll be there in time. Don't ask me how I know. Wishful thinking, I dare say." His tone changed. "If I'm not, I'll no doubt be going down there myself before long," he said softly, speaking to himself.

"Don't say such a thing, please, Christopher," said Lane. The tone, rather than the words, had sent a shiver through him. "Do you know what to do with him if you find that he has taken the tablets?"

"Not very certain, sir. Turn left here, and you'll see the bridge up ahead. Make him sick, I suppose?"

"Quite right. That's the first thing. Bend him forward, stick two fingers down his throat and tickle the back of his throat, and keep doing it until he's brought up everything there is to bring up. Doesn't matter how painful it is, just make sure he's vomited himself dry. Is this the bridge you want?" Christopher was already slipping out of his seat-belt. Lane halted the car with a jerk and Christopher was out before it had settled. "Anything else, sir?" he asked, still radiating the same strange calm.

"We should have hot coffee or tea, but I'll arrange that and we'll bring it when we follow. But the most important thing is to keep him at all costs from going to sleep. Shout at him, sing to him, make him talk, slap him, and most of all keep him on his feet, walking, and his eyes open. Keep his eyes open, keep him talking and keep him walking. Go on, Christopher, and God bless you. We'll follow as quickly as we can."

Christopher was already moving at a fast jog down onto the towpath under the bridge. He turned quickly and waved a hand, then accelerated into a run. Lane watched him cover the first hundred yards and disappear from view round the first bend, then walked rapidly back to his car and shot back the way he had come. It was 9:52.

**

Jamie, walking fast, reached the fishing place at 9:45. By the time he had slithered under the hawthorns, dropped down the bank and forced his way through to the little greensward a further two minutes had passed. He walked slowly round the little semi-circular patch of grass, looking about him, down at the rough, tussocky turf, up at the rainy sky, seeing the slender reddish branchlets of the alders as if for the first time. Lastly he walked to the edge of the water and stood gazing into the water. He felt vaguely that he would have rather liked to have seen the great old pike once more, but the water was dark and opaque under the heavy, many-shaded grey of the sky, and there was nothing to be seen.

There was a blank expression on his face, and he felt oddly numb. He knew that he was Jamie Potten, and he knew that he was not ill. He was, he thought, more or less his normal self. It was just that being normal didn't seem to feel the same today. I'm normal, he ruminated. It's being normal that's not normal today. I wonder why. He spent a few moments wondering, vaguely, but his mind didn't seem to be capable of holding on to anything much for very long this morning.

He suddenly looked about him again, and wondered how he had come to be there. Why, I walked here, of course, he thought. How silly, to walk here and then, having got here, to forget how you came. Odd. He sat down on the sodden grass a few feet in from the water's edge. Wouldn't do to loll into the water and drown. Hmmm. Funny. Why not? He was going to... what *was* he going to do? Ah, yes, he thought. And, at last, his mind settled on the purpose that had brought him. He eased the J & B bottle from his blazer pocket and propped it between two tussocks beside him, pulling the box of Panadol from the other side pocket.

Thirty-six Panadol. Should be enough, he thought, with enough whisky to wash them down. He pressed tablets out of their little recesses until he had them all cupped in his palm. He looked at his watch. It was a minute to ten. Odd that, he thought, I'd have thought I'd been here much longer than that, mooning about looking in the water for the old pike and all that. Nothing seems to be making much sense this morning.

It still wasn't when there was a tremendous crashing in the thin belt of trees and he was hit by what felt like a battering ram from behind. So that's what dying was like, thought Jamie. A loud crashing noise and something hitting you in the back. Surprised we were all so afraid of it.

***

The battering ram was in fact Christopher, bursting through the trees and hurling himself across to Jamie as he saw him prone on the wet grass with his head pillowed on his arm. Christopher scooped him up in his arms and swung him round, looking at his face. Jamie's eyes opened wide, and he gave a slow smile of delight. "Chris," he murmured. "What are you doing here?"

"Oh, Jamie. My Jamie," moaned Christopher. "What have you done?"

Jamie, who was wondering if he was in Heaven, just smiled at him, and closed his eyes in a blissful expression. Christopher shook him violently. "Have you taken those pills?" he asked, putting his hands under Jamie's armpits and jiggling him up and down like a puppet. Jamie's eyes snapped open, and Christopher was a trifle relieved to see a little more alertness in them. "What's the matter, Chris?" Jamie asked. "Why are you shaking me about?"

"Have you taken those bloody tablets?" shouted Christopher at him, shaking him even more fiercely. "Have you? Wake up! For Christ's sake wake up!"

He gripped Jamie firmly round his waist with one arm. Then he pushed his head down and worked a couple of fingers into his mouth. With some difficulty he managed to push them to the back of his throat. Jamie made little squeaking noises of protest, then was suddenly and painfully sick. Christopher, watching anxiously, saw a spirt of brownish liquid, followed by a stringy mouthful of yellow bile. He continued to run his fingers along the back of Jamie's throat, and the boy retched again, more violently, and this time Christopher gasped in overwhelming relief to see a great gobbet of white muck cascade to the grass, along with several individual tablets, fluffed and swollen as they had begun to break up. Christopher, wanting nothing more than to cradle his beloved in his arms and comfort him, hardened his heart and forced his fingers back into Jamie's mouth making him gag painfully again, and twice more, until there was nothing left but a trickle of sticky fluid. Christopher withdrew his fingers and was horrified to see they were flecked with blood; but he supposed that the violent retchings had been bound to strain something.

He noticed for the first time that his eyes were streaming, and wiped his face as well as he could with his sleeve. Jamie began to fall into his arms, but Christopher fended him off brutally and shook him some more. Jamie gazed at him, with a hurt look in his eyes that wrung Christopher's heart, but he glared at Jamie and carried on shaking him. At last he saw what he had been hoping for. An angry gleam began to show itself in Jamie's eyes. He held him away from his body with one hand, and slapped his face lightly with the other. Jamie began to look a little more awake. He started dragging Jamie up and down the little greensward, trying to make him walk.

It suddenly occurred to him, as Jamie's feet got into a tangle for the third time in ten yards, that he was probably more drunk than drugged. He lugged Jamie over to where he had found him, and inspected the scotch bottle lying in the grass. It still had about three inches of whisky in the bottom. Christopher didn't know how full it had been, but it meant that Jamie could have had a very large amount. He dropped the bottle and continued to haul Jamie up and down, seeing with relief that he was beginning to move a little less painfully.

After a few more minutes of walking him up and down Christopher decided to try to get him to the towpath. It cost him a lot of sweat, because Jamie clung to him, evidently not fully aware of what was happening, but at length, after innumerable false starts, scrapes and tumbles he managed to half-drag, half-carry him up the steep bank. He subsided, exhausted, onto the flat ground at the top for a moment's respite, but quickly scrambled to his feet, not daring to allow Jamie to rest for more than a minute. Jamie moaned and muttered something as Christopher hauled him to his feet, but he clung to his arm and staggered obediently alongside when Christopher shook him again.

Getting him under the hawthorns was the most difficult part of all, but eventually he made it, and the two of them scrambled up on the towpath side. Christopher looked at Jamie, then at himself. Their clothes were snagged and torn from the thorns and the trees on the bank, and they were both smothered in grass, leaves and mud and spotted with the blood-flecked white mess and bile vomited up by Jamie. Christopher wiped his face with a filthy sleeve, clearing some of his tears and replacing them with mud, and lugged Jamie to his feet again.

As the two bedraggled scarecrows emerged on to the towpath, Christopher more or less lifting Jamie up one side of the fence and dropping him as gently as he could on the other, Robert Rowe arrived, bouncing and jolting along the towpath as fast as he could on Christopher's bike. He dismounted and propped the machine on the fence and ran to the two boys, his face taut with concern for his son, and rather less for Jamie. "Are you all right, Chris?" he gasped breathlessly as he reached them.

"I'm all right, Dad," panted Christopher. "If you could just hold him for a minute, I'm out of breath. Just keep him on his feet. Make him walk up and down. He's drunk, Dad, I think," he said, breathing in great gasps. "He's had a lot of whisky, but I made him bring it all up again."

"Had he had those tablets as well?" asked his father, hauling Jamie up and down a five-yard run.

"Yes, he brought up a great mass of white gunge. It looked as if he'd taken a lot, but he can't have had them in him very long, because a lot of them were still whole," said Christopher more easily. He extracted a handkerchief from his pocket and wiped at his face. His father saw him doing it, and laughed shortly. "You won't do much good with that, Chrissie, you'll just spread it around a bit further." Christopher grinned weakly at him.

Robert Rowe looked at his son with affection and respect. "You're a good boy, Chrissie. You've probably saved his life, you know."

"I know, Dad," said Christopher soberly. "God, I'm glad I was in time. I don't know what I'd have done if I'd been too late and he'd... he'd been..." he left it unfinished. "Can I have him back now, Dad, please?" he said, taking Jamie from him anyway.

Robert watched him thoughtfully as he walked Jamie gently up and down. "Are you really sure he's worth all your devotion, Chrissie?" he asked, very carefully. "He's caused nothing but trouble, you know that as well as I do. And this, coming on top of everything else... You know your mother and I don't want you to be unhappy - not over anything. And if this boy had really been what you wanted, we'd have got used to the idea, I dare say. You could have worked something out when you were both old enough, I imagine. But don't you think he's caused you enough grief and pain?"

Christopher stopped walking Jamie for a moment and looked his father directly in the face. There was no anger or reproach in his face, but Rowe saw that there was a very adult look of resolve which he had never seen in his gentle, easy-going son before. "I've never wanted anything much, Dad. Not so badly that I couldn't do without it and not cry about it, anyway. That's true, isn't it?" Rowe nodded.

"Well, I want him, Dad. I know you don't really

understand this, and I know you don't like it much either, but there's nothing you or anyone can do about it - not even me.

"He's mine - or rather, I'm his. I belong to him, and that's that. We'll sort this imbecile bloody business out when I see him after he sobers up, and we'll work out how we're going to make the waiting bearable. But some time or other, sooner or later - sooner, if I can think of a way to do it without getting into more trouble - I'm going to have him." He paused for thought, still holding the sleepy, befuddled Jamie on his arm and walking him in a tight five-yard track.

He looked earnestly at his father and tried again. "You don't know him, Dad. You've only seen him in the worst possible light - now, when he's got so desperate that he doesn't know what he's doing, and in the court. The only thing you know about him is that he's caused a lot of terrible trouble and suffering - for you and Mum and Dr Lane and his wife, and everybody. But that's not Jamie's fault." He saw his father's expression, and went on, speaking seriously but calmly, offering explanation but not apology. "It's *not* his fault, Dad. He never wanted to hurt anybody. He never did anybody any harm, not intentionally. All he wanted was to be free to give me what I wanted him to give me, and to take what I gave him willingly. I love him, Dad," he ended, a little hopelessly, "and this doesn't make any difference to that - except that after this he belongs to me and I belong to him more than ever."

Jamie mumbled something incoherent. Christopher stopped and bent to hear. "There, there. Don't worry," he said gently into Jamie's ear. "He was trying to say he was sorry for all the trouble he's caused," he said to his father after a moment. "Dad, shall we start walking him back? We'll meet the others on the way, and it'll be less distance to get him to the ambulance. I suppose they did call for one?" he added.

"Yes, Audrey called one before I left," replied Rowe. "I'm surprised they're not here by now. You're right, anyway. Let's start back." He turned the bicycle round and they began the two-mile walk back, Robert wheeling the bike a comfortable talking distance behind Christopher, laboriously supporting Jamie, who was beginning to make an effort to help himself. "As you said, Chris," he said as they set off, "I don't really pretend to know how you feel. It's nothing like how I imagined - er - people like you behaved. I suppose I always assumed they were... I don't really know..."

"You thought like most people do, I expect," said Christopher, helping him. "You thought we were all limp-wristed, mincing queens..." He chuckled suddenly.

"What's funny?" asked Robert in surprise.

"Oh, it's nothing much, Dad. I was just remembering Neil when we got back from court." He laughed again and told his father of Neil's antics with his mother's handbag. Robert Rowe tried to imagine it, and suddenly laughed. "Well," he said, "I'm glad you can laugh at something like that, anyway. Good old Neil.

"Do you know what he said when we told him that you were... about you?" he said after an interval.

"I don't know, but I imagine he said 'so what?'" said Christopher. "Something like that," assented his father. "It shook me rigid. There I was, stumbling and groping for some way of telling him without upsetting him. In the end all I could say was 'Chris is gay, Neil', and he just stood there for a moment and looked at me, and then he laughed and said, 'Really, Dad, is that *all*?' It made me think, I can tell you. I thought, here's your mother and me, thinking it's the end of the world. We can't believe it, and all Neil says is 'Is that all?'"

Christopher switched Jamie from one side to the other, flexing his freed arm to restore the circulation, and said, "Dad, do you remember what the barrister said in the pub, while we were waiting for my sentence? About the notice board?"

"I do," said Rowe, "and that gave me more to think about. All this is very new to us, Chris. - I mean, we knew queers existed... I suppose I'll have to stop calling them that now. I don't quite know what to call them... anyway, it was just that I never thought we'd ever have one in the family, I suppose..."

"I can't say I like the word much, Dad, but I don't really care what you call 'them'. It's how you think of *us* that matters. Ah!" He broke off. "Here's the others." Dr Lane appeared round the next turn in the towpath, with another man carrying a leather bag. They hurried on as fast as Jamie could stumble.

"Let's have a look at him," said the stranger briskly. He set his bag down and rummaged in it, bringing out a stethoscope and an opthalmoscope. He looked into Jamie's eyes and hauled his shirt up to listen to his chest and back with the stethoscope. "What's he taken?" he asked. "He's had some whisky, and a lot of tablets," said Christopher. "I don't know how much of either. Hello, Dr Lane. I got to him in time. How much whisky was there in that bottle, sir?"

"Mmm. It was about half-full, I suppose. And we believe he had thirty-six tablets with him - three cards of twelve - but there may have been a fourth card," said Lane, looking anxiously at Jamie. "You've done very well, Christopher," he added, looking at Christopher with approval.

"Well, there was about three inches of the whisky left," said Christopher to the doctor. "Means he's had about two or three inches-worth, I should think. He's pretty pi... drunk. I made him bring it all up, though, and a lot of the tablets hadn't really dissolved yet. They were a bit fluffy, but they were still separate. Did I do right?" he asked the doctor anxiously. "You did exactly what you should have done," said the doctor, picking up his bag and setting off back the way he had come. "I'm going to go ahead and make sure the ambulance is ready at the bridge. Get him there as fast as you can. He's not out of the woods yet."

Christopher and Lane opened their mouths to ask questions, but the doctor was already striding rapidly away. They continued, Christopher helping Jamie. Robert Rowe and Dr Lane had a good deal to talk about, and dropped back twenty yards so they could converse freely without worrying the boy. Twenty minutes later they reached the bridge. Jamie was efficiently plucked from Christopher's arms and whizzed into the ambulance. Christopher stepped up to the vehicle's tail. "I'll go with him, Dad," he said. Turning to Dr Lane he added, "I'd like to come to speak to you later on, sir, if you'll allow me to. May I come to your house, please? It's very important," he pleaded.

Lane nodded kindly at him. "Of course you may, Christopher. Come at any time. Meanwhile, I think your parents and I must talk, so we'll leave you. Goodbye for the present."

"Are you sure you ought to..." began Robert Rowe, but Christopher simply smiled a thin smile and said, as he climbed into the ambulance, "I wouldn't leave him now, Dad, now would I?" He vanished into the vehicle, the crewman shut the doors, and it roared away with its blue light flashing and the siren beginning its banshee howl.

After the ambulance made its ear-splitting departure Robert Rowe and Dr Lane stood for a few minutes, watching the glittering canal flowing peacefully under the bridge, and eying each other now and then a little warily. At length Rowe broke the silence. "We *have* got to talk, Dr Lane."

"I know," said Lane.

"Your Jamie's a bit of a problem child, isn't he?" said Rowe. He had rather taken a liking to Dr Lane, and reflected that he would have put it a great deal more strongly had he not wished to spare the other man's feelings as far as he could.

"Well, Mr Rowe," said Lane, a little stiffly, "I can certainly understand your regarding him as such. He's been nothing but a series of traumatic problems for you. We know him better, and have seen many better sides of him. And, of course, Christopher sees him differently from any of us, though I have to confess that though I have tried hard to do so, I don't understand exactly what they do feel for each other."

"Nor do I, Dr Lane," said Rowe with feeling. "I wish I did. It would make the whole thing clearer if I could begin to understand just how they feel, but it's completely beyond me." He shrugged his shoulders in a gesture of defeat. "I mean, Chris has always been so... so *normal*. So ordinary.

Oh, he's bright, we saw that when he was at primary school. He's always been the brightest in the family. He was always a gentle, quiet boy. But ordinary. Just like me. Like his mother and Neil, for that matter. And then, out of the blue, this Jamie appears on the scene and he reveals this... well, I don't know... it makes you think you've never really known the kid after all..." He fell silent.

"Perhaps we'd better go back," suggested Lane. "I think, if I may suggest it, that we might all benefit from a candid discussion of both boys. We have both, after all, to work out a *modus vivendi* with one of them..."

"I beg your pardon?" said Rowe.

"I'm sorry. I meant that we both have a boy with us of whom we're exceedingly fond, but who, in one way or another, poses us problems. Different problems, because they're different and so are we, but problems all the same, and interrelated at that. At least, I have a feeling that they are going to be interrelated."

"I don't want them interrelated," said Rowe. "I hate to burden you when you've already got so much on your plate, but really, Dr Lane, it's got to stop. I mean, we've got through that awful ordeal of the trial, and then, hardly five minutes after it's all over and we think we've got something worked out to take the pressure off Chris, that boy comes along and throws another bloody great spanner in the works. I was supposed to be driving Chris down to London this afternoon, to get him out of the way until he goes off to university. Well, that's off now, isn't it? We shan't be able to go until tomorrow now, if then. I don't know how long he'll be at the hospital with Jamie, but it'll be some time, and - well, what chance would *you* give me if I tried to drag him away?"

He read Lane's face. "Exactly. I'd have to hit him on the head and knock him out. And when he finally comes away from the hospital he wants to come and talk to you. Well, all right, I suppose that's got to happen. I'm not sure what he wants to say to you, but I could make a fair guess. I shan't try to stop him, for the same reason as I wouldn't try to get him away from the hospital - same reason as I didn't really try to stop him going in the ambulance just now. He'd have gone whatever I'd said or done."

"I understand your feelings. In many ways I share them. *I* wish Jamie and Christopher were just ordinary, conventional boys, with ordinary, conventional things on their minds. But I'm afraid, Mr Rowe, that to say you don't want their problems interrelated is very likely to prove to be mere wishful thinking."

Rowe looked at him in alarm, mingled with the beginnings of anger. "Isn't it our job to make sure that's what it *isn't*?"

"Perhaps, if such a thing were possible. But the point is, is it possible, Mr Rowe? Please don't misunderstand me. The last thing I want is for anyone connected with me to be a cause of grief to you. Nor do I myself wish you and your family anything but well. You and I, Mr Rowe, are on the same side in this, whatever our boys get up to. But really, consider the evidence of your own eyes, not ten minutes ago. Do you really believe that everything will be put right by putting a little distance between your son and Jamie? You said yourself, you didn't try to stop Christopher going in the ambulance, you won't try to move him from the hospital or prevent him from coming to speak to me. Very well, I could prevent that last; but what good would that do? It seems to me that the more we set out to make difficulties for these two, the more we shall tend to drive them into each other's arms - in this case, regrettably, literally so. I think, Mr Rowe, we must consider the matter further than merely wishing it were not so. And, if I may suggest it, I think our wives may very well have some ideas that might not occur to us. Shall we rejoin them?"

Rowe looked at him in an uncertain mixture of hostility and respect. "Yes," he said unhappily. "Yes, let's get back." And grudgingly he added, "If you've got any practical ideas about what we can do, I must admit I'd be glad to hear them."

"I think we must face the possibility that there *may* be *nothing* we can do. But I hope that's not the case." They got into the car and Lane drove back to Cross Oak Gardens.

***

The ambulanceman had been busy over Jamie throughout the short journey to the hospital, so Christopher had no chance to speak to him or even hold his hand. When they arrived Jamie was whisked away on a trolley, and Christopher had hours to kill. He spent half an hour cleaning himself up as well as he could in a hospital washroom. Then he went out into the town. He blew a fiver on the *Listener*, the *Spectator*, the *New Statesman* and the *Cricketer* and wandered with them into a pub. Having wasted a couple of hours over the magazines and three pints of indifferent bitter he went back to the hospital and asked if he could see Jamie.

"Oh, yes," said the ward sister he was directed to. "You'll be Christopher, I suppose?"

"That's right. Why, has he mentioned me?"

"Yes, he's been asking for you. You can see him for a while. But you're not to do anything to upset or strain him, he's quite seriously ill." She saw fear etch itself into his face instantly like acid. "Don't worry. He's not critical. They got to him in time to save anything permanent. But it would have been touch and go if they'd been half an hour or so later." She looked hard at him, saw the rips and stains in his clothes, and her face changed. "It wasn't you who found him, was it?" He nodded, his face a mask of concern. "Oh, well, you very likely saved his life, you know," she said. "Is he a friend of yours?"

Christopher nodded impatiently. She showed him to a small room and gestured to him to go in. "Remember," she admonished, "don't let him get excited or upset, please."

"I won't," he said, and slipped into the room. The sister went away, making a face to herself. "*Friend*" she muttered to herself. "Oh, yes?"

Jamie was lying almost flat on his back in bed, with an intravenous drip leaking some liquid into his arm. Though he had been cleaned up, he was very pale, and there were puffy bluish bags under his eyes; but the vacant expression had gone out of them, and he looked much closer to his normal self than he had that morning. He gave Christopher a great smile of pure joy, and Christopher felt a shiver run through him. Jamie, and Jamie's smile, still had the power to turn his guts to water. If anything, he thought, it was increasing. He went to the bedside and gave Jamie a long kiss. "How are you?" he asked gently.

"I'm not too bad, Chris," he said in a small voice. "Chris, darling, you saved my life. I don't know how to say thank you, but you did. Did you know that?" Christopher nodded, smiling. "Never mind about that..."

"Never mind?" Jamie said. "I don't know how I'm supposed to never mind. I'd have been dead if you'd been a bit later. Oh, Chris, I'm sorry..."

"Jamie, don't be sorry, and don't thank me. You can do both of those in one, by doing two things for me. Will you do something for me if I ask you - if I ask for that thing especially?"

"Chris," Jamie said seriously, pushing Christopher away from him to let him see the sincerity on his face, "I'll do anything you ask. I promise you that. No exceptions. I know I've broken promises to everybody lately. I'm not proud of myself, Chris, though I only did all the things I've done for you - or at least, for us. But I've never broken a promise to you, and I won't."

Christopher looked firmly into his eyes. "All right then, Jamie, my dear. I said two things, and they're these. One is, wait for me, and the other is, don't do anything foolish while we're waiting. I'll explain why I'm asking you in a moment, but will you promise me those two things right now, just on the strength of what I've said? Just because I've asked you?"

Jamie took Christopher's hand in his own and squeezed it. He looked straight into Christopher's eyes for a long interval. Then he gave a long, deep sigh and, with a sad smile he said "I promise, Chris. I'll promise you those two things." He reached out and put an arm round Christopher's neck and pulled him down to himself, and held his face against his

261

own, saying nothing, for some minutes.

"I'll explain those two promises," Christopher said, gently drawing away. Jamie let him go, but curled his fingers round Christopher's and stroked the backs of them. "Yes, Chris?"

"First, I wanted you to promise to wait for me. It won't be for very long. In theory it could be for five years, until you're twenty-one, but in fact it won't be anything like that. I've got to keep my nose clean, not get into any trouble with the law, for two years, but I doubt if it'll even be that long. The dust will settle, people will forget. Maybe one day they'll even change the law. But even if it did take two years, well, I'd only be twenty-one, and you'd still only be seventeen. We'll have a lifetime in front of us. You wouldn't have seen a great deal of me in that time anyway, because I'd be away at university for most of the year.

"Now the reason. I told my father this morning, Jamie, as we were bringing you back from the fishing place: I told him that I was going to have you for my own, because I already belonged to you. I laid that straight out flat for him, and he didn't like it much. But he didn't argue, because I think he's just beginning to see what there is between you and me. What I'm telling you is that you've *got* to wait for me, because you belong to me, every last bit as much. I need you, Jamie. It's not just that I love you, though you know I do. It's much, much more than that. I need you, Jamie. I couldn't do without you. That's why you've got to wait for me, as I've got to wait for you. We've tasted what we are for each other, and now we've got to wait for the full course. But if you don't wait for me, it'll be me going off to some lonely fishing pool with a bottle of scotch and a hundred aspirins.

"And here's another reason. Jamie, I don't particularly like doing this to you, and you can call it blackmail if you like, but you've got to wait for me, because you *owe* me. Now how does that little speech make you feel?"

Jamie put his free arm behind his head and gave him a long, lazy smile, the most beautiful, Christopher thought, he had ever smiled. "I liked it," said Jamie. "You never realised, Chris, you were always so... so *polite* about us, and how we felt about each other, weren't you?"

"Polite?" echoed Christopher, puzzled.

"You never realised that I didn't want to be treated with kid gloves - as if I was breakable. I *want* to owe you, Chris. Did you really never see that? I want to be *told*, Chris, told that you love me and all that, of course, but told that I belong to you. I want to be *told*... oh, Chris, I just want to be ordered about now and again. Do you understand?"

Christopher thought he began to, and nodded encouragingly. "Okay, I won't be so polite in future. But you agree to abide by that promise? You'll wait?"

"I'll wait, sweet Christopher. I'll wait."

"Right, that's promise number one. Now number two. You must promise me that you won't do anything silly while you're waiting. I don't just mean trying to kill yourself again. I know you're not the sort to do that really. You only did it today because you were over wrought and half way out of your mind and didn't know what you were doing. But there's to be no more of it - not even *thinking* about it, you understand?" Jamie nodded gravely.

"But it's not only that. You must promise not to do other sorts of things too. There's to be no getting desperate and trying to come and find me at university, or at the old folks' place in London in the next three weeks. Agreed?"

"Yes," said Jamie.

"You *must* promise me that, Jamie, dear. I've got to make you promise that, because I know you well enough to know that I'm the only person there is you'll keep a promise to. That's right, isn't it?"

"Yes," said Jamie again. "I don't like lying, or breaking promises, but I'd always break them if I had to for you, or for us. But I won't break a promise I make to you."

"Good. Then promise me you'll behave yourself until we're together."

"I promise," said Jamie softly, squeezing Christopher's hand painfully hard.

"That's all right, then. I told you the other night, I've got to get my degree, so I can get the sort of work I want.

Remember that, and if it's any comfort, think of it that every day we're apart it's another day towards setting ourselves up the way we want to - for ever, as far as I'm concerned, my J." Jamie smiled, thinking about it. "It won't be easy," he said slowly.

"It's going to be *hell*," said Christopher, "for both of us. But we've got to do it, so we will. But I've got one or two promises to make to you, too. First of all, I'll write."

"But..." Jamie broke in.

"No buts. I say, I'll write. I know what Dr Lane said, but I'm going to fix that. I think I've gone up a few notches in his esteem today, and he's letting me go to the house when I leave here to talk to him. He's a reasonable man, Jamie, you know that better than I do. I think he loves you - he's very fond of you, at any rate. Believe me, I'll square it with him, and you'll get a letter from me... every day if you like, even if it's only a note sometimes..."

"Every day, Chris. I want a promise this time. I don't care what you say. I know you'll be busy a lot of the time, and there won't be much to say in lots of them. But just a slip of paper with 'Love from Chris' will do. Every day, Chris?"

"Every day. I promise. In return, I want a letter from you at least once a week. Tell me everything that goes on. It'll be just about what I live for, J. Will you do that for me?"

"Every day, Chris," said Jamie in the same tone as he had said the words before.

"I'd like that best of all, but I won't hold it against you if you miss a day or so now and then."

"Yes, you will, Chris. Please. You must."

"What's that supposed to mean?" asked Christopher in perplexity.

"That's what I meant about being *told*, dear Chris, about you being so polite. I want you to tell me you want a letter a day and you won't accept anything less. You're so nice to me it makes me feel guilty, and I hate feeling guilty - except over things like today, when I've really done something to be guilty about."

"All right, Jamie. One letter a day from me to you, and one

264

letter a day from you to me - without fail, both ways. Same conditions for you as me - if there's nothing special to say, just a note saying you love me'll keep me happy. Very happy. Okay?"

"Of course it's okay." Jamie stroked Christopher's face and neck and smiled up at him. Christopher thought he looked happier than he had looked for weeks.

"Another promise from me to you," he said. "We will meet, fairly soon." Jamie caught his breath, and squirmed and fidgeted, beginning to get excited. "Don't, love," said Christopher. "The nurse said I wasn't to do anything to upset or excite you." Jamie obediently lay still. "I'm supposed to be ill," he said, grinning.

"I know, she told me," said Christopher. "Did they tell you what's the matter?" He glanced anxiously up at the drip.

"The tablets I took are pretty nasty," said Jamie. "Apparently they destroy your liver. That's what that stuff is. It's got some long name. Unpronounceable. If you take too many of those Panadol they have to pour about a gallon of this stuff into you to protect your liver, otherwise it packs up and you die... Chris. Chris, what's the matter? What have I said?"

Christopher had gone white and suddenly had to prop himself with both hands on the counterpane. "It's okay," he muttered after a moment to recover. Jamie saw the colour come back into his face with enormous relief. "Christ, Chris, what was it?"

"Nothing, love. I just thought what a close thing it was, and then I thought of you with your poor liver failing and dying alone, and I... I... Well, I just had a sort of premonition - no, not a premonition, a sort of inkling of what life without you'd be like."

"What *would* it be like, Chris?" Jamie asked interestedly.

"Short," said Christopher. Jamie saw his face, and pulled him down roughly with his free arm.

"You said we'd meet, though, Chris darling," said Jamie happily when at last he let him go. "When?"

"I can't say for certain," said Christopher. "I'll be with the

265

old couple for three weeks from tomorrow. I'll send you the first letter one day early next week - give me a day or so to get sorted out. I go to the university three weeks on Monday. I'll tell you the address in one of my letters before I go there. The term's ten weeks. Thirteen weeks in all. I'll definitely see you early in the holiday, so thirteen or fourteen weeks is the longest you'll have to wait. But there's a very good chance that I'll be able to get back for a few days during the term. If I do, I shan't tell anyone except you. I'll work something out so I can stay somewhere off the beaten track, and we'll arrange something. But you'll just have to trust me to fix that nearer the time."

"I trust you," murmured Jamie.

There was a light knock on the door and the sister came in. "I'm afraid you'll have to go very shortly," she said pleasantly to Christopher, and to Jamie, "Are you feeling all right?"

"Well, not *too* bad, thanks," said Jamie, pulling a face. "Pretty sickish, I suppose. And I've still got that headache."

"That's a hangover," said the sister severely. "Your first, I trust. And your last, if you've got any sense."

"The whisky was vile," said Jamie, remembering. "Funny, Chris, I can hardly remember anything about the whole thing. I felt very funny, sort of light-headed. And that was before I'd drunk any of the whisky. I just didn't seem to be able to think straight. And I don't know how long I'd been lying there after having the whisky and taking the tablets before you got there. I thought it was me dying when you thumped me. It was very unpleasant," he said. His voice had sunk to a murmur, and there was horror in it. "I didn't need to promise you I'd never do anything like that again, Chris. I'm glad I did though. I like promising you things," he confided in a whisper. The sister took the hint, and went out. "Five minutes," she said to Christopher as she went. Then she saw Jamie's face. "Ten," she said, with a soft chuckle. As I thought, she thought to herself in the corridor outside.

They poured as much of themselves into their last ten minutes as they could contrive, like condemned men over their last meal, investing every tiny action or word with the special significance of last things. "We're not parting for good and all," said Christopher into Jamie's mop of dark-red hair. "But it feels like it, doesn't it?" answered Jamie sadly, nuzzling Christopher's throat. He suddenly had an idea. "Got your knife?" he said.

"Yes, here," said Christopher, fishing it out of his pocket. "What do you want it for?"

For answer Jamie pulled Christopher's head down to him, and Christopher felt him sawing at a thick hank of his long hair with the blunt pen-knife. Jamie sat back, with a hefty twist of the hair in his hand. He looked at it fondly. "Take some of mine now, Chris," he said. "Quick, before she comes back. I think she's guessed about us, you know," he added, grinning at him. "That's why she's being so decent about the time."

"Well, if she's decent about the time, I couldn't care less if she knows all about us," said Christopher, blessing the woman in his heart. He sifted Jamie's thick, heavy hair, looking for a lock that would not be seen to be missing. He cut a long, thick curl and rubbed it between his fingers. "Got an envelope or something?" he asked. "I'd hate to lose it or get it dirty or anything."

"There's some sort of surgical bag in the waste bin," Jamie said, pointing down on the other side of the bed. "There was a needle or something in it when I first came in here." Christopher got up and went round the bed. "Got it," he said, and he was slipping the lock of hair into the little autoclave bag when the sister came back into the room. The first thing she saw was the bag in his hand, and he had no chance of concealing what he was slipping inside it. To Christopher's surprise, she blushed. She was a pretty woman, he saw for the first time, and the blush made her prettier. He wondered how it would feel to be attracted to her. She made some excuse of having forgotten something, and left them alone again, with a brief but unmistakable look of warning. "That was bloody decent of her," Christopher remarked. "Time's up, Jamie."

They made as good a farewell as they could, and at last Christopher said, "I'll have to go. Goodbye, Jamie, my dearest. Don't forget - a letter a day, starting the day you get the first from me. You'll wait for me?"

"I will."

"And you'll be good?"

"I will. I will. My Chrissie." The name that only his father, and occasionally his brother Neil, used, stopped him at the door. He turned back and smiled to Jamie, giving permission. "Bye, love," he said. "Bye, Chris. Bye, my dearest," said Jamie. It was the last word he heard in Jamie's voice for a long time. The last thing he saw as he blew a kiss, slipped out and drew the door closed was Jamie's smile, through the first of many tears. Half-blinded, he had a near-collision with the returning sister as he turned to walk down the corridor. She looked at him with pity. "I'm sorry," he muttered thickly. He stopped and tried to smile at her, blinking hard.

They got past each other. As she was about to go into Jamie's room he turned back. "Sister." She stopped and looked back at him. "I don't know if you were wondering," he said, with a better attempt at a smile. "But the answer is yes, we are." Before she could respond, he had gone out of sight.

***

"Come in Christopher," said Edith Lane. She let him in, looking at him with interest. Apart from the hectic few minutes at his home that morning it was the first time she had seen the young man of whom she had heard so much and who had unwittingly brought such upheaval into their lives. She saw a slim, boyish figure, a pale face, pretty in a plain sort of way, but with a neat bone structure, a little ravaged at the moment by strain and anxiety; brown hair falling in a heavy mantle to his collar and curling over his forehead in a fringe; a pretty mouth, but beautiful eyes, large, dark brown, with a mildness about them that she thought women would find very appealing. She realised with a moment's shock as she appraised him that that was not a consideration that would interest him.

She immediately gave herself another moment's shock, because she realised that he was standing patiently, allowing her to take stock of him without apparent resentment. He saw her start, and smiled faintly. "Christopher, I am sorry," she exclaimed, "whatever must you think of me? I'm afraid I was a little curious about you, having heard so much. But that doesn't excuse an inspection parade in the hall, does it? Do come through." She ushered him into the living room hurriedly, to cover her embarrassment, but he just gave her a rather strained smile. She thought he had a very nice smile, and even nicer manners. John Lane rose from his chair and offered his hand. Christopher shook it delicately.

"Please sit down, Christopher," said Lane. "Can I offer you a drink? Or tea, coffee, some such?"

"Thank you," said Christopher. "I'd love a beer, if you've got such a thing."

"We can find you a lager, I think," he said. "I don't drink it myself, but most of my younger masters seem to live on it. It's always struck me as a beastly substance: nothing but gas. But there we are. Now then, Christopher, what did you wish to discuss with me?"

Christopher settled himself in his deep armchair, accepted his lager gracefully when Edith brought it, and sat for a minute or more in silent thought from which the Lanes wisely did not disturb him.

"This isn't very easy," he said at length, looking at them from under his long eyelashes. "I don't really know how much you know about what there is between Jamie and me. But I believe you understand better than my people - better than anyone else at all, I think." He paused, waiting for them to say something, but they would not interrupt him. "I'd like to try to explain it properly to you," he went on. "I would try to do this for my parents, but I'm pretty sure they

269

wouldn't understand. I think you will.

"I've just left him in hospital. He's very ill. He put on a brave face for me, but he's in a lot of pain. He's been stomach-pumped, and he's still got a hangover. He's got a needle stuck in his arm, which hurts him every time he moves. Though I don't think he's thinking about that very much at the moment."

"What exactly *do* you think he is thinking about, Christopher?" asked Dr Lane.

"Sir, I think he's worrying about whether I told him the truth earlier this afternoon." Their attentive expressions encouraged him to go on. "I told him that I was coming to see you. I said that I would fix it with you that I could write to him," he said, coming out with it baldly.

"I know you've told him that he won't be allowed to receive letters from me," he went on. "But, sir - Mrs Lane - I don't think you should try to enforce that. I've spent ages this afternoon, sitting with him, persuading him that we'll be together soon - in a bearable time - and I believe I've convinced him that it can be done - that we can wait and come together when it's safe. I really think he'll wait for me, as I've promised I'll wait for him... provided we can have some contact.

"Dr Lane, I've promised I'll write to him every day; and he's promised to write to me. What I'm really here for is to ask you - to beg you, if necessary - to let me write to him here. You know him almost as well as me. You know if you say no, we'll find some other way of keeping in contact; I don't say that as any kind of a threat, or blackmail. I'm simply stating a fact. You know how resourceful Jamie is when he needs to be. And you know that I wouldn't allow scruples to get in my way either, if he was involved.

"I don't pretend to be my own master in this - I can't resist him, and if he called me, I'd go, whatever the cost. I want to avoid any such extremes, if I can, sir. I think if he's left with no means of contacting me at all, he'll do something foolish. But I think if he's allowed just *enough* contact - like, say, a letter every day - he'll be all right. I really believe I've managed to get him into a frame of mind in which he's ready to wait, and wait in some sort of patience, for me - just so long as he's got something to wait for. Without those letters, I don't think he'll last out."

Christopher sat sipping his beer, wondering if he had made a terrible mistake in asking to see the Lanes. They made no answer for a very long time, and he was beginning to feel sure that he had put his foot in it when, suddenly, Dr Lane shot a question at him. "Christopher, how do you reconcile this attempt with the fact that you face a prison sentence if you are found - ah - consorting with Jamie?"

"Sir," he said without hesitation, "I shan't be 'consorting' with Jamie, as you put it. I'm asking you to allow me to write to him openly - instead of doing it secretly. You must know we couldn't just be apart and have no contact whatever. It would kill him, and it would kill me. We'd do it somehow, clandestinely, under the counter. There would be some sort of hole-and-corner meetings, when we'd be terrified all the time in case we got found out. But you know better than to think we could simply accept being kept apart like animals in a zoo."

He looked at Dr Lane with a great deal of pain in his pretty, pale face. Lane looked closely at him, and saw something else there also: there was a dignity there, which he had not seen in the boy before. "You're being very honest with us, Christopher," he said.

"I haven't got a lot of choice, have I?" he said, looking straight into Lane's eyes. "I've done my damnedest to talk Jamie into being sensible. I think I've succeeded. I really do think he'll wait for me, and not do anything silly. In fact, sir, I think I've done something no one else could have done - because frankly, I don't think he'd have made any of the promises he made to me to anyone else. In fact I know he wouldn't. That took a hell of a lot of doing, sir. All I'm asking you to do now is to help me by allowing my Jamie a minimum of contact - official, sanctioned contact.

"It can't possibly do any harm," he pleaded. "I'm begging you, sir. I shall be a hundred and fifty miles away. All I

271

intend to do is to write to him every day. He'd probably show you most of the letters, if you insisted. He needs some contact with me, and I don't mind admitting I need it too. I don't think he needs me any more than I need him, in fact; but he's not as good at controlling his wants as maybe I am. I hope you'll be keeping him preoccupied, sir - overworking him at school, making him play the lead in the school play and so on. But he won't survive without some sort of reassurance - some sort of regular contact with me, and I'd be kidding myself if I convinced myself he was all right without it."

He fell silent. After a long pause for thought, Dr Lane asked Christopher, "What promises did he make to you?"

"He promised me that he wouldn't try to kill himself," said Christopher, and Edith shivered a little at the starkness with which he said it. "He also promised he would behave himself, not try to come after me when I'm at university - that sort of thing. He's promised to behave, sir."

"But will he keep his promises?" asked Lane.

"I can't speak for him. He won't commit suicide, that I'm sure of. He's not the sort. He wouldn't have done what he did this morning if he hadn't been overwrought and depressed. He's far too tough to do anything like that when he's himself. As for the other promises, well, I think he meant what he said. I hope he did."

"Should I allow you to write to him, Christopher, would you promise me that you would not seek to see Jamie without my express permission?" was Lane's next question.

"Yes, sir, I'd promise you that," said Christopher, making mental apologies to Lane, for whom he had conceived a great respect. He knew he was lying, and there was a brief internal struggle between Christopher and conscience. Christopher won on points. He mentally crossed his fingers, and waited for the next question.

Lane looked very hard at Christopher. "You may have to wait for five years. Do you think you could do that, if you had to?"

"Yes," said Christopher, with utter finality.

"It can't be easy for you to say such a thing," said Lane. "How do you believe you'll cope with the waiting over the next - what? - year or so?"

"I don't know," admitted Christopher. "All I know is that at this moment, it's breaking my heart. I love him, sir," he said inconsequentially. "I've been prosecuted and tried, convicted and sentenced, hounded, assaulted, insulted and abused for loving him, and now I'm being banished to my grandparents for loving him, but love him I do, and I can't help that - not that I want to. After what I've been through, waiting a while won't be much hardship."

"Christopher," asked Edith Lane, speaking for the first time, "do you feel that your conviction was an injustice?" She watched him closely as he considered the question.

"Yes, Mrs Lane, I do. I don't deny that I committed the offence I was charged with. But I deny that I did anything wrong." He tipped his glass up and drained the last few drops of lager, then sat for a minute, pondering the question. "Mrs Lane," he said at length, "while that sadist of a judge was making me wait over the lunch-break to find out what my sentence was, my lawyer talked to us - my parents and me - about a notice board."

Seeing their puzzled expressions, he went on. "There's a park somewhere," he said, "with a notice board in it, which says 'It is forbidden to throw stones at this notice.' Mr Compton said that that's what I'd done, in his book. I'd thrown stones at that notice. He said that what I'd pleaded guilty to was breaking the law, and that I'd broken that law because it was there to be broken, that's all. He said it was being broken by hundreds of people as he was speaking, and by thousands every day of the week.

"He said this law does no good to anyone, but it puts my entire emotional life on the level of a smutty joke, or a dirty book shop. I agree with that, Mrs Lane. He said this law makes no difference to anything or anybody except the odd unlucky one like me who gets caught by chance. The other nine hundred and ninety-nine carry on just the same, hoping they're luckier than I was.

"He said I'd committed the offence of committing an offence, and all I was being pilloried for was for breaking the eleventh commandment. I think he's right, and I feel pretty bitter about it.

"But the point is," he went on wearily, "that this isn't the point. It's all true, but it doesn't help me or Jamie right now. I've said, sir, I really think I've managed to convince Jamie that he's got to behave sensibly, and I don't think anyone else could have done it. But I don't think he'll stand by his promises, not even promises made to me, if he's denied all contact whatsoever. Sir, I'm desperately anxious to get a good degree. I should think you of all people would understand that and sympathise. Well, I'm not likely to do good work if I'm constantly out of my mind worrying about how Jamie is, what he's doing, and terrified all the time in case he turns up on the doorstep because he couldn't stand it any longer. And you know he'd be just as likely to do something like that.

"I want that degree more than anything else in the world, Dr Lane, Mrs Lane - one thing excepted. The last thing I want is Jamie throwing spanners in the works. Please, sir, please help me to achieve that."

Christopher slumped back in his chair. He had been desperately tired already, what with the chaotic events of the morning, the tedium of his hours of waiting in the afternoon and the emotional overload of worry and care over his beloved boy. The long, uninterrupted speech he had just had to improvise for the Lanes had added the final touch to his weariness. He looked from one to the other of them beseechingly, but he had nothing more to say for the moment.

The Lanes sat silent, considering what he had said. Edith looked at her husband, and he saw her verdict clearly in her face. At last he spoke. "Christopher, I had felt all through this miserable business that it must probably have been mainly your fault that all this trouble arose. I thought a man of your age must have seen the problems that this affair with Jamie would bring in its train, and that it was your duty, in that knowledge, to refuse to proceed with it.

"What I have seen of you today, however, has altered my feelings about you. I still can't tell you that I approve of this relationship. To begin with, it seems to me that you are both extremely young to be contemplating the kind of lifestyle that you are. However, I don't see that there is much I can do to persuade you of that, so there is little point in dwelling on that aspect of the matter. Meanwhile, may I say that I have felt nothing but admiration for you today. I think your action this morning showed a strength and resolution of character of a very high order - one might almost speak of heroism, perhaps…"

"I'd rather you didn't," said Christopher, modestly.

"The sentiment does you credit," said Lane. "Now, as to what you have come here to ask of us, I don't pretend to understand fully exactly how you and Jamie feel. I am, of course, familiar with homosexuality as a fact - as a phenomenon. But I'm afraid it's beyond me to imagine what goes on in the head or the emotions of someone like yourselves. None the less, I have heard your plea with some sympathy, and on balance, I believe you have made out your case."

"You're beginning to sound like a lawyer yourself, John," commented Edith. They both looked across at her, and saw that she was laughing at him. "You're being most frightfully pompous," she went on. "You sound like a headmaster." She turned to Christopher. "I think I'd better deliver the verdict of the court, Christopher. Of course he's going to allow you to write to Jamie. It would be the grossest injustice to deny you that. Apart from that, it would be extremely ungrateful on our part, since you have probably done more in one afternoon to procure a peaceful next few months than we could have achieved ourselves in a month of Sundays. Am I right, John?"

He had looked a little put out at having the initiative taken away from him in so peremptory and unexpected a fashion, but he saw the humorous glint in her eye, and laughed. "All right, Christopher, there's your decision, neatly taken off my toe and delivered unpompously. I was getting round to saying exactly the same, though I should perhaps have taken rather longer to say it. I agree with my wife. I think if you have managed to talk a little sense into Jamie, to talk some of the impetuosity and wilfulness out of him, then we shall owe you a great debt of gratitude. It will make our lives a lot easier over the coming months."

He hesitated, then went on, "Added to that, I believe that it would in any case be unkind to deny the two of you the solace of writing to each other. One does not have to be persuaded by that young barrister, eloquent though he is, to feel that you deserve, at the lowest estimate, bare kindness. You have what you asked for, Christopher. I hope it will be some consolation to you both."

Christopher sat up and, for the first time, smiled, and they knew then that they had made the right decision. "Thank you, Dr Lane, and you, Mrs Lane. I'm very grateful," he said. "I won't bother you any more." He got to his feet with an effort.

"Will you let me drive you home, Christopher?" asked Lane. "You must be utterly exhausted after all the dramas of the day." Christopher gave him a grateful look. "Sit down for a minute, then," said Lane. "May I ask you just one more question?"

"Of course," said Christopher, sitting on the edge of the chair he had just vacated.

"You have, quite clearly, a great deal of strength and firmness of character, Christopher. Do you feel that you could now do without Jamie altogether? I ask only out of - ah - academic interest."

"No," said Christopher flatly. "I couldn't. If I knew this minute that I had to make a straight, single choice between Jamie and everything else - my degree, my career, being able to live in this country, the lot - I'd throw the lot up right now. It wouldn't be a choice. I'm not that strong. At the bottom of it all he'll always be the stronger. I've stepped in and taken control today, because I had to, because he took a tumble. But it was a case of him *losing* control, not me taking it. He'll be a very formidable man when he's older. I think I'm very lucky."

Lane stood up, and the others followed suit. Christopher went across to Edith and offered his hand. "Goodbye, Mrs Lane. I shan't be disturbing your lives any more after this, but I'm very glad I've had the chance to meet you. And thank you for being so kind to us." She felt tears pricking at the back of her eyes as she took his hand. Looking very kindly on him, she said, "I'm very glad we've had the pleasure of meeting *you*. I think you're a remarkable young man, and I suspect that perhaps it's Jamie who's the lucky one. I *hope* you will soon be as lucky and as happy as you deserve to be. Goodbye, Christopher, and bless you."

Lane took Christopher outside and got the car out of the garage. It was already dark. "You'll be going off to London tomorrow, I suppose?" he said as he put the car into gear and pulled away. "I imagine so," said Christopher. He was almost asleep.

Lane drew up outside Christopher's house very differently from how he had arrived there at the start of the wild and whirling events of the morning. "It seems a very long time ago, doesn't it?" said Christopher, precisely echoing Lane's thoughts. "It certainly does, Christopher. For you more than any of us, I should think. You've had the hardest work to do today, by a long margin." Christopher turned towards him. Lane could see his eyes gleaming in the darkness of the car. He took the hand Christopher held out and shook it firmly. "Goodbye, Christopher," he said. "I agree with my wife, we owe you much gratitude for everything you have done today. I hope everything turns out well. I think, if you'll permit me to say it, that with the firm and honourable character that you clearly possess, it almost certainly will. Goodbye, my boy."

Christopher got out of the car, and Lane watched him trudge wearily up to his front door. He extracted a key from his jeans and let himself in. Lane watched the door close behind him, then drove slowly away. At the end of Cross Oak Gardens he sat with his indicator casting a feeble intermittent orange glow over the road surface as he waited for a chance to turn out. As he swung out into the main road his mind moved ahead, scanning a long mental list of administrative jobs that had to be done. They had to visit Jamie in an hour or so, and there was a double period of Aristophanes with the sixth form on Monday morning to prepare.

He settled down in a queue of home-bound evening traffic and switched on the radio. The car was filled with the plangent sounds of Debussy's faun, dozing for the rest of time in his eternal golden afternoon. Lane had a sudden mental picture of Christopher and Jamie, basking and frolicking in some enchanted Tempe. "Goodbye, Christopher," he murmured to himself as he turned into the Steeple Wynton road and headed for home. "And good luck."

Postscript (June 1996)

The reduction of the age of consent for male homosexuality from 21 to 18, in 1994, would have made no difference to the legal situation portrayed in this book. Any form of consensual sex with a boy under 16 is punishable with up to ten years' imprisonment, and what the law persists in describing as 'buggery' carries a maximum life sentence. In theory, these penalties apply even when both partners are under age, and each year several youths under 18 are sent to prison for gay offences. Outrage! has recently launched a campaign 'to reduce the age of consent to 14 for everyone'. This would bring Britain into line with European norms. Outrage! further argues that 'sex involving young people under 14 should not be prosecuted, provided both partners consent and there is no more than three years' difference in their ages'. Such flexibility already exists in German, Swiss, and Israeli law. Only under this proposal, still considered daringly radical in Britain today, would 19-year-old Christopher in this book be immune from prosecution.

Mike Seabrook
OUT OF BOUNDS

When handsome seventeen-year-old Stephen Hill joined the cricket club, it was only a matter of time before young school-master Graham Curtis fell head over heels in love. Their passionate affair intensified until the threat of exposure became too great. For safety they decide to part temporarily — but their commitment is tested more than they imagined, when Stephen is courted by his clever, irresistible friend Richard, while Graham is blackmailed by a jealous former lover.

ISBN 0 85449 177 5
UK £8.95 US $14.95 AUS $19.95

Mike Seabrook
CONDUCT UNBECOMING

Bright, idealistic, and a touch naive, 23-year-old Bob Chambers seems launched on a succesful career in the Metropolitan Police. But one day he is assigned to the importuning squad, trusted with surveillance — and more —in public toilets. The drama that unfolds shows a complex conflict of loyalties, leading from Bob's operation as agent provocateur to unsuspected discoveries about his own sexuality and the inevitable conflict with his superiors.

"A psychologically spot-on thriller" — *Gay Times*, London

ISBN 0 85449 147 3
UK £7.95 US $12.95 AUS $19.95

Mike Seabrook
FULL CIRCLE

An RAF bomb-aimer in the Second World War, shot down over the Bay of Biscay, Brian Hales has already had to overcome a crisis of conscience when his lover Ronnie ended their relationship and went to prison as a pacifist. The risks of attempted escape are his next hurdle, bringing him into conflict with his superior officers in the prisoner-of-war camp where he eventually finds himself. But his most disturbing experience is still to come, when he finds himself falling in love with a young German guard.

"I loved the book" wrote Jilly Cooper on Mike Seabrook's *Unnatural Relations*.

ISBN 0 85449 242 9
UK £9.95   US $14.95   AUS $19.95

Jeffrey Round
A CAGE OF BONES

Warden Fields, an ingenuous college student from Toronto, is discovered by an Italian model agency and persuaded to work in Europe. He begins to find the love and affection he desperately seeks, but the glamorous and frenetic world of the fashion houses in Milan and London makes it hard to maintain a relationship. Warden's boyfriend in Italy is drafted into the army, while his adventures with an English lover draw him into illegal political intrigue. Sensitive and subtle, this fine new novel weaves together tragic and comic themes into a moving and delightful human story.

"A brilliant novel by a writer whose moral vision will surely ensure his place in the world of literature" — Shyam Selvadurai, author of *Funny Boy*

ISBN 0 85449 252 6
UK £9.95 US $14.95 AUS $14.95

Simon Raven
THE FEATHERS OF DEATH

An English cavalry regiment of the 1950s, sent to suppress rebellion in an African colony. In the aristocratic world of officers and gentlemen, male love affairs scarcely raise an eyebrow. But when Alastair Lynch, an attractive but cynical lieutenant, succumbs to an infatuation with an inarticulate young drummer, the tensions with his friends start to build, coming to a head when his company are besieged by rebel tribesmen. This first novel, published originally in 1959, has lost none of its power to charm.

"Entertaining, gripping, memorable" — *Sunday Times*
"An exceptional gift for storytelling" — *The Times*

ISBN 0 85449 274 7
UK £9.95 US $14.95 AUS $19.95

The Gay Men's Press Collection

Many of the most popular titles from our backlist are now being reissued in The Gay Men's Press Collection series. These currently include:

Michael Davidson
THE WORLD, THE FLESH, AND MYSELF
In the heyday of the foreign correspondent, Michael Davidson travelled the globe and campaigned against oppression and injustice. Bravely writing in 1962 "the life story of a lover of boys", his autobiography, praised by Arthur Koestler, is a classic memoir of gay life in the first half of the century.
ISBN 0 907040 63 2   UK £12.95 US $19.95 AUS $24.95

Michael Davidson
SOME BOYS
The still more revealing sequel to *The World, The Flesh and Myself*, showing an unerring personal empathy with boys from four continents and four decades.
ISBN 0 85449 259 3   UK £8.95 US $14.95 AUS $17.95

Richie McMullen
ENCHANTED YOUTH
This follow-up to *Enchanted Boy*, a "journey through abuse to prostitution", finds Richie escaping Liverpol at fifteen for a life on the game in London's West End. Though preyed on by criminal gangs, rent boys give each other comfort and support, in the excitement that was Soho in the rock'n'roll years.
ISBN 0 85449 134 1   UK £7.95 US $12.95 AUS $17.95

The Gay Men's Press Collection

James Purdy
NARROW ROOMS

A cult book that Derek Jarman planned to film, this "dark and splendid affair by an authentic American genius" (Gore Vidal) is a shattering novel of sexual passion in the remote Appalachians, and a journey into the dark night of the American soul.

ISBN 0 907040 57 8   UK £7.95 US $12.95 AUS $17.95

David Rees
THE MILKMAN'S ON HIS WAY

In the early 1980s, this best-selling coming-out novel broke new ground as a positive image of growing up gay. "The best fictional guide for gay youth that has yet appeared" (*Identity*). " Amore convincing portrayal of gay coming-of-age isn't to be had" (*Mister*).

ISBN 0 907040 12 8   UK £6.95 US $10.95 AUS $14.95

Christopher Bram
SURPRISING MYSELF

Joel and Corey are two young men trying to build a life together in New York, amid the challenges and pitfalls of the gay scene, and the problems of work and family. "An extremely impressive performance" (*Christopher Street*).

ISBN 0 85449 130 9   UK £9.95 ex-US AUS $19.95

Christopher Bram
HOLD TIGHT

An erotic suspense novel that captures the feel of New York in the forties, the intensity of a nation at war, and the passion of men for their country and each other. "The author of *Surprising Myself* continues to break new ground with this spy thriller about Nazi interracial romance in a homosexual brothel" (*Kirkus Reviews*).

ISBN 0 85449 132 5   UK £8.95 ex-US AUS $19.95

The Gay Men's Press Collection

John Valentine
PUPPIES

Fall 1970 saw John Valentinue writing for a fragile underground paper in downtown Hollywood. A decaying cardborad building housed its seedy premises, and short of anywhere else to live he made his home in the rear office. "The building was the streetkids' social and community center... It was a sexual paradise".

"Puppies is fun reading" — Allen Ginsberg

ISBN 0 85449 258 5   UK £7.95 US $12.95 AUS $17.95

Mike Seabrook
OUT OF BOUNDS

When handsome 17-year-old Stephen Hill joined the cricket club, it was only a matter of time before young schoolmaster Graham Curtis fell head over heels in love. Mike Seabrook continues to explore the conflicts and rewards of gay life in a male environment.

ISBN 0 85449 177 5
UK £8.95 US $14.95 AUS $19.95

Mike Seabrook
UNNATURAL RELATIONS

This gripping yet tender story of two young people facing together a brutal assault on their human rights highlights the iniquitous position of gay teenagers under English law.

"I loved the book" — Jilly Cooper

ISBN 0 85449 116 3   UK £8.95 US $14.95 AUS $19.95

Send for our free catalogue to GMP Publishers Ltd,
P O Box 247, Swaffham, Norfolk PE37 8PA, England

Gay Men's Press books can be ordered from any bookshop
in the UK, North America and Australia, and from
specialised bookshops elsewhere.

Our distributors whose addresses are given in the front
pages of this book can also supply individual customers by
mail order. Send retail price as given plus 10% for postage
and packing.

*For payment by Mastercard/American Express/Visa, please
give number, expiry date and signature.*

_____

_____

Name and address in block letters please:

Name
_____

Address
_____

_____

_____